Knocked

Into

Another

Dimension

By

Derek C Chance

ISBN-13: 979-8-9995074-1-9

For my girls

Table of Contents

Prologue - A shootout

Things were about to go down – for real.

We looked at each other solemnly, as we rode in our vehicle, ready for a fight.

We wore full, mostly dark brown beards on our faces, and had slightly tan skin that only moderately hid the weathering, and mostly dark brown hair capped with Gambler hats.

Barely hiding the dark circles under our eyes were our specialized glasses that helped provide Augmented Reality Assistance, such as visually marking each of us to each other with our chosen names. This was to help with identification, since each of us were essentially identical in all aspects except the origin of our timelines, our home dimensions.

I was Max, of course, because we were in my dimension.

Riding west, in a blacked-out custom autonomous vehicle (an auto-auto by our nomenclature), a driveway appeared on the right side ahead of us, as we sped across a small bridge, in the backwoods, on the edge of a small Northeastern town.

A family in their own auto-auto was just reaching their garage before we arrived, looking to be returning home for the evening. We pulled in behind them but stopped at the end of their driveway.

We were only ahead of the modified auto-van, which was racing in our direction, by about two minutes, but it was enough time to set up. The homeowners continued into their garage, about fifty yards away, unaware of the events unfolding on the road outside their house. The sun was apathetically beginning to doze on the horizon behind the thick tree line, starting to cast shadows.

The four of us exited our vehicle. A dozen drones filed out from the inside, each of us had three digitally linked specifically to us, and they all took to the sky above, training cameras in all directions and readying weapons systems. We all had long faded brown shearling coats blowing in the cold wind. We each had on special graphene gloves, fitting perfectly on our hands to maintain warmth, dexterity and a pivotal connection point for our suit systems.

On our feet, we had on combat boots, also laced with graphene, to ensure true footing and protection.

Customized sports rifles in hand, locked and loaded. These were special guns linked to us via unique pinky rings, so we were the only ones that could fire them. Each of us holstered three extra magazines clipped to our belts; two of these magazines were loaded with special bullets that were electrically magnetized, and had unbelievable precision when fired. In addition, these bullets could pass through nearby dimensions and back with ease, once locked on to their target. I asked my AI via my ear comm to launch two additional drones from the trunk and haul the weapons case to the middle of the road.

To any onlookers, or the poor family close by, this must have looked like a futuristic western about to culminate in an epic gunfight.

It was.

I took note that it felt like slow motion in my mind as we walked forward as a group, all knowing the gravity of our situation, the chance we might not make it to see tomorrow. A tune my brother and I loved as kids played in my head with a variation that emphasized a slowed down, bassier version, playing the first few seconds of the song: Next to Me, by Violet Capri Rose.

♫ When darkness falls ♫

We all crossed the end of the driveway threshold, into the road and raised our weapons as the van approached the turn.

♫ And all's so calm ♫

It hooked the turn with a lean and a screech, almost ready to tip, but held on. The husband stepped out of his garage to see what the disturbance was, the wife and son close behind.

♫ And evening shine is all we see ♫

We all walked out into the middle of the road and opened fire without hesitation, giving the cue to the combat drones above to provide additional support.

♫ Don't be scared, my dear, just stay brave ♫

The van's shell began to form with holes, but not the windshield. He must have reinforced it.

♫ Don't you cry, my dear, don't be sad ♫

We all walked in unison towards the van as it sped towards us.

♫ We'll be well, be as well, as we can be ♫

The front windshield was slightly tinted, so we couldn't see our enemy yet. We had strong suspicions who he was, though.

We didn't even hesitate. The homeowners screamed in the distance and took cover in their garage. The normal bullets couldn't reach him, and even outnumbering him by four-to-one, I knew what I had to do; I initiated the next phase.

I retrieved my digital pocket watch from my jacket pocket: it was a specialized tool we'd created called a Draw Bridge. Quickly, I dialed in the signal on the watch interface then I opened a Bridge to another dimension to the side of me. (The act caused time to slow down slightly as it was fracturing space and time harshly.)

It was like a vertical puddle formed in thin air in front of me, when I opened the Bridge. Then I leaned into the opening with my upper torso through the hole. With a quick scan, I spotted who I was looking for. I grabbed the arm of my other self, the self from this exact moment, in a parallel timeline, a parallel dimension, where this showdown wasn't occurring like this.

He was back with me in the current dimension milliseconds later and time resumed to normal speed. I took out my injection pen and popped a chip into the side of his neck, to initiate the Express Acclimation Procedure (EAP. The P could stand for Procedure or Pen depending on context).

I repeated this action five more times, in five other ideal timelines, and time only moved fractions. Even so, we didn't have enough time to pull any more resources.

I closed the final Bridge, and time was relatively normal again.

The horizontal hailstorm of bullets continued, from my other original counterparts, towards the van. The five new members of the team stood dumbfounded and looked back and forth at one another for a few seconds until the memories were restored inside their minds, via the acclimation chips. The total pause was brief, and they retrieved weapons and were joining the action soon after. Each new member sprinted toward different sides of the van, as it still raced forward, but was slowing with all four tires stripped down to rims and rags.

"Changing mags!" I yelled out to my team. They all followed suit sequentially, as if choreographed (theoretically it was on a biological level). These next set of rounds were dimension-piercing.

This next wave of bullets destroyed the van's exterior and began to penetrate the windshield, by traveling through nano-Bridges into adjacent dimensions and back to ours to get around the material of the van. After a few seconds, the windshield of the van was beginning to shred, and exposed what we were looking for. We all stopped shooting. The vehicle was at rest now. The passenger raised his head centered in the large hole.

It was another version of me, of us.

I didn't have time to process the asinine, absurd nature of seeing myself being fired upon with force. I just aimed for my forehead and took me out.

The fraction of a second I could shine with pride, beam with a sense of accomplishment in taking out an enemy, was spoiled by the bright pulse of energy that ruptured the otherwise peaceful nature of this sleepy, rural road.

I registered several thoughts before blacking out: he (this seemingly bad version of me) had gotten his hands on a modified pendant and altered the output of the Draw Bridge device because interdimensional Bridges began to open without much assistance around the van; he must have used a dead man switch (dang I'm slick and also stupid for forgetting that about myself); and finally, this was about to go horribly and catastrophically wrong.

I hope I (or some version of me) planned for this.

♫ We'll be well. ♫

♫ Be as well. ♫

♫ As we can be. ♫

Blackness settled in.

Chapter 1 - The Disappearance

I remember the day Michael disappeared, clearly.

We had just finished watching an old movie about a group of friends embarking on an adventure where they search for their missing friend. We both loved the theme. Searching for something lost. We set out to have our own adventure in our backyard.

In hindsight, it was an ominous day, presaging with an ominous sky. Murky gray mud-like smears spread across the sky in all directions. Occasional blotches of darker contrasting gray clouds were stamped out on a hoary canvas.

Every so often we'd hear grumbles of thunder in the distance.

A thunderstorm was an exciting time for two young boys to play outside. The mystery of the possibilities went beyond our imaginations' capacity, and we just gambled with any eventualities.

Our house was in a quiet neighborhood and our property extended into an area of land that was technically owned by the power company by easements. High-tension power lines ran for miles and happened to act as a property delineator for the backyards of many houses on our street. I'm sure for adults, squabbling over who was responsible for taming the tall grass and small trees, it was a nuisance. For young kids, it was a playground like no other.

My brother and I, and a lot of times other neighborhood kids, would see who was bravest to climb the highest on the metal high-tension frames. Ignoring all the warning signs, we'd head up in a race to psych ourselves out. None of us ever reached the top, or even came close, but I think the height scared us more than the prospect of dying epically from electrocution.

During a storm, my name seemed to be an imperative for having fun as if my parents named me Max because they just wanted a kid to push the limit of everything. I often reminded them of the irony when my "Maxing out" led to something like a broken coffee table or window after a stunt gone wrong.

Michael, my younger brother by four years, since I was fifteen, and he was eleven, followed me. Trying to keep up, while running as fast as he could behind me. I got a head start, in all fairness - I'd never admit that - because he had to get that silly necklace he always wore.

I sprinted full speed towards the woods behind our house. There was about twenty yards of lawn from the back porch to the tree line and our father only tamed the overgrown brush between the trees for about two yards going in, so once we were past that, we had to dodge thorny vines that hugged the trees in all directions. It was all part of the adventure though. At a point the trees and nuisances between just stopped. This was where the utility road started, that was cut out by the power company.

Then the mad dash was on.

I reached the metal structure first, as usual, and rushed to climb. Scaling to the second level up before Michael even started to follow me up.

"Told you I'd beat you!" I yelled down.

"No fair, you didn't wait for me before starting!"

"No, I didn't, stop lying," I rolled my eyes and sighed, starting to notice the sky above more clearly. "Look at those clouds over there. They are so dark. Maybe we'll see a tornado."

Not likely. Our area was too hilly for tornadoes, but nothing could stop the illusion of one.

"Woah," he said with such awe and amazement I thought it was endearing; I would never say that out loud though. I noticed he also rubbed his necklace meaningfully.

That necklace was a gift from our grandmother. It was a simple rope necklace with what looked like a simple pendant, but it was a special EMF (electromagnetic frequency) protection pendant. I guess she thought my little brother needed to be protected from electromagnetic frequencies or maybe thought it would protect him from getting cancer. I guess it was okay if I got cancer then…shrug.

The roar of thunderclaps exploded in the distance and came like a wave of sound rolling towards us, and I imagined it was like gray crested swells in an upside-down ocean creeping closer.

"Maybe we should go back inside," he said, slinking slightly into his thin jacket.

"Don't be a wimp," I said after sucking contempt through my teeth.

"I'm not!"

Thunder echoed again, for much longer. Michael flinched, and recoiled slightly, trying to look in all directions at once. Then some lightning flashes began to create electric spider webs across the sky. We were seeing a light show that was so spectacular, it challenged the 4th of July. All playing out above the houses that spanned our neighborhood in a panoramic view around us.

Our residential neighborhood consists of middle-class homes; and raised ranches that vary in horizontal shape. Despite the variety, the homes maintain a common, vertical, structural symmetry that doesn't obstruct views. We could see this show playing out for what seemed like endlessness in all directions. We were both in awe now.

Lightning webs sprawled out again, and the wind picked up and started its intimidation campaign against us. Maybe it didn't like us encroaching on its territory in the sky. One harsh bolt of lightning detached from the web of them and struck something in the distance, causing a loud explosion of sound and light.

Michael shrieked, causing me to jump slightly, and I looked down at him.

Suddenly we were higher than we realized. Suddenly Michael seemed so much smaller than me.

I felt smaller.

It was time for us to escape back to the safety of our playroom in the basement; where we could recreate this as a fantasy game where we were guaranteed to win the challenge with zero risk to life and limb.

"Okay. Let's go," I said, but Michael didn't wait for me to say the final word before he climbed down as fast as he could carefully descend. He stopped suddenly as his necklace caught on a protruding metal footing.

I followed fast to reach him when the harshest, brightest light I've ever encountered appeared below me.

Time appeared to slow down.

At first, I saw spots and tried blinking them away. I rubbed each of my eyes with the index and middle finger of my right hand while tightening my grip on the metal frame with my left. I searched below me for Michael. I could see him, frozen, staring down, but reaching back up for something. He was, what seemed like, only inches above a darkened hole that had formed. It looked like it was out of place, like it didn't belong in the view, like a sidewalk artist's drawing of a cliff to freak people out. Except, this was not an illusion. Michael was slipping down into it, his legs no longer visible up to his kneecaps.

I reached down and grabbed at him, trying to find one of his hands, so I could grip it, so I could yank him up and pull him away from the hole.

We locked eyes. Tears welling.

"Don't let me fall," I barely heard him say, but clearly saw him mouth the words.

He slipped farther away though, farther down into the hole, more of him disappearing into the darkness of a similar-looking scene; his lower body gone, then his stomach. He began to scream and cry while looking up at me with panicked and pleading eyes. His last sections stretched awkwardly up away from the hole.

"Hold on!" I yelled.

"Please stop it, it's sucking me in!"

He said 'sucking me in' as if this hole was more than a spot, out of place, overlapping our reality, and intentionally trying to take him away. Was this a black hole, like I've seen on the Discovery Channel; something from space… on Earth? This didn't make sense because it wasn't completely black, but I couldn't investigate the developing science fiction right now. I just loosened my grip on the metal frame and moved down closer to Michael. Increasing my range of reach and finally was able to grip the collar of his coat. I pulled as hard as I could, and he was coming back up to me, moving him away from imminent danger.

Except, the jacket became easier to pull, and Michael was lighter suddenly. Because the jacket was empty, he was no longer inside it. He was no longer present, no longer in reach – no longer with me.

I stared down and could see he was on the other side of the separation, on the other side of the tear in our world. It was an identical looking grassy field cast with ominous shadows like this side. I could see the legs of the tower sprouting from that field. He was staring back at me, looking so small, so terrified. Looking smaller and smaller as he seemed to move farther away from me, falling slowly toward that analogous ground.

I decided instantly to chase after him. I let go to fall to him, to fall through the hole to grab him – to save him.

As I got right to where the horizon of the hole was, it closed with a wink out of existence, and I passed through the space it used to take up and fell toward the ground. Realizing it was approaching rapidly now.

With the force of a bat to the head, the ground knocked me out.

"Max. Max, honey. Can you hear me?" my mother's voice vibrated in my ear and caused my eyes to spread open slightly. I peeked around my mother to look for Michael, fearing his absence.

"Where's Michael?" I asked.

"We wanted to ask if you knew… You don't know where your brother is?"

I could only shake my head regrettably. Knowing I wasn't waking up from a nightmare but entering one.

"He fell into a hole and… it closed up," I finally said.

"Max, what do you mean by that? We didn't see anything that looked like a hole when we found you. But we only found you and not Michael. Are you sure he was with you when you fell?" my father asked from the other side of my bed.

I could tell my parents were trying to remain calm, but the tears in my mom's eyes and the incredibly serious face of my father signaled they were about to break into a panic.

"I don't know where he is. I... there was a flash of lightning right near us, and then I couldn't see him anymore." I didn't know how to explain what I saw in a way that would help at this point. I knew I saw Michael fall into a hole that opened up out of nowhere, but I can't get clear on whether this was somehow a hallucination after the lightning strike. Maybe it knocked me out and I imagined the whole thing.

"Max. Did lightning strike near you? Were you up on the tower when it hit? We've told you not to..." my father trailed off, closing his eyes, and moving around the bed to hold my mother who was losing to gravity with the weight of the moment.

"We have to let the police know about the lightning," my father said, getting a nod from my mother, who he just helped to sit in the chair near my bed. He walked out of the room without looking back at me.

That day changed everything.

The police searched for weeks for Michael. The entire neighborhood and eventually the entire town formed together for multiple search parties. After the tenth day of searching, it ended with a candlelight vigil, and a mountain of stuffed animals and notes near the base of the cordoned-off power line tower. A month later fencing was erected along the entire path of high-tension lines for a few miles in each direction.

I snuck back to the tower in the middle of the night, a few weeks after the fencing went up. I found a weak point where I could pull back the loose chained link fence and slip under.

I went over to the spot where it all happened, creeping, as if anyone could see or hear me. (The power company did the minimum necessary to give the illusion they solved the problem). No one was watching.

I found Michael's pendant, well, half of it. The other half was probably attached to the necklace that was still around Michael's neck.

I began to remember everything again, but it was like I was watching it happen in the third person.

I stood there running through the events over and over:

I could see the pendant break away from the necklace Michael had around his neck. The pendant was broken exactly in half. I was holding the lower half and looking between it, the sky and the tower.

The lightning didn't hit Michael, it hit the pendant. It didn't make sense how it didn't vaporize IT or Michael.

What was it about this pendant that protected Michael, which caused that hole in between worlds? Was he sucked into another dimension… I turned the pendant over and over in my hand for several minutes before placing it in my pocket.

I had to dig into this more, but I got all I could get from this spot for now. I decided I needed to do research, on something. It felt like I was only going to be able to figure out what happened to my brother if I could figure out what happened with the lightning and this pendant.

That was the key. I suppose the key to another dimension, in a sense.

It would be a while before I would visit that spot again.

Chapter 2 - Lost Boy

Losing my brother meant my parents lost two sons that day.
I didn't know how to process anything. I was fifteen after all.
I was there – but I wasn't there.

Not only were they obsessed with finding Michael, which meant one or the other was gone most of the time meeting with various people vowing to "bring him home safe," since everyone wanted to help the Baxters find their lost boy, but they were also paranoid about losing me, so they became insanely overprotective. Not that this made us closer. We barely did any type of family activities.

I can't blame them, losing a son had to be hard for them, but it was also a lot for me.

I ran away every few months, just to experience a bit of freedom.

It wasn't like they kept me locked up in my room or something. They would never let me do anything though, so I'd escape to a friend's basement. He'd let me hide there as long as I needed, even at the risk of being grounded by his parents. After about five times, my parents didn't call the police any longer and would just wait until I showed up the next morning.

They finally let me sleep over at my friend Denny's house again.

He knew Michael and me well, and even though Michael was younger, he treated him nicely even when I was being a jerk of an older brother to him.

Denny knew I had changed after the disappearance, almost immediately. I had lost that flame behind my eyes that made me fun. He didn't abandon me though. He tried to be a good friend. We'd hang out at his house, watching movies or tinkering with tech stuff. I'd try to help because it was a good distraction. He loved to take a part computers and figure out how they worked and build new programs to invent new ways of doing things. There was also joking, and laughing. Yet the long hours of laughing fits were gone. The humor seized after only a few minutes passed. Once the laughing stopped, I was back to reflecting on things, lost in my thoughts again.

The laughing did remind me of Michael. The jokes, the fun, anything that was emitting happiness; it all seemed to make me feel guilty that Michael wasn't experiencing this anymore. Not with me, not with his own friends, not with anyone for all I knew.

He was kidnapped in front of my eyes, but without a face to put to the perpetrator.

Did someone open that hole from the other side, in actuality? My memories were always clear up until that point, then fuzzy and speculative.

I always wondered where he went from there. Was he enjoying life in that new place, new world (I guess you'd call it)?

Or was he a victim? Held against his will.

The thoughts were beginning to drive me insane.

I had to stop. It was hard though.

I'd sometimes fantasize about seeing him die from the lightning strike and feeling happiness about the closure it would bring, as morbid as it was.

I had no closure, and I had no brother anymore.

I had to stop dwelling backward and move forward.

I finally started the process of moving forward as I began branching out in high school a couple years after Michael disappeared. Denny and I were still friends, just not as close. I pushed him away slowly because he was a reminder. It caused me secret guilt at night, when I finally did start to move on, I started to dwell less, I started to meet new people, I started to make new friends.

When I met Tabitha, she pulled me into a bubble that seemed to form around us and protect me from my spiraling thoughts.

It felt like freedom, like the liberation from my negative self.

That was the first time feeling happy in a long time.

I was spending my lunch hour in the library when I first met her.

Libraries evolved over the years. They almost went extinct at one point, but library preservation efforts were successful. Now books as we know them are fully digital, but nostalgia held tight to the original ideals and individual digital versions of every publication were present in traditional stacks. Paper thin, "all-light" devices (devices that could be read in any lighting scenario, including the absence of light entirely) were stacked vertically next to each other.

Holographic displays projected information about the publication on the edge of the shelf, and with a swipe would grow to accommodate more accessible reading. Just pull from the shelf any publication of interest and swipe through cover to cover to consume the creation.

Summaries were present at the beginning if you were in a hurry. Trigger the Read Fast technology to speed read the entire publication. Rapid Pair an earpiece with quick device tap to hear the audio version. Of course, one major benefit was any publication could be quickly replaced. The downside was that you couldn't experience the feathery, leathery feeling of an old-fashioned book here. (You could if you traveled to the Smithsonian though.)

"Excuse me," this beautiful brown-haired girl, with clear-framed glasses, framing auburn eyes, tapped me on the shoulder. I was startled because I was lost in a book about lightning. I was spending a lot of time reading about that subject, trying to glean any kind of hint as to what happened that night.

"I'm sorry," I immediately responded and jumped out of her way, barely looking her in the eyes at first.

"You're in my science class, right?" she asked, so soft and polite.

I met her gaze.

"Yeah, yes, I am in my, your, I mean the, that science class." I was going to die alone. I struggled to form a cohesive sentence out loud, while in my head I was smoothly answering. How do people connect their mouths to their brains in this situation? "You sit behind Kal Pickens."

Okay, better.

"Yeah. Mrs. Terries is hard to follow sometimes. I don't fully understand this latest subject on cell biology," she paused, listing towards the bookshelf slightly awkwardly and looking at her hands. An opportunity for me.

"Totally, yes, she is the worst." She actually was trying to talk to me, on purpose.

"She really is," she smiled and tucked a strand of loose hair behind her ear, "I was looking for a book to help me study. The librarian said it would be in this row."

Oh, she didn't just come up to chat with me, I was in her way. I imagined a face-palming emoji and stepped aside to look at the stacks of books.

"Oh, yeah, those types of books should be here, somewhere. I was looking for one like that too…" a white lie, but maybe I was still in, "but this looked interesting." I closed the book to show her the cover.

"Lightning. That does look interesting," she was not just moving on to find her book just yet, that was a good sign. I was thinking I should bid her farewell and skulk away and wallow in self-pity in the bathroom, but now I had an opening to attempt to connect.

"I kind of understand cell biology," my famous last words.

"You do?" she asked.

"Maybe I could help you study," I have no idea where this bold comment was going. Did I have game? I'm pretty sure I did not, but somehow, I was saying words without pause.

"Sure. That would be great, and maybe you could start by helping me find this book?" Tabitha said, while she smirked and showed me a section reference number, the librarian had gave her, as the place to look for the book.

I sprang into action and searched high and low, as quick as I could, without seeming like a spaz, until I found it.

"Here it is!" I practically yelled while yanking it out and moving the digital version of the book towards her.

"Wow. You're really excited about cell biology," she said practically about to laugh at me.

I was feeling slightly embarrassed.

"Yeah, I was just eager to find the book for you, because you needed my help." I blushed, and then I started to become self-conscious. "I should probably go actually," I said and slowly turned the lightning book, opening to a random page, and stared down at it. Interestingly, the page I landed on had something written on it that immediately stood out: I could create lightning at home.

"But you haven't helped me study anything yet, and you did say you would…" She was soft again.

I was lost for a second in thought, but she politely waited for me to refocus.

"Oh, yes, yes, I can help you study." I paused because now I was stumped about what to do next. Should I schedule something? Compare calendars on our handhelds? I was so out of my element. "When should we do that?"

"I have to head to my next class, but we could meet here at lunch tomorrow…?" she trailed off with a question.

"Yes! Yes, that works," I tapered my excitement. "I'll see you then."

"Here, let me see your handheld," she said reaching out. I quickly dug it out of my pocket, unlocked it, and handed it to her. She pulled up the Contact app and created a new entry under Tabitha, then handed the handheld back with a smile.

"See you tomorrow," she said turning and heading away.

I didn't stick around to navigate any more awkwardness and headed away in the opposite direction from her, and quickly out of the library. I was smiling like a goof as soon as she could no longer see me.

All I could think about was seeing her again.

Love at first sight has a look and looking back in the memory of that moment I could see a shimmer of it.

Tabitha was a pivot point.

Even if that next day wasn't as magical as it was; just the hope she gave me of a brighter future was enough.

We studied for about five minutes before discovering we might die of boredom and saved our lives by talking for the next thirty-five minutes about our histories.

She managed to get me to talk about my brother without me losing it emotionally.

"That must have been so scary when you woke up," she said after I concluded with a description of being knocked out by the ground.

"It didn't feel real," I said, "still doesn't feel real. I keep expecting him to turn up. I can't go back to the tower because the memories are still too raw.

"Sometimes, I hear the wind rattle the chains they used to lock it up and think maybe it's him trying to get free. Not knowing how to sneak under the fencing.

"I know it's crazy." I paused a couple seconds, "I feel crazy," I spoke but had to look away for a minute. Looking out the library window that overlooked the school's almost full parking lot.

She touched my arm to draw me back.

I met her eyes. She had wetness in them.

I smiled because she was listening.

"Thank you for telling me," she said softly.

"No problem. I haven't told the full story to anyone else," I grimaced. "It felt good to tell it though."

"Is that why you're reading that book," she nodded to the book about lightning my right arm was resting on.

"Oh, yeah, I guess kind of..." I trailed off a bit wondering how much I should say about my growing obsession.

"It's fascinating, the way lightning works. It's also beautiful... from a distance."

I could tell she was choosing her words.

"I wish I knew what happened. I've read that lightning could vaporize someone, but he was still there after the strike," I said, pausing to briefly go to that memory yet again. "Then he fell away and disappeared."

22

"That does sound strange. It's so vivid when you describe it. There is no logical way to process the thought of this. It does seem like he vanished out of thin air or fell into some unknown place, somewhere where you couldn't see him after a few minutes. I fully understand why you want to try to find an explanation. It would drive me crazy as well," she said, giving my hand a squeeze, but not lingering too long and bringing her hand back to her lap.

She didn't treat me like my parents did. They would prod for alternate explanations. They made me retell the story over and over and picked apart every detail I recounted trying to find something logical hidden in my story. They were convinced he was scared off by the strike and ran away without realizing where he was going. Then was out on the main road where someone picked him up and ultimately kidnapped him.

Tabitha didn't even entertain that I was making anything up. She took the story at face value.

I appreciated her for doing that and felt closer to her, faster, because of that.

"I'm not sure how, but I will find out what happened one day," I lowered my head, slowly shaking it and beginning to laugh. "Wow that sounded like a cheesy movie line. Sorry for that."

We both laughed, then realized our location and we lowered to giggles that faded after a few seconds.

"Well," I spoke and tapped Tabitha's cell biology book, "we should probably learn something about this stuff at some point."

Chapter 3 - Research and Development

When I got home that night, I had renewed hope in my quest to learn what happened. I had gotten through that awkwardness of hanging out for the first time with a person I "like-liked," and the pressure came down a bit. I was able to expand my thinking a little beyond wondering how I was going to survive it.

The conversation about my brother triggered a memory of seeing something in the texts of that book about lightning. It mentioned being able to create lightning in my own home. It sounded dangerous, but this book was geared toward kids, so it didn't seem like it would be too dangerous.

I remember vaguely learning about lightning and thunderstorms and weather in middle school, but don't remember doing anything crazy in class like creating lightning. However, I do remember a class trip to some science place with one of those glass globes that had electricity following your finger as you touched the outside. That wasn't lightning though, as far as I knew.

I set out to collect the items I needed from around the house:

Styrofoam plate
Aluminum pie pan
Small piece of wool
Pencil that had an intact eraser
Thumbtacks

I rushed back to my room after collecting everything and began the setup. I stuck the tack into the pie pan; and jabbed the eraser end side of the pencil into the tack point.

Following the next steps, I lay the plate facedown and rubbed the wool across the bottom of the plate for twenty seconds (which was now the top face up at me). Then I gently lifted the pie pan with the pencil and placed that on top of the plate. I braced myself for the next part. I touched the aluminum pie pan with my index finger and jumped at the sharp shock I got. It worked. I continued with the instructions, turned off the lights, and repeated the steps.

Zap.

I could feel it and see it.

I made some "lightning" all on my own and it was lame. So very lame. I turned the lights back on and sat there staring at the little experiment for a few minutes.

I needed to figure out how to do the real thing somehow.

I met up with Tabitha at her locker at the end of one of my periods, in between classes. I thought I'd be sharing an impressive, crazy experiment story with her, but couldn't bring myself to say anything about it, since it was embarrassingly juvenile. Instead, we complained about so and so teacher for giving more homework than would be humanly possible to complete.

I had plans formulating in the back of my mind how I'd get a closer proxy for a better experiment, and then share with her, but had to move forward until I could solidify something.

We made plans to meet up later after school and headed to our next bank of classes.

It was feeling like I was in a relationship… unofficially, of course, because we hadn't identified it out loud yet.

At the end of school, we met again in the library to study for thirty minutes before our parents came to pick us up.

"I know we've only really known each other for a couple of days, but I was wondering if you wanted to hang out, like outside of the library." I asked.

"Sure," she said simply.

"Cool," I said satisfied.

"What did you have in mind?" I'm not sure why this question stumped me, but it seemed like I hadn't thought far enough into the future. I was content knowing that she wanted to hang out more, and not just under the premise of studying. I went with tradition.

"Movies?" I upwardly inflected my question.

"Cool," she said, smirking, knowing she was baiting me into having to think this whole thing out.

"The new Marvel movie just came out," again I went with what felt safe. "It's about saving the world, or more than one world, or all the worlds at the same time..." a curious thought occurred to me about those multiverse storylines, but I put a pin in it, "you know the theme by now."

We laughed and she nodded, and we had our first date planned.

Now we were officially dating.

The movie was good. We held hands. We shared popcorn. We watched superheroes break the laws of the universe to entertain us. We had a wonderful time together. I managed to grow a subconscious itch though. Fortunately, Tabitha having known the story of my brother, allowed me to talk freely about the crazy thoughts I had, over milkshakes at the diner next to the theater.

"I know it was just a movie, but they do make it seem so real, so possible," I said sipping on my cookies-and-cream shake.

"I was wondering what you thought about that part," she said, keeping pace with my sips. "I couldn't help but think about your story of your brother. I also was wondering if it made you uncomfortable."

"It didn't make me feel uncomfortable, it gave me hope actually," I said brightening up and taking a break from my shake. I was feeling that cold buzz coming on anyway. "There must be some science to what they are showing. I know Hollywood can make up whatever they want and sell it, but to make things believable, they do better when it has a feel of being scientifically accurate."

"I believe there are other worlds," she said with even measure and no "but" in sight.

"Really?" I was taken aback slightly.

"Yeah. I saw this video on YouTube of a guy talking about a theory of other worlds, of parallel worlds, and he was backing it up with science. Why not believe it's possible?"

I was at a loss for words, I even said the fact out loud after a few seconds.

"I'm not sure what to say," I brushed my hands up through my hair as I spoke.

26

"I mean, you believe your brother fell into another dimension, because you saw it with your eyes, right?" she asked.

"I do. I just haven't said it out loud yet," I said, shaking my head with a smirk realizing the crazy turn our conversation pivoted to.

"I don't even question what you told me, I believe you, without really even knowing you. I know we just met recently, yet I have no reason to doubt you," she said firmly, "our world is too complex to not believe in other things outside our comprehension, but then when you go down a time-travel or parallel-dimension rabbit hole on YouTube, it's hard not to imagine the possibilities with more color."

I just nodded. It was quiet for about a minute until I split the silence.

"I want to try to open the hole again. I want to see what's on the other side. I want to find my brother," I said.

She nodded, remaining quiet. Seemingly pondering the notion.

"Next time a storm comes through, I'm going to capture the lightning."

Her left eyebrow raised.

"The stuff I watched on YouTube didn't say how to open portals, or how parallel dimensions are created. That sounds a little dangerous though," she said with a grimace.

I guess she was on my side until she wasn't. I couldn't blame her though. This idea was crazy. I knew enough about lightning to know it was dangerous. I should have guessed that home experiment was for little kids, but the prospect got the best of me. Now I was talking about serious stuff; I was talking about doing something crazy on a dangerous scale. I didn't want to get Tabitha hurt, so I had to do some damage control.

"Yeah. You're right. It is dangerous. I need to understand things a lot better before I attempt anything," I said with a frown.

"I get it. I know you want to find your brother. I get that you are willing to do anything," she gave a slight smile, "just don't kill yourself in the process." She winked while reaching out and tapping the top of my hand that was resting on the table. Setting me slightly more at ease.

I was on my own to figure this out though.

She did give me a little nugget to explore though.

"What was the name of that guy that talked about parallel dimensions?" I asked while digging out my handheld and opening YouTube.

"Just look up 'other parallel worlds' or 'many worlds' I think, I can't remember his name, but would recognize the video screenshot," she said, watching me navigate.

"This it?" I turned my handheld toward her, and she glanced at it but shook her head. I flipped up several more videos with the screen still visible to Tabitha and she shook her head until the seventh one that came into view appeared to be the one. Surprisingly still around after all this time since it was from twenty-nineteen.

"That's it," she pointed, extending to touch the screen, and playing the video.

We watched for a minute, and she got confirmation that was it. I bookmarked it (and noted at some point this would become the start of my rules to interdimensional travel when I get around to writing that up) and put my handheld back in my pocket.

"Cool. I'll watch that later," I said and smiled. "What do you want to do now? Is our date over?" I half-grinned while hoping I presumed the correct answer to the latter question was no.

"I'm not done being dated yet, so no, it's not over," she said with a smirk. We left the diner, walked to the strip mall nearby, and browsed for a while.

It was a lovely, uneventful rest of the date.

We continued getting to know each other over the next few months, by meeting whenever we could during the week in the library: half-studying, half-falling in young love.

While having movie-theater-dates, dinner-dates, staying-in-watching-TV-dates on the weekends; we had lots of dates during that time. Yet, we got comfortable and started to get past the point of needing to spend every possible minute together.

It was after this I reconnected with Denny again.

Chapter 4 - Seeing Myself for the First Time

Denny stopped by randomly and knocked at my door. My parents greeted him with smiles, welcoming him in. They talked about not seeing him in "so long" and ushered him into the kitchen while calling for me.

"Look who it is!" my mother said with moderate, motherly excitement. He was that one friend that they trusted and had saved me from a life of solitude and madness.

Little did my parents know; the madness was invisible.

"Hey Denny," I acknowledged him as the non-rockstar person he was. I had come up from the basement of our raised-ranch house, "wanna watch Back to the Future with me?"

"Yes. You know I can't say no to a classic eighties movie," he said with a grin.

Even over fifty years later the eighties still ruled.

We descended to the basement.

I was watching Part II. Because of the lightning scene. This was definitely an obsession.

We didn't talk much after I restarted the movie, but I paused it at the point where Doc is sliding down the long extension cable and Marty is flying down the street toward the wire crossing from sidewalk-to-sidewalk.

"This is the best part," I said leaning forward on the couch and pointing at the TV while looking at Denny, "this part changes everything."

"OK, dude. Calm down. Three is still the best one in the trilogy," he said arrogantly.

"Yeah, but without this part, there can be no three," I said with comically wide eyes.

"OK... whatever. Can you hit play?" he said rolling his eyes.

I hit play.

I watched closely, attempting to slow the scene down in my mind so I could watch the exact moment the lightning struck the cable on the clock tower, sending electricity streaming down it.

The electric pulse flowed to the wire crossing the street, just as Marty in the DeLorean rushed under. The lightning had charged the line as the special wire-hook attached to the top of the car/time machine made contact, precisely. This gave the time machine enough juice to power the flux capacitor (the device that made time travel possible). Marty, the DeLorean, the special hook, the flux capacitor, and all, are sent – Back to the Future!

This fictional movie gave me a glint of hope.

Denny made me put on Part III afterward, and we hung out and watched that. Then three other eighties classics.

Once he left, I headed to my room and started peter-panning (which was called doom-scrolling at one point, but recently adopted this new urban definition after kids rediscovered what Peter Pan was really about) on YouTube. Then I pulled up that video Tabitha pointed me to and watched it for the hundredth time.

Even twenty years later these videos were still cranking on the platform, except the UI team at YouTube had to add more space for more commas and digits. Also, YouTube was now owned by O Media. This stood for Only Media, meaning the only one left, since it gobbled up every other tech company. Somehow, they convinced the FTC that the acquisitions were part of their "vertical integration strategy" and therefore not causing a monopoly. On paper they acquired YouTube just for its massive data cities (yes, the size of a medium city), so yeah, government nonsense never changes.

This physicist named Sean Carroll (recently a Nobel Prize winner for his work in quantum mechanics) explained to Joe Rogan (now a retired billionaire, and former Texas Senator (R)) in the video, about the "many-worlds theory" of quantum mechanics.

After this video, the suggestion engine churned up more related videos where experimental ones showed attempts to open an interdimensional portal. Some fell under the "free falling" category, while some were legit.

The legit ones were of interest, but nothing showed me how to actually do it. I knew what I saw, it opened with the lightning strike – the strike hitting the pendant. I was convinced this was the truth. I walked over to my drawer and grabbed the lower pendant half from Michael's necklace.

I sniffed it and it still smelled slightly like burning, having a charcoal and cinder smell. The end was smooth where it connected at a magnetic point of its pair. It's amazing how the lightning hit this thing directly at that connection point. Maybe it was connected to the magnets?

If I could just get lightning to hit this pendant, or a new one to be safe, I didn't want to ruin the last piece of history I had that represented my brother, then maybe I could open the portal and get my brother back.

I was a teenager, so of course I didn't think too much more about the scientific validity of my theory, or even call it a theory for that matter. I just went ahead and attempted this.

My obsession list was growing. Not only was I into learning about lightning, but I was also into learning about parallel dimensions, magnets, and now apparently meteorology. I needed to track storms in order to track when lightning would be more likely to strike and to find the best time to attempt my (insane) plan.

I had visited my grandmother seeking out a new pendant, which she had, and gave me almost instantly once I expressed interest. She was coy about where she obtained it. I think she felt guilty not giving me one sooner. Explaining she was going to give me one the next time she saw me, back before Michael vanished, because she had only just recently given that other one to Michael, and I hadn't seen her yet and she always liked to treat us evenly.

There were thunderstorms predicted in two days, so I set out to plan my experiment. I gathered gear: an unopened model rocket kit I found in my attic, duct tape, rubber gloves, rubber rain boots and goggles. I couldn't find any copper wire though. I needed enough to attach to the rocket, so that it could go high enough into the sky to draw lightning, while not reaching the end and getting yanked back down before a strike. The end which would be tied to the pendant and then the ground. I visited Denny to seek some out.

31

This led to many questions and curiosity and next thing I knew I had a new partner.

We had found that the previous owner had left some in his shed and apparently had used it to attach from the basement up to an antenna they had on the top of their roof to get signals from, I didn't know, maybe outer space?

We brought all our equipment in stages to the wood line, right at the edge before the fence that surrounded the infamous tower.

I figured why not return to the scene; maybe there was significance in the spot.

It was going to be an interesting challenge launching a model rocket, with copper wire attached, in the middle of a lightning storm. We decided to practice a little bit, to ensure at least the rocket would launch. We launched the rocket from outside the fencing a couple times under these better conditions and without the wire attached.

The rocket sailed up smoothly and parachuted back down safely.

We then secured the copper to the rocket. I then led the copper wire down to wrap around the middle point of the pendant.

When we were finished, we covered everything up with some loose dead leaves and then headed back into my basement. I turned on the TV to the weather channel and we watched for a little bit and checked the timing that was estimated for the storms to come in.

There would be no events for several hours, so we put on a movie to pass the time. This time we watched a movie new to streaming. Dead pool and Quantum Iron Man: The Portals inside Me. The latest marvel reincarnation of Iron Man mashed up with Dead pool to revive Iron Man on a different timeline. (Seriously, Marvel's slogan should be Endless Incarnations, because a multiverse was the Wild West).

Halfway into the five-hour movie (it was a game changer when movie theaters finally started doing intermissions for bathroom breaks, at the trade-off of charging triple), we heard thunder.

Denny and I popped up. I paused the movie, and we listened. More thunder. I flipped off the light switch and opened the shades. A flash illuminated the sky, trees highlighted with bushy tops blowing back and forth and three seconds later came some more thunder.

"Let's go," I said, heading out of the basement, through the garage side door, without waiting.

We rushed quietly out of the house and headed for the tower. When we arrived at our setup, the leaves had mostly blown off, exposing all our stuff. We suited up, which really was pulling on rubber gloves, rain boots and putting on goggles.

I began setting up the rocket, a few feet away from the tower, with a clear space to fire it up into the sky. I asked Denny to hold the copper wire so it wouldn't drag after me when I walked.

"This doesn't seem like a good plan anymore, Max," Denny said with some volume in his voice, while looking around at the angry sky, competing with the thunder that was getting louder.

Lightning was striking all around at this point.

The flashes were bringing back memories. I could see the scene of my brother and me clearly, then I'd blink and be back.

"Max!" Denny shouted, "Can you hear me?" He was agitated.

"Yeah, what's wrong?" I said with a startled, confused look.

"I've been yelling your name for like a minute!"

I hadn't heard him until now. I was lost in the brief memory that felt like only a millisecond.

"You have to launch it and get out of here; we can't stay here!" Denny yelled and didn't wait for a response, just started moving back to the hole in the fence we came through. I nodded and pushed the button to launch.

The rocket blasted into the sky, copper wire trailing behind.

A flash hit it as soon as it hit the low clouds and it exploded and electricity streamed down the wire, rushing towards me.

I dove back toward the fence and spun my head back to look where the pendant should have been. My arm hair was standing straight up, and I looked from my arms to the unusual spot on the ground.

The portal was there.

I could see it clear as a reflection in a mirror. I got to my feet and rushed to it. The winds seemed to slow. I knelt down to look inside. I reached my hand in and out as fast as I could. Nothing happened to it; there was no damage to my hand.

"Denny! Look at this! We did it!" I shouted out over the still thunderous storm. He didn't respond and I looked back to find him slumped against the fence. I panicked internally, gut rolling around, but couldn't pull myself away just yet to go to him.

I had to look.

I dipped my head into the hole as if dipping my head into a barrel to bob-for-apples. I kept my hands firmly outside the hole and braced myself. I could fully see the other side, a vision of the same place, same storm, same tower, but no sign of Michael. Looking around I then saw my own eyes, on a mirror image of my face.

I was looking at myself and we were both as confused as intrigued.

I took in the sight as long as I could until I heard a strange air-sucking sound. I immediately pulled my head back. I assumed the portal was closing and didn't want my head severed. Sure enough, it began to shrink like a round puddle drying up in the sun.

It was gone.

A loud clank shook me back to the trouble I was in. I heard shouting coming closer, from somewhere beyond the fencing. I noticed Denny slumped against the fence and rushed to him.

"Come on, Denny, wake up," I said loud enough for him to hear over the thunderclaps, but not too loud, cautious for whomever was on the other end of the shouting in the distance.

He wasn't waking up but could feel breathing moving his chest up and down.

"Max!" my father was shouting for me, then my mother echoed, then another voice yelling for Denny.

This night had been a considerable success, but no one else would see it that way.

Denny was fine.

He was scared so bad by the lightning strike that he ran into the fence face first trying to escape the danger. He knocked himself out, while also scratching his face up. Honestly, he looked worse than he actually was, when my parents and his mother rushed up as I was trying to drag him through the opening, we made to sneak in.

It didn't matter.

I was responsible for two events involving lightning, because of my "reckless behavior." I was no longer allowed to be around Denny, which was a ceremonial punishment, because my parents had me institutionalized – "for my own safety."

And so ended that chapter of my life. No more dancing around the awkwardness with my parents. I felt some relief with this, but at the expense of leaving Tabitha and to a lesser degree my best friend Denny, which made me kind of sad.

Yet, I was also invigorated by this and more motivated than ever to figure out how to create a portal to find my brother.

Chapter 5 - The Looney Bin Wasn't So Bad

The looney bin wasn't so bad.

Being there allowed me to focus my attention on my next steps. I was able to continue my research, in secret of course, after a few months.

Those first few months were rough, though.

When I was admitted, I thought I would be there only a week, because that's what my parents made me believe. I just held on, dazed, and waiting for them to collect me, but the doctors kept talking about their plan for treatment for me. It kept changing. They'd ask me what happened, and I'd recount everything, then they'd change the type of pills or adjust the dosage. A few days would pass, and I'd forget why I was there. Then memories would come crashing back and I'd have what they described as an "episode." The doctors would ask again and – rinse and repeat. Finally, after three weeks I started to learn what was going on. I started to tell them what they wanted to hear. The dosages were being reduced and I was no longer in isolation or suicide watch (there were some dark days).

I was allowed to see my parents finally.

"How are you feeling, Max?" my mother asked with red, damp eyes.

"I'm fine," I responded with minimal eye contact.

"Max, I hope you are listening to the doctors, they really are here to help you," my father said.

"Yes," I acknowledged with an even shorter response.

"You have to understand why we did this," my mother said.

"I do," I said.

"The doctor said the treatment appears to be working, but it takes time to complete," my mother said.

"Ok," I said, then rose from the chair I was sitting in across from the two chairs they were sitting in. Then I walked away. I heard my father say to "just let me go" that I "needed time," but my mother just cried softly as I disappeared around the corner.

It was a shame.

The place was set against a picturesque backdrop. Nestled in a wooded cluster of seemingly endless acreage. It had a large terrace out back where the "good ones" got to enjoy a bit of nature on nice days. I suppose the beauty was meant to balance, or distract, depending on if you're a patient or a visitor.

Tabitha visited me into my second month.

"I've missed you," Tabitha said as the first words to me, as she was led to where I was sitting at the corner of the "good ones" terrace. I finally was perceived this way, finally earned the status.

"Hey, you," I said, smiling and rising to meet her and look into her lovely, familiar eyes. It turned into an embrace. "I missed you too," I spoke close to her ear. This lasted only a few seconds before an orderly scolded us from a distance with a "hey" and a stern glare. This wasn't prison, but also not a high school library by any stretch. We decided to behave and sat across from each other. The orderly seemed happy we'd complied with the rules quickly, so let out a bit more to give us our space to talk privately.

"You look better than I expected," she said with a smirk.

"I had my anti-crazy pills today," I said winking.

"Very good, those are important," she said. It became silent though. Banter could only last so long in a situation that was serious.

"I am doing better. They have me on the 'right dosage' now," I said with mocking quotes formed from my fingers, "I'm thinking clearly though." I could only halfway smile.

"That's good to hear. Do you think you will be out of here soon then?" she said, perking up and leaning forward in her chair.

"I'm not sure," I said.

She just frowned and sat back.

I looked around and leaned forward.

"I'm telling them whatever they want to hear, so they'll let me go," I whispered.

Tabitha raised an eyebrow and sat forward again.

"I guess that's a strategy..." she frowned, "are you going to try to do something stupid again?"

37

Wow, she didn't sugarcoat it.

"What do you mean?" I was visibly taken aback.

"Are you going to summon lightning again?" she was visibly concerned.

I hadn't had a chance to tell her what I saw. That I saw the other side. That I saw myself looking back. My guess is my parents told her about what happened. It all happened so fast; I didn't have a chance to talk to her before being put in this place. It did give me pause as I considered if my parents sent her in here on some kind of humanitarian mission to try to "save me."

I didn't respond right away. This felt like a make-or-break moment; felt like a ride-or-die pivot point in our relationship. I couldn't help but recall the video I watched many times about the many-worlds theory. At this moment a new timeline was being born, a path down one of the forked lanes, and the outcome was unknown, yet both ways forward would play out.

It was time to define this timeline's path.

"I can't do it without help," I said, measured. Tabitha seemed to sit with her response for longer than felt necessary. She pinched her bottom lip with consideration radiating from her eyes.

"If I help you, I must be all in, fully involved. No more secret experiments," she wagged a playful finger at me. I smiled and eyed the orderly that was several feet away.

"Deal," was all I needed to say.

I raised my hand towards the orderly, his name was Bruce, like the Boss from many years back, and that sang inspired songs about America. Born in the U.S.A rang briefly in my ears when I thought of his name. Bruce in the U.S.A acknowledged me (that playful refactoring of his name in the familiar song made my inner self giggle when I thought it).

"Is it okay if we walk around?" I asked.

"Sure, I'll be nearby though," Bruce responded.

I nodded and Tabitha and I rose and started our slow stroll.

It's not like I could really do much to escape or anything. The bracelets the orderlies wore could call up "de-stim" drones that would incapacitate me relatively fast. Yet, the illusion of freedom still felt refreshing and kept me at ease.

"Do you have a plan?" Tabitha asked.

I casually looked along the wood line that boxed in the outdoor area we were contained in, making a point to gauge Bruce's distance. He seemed to take in the peacefulness as well in his own way. Must be a nice reprieve from containing disorderly patients.

It was the peak of summer and the encapsulating forest beyond was thick. I could see maybe five to ten feet in, but not much more. I wondered what secrets were held deep in hidden depths.

"I do," I smiled with a slight nod.

I wouldn't be able to elaborate much, so I couldn't explain what had happened or what I had thought of to attempt to recreate the situation again, but I did need things that wouldn't be in this place.

"Care to tell me? Remember that deal you just made, back over there, like not even five minutes ago?" She teased lightly.

"I can't exactly explain everything in detail with, the Boss," I sniggered slightly, not sure if she got the reference, but continuing anyway, "back there." I tipped my head subtly backwards.

"Okay, fair enough. How is this going to work then?" she said with a grimace.

"I was going to pass you a secret message the next time you came to visit," I said with a wink, "when do you think you'll be able to?"

"I can come next week… next Wednesday after I get out of work," she said after musing for a few seconds.

"Cool." The last sentence caught me off guard. "You started working?" I was quickly distracted by this new disclosure by my girlfriend.

"Yes… but before we head off talking about that…" she giggled, "will your," she leaned in a bit closer, "secret message," she said the words in a coy whisper, "give me all the information I need to help you?" she bumped her shoulder into mine before she returned to her normal upright posture.

"Yes. I'll fill you in on everything and give you a list," I said with eyes enlarging comically for emphasis and added humorous effect. "Something not as secret worthy, you could bring me a couple books, next visit. Something Deeply Hidden by Sean Carroll and the Emergent Multiverse by David Wallace. Also, The Warped Side of Our Universe: An Odyssey through Black Holes, Wormholes, Time Travel, and Gravitational Waves by Kip Thorne, if you can remember the title, ha-ha. They shouldn't view books as harmful... hopefully. I'd love a good textbook on lightning too... but that might be considered contraband considering." I smirked.

"Great. I look forward to starting our spy adventure," she said, pushing air out of her mouth with a low laugh and indexing emphasis on the last two words. "I'll see if I can pick up those books, if I can remember the names, Max." She just shook her head with amusement.

We walked a few more yards, tracing the edge of the courtyard tree line right at its edge, and followed its turn at the outdoor area's nadir. I stopped to look back at the magnificent, castle-like building in its full southerly panorama. Tabitha followed my eyes and took in the view with me. Bruce subtly did the same, but off to the side. I took a deep breath and released while staring in awe of the structure, thinking how it was so contrary to its contents.

"That's new," Tabitha said with a quizzical look.

"What's new?" I asked.

"That deep breathing thing you just did," she said with a raised eyebrow.

"Breathing is not new for me," I said with a smirk.

She just bumped my shoulder while scowling with annoyance.

"Yes," I conceded, "I've been doing breathing exercises with one of my therapists," I said.

"That's really good, Max," she said.

"They taught me about meditation practices to help 'calm my mind' as part of my treatment. They explained that they felt I was too caught up in the past and too fixated on that day I lost Michael. It made a lot of sense. Regardless of what happens, I was stuck on that day and not seeing what was going on in the current moment. I wasn't as present when I was with people, when I was with you, as I should have been..." I paused to look at her and frowned slightly.

She put her hand on my upper arm briefly before seeing Bruce and pulling it back down. She acknowledged me with a soft smile.

We took in the moment silently and started along the tree line slowly again.

"It started to work after a few sessions though, and I actually started to enjoy it," I continued, "it's relaxing and it did open my mind up to think clearly about everything. I don't need to keep reliving that moment, while still working towards my goals."

"I was really worried about you, you know?" Tabitha said without turning to look at me. "When I stopped by after work, that day, your parents said you were in the hospital but wouldn't give me much information. I was able to pull out of your mother that day that you were messing around during the thunderstorm and lightning struck near you and Denny. I had to push very hard to find out more, but that wasn't until a week later when I showed up at your house while your father was at work. Your mother told me the full story."

"Sorry. I didn't plan on any of this obviously. I'm so sorry I couldn't say goodbye," I said.

"It's okay. I know. And no more secrets, so it won't happen again," she said with a wink, "and I'm glad you found something that helps."

"Yeah, it's pretty amazing. I didn't realize how wound-up I was. That thing I did, that thing that almost got Denny hurt really bad, that was stupid. I see that now. I was caught up in trying to find a quick path to find Michael. Even though it worked, it was stupid, and I should have been more careful," I said, starting to walk the tree line again. Tabitha followed. Bruce trailing several paces behind now.

"What do you mean it worked?" Tabitha asked, catching that little breadcrumb I subtly left behind.

"It worked. I did what I set out to do, to see that other side. I didn't find what I was looking for exactly but proved it could be done... somewhat accidentally. I have no idea why it worked, but it worked." I said as I side-eyed back towards Bruce and he was still just out of earshot.

"Wow," was all Tabitha could muster.

"Yeah, so, next time, I'll give you more details and I'll have a list of things I need to make this happen... a lot more safely," I said, "but for now, tell me about your job."

Tabitha told me about how she started a job at a restaurant as a hostess a few weeks back. I guess she had an interview the day of the lightning adventure, so I never heard about it. The rest of her visit was casual, with us having set up our future-plans, and we wrapped up our conversation by the time we completed walking the square.

I went back to my room to write up my note for Tabitha.

I recounted the story, old school pen-and-paper style, and wrote up my list. There wasn't much to the list really. I wanted to see if I could create a "safer" scaled down experiment. I wasn't a scientist, nor any kind of whiz-kid genius, but I knew what I observed. There was a fundamental basis for my theory. I learned about the scientific method, so I was just following what was tried and true. I needed to strike that seemingly magical pendant at just the right spot with a blast of electrical energy and that apparently was the trick to opening interdimensional portals. Who would have thought it was that easy?

I requested that Tabitha get me more pendants, multiple, since I would probably burn through many more in no time. I needed the shot of electricity and had seen a video online of the advancements in nuclear batteries and speculated that maybe if I paired a strong enough one with an arc lighter, maybe I could get the jolt I needed.

I wrote out a simple list, in quantities she could sneak in:

Pendants (Grandma's Pendants)
Nuclear batteries
Arc lighters
Copper wiring, smaller gauge, at least 20 feet
Rubber mechanics gloves
Books (I already mentioned)

I couldn't wait for her next visit. Or rather, the one after that when she made the special delivery.

When Tabitha arrived the following week, she surprised me with the books I had requested. It didn't seem to be an issue, she just handed me a bag and I took it nonchalantly.

Bruce didn't even flinch.

We headed outside to the "good ones" zone and decided to just stroll. I found my opportunity when Bruce was admiring a pair of birds flittering around a feeder set near the center of the yard and passed Tabitha the note. She quickly and sneakily slipped the note into the front pocket of her jeans.

We both gave knowing smiles to each other and carried on. She told me about school, and her job, and new friends she'd made, and I filled with regret and envy. I was paying the price for my hastiness, but pushed the negative feelings down, so as not to become consumed, preventing me from enjoying my time with this lovely girl, my only ally.

After we circled a few times, our visiting hour was up and Tabitha bid farewell from the foyer.

I asked Bruce if I could return to the terrace area, since I was "extra good" today. He allowed it. I went and sat crossed legged in the grass for a while, which was about an hour. I was alone with my thoughts, and it was healthy.

I could feel things were about to change in a major way.

Chapter 6 - Reinvention

Two weeks later Tabitha returned.

That extra week in between had me a little worried, though, but I tried to consume my thoughts with what I was consuming in my new reading material. It was helpful to read a breakdown of quantum mechanics and gain an understanding of the concepts of many-world theory, but according to the scientific interpretation: there is nothing that allows for communications between the split off dimension.

How did I see my other self then...?

I needed to find internet access if I was going to fast-track getting to a prototype, so I set out to do that. It wasn't terribly difficult to find access, when I found the "teachers' lounge," as I liked to think of it, while wandering around one day. It was essentially where employees went on breaks and to escape the asylum I lived in. I noticed consistent periods of time when it was unoccupied and took advantage of those gaps to sneak onto the widely open, severely insecure QC computer (Quantum Computer, as it's called, which always annoys the department of redundancies redundancy officer) in there, not that it wasn't heavily encrypted, it's just that someone had scribbled the password down next to the keyboard on the Digi Post (digital Post It).

I started my search following keywords I'd jotted from the text I had noted while reading. I scurried across scientific sites and scoured scientific journals, attempting to comprehend deep concepts around quantum mechanics, superposition, decoherence and wave functions. This would take years of studying to fully grasp these concepts. It was useful to see there's actual support of the theory of parallel dimensions, even after years passed since the theory O.G.'s first wrote about it, and folks like Hugh Everett and Max Tegmark laid invaluable foundations, in addition to Sean Carroll and David Wallace. However, I didn't have the kind of time, nor patience, to reinforce my already known knowledge that parallel dimensions existed. I guess I was really trying to find out if anyone else had experienced what I had and if there was a little-known and/or quicker method of accomplishing travel in this space as an operationalized concept.

No luck. No time.

I stewed for the rest of the week until Tabitha returned with my scientific cache and managed to survive.

"This was the weirdest shopping list I've ever shopped for," Tabitha said when we met on the terrace. It was hard to tell if she was really perturbed, but I played it off apathetically.

"That's for sure," I said eying the lack of any type of bag in her hands, "but usually shopping yields products... maybe a little buyer's remorse, as well..."

"Yes, usually. And it did," Tabitha looked around coyly, "I didn't think these items would get through the checkpoints though."

I was caught off guard by this "checkpoint" comment. I didn't know that was a thing.

"I see," is all I said.

"Don't worry, I have it covered," she smirked, "Let's go for our walk."

So, we walked.

I obviously couldn't help but wonder what she was up to, but I resigned to trusting her and didn't push the topic further. We made small talk and did a few laps, and with stealth, she slipped me a note before kissing me on the cheek and bidding me a farewell seasoned with a good luck.

I returned to my room, devoured the note, taking in the sweet sentiment she infused it with, and then jolted up when I realized she had hidden my cache at the edge of the wood line at the far end of our outdoor walking route. I couldn't risk being seen grabbing a mysterious bag or package, not knowing how she packaged my goodies, by anyone here, so I had to wait until it got dark.

I had learned that some lower-level windows were unlocked in the activity rooms, during my exploring. I snuck down to the Arts and Crafts room and waited for thirty minutes to ensure I wasn't noticed, then I lifted the window open and climbed out. Slowly I made my way along the tree line, only able to see by half-moon light, to the location Tabitha specified. A black bag was stashed behind a tree, right where described. I retrieved the bag and worked my way slowly back along the tree line. I heard a faint sound at one point, and stopped, it was a hum of some sorts but I attributed that to some machinery coming to life in the building and this being just residual echoes.

I climbed back through the window I exited, lowered the window carefully, and made my way back to my room.

She got me everything from my list.

I was in business.

I began piecing together something I considered the right device to open a parallel world. My experience during the storm had channeled lightning, or better yet, high amounts of direct voltage, to the middle of the pendant. The pendant had its own qualities as a heavy metal as well as some magnetic elements and my guess, was that hitting the center, where the magnet connects, held some of the reasons behind the split opening.

My smaller scale test was to wrap the copper around the exact middle of the pendant, just like before, and then each opposite end of the copper wire would be attached to the tips of the arc lighter points. The nuclear battery powered the arc lighter by me essentially hot wiring the battery via more copper wire to connect to the positive and negative points in the lighter. This was why I needed the rubber gloves. I saw sparks a few times while trying to attach things. I also really needed a soldering gun. That would go on my future shopping list.

It was time to test.

I waited until after midnight to take it for a test run.

It blew up.

Melted my right-hand glove, index, and middle finger slots. Singed my right eyebrow hair. Burnt a black stain on my desk and left black stains licking up the wall. It was my first fail, but I had an idea of why it failed. I had wired it backwards.

It was pretty loud and left a strong burning smell lingering in the air. Once I gained my senses, I quickly cleared away all my necessary gear, hiding it under my bed, and hurried to move my desk lamp over the stain, and punctured the bulb with my pen.

When a nightshift orderly rushed in five minutes later, I told her the lamp shorted out. Fortunately, the shadow cast by the light of my remaining lamp obscured my battle scars.

She could only believe me, because what else could have explained the noise and I said it rather frazzled and believably. She checked around the room and saw no imminent danger, and in an effort to not have to do any paperwork, left it at that, and left me alone.

I went back to work. By the light of my remaining bedside lamp. I rigged up another device in about thirty minutes and thoroughly checked my work.

I leaned away, looking with just one eye, my right eye with the burnt brow above it, figuring it was already willing to sacrifice, and hit the button on the arc lighter.

Nothing happened.

Success!

Success, in not blowing up again, so I felt excitement that subsequently dissipated, along with the scent of ozone.

Nothing happened.

I pushed the button again, less carefully, with both eyes facing, both eyes watching and held the button down this time. The arc of electricity flowed.

Something happened.

I watched light, in the form of electricity, glowing in a pulsing somewhat-crooked-line crossing the arc of the arc lighter and then it followed the copper wire down on both sides. Traversing the copper and meeting at the coil wrapped around the center of the pendant. The pendant began to glow at its middle and it started to separate at the pole of the magnets. The electricity was getting more intense and began to push the magnet apart. As the separation formed a light, like hot white, as if it were the concentrated point when the sun shines through a magnifying-glass to cook an ant. The magnet was starting to vibrate and shift from being centered, but the polarity was pulling it back in alignment. The gap grew ever-so-slightly, and a hole was forming in the middle. As it grew, the hole pushed out from between the center and floated to the side. It looked like it was being pushed as well as pulled at the same time, but the pushing force was winning.

It was the size of a quarter at first, then a half dollar, then a Frisbee. It stopped there. Looking as it was trying to grow larger but ran out of grow-juice (best name I could think of at the time).

I watched as the hole floated, and a scene formed through it, to what looked like the other side of the hole. The scene was looking fuzzy, but I could see through like it was a dirty lens. I tilted my head to view the other side, which was the bottom side of the hole. The hole was almost perfectly horizontal and was as thin as a thin-crust New Style pizza (my stomach rumbled reminding me I hadn't eaten in a while, so preoccupied).

With my free hand I poked a finger through, half expecting it to come out the other side, half expecting a different hand from my own to poke through upwards towards me. The air split gently, like dipping a finger into a puddle of water that didn't cause rings, it didn't feel like anything but, er, air, but I could see the split visibly. I pushed my hand forward, creating a fist and going through up to my elbow. The ripple closed around my arm and was clearly showing a ring wrapping it. I pulled it back out realizing I could not see what I was actually reaching into at this angle. My thumb that was pushing the arc lighter button was tiring, so I stopped pressing and the hole slowly closed until it wasn't there anymore, and the magnet ends reattached.

"That was amazing…" a voice behind me spoke softly, causing me to jump and drop my newly concocted device to the desk. The copper disconnected and it looked like the whole device was broken now, "I've never seen anything like that in my life. How did you do that?"

It was Dr. Zine. My primary physician at the facility. The one that would not believe me about my brother and insisted on trying to drug me until I would forget about it all.

I didn't say anything. I just eyed him guardedly.

"Max. I never imagined you could be telling the truth," Dr. Zine said.

"Well… I was," I said, then looked back to the now broken device.

"I can see that. Did you create that device?" he asked.

I didn't want to tell him anything, but saying nothing might cause him to do something hasty, so I gave him as little as I could.

"Yes," I said, looking at him briefly, before returning my focus to the desk disaster.

"Where did you get the parts?"

"Are you going to take it away?" I answered his question with the only one I cared about an answer to.

"No, why would I do that?"

I shrugged, looking at him again, "does it really matter?"

"No, I suppose it does not," he said, moving closer, but slowly as to not seem like an aggressor. He only stepped forward halfway, then I suppose realizing that an orderly might be nearby, he stepped back to the door and peeked out. I just watched him cautiously.

"Listen, Max. Could you do me a favor?" he asked.

"It depends," I said.

"Could you put all this away? Hide it, if you must, and wait until morning when we can chat, preferably in my office where we'll have privacy," he asked sincerely.

I gave it consideration. I probably couldn't do much more anyways, and I was tired. He didn't seem to want to take anything away, and I'd sleep atop my cache in case he tried to snatch it while I slept.

"Ok," I agreed.

"Thank you," Dr. Zine said, "I'll see you first thing in the morning."

Chapter 7 - Unexpected Partnership

I met Dr. Zine in his office, carrying my science cache in my pillowcase, because I didn't trust leaving it in my room. I weighed the possibility of having it confiscated, versus toting it around awkwardly, as the lesser risk.

"I minored in physics in college, Max," Dr. Zine said as I took a seat opposite him sitting at his desk. He had a book laid open in front of him and he pointed down at it.

"David Wallace was a great philosopher and physicist in the field of Quantum Mechanics," he continued. He flipped the cover so I could see the author's name: David Wallace. (It's hard not to hear that name and think of the famous fictional character from the TV show The Office and think of all the awkward "Michael Scott" moments and laugh and die a little inside, but I digress.)

"I read a bit about him, and watched a recorded lecture by him online," I said, "he defends the Everett theory. There seems to be solid science around the parallel dimension theory, but no one has proved it could be done yet."

"I guess that's not true anymore," Dr. Zine said with a smile. "I'm impressed, Max. Not many people fancy themselves knowledgeable in this area, and you seem to even comprehend these concepts, even high level, at such a young age."

This felt condescending, but I suppose me just spitting out physics terms like this, would seem odd for a teenager to say out loud. Also, I was a patient in a mental facility.

"I wasn't lying," I said flatly, with maybe a slight air of contempt, "I know what I saw when Michael disappeared. I saw him disappear into another dimension. I know how it sounds to anyone that hasn't seen it, but I saw it, like I'm seeing you in front of my face. I saw it just like I saw my hand pass into an unknown space last night."

"I saw the whole thing. That was amazing," Dr. Zine said.

"Do you believe me now; do you believe me about my brother?" I said as I sat forward.

"Yes. I do believe you, Max. I'm sorry for not believing you before," Dr. Zine said, nodding, "you do understand why someone would have trouble believing you though, right?"

I guess I was in a therapy session.

"I do understand that, but I would expect my parents to believe me," I said.

"Fair enough. They discounted you too soon, I can agree with that. More so now, of course, and hindsight is twenty-twenty. Do consider that they were also dealing with the loss of a son, though."

"Yeah. I have a hard time with that one, because they seemed to obsess with that and forgot about me. I know that's selfish and can't imagine how they feel, but I also lost my brother and feel like I'm the only one trying to get him back," I said.

Dr. Zine nodded thoughtfully and there was silence for a few beats.

"Your feelings are completely valid, Max," he said after the pause.

Another pause ensued.

"So, where do we go from here?" I finally asked.

"What do you mean?" Dr. Zine asked.

"You saw what I did, saw the 'interdimensional' portal..." I said, and wrapped the crazy term in air quotes, since it still sounded crazy out loud, "Which I do hear how this sounds..." I said, smirking slightly, "are you going to take away my device, take away my parts?"

"No. That's yours. I don't have a right to that," he said, smiling, "I do have a proposal, however."

"Ah, okay, here's the catch," I said, shaking my head slightly, "what's the proposal?"

"Let me help you," he said.

This caught me off guard, and it showed on my face.

"Help in what way?" I asked, but could surmise what he might be suggesting, since he not-so-casually mentioned his experience with physics.

"I can help you not blow yourself up, or our facility either," he said with a wink.

"Okay. That could be helpful. I'd like to not blow up. Can you get more equipment?" I asked.

Our unexpected partnership began at that point.

Dr. Zine commandeered an abandoned room in the basement that had its own entryways. It reminded me of the woodshop/tech shop rooms in my high school, where they had a regular door to the outside as well as a full garage door that retracted up to the ceiling, to allow for pulling in a vehicle for educational dissection.

The room was largely empty, with metal tables lining the perimeter, and cobwebs and dust lining the tables. I walked along the edge and picked a table on the inside wall and brushed across the top with my hand, stirring up a little cloud. I coughed and walked back towards the middle of the room where a lift sat idle, not having done a pull up with a vehicle in a long while.

"This will do I suppose. Seems like no one has been down here in a while," I said, looking around and looking at Dr. Zine.

"No one has. Not since a patient was crushed under a vehicle when another patient hit the lift release intentionally," he said so matter-of-factly I got chills. I didn't push for any further explanation.

"So... should I just rebuild the device?" I asked.

"No, Max," Dr. Zine said slightly shaking his head with a smile, "this is how I'm going to help you out. I'm going to establish guidance to ensure safety. We'll work through a process following some minimum scientific principles. First being we don't just throw something together and press a button."

Dr. Zine walked over to the table I had started to dust off and tapped it.

"We'll start by laying out all the equipment, cataloging everything, and writing up some notes on the purpose of each item and then we'll draw up our plan to test. From here on out, we both talk about the steps we're going to take before we take them."

I fell into student mode and nodded.

I knew this structure was going to be good, so went forward with the process he described.

By noon we had everything laid out. We logged on to a couple of rolling digital whiteboards he had went to retrieve. They were positioned near our workstation. These boards were great, since they maintained version history and synced back to the whiteboard application we used. You just drew whatever with the stylus and it would show up in real time on any digital screen that was also connected with the whiteboard session. He drew up a rough sketch of the device I had built and labeled elements of it so we could define what each piece was doing.

After talking through my first failure, he suggested that we use colored duct tape to mark the wires for positive and negative sides and increase the number of nuclear batteries. This felt like 101-stuff, but it highlighted that I was an amateur. He actually did out the math, all officially, like a real scientist. I had questioning thoughts but didn't say them aloud because I was in awe and took in everything he said with thoughtfulness – I could learn a lot from this man.

After two full days of planning and then building a prototype, we were ready to test the newly made device.

"This is a little bulky," I said, raising it up and down in my hand.

"It has all the necessary parts, though," he said with confidence, "and it's just the first iteration."

"I'll be honest, I was imagining this device being very portable, so I could easily carry it around and quickly open interdimensional portals... which, continuing to say this phrase makes my mouth and brain hurt... there has to be a better term..." I said looking off in distracted thought.

"Let's brainstorm some ideas about names," Dr. Zine said as he approached the whiteboard and created a table to write ideas in, with proper column headers and one that said "Other Potential Names."

I couldn't help but roll my eyes, because I was anxious to just test, but I realized I fueled this with my abstract questioning. I let

53

the fact that he ignored my portability concerns sit in the parking lot for now.

"Okay. How about: Dimensional Gate, Interdimensional Gate, Interdimensional Portal, Interportal, Interzone, Portal Hole, Portal Zone Hole, World Hole, Worm Hole, Time Gate, Time Door, Time Doorway, Doorway Zone..." I listed off every name that popped into my head just then and Dr. Zine listed as fast as they came out my mouth, until I paused to think a bit before continuing, "Time Slot, Slot, Door, Portal, Gate..."

I paused to review what we had so far.

"None of these are jumping out as ones that feel right, but let's go through and cross out the ones that definitely don't work," he said, marker at the ready, waiting for me to speak.

We crossed out all but: Dimensional Gate and Interdimensional Portal.

"Why is this even hard? Ugh," I said with audible frustration.

"Naming things is hard," he said.

"Yep," I agreed.

We both looked at the board for a few minutes in silence.

"How about we incorporate the word bridge somehow?" I finally said.

"How about we just call it a Bridge," he said with a chuckle.

Wow. Sometimes it is hard to see the forest through the trees.

"Yes," I said with a smile "and what if we call the device a Draw Bridge," I said with radiating excitement and emphasis on the last two words.

"Brilliant," he said, writing this on the board and circling it, "let's test our Draw Bridge."

We had rigged the device with a remote button we could hold down from a distance. Rewiring the arc lighter is what took the longest. With proper equipment, we were able to solder the copper wires to the ends of the electrodes and create a rigid holder for the pendant, all fit into a 3D printed metallic casing that made it look just like an old-fashioned pocket watch, albeit, a lot larger. It was more like a grandfather clock of a pocket watch in this iteration.

We placed the Draw Bridge in a stand we fashioned and had setup on a metal table we dragged to near the vehicle lift in the center of the room. We also had the garage door opened in case some kind of event needed "airing out" and to let in the nice cool breeze.

We donned safety glasses, stuffed ear plugs into our ears, looked at each other and nodded. Then I had the honor and pressed the button on our remote trigger device. It first was the faint glow of the arc lighter stream and then the glow of electricity illuminating the center opening of our Draw Bridge, which exposes some of the components. The gaze on the device was brief once the Bridge formed vertically behind the device. We had positioned small mirrors inside the device to deflect the energy and guide where the Bridge would form. With the increased power from the additional nuclear batteries, the interdimensional hole (now known as the Bridge) was much larger than the one I generated a few days back, and the other side was clearer. This was at least the size of semi-truck tire and in pulsing fashion grew and shrunk back to that size. With the added measures we put in place to stabilize the current, it seemed to allow for the proper steady growth. I wanted to walk up to it and stick my head in to peek inside so badly, but I had promised Dr. Zine I would follow our new protocols. We did have a plan to look through it though.

"It looks stable now. Let's commence phase two," Dr. Zine said.

I extended the telescopic arm of the selfie-stick we had on hand and pinched into place a cheap digital recorder (these things will be around for cockroaches to keep reality TV culture alive well past the extinction of humankind). We walked up closer to the Bridge, and I was going to continue to step forward, if not for Dr. Zine's arm reaching across my chest keeping me back. He looked at me and nodded at the camera. We were close enough for me to reach the camera into the Bridge with the selfie-stick fully extended. The camera disappeared through the Bridge, taking in angles we couldn't see from our vantage point.

I held my arm still.

"That should be good enough," Dr. Zine said.

I brought the camera back to this dimension.

We couldn't resist watching the replay as soon as we turned off the Draw Bridge. It was hard to see on a three-by-five-inch screen, but we were impatient. Once we got the full glimpse of the other side, in that small view, which was not surprisingly like this dimension, we decided to hook up to a larger screen. We headed to an adjacent room, which had a large digital screen attached to the wall, and we tethered the camera.

We watched the view move up to the Bridge slowly and pass through. We could see the details very clearly defined. The camera passed through the center axis and to the other side and it was almost like filming while passing through the surface tension of water. Except there was no cloudiness and the other side was clear as this side. On the other side of the Bridge there was an empty room that looked like this one, but no people, no Dr. Zine or me looking back at us. This realization got Dr. Zine's wheels spinning.

"This is fascinating," he said, "I'm still in awe that this worked. I have to say you're very innovative coming up with this idea on your own while essentially basing your testing on speculative observations."

"I just approached it following things I knew," I said, "once I realized the key element was that pendant, I worked backwards from there to send enough energy into it figuring it should do the same thing the lightning did."

"Okay. Let's talk out our observations," he started, "we built a device, opened the Bridge with our Draw Bridge, and entered the Bridge with our video recording device. It recorded a scene that was similar to this one, but neither of us were on the other side of the Bridge; we didn't see anyone on the other side in fact.

"One explanation could be the fact that we 'made a decision'. We decided to open the Bridge, and did it in our dimension. We created a decision point. The other dimension they didn't decide to open a Bridge. Maybe they never went to the basement to try it?"

He paused in thought.

"That lines up with the Many-Worlds Theory," I said.

We both thought for a few moments.

"Maybe we should look through again," I said.

"What do you mean, 'look through'?" Dr. Zine asked with concern.

"The first time, under the power lines, I poked my head through and saw myself on the other side," I said casually.

Dr. Zine stared at me thoughtfully, scratching his chin, but didn't say anything.

"It was pretty surreal, I didn't feel anything when passing through," I said, "maybe being in the dimensions has an effect on what we see."

"Fascinating," he said, "I'll do it then."

He then turned back towards where the remote switch was resting.

"Wait, you?" I asked.

"Yes. I can't knowingly put you in danger."

"But it should be me, to test my theory about seeing myself again."

"You have no obligation to do this, but I have an obligation to keep you safe," Dr. Zine spoke while picking up the remote, "put on your safety glasses. In theory, I should see me then, thus proving the theory either way."

I couldn't argue. I supposed he could also experience this too, and once he saw it was safe, he'd let me do it too.

We took up our ready positions. He went to press, then paused and looked at the remote.

"We need to make a modification," he said, turning to the table behind us and placing the remote down. He retrieved the tool kit and took the remote's back off.

"We need to make this an on/off switch, so we don't have to hold the button down," he said while working to change around the wiring configuration, "this way we don't have to focus on holding down the button and can focus on making sure this thing doesn't chop off my head."

The power of iterative development.

He smirked and readied the remote. I smirked and nodded, and we both faced the Bridge zone. He switched on the Bridge, and it glowed to life. We waited for a minute then approached it slowly. He handed me the remote and signaled for me to stay where I was as he walked closer. Dr. Zine got right up to the Bridge and looked back at me before turning back towards it and slowly putting his finger to it. His finger passed through, then his wrist, then his elbow, then his torso. From my vantage point I just saw a belt pressed against the Bridge nexus and small areas of the room on the other side.

I held my breath.

He was in the Bridge for a full minute before pulling back. Dr. Zine's face was wearing amazement when he returned.

"Should I shut it down?" I asked.

He didn't answer.

"Dr. Zine," I asked a little louder.

"Oh. Yes, shut it down," he snapped out of it.

"What did you see?" I asked after closing the Bridge.

"I saw a field of golden wheat through the door."

My jaw went slack.

"A what?" I said looking sardonically at Dr. Zine.

"I saw a field of golden wheat on the outside of the building, through the open garage door. The wheat was waving in the breeze. I looked around as much as I could from my vantage point and didn't see anyone else, but was fixated on that field, because there was no forest in sight," he said.

That's why he was so amazed, the landscape was different in that dimension. We didn't see that field on the camera, but it might have been because I passed the camera through in a way that made the view facing to the left or right and not straight ahead. We had so much to learn about this and had endless experiments we could conduct.

"Can I peek through now?" I asked somewhat impatiently. It was childish, but I felt like being an impatient jealous child right now.

"Yes. The experience caused me no harm," he said, coming back to the moment.

We set up again, opened the Bridge, and I passed my torso through and took in the view. It was not of a golden wheat field through an open garage door. The garage door was closed now. I leaned left and then right and could see no other people in the room. I leaned harder to try to see what or who was on the other side of the portal.

I fell through the Bridge.

I heard Dr. Zine start yelling for me, but my name was cut off. I landed on the floor and immediately jumped up thinking that I might not be able to go back. I looked at the Bridge, but my fear dissipated as it looked stable. I stepped to the side to look behind it. No one was there. I walked back to the Bridge and started heading back to cross back, about to lead through with my hand, but paused. I searched with my eyes for the garage door opener and found it. I rushed towards it and pressed it. As it opened, I backed up to the Bridge and readied myself to dive back through.

I was inches from the Bridge and watched as a golden field of wheat appeared.

I could see why Dr. Zine was awe-struck. I was too. I snapped out of my gaze and turned and stepped back through the Bridge. I bumped into Dr. Zine who was about to come through after me.

"What happened?" he asked.

"I fell forward," I said.

"You had me worried," he said releasing his breath.

"I'm okay," I said.

We both moved away from the Bridge and Dr. Zine powered it down to close it.

"The garage door was closed when I went through, so I opened it and saw the same field you described," I said, "it was amazing."

"Interesting," he said, "so we might have experienced two different universes."

"But I saw the field of wheat instead of trees like you did. Were they just closely linked?"

Dr. Zine didn't respond and walked over to the whiteboard lost in thought. He started scrawling notes on it. He wrote about both of our experiences, drawing out the two parallel columns of data, and delineating the difference.

"We need more data," he said.

This is when we accelerated our testing speed. We ran several experiments in succession as quickly and safely as we could open and close the Bridge while noting the new data points we discovered.

This is a high-level list of the experiments we conducted:

Dr. Zine returned to find the garage door open and then he closed it. No other people were found.

Dr. Zine returned right after coming back and confirmed the door was still closed. There were no people still.

I returned ten minutes later and confirmed the door was still open for me. I closed the garage door. Still no people.

I returned a minute later and confirmed the door was closed after shutting it.

I returned ten minutes later with an object from our side and placed it on the nearest table on the other side. Still no other people were around. I stayed for ten minutes and made more observations, making notes on a digital tablet. I heard no sounds coming from anywhere nearby on the inside. I heard nature sounds coming from the outside.

Dr. Zine returned with the object I had left on the other side, after ten minutes of observation. The garage door was closed. No other people were around. He confirmed no sounds inside, but heard the nature sounds outside.

We had to evaluate the new data sets thus far, after the last test, to test our theory of the two of us entering different dimensions out the window.

"I don't understand this, I thought we were entering two different dimensions, but you found the object I left..." I said as I took a seat near the whiteboard.

"It's the nature of experimentation," Dr. Zine said with a smile.

We had started to build out the equipment in our makeshift laboratory over the course of several days. We'd work for around ten to twelve hours a day and then rest, our bodies and minds.

Dr. Zine had explained to his staff that he was trying out an innovative, cutting-edge type of therapy based on teaching patients about science to help them better understand their minds. Since I was "inquisitive" and a "perfect candidate" for this trial, it explained away skepticism.

They seemed to buy it because we were left largely uninterrupted. We had setup a camera system pointing at our whiteboard work area, with the Bridge completely out of sight (the camera setup also gave us another idea, and we setup a separate secure feed, only we could view, pointed at the Bridge, so we could monitor things immediately visible on the other side [It helped with our retrospectives at the end of the day].) This way staff could see us working at the whiteboard if they felt like checking in; this gave anyone that was skeptical or concerned peace of mind.

We were allowed to conduct our experiments in peace.

Chapter 8 - Turning Point

Tabitha came to visit. It had been a month since she dropped off my science cache.

So much had changed since then.

"You look older," she said and then scrunched her lips to one side and touched her chin, "or just tired as hell."

"The latter," I said and signaled with my hand towards the usual direction to take. Bruce followed behind at a respectable distance, slightly further than normal. Maybe Dr. Zine told him to give us our space.

"I'm going to guess you made good use of my gifts?" she said still looking inquisitively at me.

"Oh yes. A lot has happened since I saw you last time," I said, "we're full-on experimenting with Bridge crossing."

"With what?" she asked.

"Sorry, new nomenclature," I said with a shrug.

"Who are you, and what did you do with my Max?" she said. Awe, she said "my" and that melted me a little and reminded me of who I was talking with.

"Let's sit over here," I signaled to a pair of chairs in the center of the rectangle walking area.

We sat and I explained everything to her. Bruce seemed to just want to continue walking, so was the perfect distance away from us.

"When can I see this thing?" she asked.

"Maybe next visit. I'll talk to Dr. Zine. He might be able to pitch it as seeing his experiment in action or something like that," I said.

"Okay, that would be cool," she said, "also, Denny wants to see you."

This was the last thing I expected to hear come out of her mouth.

"Really? He doesn't hate me?" I asked.

"Why would he hate you?"

"Because I got him hurt."

"Not on purpose though, he knows that. He's worried about you. He reached out to your mom and your mom told me he wants to come visit you. I told her I'd check with you," she said and tipped her head, smiled, and shrugged.

"Interesting," was all I could say.

"What's interesting?" she asked.

"My mom doesn't want to visit me?"

"Oh. She didn't say anything about that to me," she was visibly uncomfortable now. Awkwardness blew between us.

"I'll talk to Dr. Zine. Maybe you both can come see the Bridge," I said after a few beats.

"Okay," she said with a small smile, "and maybe then I'll find out what the heck a 'bridge' is."

"Yes, yes you will," I said smiling back, "enough about me. How are things with you?"

"Things are good. It's not fun being part of the working world, I'll tell ya. Once you start making money, you want to use it, and then you need more to use and the cycle repeats," she giggled to herself.

"What?" I asked.

"I almost said you had it good being in here," she said.

I laughed because it was a funny thought.

"Lucky guy, I am," I said.

She shared some stories about work and how she was doing in school and then our time was up.

I said goodbye and headed to the basement lab.

I told Dr. Zine about what Tabitha and I spoke about, and he was surprisingly open to the idea.

"That might be okay," he said, surprising me.

"It would help my relationship with her if she saw for herself what I've been telling her I've seen," I said.

"Yes, I agree. I would classify it as part of your therapy session as well," Dr. Zine said matter-of-factly.

I didn't need to plead my case, like I had thought I would have to, so didn't need to say anything else about it.

We went back to work.

Tabitha and Denny wouldn't be visiting for two weeks, so we continued our experimentation, gathering further data points.

We learned that the Bridge was creating an opening between several dimensions, and we couldn't control which one presented. We were proving solidly the existence of the multiverse. (I leaned towards calling them dimensions, as much as Dr. Zine leaned towards universes, but I thought universes sounded confusing as it relates to the multiverse, but to each their own.)

We did see dimensions we had already seen, so they were repeating, albeit randomly. We knew this because we developed a system of placing objects each time we crossed over. We would see these objects again. Strangely, we didn't see any other people during these visits.

Dr. Zine theorized that these dimensions were adjacent to each other, but in all of them, the versions of us in these dimensions hadn't made the decision to go to this room in the basement and conduct experiments. They might not have even invented a Bridge yet.

We were dealing with some heavy concepts and my head was starting to hurt trying to wrap around the ideas he was presenting. I just trusted his expertise and we carried on.

After a week and a half of testing, Dr. Zine was feeling comfortable in our understanding, and we had only seen one anomaly he couldn't explain. Up until this test, we had been able to document being able to retrieve every object we left on the other side of the Bridge, after enough attempts. This one anomalous case happened as we opened the Bridge to a dimension where we were expecting to see an object we had laid, but there was no object at all. Since we were leaving one in every visit and finding one as well upon returning. Not seeing one this time took us by surprise. We logged it and continued.

After a few more days of testing, we didn't see that "empty" dimension, so chalked it up as just an anomaly.

This gave Dr. Zine the signal that it would be okay to invite our guests down to check out the setup.

When I met Tabitha in our usual meeting spot, Denny was with her. He was smiling sadly at me, a little bit of pity in his eyes.

"Hey man," I said to Denny after greeting Tabitha.

"Hey Max, how have you been doing?" Denny asked.

"Good, how have you been?" I asked going through the platitudinous exchange.

"I've been ok. Tabitha said you had something exciting to show us," he said with a weak smile, looking over at Tabitha for validation.

"Are we still going to check out your new therapy room and meet your doctor?" Tabitha asked me.

"Yes, follow me."

They followed me and I didn't even have to awkwardly redirect Bruce, he just stayed where he was.

We got to the room, and Dr. Zine was waiting patiently for us, near our blank whiteboards. We had decided to clear our notes from the day from the whiteboard, having filed the digital copies away earlier.

Tabitha and Denny looked around the mostly plain-looking room and then at each other, as I led them up to Dr. Zine.

I made introductions.

"Very nice to meet you two," he said to them, "I've heard so much about you." They returned friendly greetings.

"Can we show them?" I asked, eagerly.

"Yes, let's show off our progress," Dr. Zine said.

"Everyone has to put these on," I said to Tabitha and Denny, handing them safety goggles. They donned them compliantly.

I signaled for them to stand behind a line we created earlier with duct tape. They complied.

I looked at Dr. Zine and he handed me the Draw Bridge remote and nodded.

I opened the Bridge and heard two audible gasps from behind me.

It was silent for a few moments, then I turned to look at Tabitha and Denny. They were awestruck, as I had expected they'd be.

"I can't believe it," Tabitha said finally breaking the silence, "it's just not real until you see it for yourself."

"It is indeed," Dr. Zine agreed.

"Yeah, I always believed it," I quipped.

Denny was still slack-jawed.

Dr. Zine closed the Bridge.

"Can I get a closer look?" Tabitha said, wanting another neurological rush.

Dr. Zine and I looked at each other. I could tell he was resistant on the inside, but then he nodded.

"You can get close to it but keep at least two feet from the Bridge and don't give in to temptation to reach through," Dr. Zine said with a wink.

Tabitha and I moved closer, right up to the "two feet" edge. I looked back and noticed Denny hadn't budged. I didn't even mention it. I looked at Dr. Zine and he opened the Bridge.

It opened in front of us, and I felt a figurative wave of energy, just like every time I was close to it, witnessing its force.

I peeled my eyes from it to look at Tabitha. She was in such a state of peace staring at this beautiful sight. I smiled.

I was about to comment about this to her and heard a low whining sound, like the audible version of a flashlight dying. The Bridge started to shrink slightly but persisted open. I looked back at Dr. Zine, and he looked down at the remote, then at the Draw Bridge edges. All of a sudden, I felt the wind of Tabitha falling towards the Bridge fast. I looked back and saw two arms wrapped around Tabitha as a body had come through the Bridge, and was now yanking Tabitha away from me. I didn't have time to process who the body belonged to. Her arm extended towards mine, this other person's hand was suppressing her arm from the other side and I managed to rush forward and grip her wrist. I felt my fingers on her bracelet, as well as on the sleeve of the stranger.

She was suddenly on the other side now, being pulled farther away...by the person I suddenly recognized as myself. I made eye contact with the Max on the other side and could only blink. My instinct was to yank Tabitha back towards me by the wrist, but she slipped away, a torn piece of shirt and her bracelet left in my hand. I was left with the last sight of her being a haunted, terrified look of confusion in her eyes, as if her last blink at me translated to the phrase "help me."

Suddenly the Bridge closed.

Tabitha was gone.

Taken to the other dimension...by me.

I looked back at Dr. Zine and then at Denny standing next to him, and back at the place where the Bridge was open seconds ago.

I could raise no words from my throat.

Chapter 9 - The Search Continues

Ten years after Tabitha was taken, I was no closer to finding her or Michael.

I had a lead though.

I was in a dimension roughly twenty-one steps removed from my home dimension, in a southerly direction. To help conceptualize, we referred to the "position" of the step like you would a location on a map, if you based it on compass coordinates. Technically, this didn't account for the "up" or "down" directions, and those could be "north" and "south" as well, but then your head explodes when you try to think about it. For all intents and purposes, I was "south" in the sense that I headed in one direction hopping from one dimension to the next staying as linear as possible to try to follow a specific path. It's complicated.

We had figured out how to isolate and travel to specific dimensions, but it took some finesse and required travel through other dimensions to get to the desired dimension. Lots of "mathy-type" stuff on Dr. Zine's part and lots of tests.

The important thing was that I was here and needed to focus on the current task at hand.

I walked into a bar that was under a very tall building. Inside the white neon-colored light came from the illumination ceiling panels, like back in the old days. Up-tempo jazz music was playing, it was the song Petals on Mars by The New Travelers. I took a seat at the bar and ordered a drink. As I waited, I unsuspiciously scoped out the bar. It was more spacious than I was expecting, as in it spread out behind me and had corners, I couldn't see the edges of. The motif was western with reddish brown leather booths running around the edges, and tan four-top tables with faux-handmade ladder-back chairs. There were maybe ten people in here, with a fire-marshal capacity of two-hundred and fifty; this place was empty. It smelled of burnt crayons, probably because of poorly electrified heated floors. I leveraged the mirror behind the bar to surveil. It was a slight challenge since eighty percent was obfuscated by dusty bottles.

The barkeep obfuscated it a hundred percent when she delivered my glass. I gripped it and watched it turn green then took a sip.

These glasses were great until they signaled to the barkeep that you'd had too much to drink. They were designed to measure your levels. It was convenient to share the calorie count of the beverage in the glass, but annoying when you were cut off, if you didn't have time for lunch and your levels were prematurely inflated.

When I first started traveling the multiverse, I thought money was going to be an issue, and I'd have to steal some to survive, but then I found out a multiverse hack. With digital currency on the blockchain, I could spend money in another dimension, that I had purchased in my home dimension, and not have it affect my balance in my home dimension. It recorded the transaction here but wouldn't reflect there. The only times I had issues were when the dimension I was in happened to have misaligned ledger records, but that only happened one time and I was forced to exit quickly after excusing myself to the bathroom.

"Brooklyn, scan area for scents," I said in almost a whisper to my BridgeAI assistant. (I preferred Brooklyn over Fremont, because the sound of her voice has become my north star in finding Michael and Tabitha.)

"Scanning for scents, Max," Brooklyn responded. Scent tracking technology had come a long way in the past ten years. Bloodhound AI (every new technology since the mid twenty-twenties appended the letters "AI" to make the company's valuation instantly triple) had revolutionized the technology for detecting and analyzing scents in a hundred-foot radius indoors and roughly fifty-feet outdoors. We had been able to scan a ripped piece of fabric that tore off when I tried to save Tabitha from being pulled to the other side of the Bridge by my doppelganger.

After that Max (I called him Bad Max now) had grabbed Tabitha and kidnapped her, he had taken her almost immediately through to the dimension "next-door."

It took us almost two years to figure this out.

It took us a while to figure out where a lot of things went wrong that day. It turned out the nuclear batteries in the Draw Bridge had died, at the worst time. As soon as we could get the Bridge open again, I went through and tried to search for Tabitha. It was fruitless though because we didn't know the exact dimension she was lost in, and I immediately spotted a familiar object we had placed during testing. We speculated she was lost in the anomalous dimension eventually, since we had no record of any objects, we placed in that one. I must have replayed the video of the event over a thousand times looking for clues, seeing the table we placed objects on sitting empty. In all reality, it could have been a new one we hadn't even explored before, but we went with what was known to us at that time.

Dr. Zine was fired from the mental health facility after we lost Tabitha, but not before we covered up the situation by staging a massive explosion, that allegedly also killed me.

Denny debated having it also kill him, so he could help me search for Tabitha, but I argued that I needed him to help Dr. Zine on this side to figure things out and get organized to advance our technology as fast as possible. After the initial panic cleared, we got the Bridge open again. Figuring out that the batteries had died was easy as soon as we tried to fire it up again and the Draw Bridge had no juice. We replaced the batteries with a set of backups we had. Then we proceeded to test until we could open the Bridge to the dimension, we had first placed an object in, because we knew it was unoccupied (at least in the basement lab). Then I crossed over and they handed me all the equipment, including the Draw Bridge and two extra sets of batteries in a backpack which I immediately put on (partly to make sure the Bridge wouldn't just close once the Draw Bridge passed through and partly trying to avoid making a movie-mistake). I crossed back, keeping the Bridge open, while gathering enough gear for me to survive with until they could reopen the Bridge again after the dust settled. We planned out how to accomplish the explosion and made plans to meet at a point we found on the map. It was where an unused barn Dr. Zine knew of rested half a mile into the woods of the home dimension, and hopefully half a mile into the golden wheat field (we didn't have time to verify anything). The backup plan was to check-in by long-range (HF) radio, weekly at eight P.M. on Monday's (High Frequency radios were old school, functional technology still used by the military) once they were able to safely build another Draw Bridge and open it.

I waved goodbye and triggered the Draw Bridge to close the Bridge, for the first time from the other side, from another dimension.

Having fed Bad Max's fabric into the Bloodhound AI system long ago, I was able to just ask Brooklyn to test for matching scents wherever I was, and she could run scans. I could have her running this scanning continuously, but that took away from other important tasks, so did so only on demand when I felt close.

I was given a lead by a contact that told me Bad Max frequented this bar in this dimension and was feeling good that I was on his trail.

I showed a picture of Bad Max to the barkeep after pulling one up on my handheld.

"Have you seen this man?" I asked.

"He's in here often," she said.

I looked around the room again but didn't see him.

"Not now though, haven't seen him this week yet," she said.

"Was he here last week?" I asked.

"Yep."

"Was he alone?"

"No."

"Was he with this woman?" I asked while flipping to a picture of Tabitha. Noting to myself that the last time I saw her, she wasn't officially considered a woman yet.

"No."

I deflated a little.

"Okay, thank you for your help," I said. I then called up my payment app and tapped a small reflective square in front of me. The glowing border of the square section that indicated my personal consumption area turned from blue to green, to indicate I was now squared up on payment.

"One more thing," I said, pulling the barkeep back with my words. I showed her one more picture. This was a generated photo of Michael simulated to make him look older, make him look more like he would today, "have you seen this man?"

Calling Michael a man after last seeing him as little boy caused an ache in my heart.

The barkeep shook her head and then echoed a frown like the one that formed on my face.

I finished my last sip, and walked back out into the cold, zipping my inner coat liner up and then buttoning up fully the outer coat flaps.

As I walked over a puddle in the alley, I stopped and took note of my reflection. I had my black Gambler hat low on my brow, there was a glint from the silver hatband. The dark circles under my eyes were darkened further by the shadow my hat cast. My eyes were heterochromatic, green and blue, like a Siberian Husky, but not truly, because they were altered by contacts as a tactic to obscure my looks (with additional help for holographic project tech that would change the way my face showed up on camera). I knew there was another Max in this dimension and didn't want to show up on facial scans, making his life more challenging. I had learned that in this dimension, Tabitha didn't exist. Max's love interest was named Samantha, and they were happily attending the same college together a couple states over. Learning this was a reality-slap that there were variations to the dimensions that were more major than I expected. Except. Michael was missing here. He was always missing — everywhere. He didn't exist in any dimension I visited so far. I always checked for him though.

I also noticed in the puddle, as the alley lights shone down, that my long shearling coat was faded from its original dark brown to a much lighter variant. It reminded me that I probably should get other clothes, new clothes. I didn't care too much about how I looked. I did stay clean though, I did shower. I wasn't trying to be too identifiable by my scent. Not that it mattered too much, scent tracking was a science now, like fingerprinting was at one point. (But, of course, we had some tech to obfuscate my scent to some degree when needed.)

I had used the dimension two steps from my home dimension as my base of operations these days. The mental facility there was completely abandoned (shut down by the state after Dr. Zine accidentally killed Tabitha and I). It was a quick jump back to the dimension before that one when I needed to communicate home. Although, after my last visit home Denny told me that Dr. Zine had figured out how to project the radio frequencies across dimensions as far removed as ten. Of course, I was twenty-one steps away now, so was out of contact unless one of them crossed far enough towards me.

I stepped forward into the puddle, disrupting the stillness, sending ripples exploding to the edges.

I continued walking to the end of the alley, far out of sight of the bar entrance that was about three blocks back and then glanced around and asked Brooklyn if there were any prying eyes.

"Any surveillance camera field of visions in this area is as predicted, nonexistent, and no other people are in range. You are clear to continue," Brooklyn reported.

I pulled out my Draw Bridge. It was improved in so many ways. It was portable enough to fit in the palm of my hand now and packed with many newer features since the upgrades, including Brooklyn. Mine was encased in the shell of a pocket watch, which I customized to maintain that Old West-style look (because I loved the era and felt like a bounty hunter, which incidentally wasn't even a term used during that era; bounty hunters were referred to as manhunters back then). The watch face was all digital, but I maintained the traditional chain that stemmed from the top and clipped to my pants belt-loop. I had the Draw Bridge synced with my watch and handheld, so it only worked if one or the other was in the proximity of it (it was a paranoid precaution). The Draw Bridge really couldn't be attached to the body because it had to be positionable in any direction, which is why it wasn't a wrist gadget.

I checked the time on my watch, it was 22:05:00 hours, telling me it was time to settle in somewhere for the night.

I turned the bevel to the frequency of the dimension I desired to travel to (the watch face was constantly updating the frequencies to match against my current location and relative connected dimensions). I was heading to the one that was only one removed from the one I was in. This one had my current nearest hideout and... the best Fettuccine Alfredo you'll ever taste.

The Bridge opened against the brick wall, and I saw an empty room on the other side. I stepped through and the lights automatically turned on, then I cleared the room with a cursory glance with my eyes (knowing Brooklyn was also scanning) and closed the Bridge.

This dimension contained my hideout, which was a storage room, in an abandoned building, with the door dead bolted tight from the inside. It was where I had stashed a bunch of gear before crossing into the +21 South dimension. I referred to it as +21 South for ease of speaking of it and to remember it more easily. However, if it were written out it would be more like 21.5.6.5.4.5.6.5.6.5.3.5.5.5.4.6.5.5.5.5.5 in its semantic dimension version. As mentioned before, it's complicated. Hence why the BridgeAI did all the heavy lifting calculating and displaying it on the Bridge watch face and Brooklyn translated it to a simple number audibly for me.

My storage hideout was cozy.

I had stashed an inflatable memory foam-topped bed, in this grey-walled space, with my sleeping bag and memory foam pillow against the inside corner. I turned on the space heater and the room quickly became warm. I sat on the bed and unlaced my combat boots (I never found cowboy boots comfortable, even though they would have matched my theme better) placing them off to the side. Tracing the metal shelves along the outer wall with my eyes and did a visual inventory. I always traveled with enough equipment to repair or replace the Draw Bridge as well as assorted items for accomplishing the different missions I staged for myself. Since I felt closer to Bad Max than I had ever been, I had loaded up this room with enough to survive for at least a year in this dimension.

Fortunately, I didn't have to use my food stores, since I could afford to eat out with my digital currency hack, but it was always good to be prepared for anything. I never knew if I would have to hideout in my hideout for extended periods of time. Bio disposal wasn't pleasant but was manageable with the containment units I also had in here.

"We're getting closer, Brooklyn, I can feel it. We know that bar is where Bad Max frequents now, so we'll setup some visual monitors in the morning and wait for him to return," I logged my final thoughts with Brooklyn, almost ready to turn in for the evening. Looking forward to fettuccine for lunch tomorrow.

"I've noted the progress and backed up to the BridgeAI Span, Max," she noted. The BridgeAI Span was our Cloud system that would transmit periodically for syncing through microscopic Bridges opened in sequence all the way back to the Alpha BridgeAI Span in the home dimension. This way Dr. Zine and Denny had all the latest data (we had it programmed to only go in one direction to protect me). Pretty neat stuff we had at our disposal these days.

"One more thing, Brooklyn," I said, "send the guys a note from me that says 'Hey guys, I'm close, I'm finally going to get Bad Max. See you both soon' and deliver it via my holographic avatar for fun."

"Sure thing, Max," Brooklyn responded, "anything else?"

"No. I think that's it for tonight. Thanks Brooklyn. Good night," I said, knowing she didn't sleep, but it felt good to say it.

"Good night, to you as well, Max. Don't let the bugs bite you," she said.

"Oh my, okay, yeah, tomorrow I'll make some tweaks to preset colloquialisms. Er, remind me to do that," I said to Brooklyn laughing to myself.

"Will do," she said.

One last thing before settling into sleep, I brought my legs up onto the bed, tucked my feet beneath my opposite knees and began my nightly-wind down by doing a twenty-minute meditation. I started with some deep breaths and then settled in to observing the natural rhythm of my body. Even after all the years of doing my meditation practice, I still got lost in racing thoughts. I just was better at refocusing on my breathing sooner.

I was fully relaxed for the night and tucked myself into my sleep bag and dozed off for the night.

The restful sleep lasted only a few hours.

I was practically wet and breathing heavily when I sprung up suddenly.

"Is everything okay, Max," Brooklyn asked, "I'm detecting elevated pulse rates."

"I had another dream about Michael," I said.

This was happening a lot more lately. The dream would start off with Michael and me playing on the powerline tower. Then the events would unfold to him disappearing. I'd relive it over and over several times. Except this time. I saw him when I returned to find his broken pendant. His back was to me. I couldn't see his face and I'd rush to him, but when I spun him around to look at his face, it was still the back of his head. I'd move to the other side of him... still seeing his back. I'd do this over and over until I'd collapse and hit my head.

"I could only see the back of Michael," I said to Brooklyn. "I keep having this dream. What could it mean?"

"I'm not sure, Max, but I'll log it for further analysis," Brooklyn said.

"Okay..." I said, unsatisfied, "there has to be a meaning..."

"Do you remember anything specific from the dream, Max?" Brooklyn asked, "I can add that to the log."

I thought for a few moments about what I saw. With eyes closed I visualized the field and Michael standing there. Only his back was visible... but I could see the pendant hanging from his neck down his back. I opened my eyes with a flash of an epiphany. As quick as I could I rushed to turn on the desk lamp and pulled the broken pendant that hung on my necklace out from under my shirt.

I always wore it. I spun the pendant so I could see the backside of it.

There was a minus sign etched on it.

Chapter 10 - Bon Appétit

First thing in the morning I sent some drones out through a mini-Bridge to setup our surveillance operation, while I got ready for the day. They were digitally camouflaged and worked quietly and signaled when they were done so Brooklyn could let them back into the hideout. I checked the camera feeds on my handheld and on the independent monitors I had setup in the room, and everything looked good, so I was now free to leave until the sensors alerted me of a Bad Max sighting.

I slipped out into the alley.

It was a beautiful cloudless day and was perfect for walking downtown to Alfredo's, best known for its pancakes, just kidding, that's where the best Fettuccine Alfredo in the multiverse is (at least the dimensions I've visited so far, which has been a surprising amount, but surely a fraction). I pulled up the app for Alfredo's and made my reservation for one, for the earliest available, which was an hour from now. Even at 10:00 AM it would be packed. It would take about thirty minutes to walk there anyways, and I decided to hoof-it. I could have used the collapsible auto-scooter I had in my shoulder-bag or called for an auto-auto (automated automobile), but walking worked better with the timing and kept me in line with achieving my daily step goals.

I turned the corner coming out of the alley and was taken by the many lights of Boston Times Square, even during the day. This strip was named after The Boston Times acquired The New York Times and decided The Times Empire hadn't created enough landmarks. Digital billboards were the facades of most of the buildings on the five-mile stretch (fun fact about Times Square in NYC, it used to be called Longacre Square, and one could think the Boston version might have been overcompensating for something by making it three times larger).

It was awe inspiring how they integrated windows around the billboards, so occupants could still take in the sights of the street from inside their high-class restaurant space, high end office space or luxury apartments. This strip could be called Monopoly Row since Only Media owned ninety percent of the digital ad space on this street, as well as office space spanning two and a half of the five miles.

A wild experience is when ads start following you while walking down the street, when the sidewalk's not too busy, after detecting your digital tracking marker from your face or even your scent (Bloodhound AI Inc. had a trillion-dollar market cap for a reason). My ads varied because the tech had a challenging time pinpointing my markers and I did a lot to obfuscate those (another trillion-dollar industry was high tech perfumes). Right now, I was seeing streaming ads for the best uses for drone companions.

The Reese's store took up half a block, and I couldn't resist popping in. Needed me some Pieces. The entryway was expansive, large glass windows went floor to ceiling, and there were transparent orange and yellow tubes that zig-zagged upwards. Kids could go up to the upper level and drop large fake Reese's Pieces in the tubes and watch them race down to a giant pit. I bought some varying styles of candy, along with some high fiber, protein gummies that were near the checkout, good for slowing the sugar metabolism.

Once my snacks, for later, were packed safely in my shoulder bag, enough time was killed, so my reservation time was approaching fruition. I headed to Alfredo's and waited only a few minutes for my seat.

The restaurant had some awesome seating. I had reserved a Solo Pod on the third floor; it faced the street, dead in the middle of the five-mile stretch. The pod rotated on demand and the starting position was facing inwards into the restaurant, so a waitperson could greet you, take your order. You were able to rotate your pod to view Boston's Times Square and take in the view up and down the strip. I loved to watch the people walking. It was always fascinating to watch people being stalked by advertisements.

I would rotate as soon as my order was taken and stare off along the strip, out through the large glass panes, and when the waitperson returned, they could just gently ring my pod signaling to me to turn around.

I got my drink and spun back around to watch the reality show unfold before me. Even this early in the morning on a weekday there were throngs of people in this section of the strip. The popular attractions I could see from this vantage point, aside from the Reese's Store (Hershey had apparently had to divest some of its sub-brands in this dimension), were the Disney Store, the One Store (One Media's handheld store, rival of Apple) and the Drone Store. The Drone Store was the most popular since personal drones had reached mass adoption. I would pop in if I had time after eating to see what new tech options were being offered.

The waitperson signaled me to spin, and I saw the magnificent dish I had been watering at the mouth for since I arrived here last night. She lowered it to my table, sprinkled some shredded parmesan cheese on top of my fettuccine and waited for me to say I was all set for now and left me in peace. I rotated and dug in.

The thing I loved most about these Solo Pods were how they closed me off to other guests and let me slurp as much as I wanted to as I sucked up strand after strand of this delicious dish. It melted on my tongue. The whole meal was gone so much faster than it should have been, even though it was a plentiful dish and more than could comfortably fit in my stomach. I managed to fit the side dish of garlic bread in as well and then sat quietly for a little while digesting and watching people traffic.

Once resigned to the fact the experience was over, I paid on the armrest of my Solo Pod and excused myself from Alfredo's.

I headed over to the Drone Store.

In my collection, I already had several types of drones and many multiples of those types. The most useful were the digitally camouflaged ones for obvious reason, but those were banned in the U.S. in this dimension. They operated with a technology on the skin that repeated the surroundings in real time and filled in gaps, removed anomalies as it flew along – more AI driven technology of course. Four Guard drones were following me at a distance as I journeyed downtown today, instructed to stay outdoors.

They were nuclear battery powered and could replace batteries themselves when energy levels warranted (sometimes it required slight petty theft, since nuclear batteries could not be recharged. The "petty theft" logic was more customized software from Denny... Denny was a wiz with software, he built all the AI integrations as well).

The Drone Store was packed, and it felt like there was a two-to-one ratio of drones-to-people. Sales drones flew around trying to sell themselves by showing off their neat features. I headed first to the back of the four-story store, where they kept the Drone repair kits. The lenses were the weakest part of these things, in my opinion; the lenses always got scratched and/or cracked, so I could always use replacements.

I bumped past a teen who gave me a funny-eyed look and I noticed him look at his friend with a smirk. Pickpockets evolved to use digital wallet skimmers, by getting close enough to handhelds to tap their device against yours, to activate and make away with funds, from whatever payment account was the default. I had no wallet. The pickpockets would have to find a new mark today.

Adjacent to the repairs sections was a somewhat discreet section that looked new. Items were behind locked glass with stickers that said "bullet-proof" for some reason. I noticed a new type of drone I hadn't seen before. There was just a flyer since the real merchandise was held safely in the back. They told me it was a Bloodhound AI 10000 aerial drone (they had drones for water and land in addition to air, but air ones were the most popular amongst the populace), which was billed as "the best drone for sniffing things out from a thousand feet away like a true bloodhound."

Shut up and take my money.

I found a sales associate and made the purchase. The box was about the size of a men's size twelve shoe box but described the actual unit as only "slightly bigger than your hand," which was such a relative measurement.

I tucked the box to my armpit, after checking out and refusing a bamboo shopping bag to carry it in, then headed back into the madness of Boston Times Square. It was afternoon and around the peak time of pedestrian overflow. I was trying to cut quickly through the crowds on the street but kept hitting thick spots that simply would not allow me to travel very fast. Not that I had anywhere important to be at the moment...

"Max, Bad Max has been spotted at the Under Belly Bar," Brooklyn said, interrupting my anxious thoughts about this foot traffic. I grinned when I heard her call my quarry Bad, like I've said out loud a few times, while doing audio logging.

"Brooklyn, what's the quickest route to the bar?" I asked, looking for any openings.

"Scanning," Brooklyn said.

I pushed through a brief opening and cut my way to a crosswalk where the holographic crossing guard danced in the middle of the intersection, waving for people to cross.

"The fastest route is through the alleys, but the risk of bad actors is high," she said, with a flicker of concern in her voice.

"Got it. Heading for the alley. Scramble ten drones for support. Half armed with lethal attachments in stealth mode and flying higher," I requested.

The alleys were the main throughways for the thieves that feed off the tourists on the main street, or in the retail stores, like those teens.

They also could stick up someone carrying a thousand-dollar drone.

I paused for a second as my gut clenched slightly as I thought of those teens and looked back towards the Drone Store entrance. I saw the faces and recognized I was still their mark.

I flipped across my watch face to pull up a map that showed my current position relative to the location of my drone pack. It was showing ETA five minutes. I also could see my four that were already nearby.

"Brooklyn, keep watch of my eager followers," I said.

"Will do. They are being held up by the same throng that slowed you down. Keeping a close eye on them," she said.

As soon as I crossed into the alley, the awkwardness of sharing oxygen dissipated. Quickly, I moved twenty feet to the alleyway intersection and turned east towards the direction of the bar. There wasn't a straight path though.

"Brooklyn, display the route on my watch," I requested.

"The route is now displaying for you," she said.

The path was not straight, for sure, I would need to make a couple of lefts and rights. Remembering my auto-scooter, I stopped walking and retrieved it from my bag and dropped it down. I stepped around to the front and placed my feet on it, letting the holder grip my back, and started gliding down the alley at double the speed I could go on foot.

The auto-scooter was odd looking, compared to its ancestors, not in that it hovered above the ground (that was normal), but that it wasn't a single platform where I would put one foot in front of the other. This was designed to have both feet side-by-side and a bar extended up behind me where a brace extended and hooked around my mid-section just above my hips automatically as soon as I stepped on it; it looked like a floating Segway with no handlebar and no wheels (maybe it looked nothing like it actually but helps with the visual). It ushered me forward at about twenty miles per hour when I leaned forward to engage full speed. The magic that made it hover was magnetic propulsion. Same thing that propelled all the auto-autos in the city, but they had the help of C-V2X (cellular vehicle-to-everything) tech helping those navigate. (At some point in the past, governments mandated that electro-magnetic strips be embedded under all pavement, everywhere. I couldn't take my auto-scooter off-roading in the desert, but that didn't bother me or many others.)

"You've put some distance between you and your pursuers, Max, but not a lot," Brooklyn reported, "but more bad actors are detected ahead," Brooklyn said.

Two of my four companion drones that had been following me immediately took off ahead to do recon.

"How many?" I asked. Just because they were detected, didn't mean we were going to have an imminent issue, but I needed to be prepared. Although, it was highly likely the teens from the store called for backup of their own.

"Four," Brooklyn said.

"Are they carrying any weapons or showing any elevated signs of aggression or excitement?" I asked, knowing this was hard to detect, but hoping the AI could deduce if things like over excitement could be detected, either by raised thermal readings or body language.

"No concerning signs detected yet," she said.

I leaned into the left turn, slowing only slightly, and had a short distance to the next right, where the potential threats were. No doubt as soon as I came around that turn and was spotted, they would fan out and cause me to slow down, to try to prevent easy passage.

Sure enough, it played out as expected. I slowed. I was gliding steady at about a mile per hour now. They had fanned out wearing grins.

The pursuers were showing on my watch map as still far behind but closing the distance quickly.

"Brooklyn, run an analysis of area where I can open a Bridge to bypass the threats," I requested. I didn't have time to play games. It took Brooklyn thirty seconds to calculate.

"I can recommend opening the Bridge under the pavement ten feet ahead, five feet in front of the center two threats. This will send you into a sewer in +19 South that is currently unoccupied, where you can open the Bridge again to return to +21 South," she said. I didn't have long.

"Execute your recommendation, override granted," I said. I didn't have time to pull out the Bridge, so granted Brooklyn privileges to help me. The Bridge opened just as I cruised up to it and I dropped through, looking up, watching the Bridge close in a flash. That had to have freaked them out.

"Wow, you picked a lovely sewer route, Brooklyn," I commented.

"Of course, Max, only the best sewers for you," she quipped, "recalculation shows you can continue on this path further down the alley before, and turn left safely, before you need to emerge."

"Excellent news. Engage autopilot on the auto-scooter. I need to adjust my hold of this drone box, it's killing my pit," I said.

I made the adjustment and shook my left arm to attempt to relieve some of the pain. I had been really gripping the box during my escape. I could not lose my new toy.

"Emerging to +21 South now," Brooklyn said.

I was above ground again and had a clear path for the final stretch.

"Any other threats detected between me and bar, Brooklyn?" I asked.

"Looks all clear," she said.

"Great, thank you Brooklyn," I said.

The rest of the way was in fact clear. As I reached the entrance of the Under Belly, I stopped to pack away my scooter. I manually called a carrier drone to me to retrieve my newly acquired drone, and it flew off to store it back in +20 South's safe house.

"Keep the protection drones active, Brooklyn," I said, "he most likely won't be surprised to see me and might have set a trap. Have four Cloaked Spiders follow me in and station them a few feet within range of me at all times."

"Roger that, Max," she said in her cheeky mode, which sometimes came out and I thought of Real Denny's sense of humor.

"Where is Bad Max now, Brooklyn?" I asked, using the codename to not raise suspicion if overheard, even though I was alone in the alley right now.

"He is in the far back corner, alone," she reported.

"Got it. Here we go."

Chapter 11 - A Bad Max

I didn't hesitate and went straight to where Bad Max was sitting in the Under Belly bar. I confirmed he was alone and sat down across from him. He jumped at the suddenness, but then smirked when he saw my familiar face. His face.

"Took you long enough," Bad Max said.

"I was waiting for the right moment," I returned.

"Max, there are three males in the room that pose threats. They all are very focused on you but have yet to move from their positions. I can see elevated heart rates on all of them. I detect heavy metal objects on them, and I would calculate a ninety-eight percent probability of those being guns," Brooklyn said in my ear. I took note, looked back over my shoulder and back at Bad Max.

"I wouldn't signal your friends to do anything. I wouldn't visit you unprepared," I said.

"I'll only introduce you to my friends, if necessary," Bad Max said with his smirk dissolving. We both had set our terms.

"You know I just want Tabitha back," I said.

"Of course you do," he said. I noticed him look past me, so I turned to see what he was looking at. A waitress placed dishes in front of me and Bad Max.

"Fettuccine Alfredo for Max's guest and Penne Alla Vodka for you, sir," the waitress said, smiling at me and nodding at Bad Max. She then walked away.

"It's not as good as Alfredo's in the dimension next door, but still pretty good. But maybe you're not hungry... since you just ate a little while ago," he said with devilish smirk.

He knew I was in the neighboring dimension. He knew I was coming. He must have been watching me.

"Checking drone footage from this afternoon, Max," Brooklyn said. She was analyzing our conversation and recognized the implications of what Bad Max was stating. This was the beauty of having an intelligence attached to me.

I didn't respond to Bad Max. I just pulled a multi tool from my inner coat pocket and flipped out the fork implement. I stabbed at a bit of the fettuccine and held it on the fork for a second, watching for the light on the multi tool to turn green, then took a bite.

"A little too milky for my taste," I said after chewing and swallowing the little bit.

"Ah, come on Max, you think I'd poison you? I'm hurt," Bad Max said with an evil shake of his head. Really trying to pull off a "mob guy" persona. He was so comfortable calling me by my name as if it was his as well. He then took up his fork and took a bite of his own food, "killing you doesn't solve my problem," he said with food still being masticated and swallowed. Bad Max also didn't have table manners.

"You never know," I said, while tapping my fork clear of pasta and then using my napkin to clean it off so I could put away the multi tool. "In some dimension you did."

"Those pickpocket-attempting teens were watching you since you entered Boston's Times Square," Brooklyn reported, "and it looks like they signaled the others in the alley. After you vanished, they called Bad Max to report you were on your way."

I should have known. I should have been more careful.

"Did your lackeys enjoy watching me eat lunch earlier?" I asked.

Bad Max raised an eyebrow after taking another bite of his meal. He finished chewing and wiped his mouth before speaking this time.

"You didn't think you could come into this bar, start asking about me and how often I come here and not have that get back to me, did you?" he said.

I had only speculated it might happen, and it was obvious now, but my lead came from an internet hit where Bad Max had posted a comment on social media about this bar being one of his favorite places to "sip licky and get lucky" in his words (whatever the heck that meant). It was a solid clue since it showed up in multiple dimensions. It was also the first solid clue I'd had in six years, so I had to chase the lead, even if it made me vulnerable.

"Let's stop slow dancing Ba... Max," I said, catching myself.

"I know you all call me Bad Max, Max," he said, "I know more than you think I know."

He narrowed his eyes.

"You want to stop slow dancing, as you said, okay, let's skip to the dip. If you want your precious Tabitha back, you need to give me something that I need," he said, letting the sentence hang, luring me in.

I had no choice but to bite.

"What do you want?" I asked, lowering my hands to my lap and leaning back in my chair.

"My own portal maker."

He said a lot with this one sentence. He told me he didn't know what we called our "portal maker" and that he didn't have access to one. He also told me he was likely not Bad Max original recipe, because from what I knew of the prime version, that one could travel between dimensions. It also raised more questions; I'd have to dig into later.

Right now, I had to stop this fake mobster game. With my hands out of sight, I opened the Drone Commander app on my watch and activated the Cloaked Spiders (yes, they are as scary as they sound) to move in. They were the size of rats, if you could see them, they were near invisible right now. In addition to being threat suppressors they were transport vehicles for a nano Spider Drone army. Each one equipped to inject threats with doses of chemicals that could either kill or subdue.

"I don't have time to unpack that statement," I said flatly, as I stood and backed away.

"You will have..." Bad Max started to say before horror took over his face along with a hundred tiny Spider Drones.

Screams filled the bar. Patrons rushed to escape. The bad guys hit the floor in slumps. Bad Max face planted in his Penne alla Vodka.

"I'll give you one opportunity to tell me where Tabitha is," I said as Bad Max came to.

The bar was quiet, and clear.

The barkeep was slumped over the bar, the bad guys lay in heaps in their respective areas, and Bad Max awakened to the nightmare, with his hands zip-tied in front of him. He was a little groggy and looked around the bar, then down at his hands. Pieces of pasta stuck to his face, and he raised his hands to knock them off, surely testing the strength of the ties with the motion.

He remained silent though, calculating his probability of coming out on top of this situation. The odds were not in his favor and his face showed his hand.

"She's not here anymore," he said.

"I asked where she was," I said.

"I don't know!" he said raising his tone; frustration, and fear exuding.

"When was the last time you saw her?" I asked maintaining calm.

"About a month or two ago," he said.

"Who was she with, where did she go when she left? Cut the short responses."

He sighed and dropped his face to fit as much as he could into his slightly open zip-tied hands.

"Alpha Max, the other Max. He makes us call him that... it's ridiculous," he began, "he brought her here, on a..." he said then stopped to look at me. I just looked expectantly at him.

"He brought her here on a date," he said, pausing, waiting to see my reaction. I gave him none.

"After the initial shock of a doppelganger showing up out of the blue and some explaining all around. Plus, the initial fanfare wore off. We sat down, right at this table, actually, and he told me that he had heard that I, me, the Max from this dimension, loved this place. He wanted to test his theory that something, a different version of him had said, in a dimension far removed from his own or this one, could be accurate. He told me he was experimenting with 'divergence theory' that could occur after a dimension splits, or something along those lines. It wasn't exactly clear to me, but after he explained it a third time to me, it seemed like he was testing what effects decisions made regarding heavier things had on inconsequential things. It was inventive but had to be labor intensive."

I just nodded and listened. Waiting for him to continue to the part about where Tabitha went. I really wasn't going to ask again.

"Anyways, he did love this place, and said he loved it in all the dimensions along this path. I wasn't sure what he meant about 'along this path' but I just went along with it," this Bad Max continued, looking at the table as if revisualizing everything, "we ate dinner and drank, enjoyed ourselves and when he was a little drunk, I started asking questions about how he got here."

"And?" I asked, growing impatient.

"And he told me all about the portal maker he used to travel here. He told me about Tabitha, how he had grabbed her from another dimension and was keeping her to lure you here. And that you would come here soon," he said, then paused a beat, "she listened to everything we said but didn't say a word. She didn't look scared, but she didn't look happy. I wasn't sure why she didn't just run away or something. She just went along with him," he said, looking up at me and stopping.

"Conduct a truth analysis, Hal," I said out loud, directed at Brooklyn, but masked behind our predefined codename to protect her identity.

"Running analysis, David," Brooklyn responded, playing along. Not that anyone else could hear her.

"Who are you talking to?" Bad Max looked around seeing no one.

I didn't respond.

"It appears everything he's said so far is true. I also confirmed his scent-markers are slightly off, he's definitely not the Bad Max we're looking for," Brooklyn reported, "and Max, there's a 97% chance this is a trap."

"Great," I said, confusing Bad Max further, and making him show signs he was getting uncomfortable, "continue."

"Okay..." he continued, "I'm not sure where he went exactly, but he made it sound like he was going to continue on 'this path' a little longer to see if he continued to like this bar, or to keep testing his theory, I guess. The whole experience was weird, he had a bunch of people in his entourage that looked just like me and looked out of place and confused. Right before he left though, he gave me some money and some instructions."

"What did he tell you to do?"

"To signal him when you got here and to keep you here as long as possible."

"Hal," I said to Brooklyn.

I quickly moved away from the table and looked around the room. A glowing oval vertical puddle formed near the opposite corner near the bar.

"Opening Bridge on the floor to your left, in three, two, one," Brooklyn said then executed.

"How twisted that we're using ourselves as a pawn," I said.

Then I stepped to my left and fell into the Bridge opening, seeing Bad Max out of the corner of my eye. I assumed this to be the Alpha Max (he's not the Alpha though, more like the Beta, since I was technically the Alpha Max), emerge into the bar with a pistol pointed in my direction.

Then Bad Max, Alpha Max, fired, except I was falling through the Bridge out of this dimension. The bullet whizzed through the air and clipped the curved corner of my Gambler hat, making a perfect little hole, and before the Bridge closed above my head, I heard the dull plunk of the bullet hit +21 South Bad Max – likely killing him.

I was standing in the basement below the Under Belly Bar, in +20 South, staring up at the blank ceiling and side-eying up at the hole in my hat.

That was close.

Chapter 12 - Retreat

I had made my way to +10 West, by heading backwards through dimensions, and established a new safehouse.

Several different auto-autos took me by highways until I reached Hartford, VT, passing me off at rest areas along the way, after draining down the batteries.

Once the "normal" autonomous vehicles could no longer transport me, I switched to an offroad-auto (not an offroad-auto-auto. Don't get too confused, I guess branding experts thought three-word-hyphenated names did poorly in robot focus groups), to take me the rest of my journey to my new place in Killington, VT.

During my drive up, I had made a digital purchase of a nice three-bedroom cabin in the mountains near Killington, through the Zillow app.

"Brooklyn, help me find a new home," I said.

"Certainly, Max. What are you in the market for?" she asked.

"I'd like something in the mountains of Vermont, maybe midway up. I want a cabin, with a wood stove. A couple acres would be nice, ideally having some distance from neighbors."

"I'm finding at least ten ideal properties, based on these requirements."

"Great, any that are not too close to any major highways?" I asked.

"Narrowing search," she said.

I waited for updated results.

"I found a nice three-bedroom cabin with ten acres, near Killington, VT. It sounds like something you might be interested in. I'm sending the listing to your handheld now," Brooklyn said.

"Boom, that's the one," I said, and made it mine.

After many years of leveraging my digital currency hack, to purchase physical products I could resell for physical gold, and then carry said gold through to another dimension to sell to build my digital wallet, I had accumulated some wealth – wealth that never dwindled (No, I'm not Batman).

Buying my new cabin was a breeze.

I was sent my digital access code with an hour to spare, so I could take in the scenery, and do a little online shopping, the remainder of my ride.

"How do you like our new home, Brooklyn?" I asked.

"It's very nice, Max. Shall I send up surveillance drones, to ensure all is well?" she asked.

"Yes, please do."

After a quick inspection of the property grounds, I made my way inside for the interior inspection, four small drones following close behind, then two breaking off to inspect the house.

"Oh, this is very nice," I said, essentially to myself aloud, but felt like with Brooklyn always listening, I was not alone.

It had lovely golden-brown knotty pine wainscoting throughout. It looked freshly remodeled. It had that mountain-cabin-look people loved.

It was fully equipped to accommodate off-grid living, with a solar array and two large windmills on the property. The massive battery backup array inside of one of the large outbuildings was impressive. A family of five could power their technological pleasures for several weeks without sun.

It was a great getaway location; I would keep it, and hopefully I would have time to enjoy it too.

My new cabin started to warm up quickly after I got the wood stove loaded and fired up, from a nicely stacked pile of split wood the previous owner had left behind, probably there for aesthetics for the open houses. The temperature outside was around ten degrees, and the windows had a nice crystallization forming around the edges. Snow was sprinkled on the outer ledges and dusted the trees.

I had ordered some gear from Tarzan (Amazon had bought Target and rebranded as Tarzan, operating with eighty percent of deliveries being handled by drones), while I was on my final approach into town, after I received my ownership confirmation for my new property. On my handheld, I was tracking the drone delivery and expected several packages to arrive within the next hour. (It was always so cute to see four quad copters cooperating to carry the corners of large packages, and gingerly lowering them to a safe location on the ground.)

"Your Tarzan delivery is approaching, several drones are in route," Brooklyn alerted me.

As they approached, it sounded like an aerial drone assault coming in for attack, with the combined rushing of wind caused by so many objects pushing condensed air in the same direction, but they were gentle as flying puppies. It was noisier than usual since I had ordered so many items for same-day delivery; about fifty drones were descending on my location. Normally, with the toroidal blades being standard on quadcopters these days, five or ten would be barely louder than the wings flapping on a butterfly.

To fend off the cold, I pulled my coat back on, returned my hat atop my matted hair, and headed out to the gravel driveway. The sun would start setting in an hour or so, and the trees around the property had shadows starting to play hide and seek.

The mini army of Tarzan drones placed all the packages neatly in a grid layout in the driveway. It was like a relay race, because I had several of my drones then move the packages from the driveway to inside. (I had lots of drones. If I were Heinz Doofenshmirtz I'd break out into a song and dance about all my drones and their specialties and names, and you would quickly spot how my evil plan might fail before even hatched, but I'm not him. Thank goodness. My plans always worked sometimes. I consider myself more of a Ferb…) I had ordered camping supplies, like a sleeping bag, an axe, and canned goods. As well as some household items, like pots and pans, several jugs of water, plates and silverware, a couple memory foam mattresses to stack for sleeping, bathroom toiletry items. I also ordered some winter gear and additional clothing. I was setup to stay here for a few months, if needed, even if I was traveling between dimensions.

By the time I was done arranging all the boxes to their final positions in the house, I was tired and hungry. I ate a little bit, locked up, and washed up, while my drones settled into their charging docks, like dogs upon their dog beds for the evening.

Then I hit the memory foam soon after it finished expansion, in the corner of the downstairs master bedroom. I realized I'd need to order some blackout blinds first thing tomorrow, as moonlight painted my closed eyes with light. I rolled over and went to sleep.

I would have plenty of time for setting everything up, to my liking in my new hideaway, while I waited for Dr. Zine and Denny to arrive.

The next day I settled into my new home.

It was still empty but feeling a little more "homey" to me. I had ordered more stuff from Tarzan, more necessary equipment, like monitors and cameras for the property and ones for adjacent dimensions when necessary. Also, I needed to build out my personal drone army further, so ordered the parts to assemble them myself. I tended to only keep about a dozen or two drones with me when I traveled, of varying skillsets, and left behind necessary versions in all my hideouts. Since I had time, I was also experimenting with building some drones that could build other drones. I had a couple in the fleets and convoys that could repair other drones, but nothing that could quite build entire new ones from scratch. I had Brooklyn working out software to install in the new builder-drones as soon as I assembled a couple.

My new Bloodhound AI drone also needed a test drive, so had to make plans to do that as well.

I had a couple weeks before my guests would make it up here.

The next day I received my next delivery, which had most of the remaining items I needed; the straggler packages for stuff I had ordered would arrive in the coming days.

I had opened mini bridges back to my home dimension, creating what we called a Bridge Tether Line, passing through a nano drone carrying just the radio antenna wire through, to broadcast a signal back to Dr. Zine and Denny. The first time I looked through at all those dimensions lined up in a row as a tiny drone passed through moving further and further away, it made me think of a fun house and those endless reflections.

My ham radio was setup, connected to the Bridge Tether Line via the antenna port, and the radio would be connected to a QC

(Quantum Computer), once I set that up. I had an app setup on that that would notify me and transmit to my handheld.

One of the upstairs bedrooms served as a good command center. I assembled my new desk and chair in there, centered to the window, so I could enjoy the view on nice days. I built the frame for my screen by starting with the top bar attached to the ceiling, and adding the supporting framing running down the sides, with the bottom framing fastened to the floor. I attached the ultrathin transparent Quantum Dot NanoLED screen to the framing, just behind my desk. I could issue a command to turn the screen opaque for displaying from my Quantum Computer, and just as quickly revert to fully transparent and see the lovely view beyond (or find a happy medium of 50% opacity to get the best of both worlds).

I installed blackout curtains as well and a solid lock and deadbolt on the door (not that I was too worried someone would get up here, get past the drone minions, but still…). The ceilings were slanted due to the roof, so I centered everything to where I would be able to stand up without banging my head. My favorite drone had to be the "handyman" drone I had built, I named him Jack, and I requested him to replace the ceiling fan in this room with a more low-profile one. (I mean, I really didn't have favorites, I loved all my drones equally, and thinking this way made it feel less like I was building digital age slaves…). I wasn't terribly tall, but at six foot two, I could get an unplanned haircut if I stood from my chair and stretched upwards without thinking.

The edges of the room were where all the wiring ran, and all the charging stations were running in even lines.

This was one tech filled room.

The other bedroom upstairs, the only other bedroom upstairs, was perfect for setting up a place for me to unwind. I limited the electronics in this room; just a rug in the center and two small coffee tables on each side under the sloped roof. Each table had a couple candles, and one table had a small sound device that just played a playlist of relaxing sounds. Jack updated the lighting so I could dim the lights if I so chose. The rug was where I could sit to meditate and clean my mental slate every day. There was the loneliness, and stress of finding my missing family members, and the toll of constantly walking into unknown situations that no human has ever walked into that required me to have to keep mindfulness as much as possible. Although, with Brooklyn and my drone friends around, I didn't feel fully alone.

While the Quantum Computer was being setup, in the other room, I took some time to sit, alone with my thoughts, trying to see past them briefly, taking an opportunity to rebalance my mind. Twenty minutes would be good, so I asked Brooklyn to hold on any notifications until I was done.

"I've finished setting up the Quantum Computer, and synced with the Span. The fully compiled and reanalyzed footage from the Under Belly is available for you to review when you are ready, Max," Brooklyn said with some cheer in her voice, "the last remaining footage was recently uploaded and combined. One of the Cloaked Spiders was low on battery and had to escape to a secure location outdoors to do battery swap, before traveling back to the +20 South hideout."

"Excellent, thank you, Brooklyn," I said floating gratitude in my voice. I headed back into the command center.

"Anything immediately jump out as interesting, Brooklyn?" I asked, knowing she would have reviewed this during the sync, out of routine.

"Bad Max confirmed that he accidentally killed the +21 South Max," she said.

"That sucks," I said, "any further audio after I left the bar?"

"I must ask, have you even tried out your new desk chair?" Brooklyn asked, "those X-Chairs are top of the line, and I'm integrated, so it's even better."

"No, I haven't sat in it yet..." I said.

It was odd that she didn't respond to my question, but she'd do that sometimes, it was an elemental part of her personification settings.

"Why don't you take it for a spin? I can preheat it if you desire," she said.

"Why do you seem concerned with me sitting in my new chair, Brooklyn?" I asked, physically rubbing my chin, and looking at my chair before moving closer and inspecting it. Only one time did she attempt a joke with me, but that was within a conversation, and it ended with a terrible dad joke (I'll have to tell you later ;).

"Are you trying to trick me into sitting in gum or on a whoopee-cushion? Or..." I asked and paused as a thought occurred to me, then sat in the chair, "are you having me sit for what you're about to report?"

"Yes," she said without much pause.

"Tell me, I'm ready," I said.

"I'll just show you the playback. You'll want to see it anyways after I tell you," Brooklyn said.

"Go ahead."

I watched the screen become solid and come alive with the playback of video from four different angles spread in four two-by-two quadrants. After I left +21 South, my Cloaked Spiders had remained cloaked and in position to capture footage from four different angles. The nano-spiders had all evacuated out of the bar and retreated to the area of +21 South where a Bridge would open to the +20 South hideout, once the coast was clear. The Cloaked Spiders were equipped with Draw Bridge technology for emergencies and would eventually retreat to the +20 South hideout, awaiting their next orders.

The top left video was where I paid my focus. It had the most direct view of Bad Max standing inside the bar with a Bridge open behind him. I heard him speak and it seemed like to himself, "I hate to call myself incompetent, but this dead nitwit in the corner makes that kind of hard."

Then Tabitha appeared at the edge of the Bridge, barely stepping over to this side, and Bad Max turned to face her.

"I thought this was all going to be over. I thought we were finally going to be able to stop running. But you couldn't even capture him when he was presented to you on a SILVER PLATTER!" Tabitha said, fists clenched, and shouting the last part of her sentence.

Bad Max looked down.

"Did you even scan the room for his drones?" she asked, sighing, and tapping a device on her wrist, "there are four in here right now, probably recording!"

The four feeds on the screen went dark.

The four Cloaked Spiders had activated emergency withdrawal protocols, skittering away at accelerated speeds, while still cloaked, upon detecting they were scanned.

I just sat and stared at the black screens.

"I'm sorry, Max," Brooklyn said. She could detect my angst.

It was a good thing I was sitting down.

Chapter 13 - Retrospective

Brooklyn analyzed the videos, and I asked her to reanalyze them two more times. It's not like she was going to come to any new conclusions. We really didn't know any more than what I witnessed, but I felt a need to reconfirm what I heard and saw.

Why was Tabitha talking about capturing me?

Why did it seem like Bad Max was reporting to her?

My mind was running around in circles trying to understand. This couldn't be my Tabitha. This couldn't be Tabitha from my home dimension.

Was this Bad Tabitha?

I cringed at the thought and pushed it from my mind. There had to be another explanation. Indoctrination. Bad Max had to have indoctrinated her over the past ten years.

What did they want with me?

Something was not right, and I couldn't wrap my head around it at this time.

"Brooklyn, what was the analysis of their Bridge?" I asked.

"It's like ours. Likely using the same basic Draw Bridge technology as ours. I don't detect any major differences. The energy to keep it open is similar," Brooklyn reported.

"Was there any angle to see more of the other side?"

"No, unfortunately, we didn't have an angle to capture more than what was just in view on the other side, where we saw Tabitha come through. Then she was blocking anything behind her."

"Ok."

I thought for a few seconds about what we had at our disposal.

"How about scents? Were we able to pick up anything from Tabitha?"

"I'm sorry Max, she wasn't far enough on this side," Brooklyn reported.

There wasn't much use trying to continue to spin my wheels on the same analysis. It was time to move forward.

The remaining days, before Dr. Zine and Denny arrived, I got to work building out everything I'd need for the next phase of my operation. I focused myself on the work I needed to do, to distract myself from what I'd learned, but also to prepare. I would need to journey to the dimensions where Bad Max had already been, to see what he was doing in them, see if there were other Maxes he's interacted with.

First, I needed to do a retrospective with my team, though.

"Max, you look like a mad scientist, a crazy cowboy mad scientist," Denny said after giving me a hug and pulling back to inspect me.

"You aged, son," Dr. Zine said while shaking my hand, "but still, you look good, like you're eating enough."

He sounded like a father.

We hadn't seen each other in five years. Not since I reached that dead end, traveling aimlessly from dimension to dimension trying to find out where Tabitha was taken. I mostly wandered around during that time, showing anyone I came across pictures of her to see if they recognized her. No one had. It wasn't a complete bust; I did learn to live between worlds during that time. It also afforded me time to build out some strategies for living unchecked in places I didn't belong and to gather gear.

The two had arrived at noon, a couple hours later than expected, due to the weather. I was pacing around during that time worrying where they were. I couldn't contact them, because we didn't want to risk opening a channel that could give away the location of my hideout. Brooklyn encoded a message via the Bridge Tether Line back to my home dimension, to pass along the address. They would have left to travel and would have had to change vehicles a few more times than necessary, out of an abundance of caution.

"I ate at +20 South Alfredo's the day before, you know…" I said with a smirk.

"How dare you?!" said Denny with mock anger.

"I would have brought you guys some, but I didn't have time after Bad Max tried to kill me," I said with a shrug. Denny rolled his eyes and Dr. Zine nodded.

I led them from the foyer into the open area where the dining area and living room were. There was drone building materials spread out on the table and across the floor. Small drones were flying about assembling more friends.

"My, my, Max, you're really maximizing your efficiencies," Dr. Zine said looking around the organized chaos of my make-shift factory.

"Welcome, Dr. Zine and Denny," Brooklyn said, her voice coming from a unit I had built and was currently in the living room. She was contained in a modified ground drone, with a body that was mostly speaker sitting atop tank treads. It had two camera lenses attached to what looked like a head atop the speaker. The unit's head rotated 360 degrees, independently of being able to rotate with the treads. She always made a point of looking at you as she spoke, so polite.

"Brooklyn, so nice to hear your voice," Dr. Zine said, "and very interesting to see you in a physical form now." (Dr. Zine favored Fremont for his AI voice persona, probably because of the British accent.)

"Nice to hear and see you as well, Dr. Zine," she responded.

"Hey Brooklyn, long time no talk," Denny said, "well, long time since talking to this version of you." He giggled to himself.

"I suppose Brooklyn is as good a companion as you could ask for, while you are out here, journeying alone," Dr. Zine said.

"I recognized I could not do it alone, so decided, why not leverage the tools and resources I had on hand, and why not have a friend to help?" I said.

"Well, this is as good as any point to segue, then," Dr. Zine started, "you are obviously a bachelor. It shows. I'm going to guess you don't have two extra beds for Denny and me?"

Nuts. I thought I had thought of everything.

"No," I said, slinking my posture slightly with embarrassment.

"I figured as much," Dr. Zine said. Denny just bounced quietly with laughter, "Brooklyn, would you be so kind as to order two extra beds for Denny and me, please? Two twins would suffice."

"Certainly, Dr. Zine," Brooklyn said, "those can be here by this evening."

"Thank you, Brooklyn," Dr. Zine said, "Max, you've been on your own for a long time, you should lean more on Brooklyn to help you not become too far removed from civilization."

"Yeah, you're right. Thank you, Brooklyn, for placing that order, and... maybe reconfigure a little bit to help me be a better host," I said, sighing slightly.

Then I remembered one considerate thing I had cooked up.

"I do have something for you two," I looked over to the kitchen and nodded.

A medium sized drone with two arms flew over and approached holding two cups of coffee and extended them out towards Dr. Zine and Denny. Another smaller drone approached carrying mine, in similar fashion.

"Care for some coffee, Dr. Zine and Mr. Denny?" medium drone asked, in a British voice. I had been busy while waiting for my guests and really got into personalizing some of the drones. I called the new Waiter Drones Jester and Jasper; Jasper was the smaller one.

"Mr. Denny?" Denny asked, side-eying me.

"May I call you Mr. Denny, too, Denny?" Brooklyn asked.

"Umm, no," Denny replied, and side-eyed the closest camera to send it specifically at Brooklyn.

I laughed out loud. It was fun to program stuff.

"Thank you, Jester and Jasper," I said to the wait staff and then they spun on an axis and headed back to the kitchen.

"This is an interesting use for these resources, Max," Dr. Zine said and then took a sip of his coffee. He smiled, "an interesting, but excellent use." He took notice of the wall of white boards I had lined up in the living room and walked over to read through the notes I had transferred to them from my handheld detailing the events that had occurred around the Under Belly incident.

"A British accent, Max, really? Isn't that a little on the nose?" Denny asked while shaking his head and moving closer to the dining room table to inspect some of the completed drones. His eyes grew when he saw the Bloodhound AI drone sitting there, taking up the farthest quarter of the table. "Where did you find this?"

"In +20 South. A store in Boston Times Square," I said grinning, "and isn't saying 'on the nose' on the nose?" He just rolled his eyes.

He ran his hand along one of the quadcopter's toroidal blades and leaned down close to the front where the "sniffer" unit was. He stared at it thoughtfully and skipped with the foreplay and grabbed the drone and flipped it over.

"Not going to buy her dinner first?" I asked shaking my head.

"Max," Dr. Zine said from the living room, "this is impressive." He gestured at the whiteboards.

"You taught me well," I said, walking over towards him, sipping my coffee.

"I suppose I could be due some credit here, but you really elevated your process since we last 'white-boarded' back home," he said, a cocktail of prideful and nostalgic tones pooling in his throat. He cleared them, then continued, "so you and Brooklyn have determined that you did finally catch up with the Max doppelganger that took Tabitha, but are now suspecting some version of Tabitha looked to be a part of something more nefarious, but maybe not our Tabitha?"

"At this point, I have no other conclusive information," was all I could say.

"That's good, you're working with the current known facts. That's okay," Dr. Zine said, "and the other Max from +21 South said that the one who we call 'Bad Max' is conducting some kind of experiment with 'divergence theory' across universes?"

"That's what he said, but I'm not exactly sure what it means," I said.

"I've been feeding all the footage that you've been sending back all these years into the Quantum Computer and having the BridgeAI analyze it. One of the things I've had it looking for are the differences between universes.

104

"When it detects differences, we open Bridges and send out Scout Drones to collect more data to add to the analysis. What we're noticing is that as you head down the linear tract of universes off the adjacent universe, following the semantic version line, things stay pretty close in line to the timeline of the initial adjacent timeline of the home universe, but as you go in other directions like 'east or west', we detect more extreme divergences from the origins.

"I'm speculating it's like a universe that was created from a universe where a significant decision was made in that adjacent universe, then another significant decision was in the universe adjacent to that one, and that causes significant alterations to the timelines.

"My thought experiment around this is a scenario where someone decided to kill someone in the home universe, and in the adjacent universe, let's say the 'west' version, that person lived, but decided to kill the attempted murderer first. Then in the next universe over, say 'north' of that 'west' version, they both die because they shot at the same time. Yet, 'south' of the origin version, which I'm calling the least varying version now, they reconcile before shots are fired, and it just terminates the relationship, and they move on apart from each other's lives. This is what I would call a divergence theory."

"Wow," was all I could muster as a response.

"It's a lot to process. I've been thinking about it for a while. Maybe that's what Bad Max is attempting to understand. And, I fear the reasons," Dr. Zine said and paused, and I thought he was waiting for me to ask "why" but he continued, "he might have *Knocked* others from these dimensional timelines to recruit them to follow him for some nefarious reason. And since they are not too far diverged, they would understand the agenda."

This was profoundly concerning, but I was hung up on an unfamiliar term.

"*Knocked*?" I asked.

"Oh yes, Denny coined this term describing someone unexpectedly falling from their home universe. Like Michael was knocked into another universe by the lightning strike and Tabitha was knocked out of our universe by Bad Max. It's a very apt term," Dr. Zine said cavalierly.

Man, I wish I thought of that term, it's perfect.

"Dang, great word for it. Can I say I thought of it, Denny, when I get a chance to write a book about all of this?"

"Nope," Denny said from the dining area, and I took notice that my brand-new Bloodhound AI drone was in several pieces, some on the floor, while Denny was pulling out the micro board.

I was going to steal it now either way because of that. I just smiled and shook my head.

I got back to matters at hand.

"Bad Max is possibly building an army from other dimensions?" I said snapping back to the heaviness of the moment.

"It's speculation, at the moment, but we have to assume that as the most extreme scenario and plan accordingly," Dr. Zine said, "our next step should be for you to head out and find out who has been knocked from the universes Bad Max has already been to. Also, you should talk to yourself across these universes and propose they consider joining us to help in the fight that might be coming to us sometime soon."

"Okay. I guess we should come up with a plan for where to start," I said, pressing a button on one of the whiteboards to make room, and it did a fancy "page flip" as if it was moving to a new page for me to write on, "let's list out the dimensions to start in."

Chapter 14 - Me, Myself, and I

"We'll take good care of your new house, don't you worry, Max," Dr. Zine said as I packed gear into two duffle bags.

"I know you will. I'm glad you guys are staying here. It certainly makes a lot of sense to stay clear of our home dimension for a while, in case Bad Max does something crazy. You know my only worry is no one being there if Michael returns," I said, while carefully packing the Bloodhound AI drone into one of the duffle bags. (Denny had completely refactored this bad boy and uploaded his own software modifications on top of it, so it would work across the multiverse.)

"We have that covered. Denny is working on building some nano Cloaked drones that we can send back home, where we can station them in locations where we can monitor if Michael happens to come back. We'll keep a respectful distance, but we'll station a couple near your folks' house," Dr. Zine said. I looked up and nodded with understanding.

"Yeah, by the way, I have a better solution for communicating between dimensions now, using our own low orbit satellites, cloaked, with nano receivers positioned in each dimension through nano Bridges. And don't bust my chops about throwing 'nano' in front of every piece of small tech we use, again, Max," Denny said.

Denny was always good with tech growing up. He would take apart computers and reassemble them for fun when he was like seven years old. It sounds like hyperbole, but his access to endless piles of old Personal Computers (PCs) allowed him to start by just destroying a bunch before perfecting the reassembly techniques. After that, it was only natural to move on to learning to program them and all things that used software. He built simple robots at first, then moved on to ones that fought each other, to ones that could fly out and pick up some snacks for him, all before he turned fifteen.

He introduced me to coding when we first met at twelve, when he moved into our neighborhood. We'd compete in AI gaming challenges where teams would attempt to create AI chat bots that would make the other teams' AI chat bots self-destruct.

Whenever I was on Denny's team, we won first place.

When I shut him out after Michael disappeared, he closed up as well, in his own way. He buried himself in tech. He buried himself in learning, in experimenting, in trying to understand what was possible with technology. He didn't understand the science behind multiverse travel but had an inkling that technology might become an integral part of it one day, so he began to build knowledge early.

"How far away can we keep the communication channels open now, then, with these satellites?" I asked.

"With attenuation, probably twenty removed from the broadcasting dimension," Denny said, "and with electromagnetic wrapping, I could get it as far as fifty if we push it. And, if I figure out how to leap comms off each other interdimensionally, we could go out as far as we wanted, in theory."

"Good to know," I said and zipped both bags up and stood, lifting one in each hand. I headed to the foyer and dropped them down.

"Marcus, Kip, please take care of carrying these, when we're ready to leave," I said, speaking for my latest personal worker drones to hear. The two carrier drones flew over and came to rest on the ground next to the bags. In theory I could have just centralized all communication with my drones through Brooklyn, but I viewed us as a team and felt better delegating directly to the individual drones I needed to command.

"I think I'm ready," I said while pulling on my coat I took from the coat hook, and I placed my hat on after.

"Everything is all set up in the new workshop," Dr. Zine said.
I nodded.

"Time to go," I said, looking down at Marcus and Kip. With virtual eyes, they were effectively watching me and rose and took hold of their cargo.

With the three of us organic bodies and several dozen drone variants now occupying the main house, we set up one of the outbuildings to be our Bridge workshop, where we would be able to easily open the Bridge when needed, and have any supporting materials staged around it.

We all headed to the workshop.

We didn't wait long and said short goodbyes.

"We'll be able to stay in contact, you can just ask Brooklyn to open a channel back to us, whenever you need," Dr. Zine said, gripping my shoulder gently and briefly with one hand, while smiling, "and we'll do whatever we can to support you from this side."

"Sounds good," I said nodding.

"I've narrowed down three locations where you can start searching, all info uploaded to the Span and available to Brooklyn," Denny said, typing into the QC that was near the workshop wall. This quickly became a second command center.

"Got it, thank you," I said, "ready to open the Bridge."

Denny fist-bumped me, and I walked to where the Bridge would open and looked over at him and Dr. Zine. I nodded and Denny pressed the button on the Draw Bridge we had constructed here, to open the Bridge. It glowed to life, and I could see the back of the workshop in +9 West.

I crossed through, and Marcus and Kip followed me. Then I turned back, and Dr. Zine passed me another bag.

"What's this?" I asked, eying the duffle bag that was similar in size to the other two.

"Your new approach to having drones build drones was an intelligent approach to scaling up your support resources quickly," Dr. Zine said, "so here is a gift bag I put together that will help you get going as soon as you 'land' at your destination." Dr. Zine made a show of his air quotes.

"Thanks," I said with a smile and nodded as I backed away from the Bridge.

It closed with a wink, and I was alone, relatively speaking; Marcus and Kip floated in the air still holding their cargo. No one was here, of course, since I was heading into a dimension that already existed, and the versions of us wouldn't be here since this wasn't a decision-point-dimension for us. The outbuilding and subsequently the property here, was not my property, and was still up for sale. The first thing I did after crossing and closing the Bridge was purchase it again, to eliminate any chance of someone else buying it and creating issues with this staging area.

The plan was to use this side to jump off quickly to my destinations in search of myself without compromising our new temporary home base. This building would stay empty.

After I got the confirmation that my property was now my property, again, I dialed up the +9 South dimension on the Draw Bridge, opened the Bridge, and crossed. I looked around and confirmed all was effectively the same. For good measure, I stepped out of the outbuilding and made sure there was still a house; all was the same, all was quiet and good. I then continued to cross through dimensions, completing the same steps, until I was finally in +3 South. As I traveled through, my gear followed. Marcus and Kip awaiting my command to settle down.

"At ease, men," I said aloud, the drones didn't budge, "Brooklyn, help me out."

"Sure, Max," Brooklyn said, and Marcus and Kip lowered their cargo, and landed next to it. Brooklyn updated the command list in their software systems, so the next time I made that cheeky command, they'd listen. I really wanted all my drones, bots, and digital companions to have personality. It made me feel less lonely.

I lowered and opened the bag I was holding and sifted through the gear. Dr. Zine had packed all the necessities for me to start having Marcus and Kip start building more resources. Some with weapons, some with only surveillance equipment. After I laid the items out, things came to life. I emptied the other two duffle's and had my Guard drones up and running in minutes. I kept my new Bloodhound AI drone in the bag for now.

I opened the app to call for an auto-auto, ordering a long-term rental, and expected it to arrive in roughly forty-five minutes. I made sure to get a larger SUV to help with transporting all my stuff. I had lots of stuff for the expedition, lots of fun stuff.

The first phase, and easiest phase, was complete.

Finding myself was the next phase.

It took a few days to travel and track down +3 South Max based on Denny's suggestions (it was weird to refer to myself in the dimensional sense, but it helped me process it better psychologically). Denny said, he and Dr. Zine decided they should start tracking the other versions of me in the closer dimensions and find a way to "tag" them so they would be able to distinguish between them and me.

I was offended at first, but came around to the idea, since it was essentially what I was doing with Bad Max. Hence the invention of the interdimensional scent tracking system, based on Bloodhound AI technology and fully integrated with our BridgeAI.

After a few years of data collection, parsing and classifying, they knew generally the distinguishing scent markers of all the Maxes in a twenty-step removed "radius" from our home dimension. And after just over ten years, they had "tagged" all the Dennys, Dr. Zines, and Tabitha's the same, well, all the ones they could find. Out of hundreds, they never found even amounts of everyone. The working theory was that Bad Max was killing off some while kidnapping others; with the new finding at the Under Belly Bar, who knows now if Tabitha was ordering this nonsense. We think Bad Max (or Bad Tabitha) couldn't kill off many Good Maxes because most Maxes knew it was coming and were actively moving between dimensions. Well, the ones with access to Draw Bridges.

The showdown at the Under Belly confirmed something was up, so that's when we decided that Dr. Zine and Denny would be safer in a random location, my new house in Vermont, and to avoid the risk of decision splitting causing other dimensional versions that could expose us, we leveraged a clever method we all had invented to randomize decisions and remove chances for "either/or" scenarios that would cause the split. Essentially, we created a bit of software that would leverage AI to help make decisions for us. All we had to do was feed ideas into it, many ideas, and it would settle on the most reasonable, logical choice, and let us know what was happening. Of course, the question to lead to the decision was delivered by Brooklyn, so we'd jokingly begin with "mother may I" when we stated it.

The Max of this dimension was in Connecticut. Where's that, you might wonder? It's somewhere between Boston, Massachusetts and New York City, New York. It's a perfect place to hide from a city. It was apparently where +3 South Max was living, quietly, having lost his Tabitha, but having no means to search for her. This dimension was branched off as one where pursuing Bridge travel didn't happen, so the tech didn't exist here. We suspect that made this a prime target for Bad Max to come here and take the Tabitha.

"Brooklyn, what's our ETA?" I asked.

"We should be arriving at +3 South Max's last known location in about twenty minutes," she replied, "our Scout drones haven't seen any signs of him yet, though."

Interesting. We had Scout drones following all our targets and reporting back weekly. Our last report stated he was at the location I was heading to, as of the last check-in. The system wasn't always a hundred percent.

"Understood," I said.

The house Max was supposedly staying in, was nice; a cape, white with black shutters, typical new England house, residing in a quiet part of eastern Connecticut. It sat on half an acre, and only had a detached garage. I pulled it up on my handheld map and zoomed out a little and noticed something great.

"Brooklyn, Max is living near Brooklyn, Connecticut... what are the chances?" I mentioned with a smile, "Should we visit that eponymous town?"

"Do you want an actual number on the chances, or are you being comical?" Brooklyn said.

"Comical," I said.

"Yep, sarcasm," she responded. She was still learning to be like-human.

"What's the status of this dimension? In terms of targets?" I asked.

"As far as we know, Max is alive, Denny is dead, Tabitha is missing, and Dr. Zine is status unknown," Brooklyn said.

"Roger that," I said, then rested my head back in my seat and watched the scenery pass, for the rest of the ride in my auto-auto to Max's place.

"We're not detecting any sign of Max, and no persons look to occupy this residence currently," Brooklyn reported as we pulled into the driveway.

"Heat sensors?" I asked.

"Yes, no heat detected," Brooklyn replied.

"Interesting," I said, "was it faulty reporting from the Scout drones?" I asked.

"Hard to tell, they don't go inside the premises and only reported seeing Max a few days ago on a check-in scan," she said. We couldn't just station the Scouts permanently outside of a target's location, else we'd raise suspicions, so they checked in in loops on a schedule. As if they were doing welfare checks on the elderly. Which was a common use of these type of Scout drones, in this day and age. State agencies had their own drone armies, for just this reason, it had tremendous cost savings, and worked very well in inclement weather.

"Load up the last footage of +3 South Max on my handheld, if you could, please, Brooklyn," I requested.

"Sure thing. It's available now," she said.

I watched the video feed close in on the property from about a hundred feet away and zoom in on Max's face as he looked around before entering his front door.

"Show me the second feed alongside the first," I requested.

"Running now," she said.

I could see the second feed now, an angle from the opposite side of the house, which was zoomed in through a window. I could see Max in what looked like a living room, peering out the window on the opposite side of the house. Then he quickly closed the curtains and rushed to the other side and closed that curtain. Our view of him was now completely obscured.

"We've been made," I said, then closed out of the video.

He was I and I was him, slim with the tilted brim… not really, but he probably understood the situation, I believe. He knew he was being watched.

Then where did he flee to? I would have tried to trap the drones and send a message to the voyeurs if it were me.

That's when the plinking of gun shots started hitting my auto-auto's windows. First the windshield, then the side glass; only slight fracturing occurred, since auto glass was much stronger than it used to be.

I dropped to the floor.

"Talk to me, Brooklyn," I said.

"+3 South Max is shooting at the auto-auto. I've scrambled some Guards," Brooklyn said.

Six Guard drones flew out of the auto-auto's back door, which had just popped open and swarmed on the location of this Max.

"Use non-lethal suppression," I said.

In less than a minute, the firing stopped.

"Clear," Brooklyn said.

I crawled out of the auto-auto cautiously, staying low. Looking around the door, using it as cover, I spotted the cluster of Guards hovering above +3 south Max. I made my way over to him. I didn't carry a firearm most of the time since I had my "flying protection squad." Max was unconscious on the ground, but his chest was clearly moving up and down, so I knew he was still alive. The Guards just sprayed a concentrated benzodiazepine gas to knock him out briefly.

"Hey, why are you shooting at yourself?" I said, leaning down over +3 South Max, then patting his face. He didn't respond.

"How much did they hit him with, Brooklyn?" I asked.

"Each fired a single dose, for efficacy, but if he gasped, he would have taken in more than the recommended dose," she responded.

"Awesome," I said.

"Keep eyes in the sky, Brooklyn, don't want any more surprises," I requested.

About thirty minutes later he woke up.

This gave me enough time to remove his weapons, only a single rifle, and a pocketknife. And move him inside his house to his living room. I had left his weapons on the kitchen table. The view of them was within sight of the kitchen chair I had secured him to in the living room. I sat on his couch, to the left of him, waiting with my hands folded, resting on just above my knees.

"I'm not going to hurt you," I said first thing when +3 South Max came to. He blinked his confusion into light. Then he started to struggle against the zip-ties I used to hold him to the chair.

"Why am I tied to this chair?" he said, calming slightly and glaring at me.

"You were shooting at me," I said.

"You were spying on me, with drones," he said.

"I was checking up on you," I said.

"What does that mean? Why would you think you should do that? Isn't that a little weird, man?" he said.

"I needed to talk with you," I said.

"You could have knocked," he said shaking his head.

"True," I said, "but I needed to make sure you weren't compromised."

"Compromised?!" he shouted, "What does that even mean? You're obviously me, but you talk in riddles," he said a little more calmly.

"Let me explain," I said, holding my hands out.

"Fine," he said.

I stood and pulled out my pocketknife, flipped out the blade, and stepped closer to him holding it, but open-palmed to show him, thumb over the hilt, moving forward peacefully. He nodded and I cut his ties to free him from the chair. He rubbed his wrists as I took a seat back on the couch.

"I'm from another dimension," I started, "one where we invented a device that allows us to travel between different dimensions.

"In my home dimension, while we were demonstrating to Denny and Tabitha the Draw Bridge we invented, and how we could open a Bridge to another dimension, a bad version of us reached through and knocked Tabitha from our dimension into another one next to it," I said, thinking for sure he'd ask what "Knocked" meant, and I'd start my campaign to make it my original thought, and not Denny's (yeah, kind of a klanker move). He didn't even flinch though.

I paused to see if he was digesting it all.

"I know about the portals to other dimensions," he said, "that's what Michael fell through."

It had been so long, I forgot that was the common thread for all Maxes in all dimensions.

"Okay that saves me some explaining, "I said," I sometimes forget we all know."

It was quiet for a few beats.

"You haven't seen him, right? He hasn't come back in this dimension, has he?" I asked with measured hope.

"No," he said with a frown.

"I figured, but I always have to ask," I said matching his frown. More silence.

"Why are you here, though?" +3 South Max said, breaking the silence.

"I'm trying to find out what Bad Max has done in all the dimensions that we know he's been to," I said, "also, I'm looking for allies."

He gave me a quizzical look.

"Allies against what?" he asked.

"We think Bad Max might be building an army," I said, "he also might be taking out people that know about the Draw Bridge and Bridge travel…"

"Awesome," he said.

"My sentiments exactly," I said, "so I wanted to make sure he didn't already do that, to you, and to warn you, if he didn't. So, here I am. Here we are."

"Tabitha went missing about ten years ago. Her and her friend. We were never able to find out what happened to her," he said, "I went away with my parents and Denny for the weekend, camping, out of range. When I got back into range, I tried to call her, and her parents answered. They thought maybe the two of them had snuck off to meet me and Denny on the camping trip."

He got quiet.

"I'm sorry to hear that," I said frowning after a few moments.

"Yeah, it was fresh sadness for my life. I felt like I was cursed," he said, "I decided to leave home after that, to try to save the rest of my loved ones from my curse. Denny was murdered when away at college. Just knowing me cursed him."

"Don't do that to yourself. You cannot really believe that. You had no control. Remember what we learned about impermanence and dwelling on the past events and things we can't control," I said with a smile.

He just stared at me with confusion lacing his face.

He wasn't taught that, like I was. He was never committed to the mental facility.

"Ah, you didn't learn that... I did in my timeline," I said, looking at the ground.

"This is all very weird," he said, standing up walking to the kitchen. He opened a cabinet and grabbed a couple mugs.

"Want some coffee?" he asked.

"No. I don't drink coffee, only tea..." I said, frowning.

So different.

"I have some English Breakfast tea if you want. I can put on the kettle?" he replied.

"That would be nice," I said politely. I didn't really like black tea, but it was certainly better than coffee.

"We have incoming threats, Max," Brooklyn said in my ear.

"How many?" I asked.

"I think I have a few bags of the English Breakfast tea... do you want more than one bag in your mug?" +3 South Max asked, sounding perplexed.

"No, no tea now, we have to go," I said standing up quickly and moving to the living room window to peer out.

"Go where, go why?" he asked, stopping the water as he was filling the kettle.

"Someone is coming for us—" I started but was cut off when the sound of gun fire rang out outside. My guards were firing on some threat out there.

"There are five threats heading towards the house, the Guards are engaging four but are outnumbered with the fifth. All appear to be drones, but I detect a vehicle is rushing this way. I've scrambled more support, but we might be outnumbered here," Brooklyn reported in my ear.

"Okay, we're going to cross over from here," I said. I didn't hesitate, didn't stop to explain anything, I just pulled out the Draw Bridge, dialed in +3 West and opened the Bridge.

As it glowed to life, +3 South Max dropped the kettle into the sink and stared.

"We have to go, now!" I yelled.

The Bridge was open against the inside wall of the kitchen. I rushed over and grabbed him and pulled him through the Bridge.

"Retreat all resources. Have the auto-auto return to base," I said to Brooklyn.

Just before I closed the Bridge, other Max and I looked back as an object broke through the living room window and rolled to a stop. I closed the Bridge just as something exploded.

I really hope it didn't destroy other Max's house.

Chapter 15 - Lesson Number One

Other Max (the +3 South Max) and I, stared at the living room window. It was untouched. No cracks existed. No hole from where an explosive device entered. No bright flash, no fire, no disturbances at all. The living room was as quiet and clean as it was twenty minutes before the attack.

"What the hell just happened?" other Max asked, walking into the living room, "did someone just blow up my house? My real house?"

"Maybe," I said, pulling out my handheld and calling up the application where I could retrieve the footage my drones had captured. I didn't see the recent footage yet.

"Hal, status on the sitrep," I requested.

"We need a link between dimensions to retrieve it," she said.

"I forgot that. I'm rushing the process. Okay," I said, and pulled out a nano-drone from inside my coat pocket. I rested it in the palm of my hand and pushed up to kick start it flying to the ceiling. It flew up and opened a nano Bridge and fed a tiny line and receiver through. I looked back down at my handheld and refreshed to see the footage files. I picked the file that would show me the footage of the drone closest to the living room window where the object broke through.

"Why did they do that?" other Max asked, now over at the window looking outside in a panic, "are they coming here?"

"No," I said, concentrating on the video.

"How do you know? You didn't expect them to show up back there, but they did," he said, rushing over to the window on the opposite side of the living room.

"I brought us to a direction they can't travel to. Well, at least I don't think they can," I said.

"What does that mean? You're speaking in riddles again, Riddler," he said, sounding frustrated, "...at least say 'riddle me this' beforehand," he then said under his breath.

"Listen, just give me a few minutes to see what happened and then I'll explain," I said, pinching my screen to zoom in on the drone with the grenade launcher at its base.

They came to do damage. They came to kill – to kill me.

"Okay, we're going to move, just in case, we'll go to a safehouse I have a couple hours from here," I said.

Other me walked back over to me and peered over my shoulder at the video. I replayed the video for him. He looked at me in horror at the sight of the front of his house exploding.

"My house..." he said at just above a whisper.

"I'm sorry. I'm not sure if they were tracking me and tried to kill me, or if they were just trying to track you and kill you," I said frowning.

"Can you please explain this all in more details on our way?" he asked with earnest.

"Yes."

I called for an auto-auto.

It arrived and we were on the road in less than twenty minutes.

"Hal, retreat all resources to +4 West," I requested. I pulled up the listing for my Vermont property in that dimension and was relieved to see it was still for sale, so promptly made the purchase.

"Hal, send them all to the property and send a status report to my handheld on the details of this dimension," I requested, "oh, and order similar load as we did in +10 West, but account for a second person."

"Got it, Max, processing now," she responded in my ear.

"Okay. I've been patient. Please explain," other Max requested, "and who's Hal? Someone at your 'base command' or something?" he said making air quotes.

I looked up from my handheld and nodded apologetically. Then held up a finger indicating to wait a second.

"Hal, take note that we really could use some kind of magic pill we could give future maxes to help them learn the whole backstory instantly," I said to Brooklyn, but winked at other Max.

Then I explained everything I could with as much detail as I thought I could deliver without his head exploding. I definitely pushed his head right to the brink though.

"You think some version of us and Tabitha are doing all this then? A bad version from your home dimension?" other Max asked, still trying to untangle the thoughts in his head.

"Not my home dimension, a branch from it. Although since Tabitha was taken from my home dimension, we're not sure if the one we saw in the video is the same one. These are all just theories though," I said, "Dr. Zine said 'lesson number one' is to work off the facts, whatever the current facts tell us, otherwise we get lost in speculation and work less efficiently. I like this approach because it helps us focus. It's also in line with the Buddhist teaching on impermanence since we can't control the ever-changing nature of life," I said.

"There's a lot to digest, so I'm sure I'll have more questions, but the hardest part to wrap my head around is how we're like different people, even though we're the same person," other Max said sincerely.

"It appears we are, I haven't really thought much about it until now, though. I guess we'll learn some interesting things in the next few days," I said.

"So, we're heading to Vermont? Where exactly?" other Max asked.

I looked at him in the eyes and hesitated to answer at first. All these "bad" versions of people running around, I started to wonder who I could really trust, but decided, I'd just have to trust myself here.

"I have a cabin in Killington. It's empty in this dimension, but we'll build it up, already have gear on the way, so we can settle in and try to unravel the events we just lived through. I'll teach you about the digital currency hack I used," I said.

"Digital currency hack?" other Max asked.

"Yeah, I can spend against digital wallets across dimensions, without affecting my real balance," I said with a big grin.

Other Max's face turned to stone and his eyes narrowed.

"Something wrong?" I asked.

"You're the reason the IRS fined me!" he yelled.

"Umm, what?" I asked, getting a churning feeling in my gut.

"The IRS fined me for not reporting the digital currency I owned. Even though I didn't!" he said, voice only slightly lower.

"Oh. Hmm. Okay, I hadn't considered that," I said, feeling my face turn flush.

"Yeah. Well..." he said, with his voice back to a normal timbre, "I was able to call the exchange and gain access and transferred money to the IRS to pay the fine, but it was an unexpected pain."

He kind of smirked.

"Wait, you gained access? So, you saw how much you had then...?" I said, licking my bottom lip and smiling.

"Yeah. It still was a pain though, so thanks for that," he said with a friendly huff.

"We're cool, then?" I asked, shaking my head slightly.

"Yeah, it's fine," he said, "but will I be able to go back home again?"

"Once we know you're safe, sure, if you want," I said, "but, you could help me out, if you're down for that."

"I guess we'll have to figure out what that would mean, but yeah, I'll help you."

We smiled in agreement.

We rounded the bend in the road, and I could see my property coming into view. The house was pretty much the same, although there was an old school tall radio antenna, and the color was a slightly lighter brown. The auto-auto pulled up to the front door and drones were already busily working to move gear into the house. I could see the look of amazement beaming on other Max's face. We exited the auto-auto, then I started for the front door, while other Max just took in the sights: the house, the land, and the drones.

"I feel like I should have been more productive in life," other Max said, finally walking in through the front door as I picked up a large, long, but light vacuum-sealed memory foam mattress, and hefted it onto my shoulder.

"Probably," I said with a smirk, "in my other house, like this, I had my bedroom on this floor and used the rooms upstairs for other things. What do you think? Each take a room upstairs?"

"I was hoping for bunk beds, ones we make by stacking two single beds on top of each other. You sleep on the bottom, and when I jumped on top it collapses," he said, so very casually.

"Stepbrothers. Great classic," I said, nodding with approval, "but seriously, this isn't heavy, but it isn't light," I said nodding my head up to the plastic log on my shoulder.

"Ah, right. Sure, sounds good," he said. I'm not sure he understood my question, I think he was too busy running his joke through his mind.

"Alright," I said, then headed upstairs. Other Max instinctively saw the other rolled up mattress and picked that up and followed me. We dropped them in the opposite rooms upstairs.

"Brooklyn let's get a few workers building the frames for these," I requested.

"I'm not sure I'll get used to that," other Max said from the other room.

"We'll get you hooked up so you can talk to her as well, don't you worry," I said.

"Can I choose a different name?" other Max asked.

"What do you mean? What's wrong with Brooklyn?" I said, walking into the hall, directing my question into other Max's room.

"Nothing. It just feels like it might be confusing," he said.

"Hmm. Fair enough. What name would you want to use? Also, sorry Brooklyn, but I still love you," I said.

"I was thinking of London," he said.

"Not bad, not bad," I said nodding with approval, "okay, we'll get you hooked up and establish a new persona for London. You know how to code still, right?"

"Yes. I may not have built a drone minion army, but I'm still smart," he said.

"Sorry. Didn't mean anything by that," I said.

"No worries," he said.

We all worked into the early evening getting the "new" house all set up how we wanted it. Deliveries had continued throughout that day, and most of what we needed was in house now. We set up the command center in the first-floor bedroom, which was much larger than either bedroom upstairs, so it allowed room for us to set up two stations. We had our chairs back-to-back. For fun we also provisioned gaming capabilities into our QCs.

"The QCs are loaded and ready to display the analysis from +3 South," Brooklyn said in my ear.

Other Max jumped, suddenly.

"Woah," he said, "I wasn't ready for that."

"Oh, yeah, it can be disconcerting at first," I said, "but don't forget to thank your AI. Also, they will only read out something like this when we're waiting on community info. If you ask her a question, only you'll hear her responses."

I turned my chair towards other Max.

"Er, thanks, London," he said awkwardly. I saw him nodding, so assumed she was speaking in his ear.

"I guess London is like your sister, huh, Brooklyn?" I said aloud.

"I suppose so. I always wanted a sister," Brooklyn said.

"So, I can just request London do things?" other Max asked.

"Yes..." I said with a concerned smirk.

"Just trying to wrap my head around this, you know." other Max said.

"London is linked with Brooklyn. It's all the same AI network, really, but different voice programs and personas. You can open and close a line directly to me and as long as we're somehow connected to the same network. Generally, when we're in the same dimension, we can be almost anywhere on earth and have a channel to communicate. And with the help of the new satellite tech Denny invented, we can talk across nearby dimensions once the channel is opened via nano Bridges."

"That's freaking insane sounding," other Max said wide-eyed.

"One hundred percent," I said.

"Ahem," Brooklyn said.

"Did you literally say that phrase, Brooklyn?" I said, laughing a little.

"Yes, yes I did, Max," she responded.

"Okay, okay, let's see what we got," I said, spinning my chair back to face my screen.

Brooklyn loaded up the footage from a couple different angles on the screen. Then she loaded up a document with a written breakdown of what came out of the analysis. I started reading through it, then air-tapped at the play button on the top left video. I pinched the air to zoom in on the grenade drone.

"Is that what it looks like?" I asked aloud.

"B M," other Max said, very close to my ear causing me to jump.

"Dude," I said, looking up at him.

"Bad Max?" he asked, ignoring my annoyance.

I looked back at the screen and pinched more to zoom further in.

"Did he create a logo?" I asked, leaning in slightly, eyes wide in disbelief.

"He created an evil logo," other Max stated.

"Hey, he's bad, not evil, remember?" I snapped, "I. P. rules and whatnot."

"Okay..." other Max said, side-eying me briefly, then looking back at the screen.

"Well, then, looks like he's branding his drones," I said, "that, might be concerning."

"Yep," other Max concurred.

This wasn't the most concerning thing though.

"Brooklyn, did we capture any of Bad Max's drones?" I asked.

"We were able to retrieve the two we downed, they are on the dining room table," she said.

"Thank you, Brooklyn," I said and rose from my chair and headed for the dining room. Other Max followed me out of curiosity. We both inspected the two drones that were laid out on each half of the table. Both had holes with melt marks in the center, and bottoms where the circuit boards would be removed.

"These were already inspected for tracking chips?" I asked Brooklyn, aloud. Other Max eyed me suspiciously at first, but realized this wasn't weird, now that he was linked up to an AI too.

"Of course," she said with an air of annoyance in her tone.

"Yes. Of course. Did we learn anything interesting about them?" I asked.

"Hey, can we have a party line with you, me, London and Brooklyn?" other Max asked.

"Sure. Brooklyn, hook that up," I requested.

"All set," Brooklyn said.

"Thank you," other Max said with a smile, now he could hear the conversation in my head.

"Could we see any people out there with these drones?" other Max asked. I could hear him in my ear at first as he started talking, but the volume auto adjusted down to prevent an echo, since he was in the same room.

"There was a woman caught on video by one of our surveillance drones running away," London reported.

"Wait, how does this work? Do you hear Brooklyn or London in your ear when they respond?" other Max asked.

"You hear London because we're in the party line and you asked the question. Your AI, London, will just respond for your questions, but I can hear her now. I hear her clearly in her British accent and all," I said, smiling and snickering, "and when I ask a question, unless I asked London directly, Brooklyn would respond. Can we get back to the matter at hand?" I shook my head playfully and gestured towards the table.

"Yes, yes we can," he said with a nod.

"Were we able to scan the woman's face, or scent?" I asked, "I didn't see anyone in the footage from the grenade drone side of the house."

"She was out by the street, operating one of the drones with a handheld controller," Brooklyn said.

"Wait, what? A handheld controller? What year is it in that dimension? Sheesh," I said shaking my head in semi-mock disgust.

"It's pretty offensive to AI assistants, that's for sure," Brooklyn said cheekily.

Other Max laughed out loud. I just nodded thoughtfully in agreement.

"Do we know who she is?" I asked.

"No scent trail, but her face matches the face of Tabitha's friend that was taken, from the missing person's report I was able to pull from that dimension," Brooklyn said.

"What?" other Max asked, "That doesn't make any sense."

"It never does," I said shaking my head. All of this was hard to wrap your mind around.

"But she went missing, with Tabitha, they were both last seen together, according to the reports," other Max said.

"We don't know if that's the same woman," I said flatly.

"I guess..." he said.

"I think we should go visit the family. We should see if maybe they have seen her again. Maybe she's not missing anymore. Maybe the police records have been updated. Can you check, Brooklyn?" I proposed, "did you follow up with the woman's parents, Max?"

"No," other Max said and then grimaced, "I figured if Tabitha was found, then I'd hear about it and just assumed I might hear about her friend too, but I guess her parents wouldn't have any obligation to try to track me down."

He paused and looked at me.

"I didn't even give my new address to my parents," he said then looked at the ground.

"It's okay. We have the best resources to try to find her – if she's findable," I said.

"The police still have her listed as missing, Max," Brooklyn said.

"Thank you," other Max and I said at the same time.

"Let's see if we can track her down. It's a good lead," I said.

"We can be like interdimensional private investigators," other Max said, with a smile growing on his face.

"Yes, well, I've kind of been doing that for a while, while trying to track down Bad Max," I said, smiling back, "but yeah, that's a good way to look at it."

"The idea is new to me, and I'm getting excited about it," he said, pondering, "we could have a cheesy name like 'Maxes Interdimensional Detective Agency' since we're plural." He winked at me.

"Sure," I said, "why not?"

"Incoming communication," Brooklyn said interrupting us as we each scanned through the footage on our separate screens, looking for any more clues to help us identify more details about Tabitha's friend.

Dr. Zine and Denny's faces showed up on the screen.

"Hey, can you see us?" Denny asked as the picture blipped and bent sideways for a brief millisecond. Then it was clear again as I saw Denny adjusting something on his side.

"Yes, I can see you," I said then looked over at other Max's screen.

"I see you as well," other Max said.

"What? Did you say you could see us twice, Max? We can see you," Denny said.

I didn't think to set up cameras in our command center setup, since I wasn't expecting to do video conferencing.

"Brooklyn, can you dispatch two surveillance drones, so they can stream both of us?" I requested.

"Yes, Max," Brooklyn said, and two drones flew in, "transmitting feed to the QC now. I just received an update from the Span and can now feed these feeds back through the open channel to Dr. Zine and Denny's dimension."

"Really?" other Max asked, "holy wow."

"We've been busy man. A lot has happened over the years," I said adjusting the video window size on my screen by pinching the air in front of me. The hand gesture controls were way better than old school mouse controls.

"We can see you both now," Dr. Zine said, "you'd think I wouldn't find it odd seeing two of you, but I do."

"Yeah, it's pretty wild," Denny said, "nice to meet, umm, see you Max and other Max."

"I'm just learning about you two. And yeah, it's weird seeing myself over there," other Max tipped his head towards me, "but this is all pretty cool stuff. I'm learning relatively quickly, I think."

"Okay, we have some news," Dr. Zine said and broke up the casual introductions.

"What's up?" I asked.

"We've been able to establish connection channels across over a thousand universes now, by leaping dimensional comms, and the data has started to flow in very rapidly," Dr. Zine said, "we should be able to start parsing that data for patterns very shortly."

I could feel other Max turning to look towards me, inferring he had a shocked expression on his face.

"Don't look too shocked, Max, er, other Max. You'll be up to speed soon enough, especially if you've installed the AI-com," Denny said with a wink.

"Yes, anything is possible, when you explore the art of the possible," Dr. Zine said. I rolled my eyes.

"Anything of interest yet, Dr. Zine?" I asked, ignoring his grandiloquent statement.

"We did confirm there are many universes where Tabitha's friend also disappeared, but we don't have enough data yet to know who took her," Dr. Zine said, "the bigger thing of interest is in a few hundred-dimensional versions out, there are some odd readings on Bridge usage. I hope to have more info on that soon. Oh, and we've tracked down a universe where there is tech that does memory restoration rapidly and with precision. That was a great request, Max, even though it was requested in jest." Dr. Zine smirked.

"I have good ideas," I said with a straight face. Dr. Zine nodded.

"That would come in handy right about now," other Max said.

"Should I check out the dimension? I could see if anything really is out of sorts," I said.

"I think it's important to find out who initiated that attack, first, but after that, you should. We'll have more data by then too," Dr. Zine said.

"Okay. Sounds like a plan," I said, "looks like we're going back to +3 South, other Me."

"Where?" other me asked.

We really needed that new rapid memory restoration tech as soon as possible.

Chapter 16 - Maxes Interdimensional Detective Agency

"I sat at my desk. Gambler hat low on my brow, cigarette hanging from my lip. A pretty little dame walked in through the front door of my office. She was all grey looking, because there was no color, we were living in black and white, and grey, I guess. I sucked the cigarette into my mouth and started to chew it, because it was candy, nice and sweet, like this dame's pretty round face," I said in my best old-timey-detective-narrator-voice.

"Hello?" the dame asked.

"I chewed my cigarette gum's flavor away in three jaw motions," I said.

"Hey!" the dame then shouted, "who are you talking to? Did you call me a 'dame'?!"

She walked closer to my desk and waved a hand in front of my face.

"Hi ma'am. I apologize. Just ignore him. He's addicted to schticks," other Max walked into the room and killed my old detective agency vibe.

We had tracked down employment records for Tabitha's friend. Her name was Blaine. Oddly enough, the records showed she was working at this real estate office within the last year.

"I sat up and tipped my hat up and then pulled the already hardened gum from my mouth and tossed it into the trash under my desk. I leaned forward on my elbows, hands clasped, and smiled," I said, "welcome to Maxes' Interdimensional Detective Agency, what can we do for you?"

"What? What are you talking about? And do for me? This is my office. What are you doing in here?" the woman asked, looking between me and other Max and then around the office, "how did you even get in?"

"The back door was unlocked. I'm sorry. We are looking for this woman, have you seen her?" other Max said and slowly moved closer to the woman, with his arm stretched forward holding a picture. She shook her head, barely looking at the picture.

"No. Now please leave. Before I call the authorities," she said.

"Are you sure? Look closer. We know she worked here. Her name is Blaine," other Max said, and now I stood up and walked towards the woman, slowly though, "red hair, brown eyes, maybe five-six."

"She's missing and we're just trying to help find her," I said sans-schtick.

The woman sighed and relaxed slightly, but crossed her arms, and squinted at the picture.

"Can I see it closer?" she asked and reached out. Other Max released it into her hand. After a second or two of inspection, she handed it back.

"I do recognize her. She was a greeter, but she doesn't work here anymore. She worked here for one day and then never reported for work again," the woman said.

"How long ago was that ma'am?" other Max asked.

Other Max seemed to be taking the lead and playing Good Cop.

"The last time I saw her was maybe two weeks ago," she said.

"Thank you for your time," I said and headed for the door.

"If you see her or hear anything, please let us know," other Max said and sent his info from his handheld into the contact collection unit near the front door.

We left and walked up the block.

"That confirms it, Blaine is alive and apparently back in town," other Max said.

"Let's see if we can find anyone that will talk to us at her family's house," I said.

When we first crossed back to +3 South, we learned that Blaine's mother and father sold their home and moved to Pennsylvania, closer to her mother's mother. We traveled there and spent a week setting up shop in a vacation rental house one town over. We gathered as much information as we could from online sources into a profile on Blaine and found out she had shown back up about two years ago. The only employment records were for that real estate office, and she apparently only worked there for one day. There was a good chance she only worked there to try to find out info on other Max's house, which would seem unnecessary, since all house information is freely available to anyone. The other odd thing was that the police still had her listed as missing.

Once arrived in their town, we stopped by her family's house, but no one was there. We were hoping for better luck this time. Our auto-auto was parked about a mile away, on the side of the road, up on a hill that gave us a great view of Blaine's parents' place.

"Should we just go down and knock and ask about Blaine?" other Max asked.

"No," I said, "that's not how I do things."

"Okay... then what are we doing?" he asked.

"Well, now that we're in range, we should send out surveillance drones to get us some intel first," I said.

He just nodded and stared at me.

"So, we should launch a couple," I said raising my eyebrows.

"Yes, that sounds good," he said.

I sighed.

"Brooklyn, launch four drones to get us some footage of Blaine's parents' property," I said.

"Did you want me to do that? Because that wasn't clear," he said with a grimace.

"Still learning our differences," I said. Other Max just nodded.

We didn't hear anything for about twenty minutes and just sat in silence.

"Detecting two people inside the house, and two inside the detached garage. The two in the house seem to be just sitting in the living room, watching something. There's lots of movement inside the garage though. The two individuals in there are moving around somewhat erratically," Brooklyn reported.

"What do you recommend we do next, Max?" I asked other Max.

"Oh," he started and took a beat and then said, "I'd deploy an invisible drone to sneak inside the garage to get a better look at the two in the garage."

I smiled and nodded.

"London, deploy a drone, the invisible one, to go and, a... spy on the people, er, targets, in the garage," other Max waded through words but got it out.

"Deploying Carrier drone to transport Cloaked Spider to the target, Max," London relayed over our group channel. The Carrier drone flew out from the trunk as soon as it opened. Inside the body was the Cloaked Spider. And inside the Cloaked Spider were the nano drones (as previously mentioned from the Underbelly). Yeah, we had a nesting doll thing going on, fo shizzle.

"Here, put these on," I said handing other Max some glasses I pulled from my inner coat pocket.

"What are these?" he asked.

"For seeing invisible drones, man," I said with a smile.

The Carrier hovered above the garage and the Cloaked Spider lowered itself via its silk line to the roof. It scurried along the shingles to the soffit vent and worked its way into the garage.

"And, to see what the invisible drones see, man," I said, and as other Max looked over at me, I tapped the right arm of the glasses. Instantly I could see inside the garage from the view of the Cloaked Spider.

"Awesome," other Max said with a huge smile.

Indeed.

Inside the garage was a workshop. Workbenches around the outer walls, tools hanging from metal hooks embedded in the pegboard. Digital whiteboards in spontaneous positions around the floor. Very clean, especially around the center... something felt familiar.

"This is odd," I said.

"Yeah, it's weird spying like this," other Max said.

"No, the arrangement of the garage," I said, "Brooklyn, does this seem incidental or does this look like an experimentation lab of some sort."

"Max, this has likeness to the original home dimension lab," Brooklyn said.

"That's what I was thinking," I said.

I could only wonder how many alternate versions existed.

Maybe they had to flee to this dimension for some reason to build the Draw Bridge. But only two heat signatures were read. I was standing next to this dimension's Max, and he confirmed he never pursued the Bridge. But just like I traveled here via a Bridge to check out what events took place; in theory, any other Bridge traveler could visit here as well. We needed a better look.

"Brooklyn, deploy two more Cloaked Spiders," I requested.

Two more Carriers took to the sky to deliver the Cloaked Spiders, posthaste. Within four minutes we had two more feeds from different positions in the garage feeding video to our glasses.

"This is making me dizzy," other Max said.

"Yeah, trying to balance where to look at different videos, only inches from your eyeballs, is a little jarring. It took a while for me to get used to, but you'll have to adjust quickly. I see Tabitha," I said blinking my eyes to make sure I wasn't seeing something incorrectly, "except, she has blonde hair."

"Brooklyn, launch the Bloodhound AI drone," I said, feeling a sense of grandeur welling inside me.

"Wow, that sounded cool and corny at the same time," other Max chirped.

"It one hundred percent did, and I stand by it," I said with my chest slightly puffed out.

"Bloodhound AI drone is inbound and scanning for scents," Brooklyn said, "I'm already getting a reading."

Impressive since it was half a mile away at that point and scanning from outside to inside.

"This Tabitha is not your Tabitha, Max," Brooklyn said.

"What about his?" I asked, tipping my head towards other Max, knowing Brooklyn wouldn't 'see' me do it but would sense the tilt with the gyroscope sensors in my glasses. (I didn't really like to wear the glasses because they felt restricting in some sense, but they certainly came in handy sometimes.)

"I'm not sure, Max. We would need something from this dimension's Tabitha to scan first for comparison," Brooklyn said.

"Do you have any of Tabitha's old clothes, Max," I said to other Max. This was going to get confusing.

"Brooklyn, take a note for us to figure out nicknames or codenames later on to help us distinguish better," I requested.

"Noted," she replied.

"That's so weird when you do that," other Max said.

"Would it not be useful?" I said.

"I didn't say that. Anyways, yes, I have at least one old sweatshirt of hers in storage," other Max said.

"Great, we need that," I said. I wished we could use the Draw Bridge to travel fast between different locations, but it currently didn't do that. We would need to order up an auto-Air (again, marketers, shrug), but this sometimes drew attention outside of areas where they flew routinely. "Brooklyn, send a Retriever drone for that, so we can add the scent to our database."

"It's like six hours away," he said.

"Yes. Still useful to have. Okay, let me think," I said. I needed to know what Tabitha this was.

"Let's just go down, knock and ask," I said and took my glasses off and put them into my coat and used the door handle to exit.

"Wait. What?" other Max said following suit and taking his glasses off.

"What?", I said.

"I suggested that earlier and you said, 'that's not how I do things' to me," he said mockingly for the last part.

"Ah, well... we're the same person. We're bound to have similarities," I said shrugging off the comment. He clicked his tongue on the roof of his mouth to tsk at me.

"Do you want to find out if your Tabitha is still alive or not?" I asked.

It didn't take any more convincing. He exited the vehicle as I did.

We headed down the hill a bit then walked over into the sloping hillside that ran down to the edge of the garage. From there we crept slowly and low all the way down the hill, trying to stay in line with the blind spot provided by the gap between windows. Once at the garage wall we each took up a position at different windows and peeked in at the same time. I could see the backs of two women facing towards the work benches.

"Stay out here, I'm going in," I said and turned and walked to the side door.

"Okay, not sure what I'll do, but I have your back," other Max said keeping his eyes trained on the women.

I opened the door and walked into the garage.

Tabitha and Blaine turned briefly to face me. Tabitha had a device that looked sort of like the Draw Bridge (slightly cruder and looked to be held together with duct tape in one spot) in her right hand, which she quickly triggered to open a Bridge. Blaine drew her pistol and aimed at me.

"Wait, Tabitha! Please!" I yelled and put my hands in the air.

She looked like she was about to rush through the Bridge but paused at closer inspection of me.

"You... you're not the Max from this dimension, are you?" Tabitha asked.

"I am not. Are you the Tabitha from this dimension?" I asked.

"No, I'm not," she said.

"And what about her?" I asked tipping my head towards Blaine.

"This isn't my dimension either," Blaine answered.

"Okay, glad we all know the score now," I said, "Max, why don't you come in now?"

"Max?" Tabitha asked with a confused look.

"Other Max," I said.

I watched Tabitha's eyes get wide at the sight of other Max coming into her view.

I thought now would be a fitting time to play out the old Spiderman meme, so I pointed at other Max. He followed suit and pointed at me, perfectly executing the bit. Gaining smiles from the ladies.

"Are you the Max of this dimension?" Tabitha asked after she finished shaking her head and sighing.

137

"Yes," other Max said, "and why did you try to kill me?" he pointed at Blaine and glared.

"Excuse me?" Blaine questioned.

"You blew up my house!" other Max shouted.

"No, I didn't," Blaine said putting a hand on her hip, other arm still holding her pistol at her side, "we just got here."

"I think we all need to talk, get out the backstories and whatnot, but we need to talk somewhere else," Tabitha said, "because the Blaine from this dimension, the one that did blow up your house, will be back any minute. And if you don't want to see Blaine doing the Spiderman meme with guns, we should step over to the next dimension right now."

"Hal, any sign of her?" I asked.

Blaine and Tabitha furrowed their brows. I guess they didn't have an AI companion. Other Max did as well. I just realized I didn't teach him the codename protocol for our AI when around others. He looked at me in confusion but didn't say anything. I chalked it up to the mostly same brain.

"There is no sign of another Blaine, or any other bodies within the range of the garage. Other than the two inside the house, who haven't moved much," Brooklyn said in my ear.

"Thanks, Hal," I said to Brooklyn. To the others I said, "we have an 'eye in the sky' and they said we're all clear. I'd prefer to stay in this dimension until we track down the Blaine that tried to kill me, er, us."

"So many questions right now, but okay, fine. We can stay, but not here. We're too vulnerable here," Tabitha said.

"We have an auto-auto about a mile away," I said.

Chapter 17 - Team Up

"I'm sorry. I'm not going to be able to keep up with who's who. One of you needs a nickname," Tabitha said.

We were sitting in the auto-auto facing each other. Tabitha on the same side of the vehicle as me, but able to talk face to face. Blaine sat next to Tabitha, and facing across from other Max. Since the auto-auto drove itself, there was no need for anyone to pay attention to the road as we drove. It allowed for a more personal experience during the ride. Like riding around in a little sitting room.

"Fair enough," I said, "I had the same sentiment."

"What's your middle name?" Tabitha asked, not directing the question to either of us in particular.

"Kel," other Max answered.

"Okay, one of you is now Kel," Tabitha said without much pause for deliberation.

Other Max and I looked at each other and he shrugged.

"Fine with me, I always liked my middle name," other Max said.

"Nice to meet you, Kel," Tabitha winked.

"Thanks, Kel," I said to other Max, glad I didn't have to call him other Max anymore. We were different in more ways than I expected; I hated my middle name.

"Great. Glad that's out of the way," Tabitha said.

"Now, which dimension are you two from? Same one?" I asked.

"Same one," Tabitha answered, "but explaining 'which one' might be tricky."

"Does your dimension have a Max? A Denny? Or Dr. Zine?" I asked.

"Max is missing from our dimension. Denny was accidentally killed. But Dr. Zine is back there, though," Tabitha said, slightly frowning, "he built our portable interdimensional portal opener."

Wow. Denny was dead. The other version of me missing...just like Michael.

"I see," I said, "what happened to Max?"

"He fell through the portal," Tabitha said, "he and Dr. Zine were conducting a test to expand the number of nuclear batteries and one exploded after he had crossed through. Denny was standing too close to the battery array and was killed instantly. The portal closed and Max was gone. Dr. Zine speculates he had set the wrong configuration to accommodate the battery expansion."

The cab of the auto-auto fell silent for a few minutes.

"My dimension didn't have a Blaine," I said, finally breaking the silence, "only a Tabitha, Dr. Zine, Denny and myself."

"Blaine's my best friend," Tabitha said, "she helped me get through the loss of Max. She also has been traveling with me to find him."

Tabitha was on a journey like I was, looking for her Max like I looked for my Tabitha and my Michael.

"Blaine was my Tabitha's best friend, as well, in my dimension. She was assumed to be kidnapped along with my Tabitha," Kel (formerly other Max from +3 South) said.

"I'm sorry," Blaine said to Kel with a frown.

"This whole thing is a mess," Tabitha said, "we've been searching for so long for Max. That was over ten years ago. Once we got a handle on using the device. We started traveling farther and farther through to look for him."

"Are you able to control which dimensions the... portal opener, opens up to?" I said, trying not to cringe. I wanted so badly to introduce them to the Draw Bridge nomenclature but resisted until I knew them better.

"To some degree," Tabitha said, "Dr. Zine refined the device to open portals in an order, like one after another. We can move backwards and forwards like going through doors into other rooms of a house. In a gigantic house."

I nodded. I was surprised other dimensions didn't have our technology to move multi directionally. They didn't have a Denny though. Which only made me wonder. Were there dimensions where no Maxes existed? Curious.

"What about you?" Tabitha asked, looking at me.

"We have a device, as you can guess, and it does similar things," I said, "How do you label the dimensions you travel to? Do you number them?"

"We say we're in a plus 'x' number dimension. Like this one we call +2 since it's two steps from our home dimension."

Fascinating.

"We do something similar, but we call this dimension +3," I said. I was still careful how much information I shared.

"Fascinating," Tabitha said staring at me thoughtfully. I held her eye contact until Kel coughed.

"So, where are we going?" Blaine asked interrupting the moment.

Tabitha was finally sitting only a few feet from me. A moment I had been dreaming of for ten years. Seeing her beautiful face again. I spent so many nights dreaming of her face, this face. I was so caught up in this chase, this mission of tracking down of the demon that stole her, that I couldn't even savor seeing her. No matter what version of her. I loved her.

"It's really good to see you," I said, continuing to stare into Tabitha's eyes, ignoring Blaine's question.

Kel cleared his throat.

"Soooo... where are we going?" Blaine asked again.

"To our safehouse," I said, still holding my eyes straight.

"Where's that?" Blaine asked.

Tabitha held the eye lock with me. We were playing a game of chicken with uncomfortable tension. Both of us grew smirks.

"It's less than twenty minutes," I said, finally redirecting my eyes to Blaine's, "we are set up in a nice quiet vacation rental."

"It has a hot tub," Kel said to Blaine with raised eyebrows and a smile. I gave a soft snort at this. I could see Tabitha giggle quietly.

"I hope you have food there, I'm starving," Tabitha said.

We were having an interdimensional double date. Maybe the first of its kind.

I ordered some Chinese food ahead of our arrival at the safehouse and we ate in the living room.

Kel seemed to sense my chemistry with Tabitha, and recognized this wasn't his Tabitha, but it didn't seem to bother him. Maybe their relationship wasn't as developed. He seemed interested in Blaine, although it could have been because he felt an innate desire to pair off. I was sitting on the couch with Tabitha, finishing the last bites of Lo Mein, and Kel very smoothly mentioned the hot tub again. Leveraging a casual joke about the fact that the "waiting thirty minutes after eating" warning doesn't apply to hot tubs. It worked and Blaine and Kel headed to the back deck to check it out. They were adults, they'd figure out the bathing suit situation.

"It's interesting to me that you two are the same person, but different in many ways," Tabitha said once we had the room to ourselves. She placed her empty container on the coffee table and then sat back against the couch cushions with her head pointed to the ceiling.

"It is," I said, "I never could have imagined a lot of things I've seen over the years of crossing dimensions."

"How many have you been to?" Tabitha asked, looking over at me. I placed my container next to hers and leaned back on the couch, looking back at her.

"I lost count, honestly. Hundreds. If I had to put some kind of number on it," I said.

"Wow," she said.

"Some of them I jumped into and out of pretty quickly, not staying long," I said, realizing that I was showing my hand a bit and trying to downplay what I said. It would be hard to explain the mechanics anyways right now, without explaining the "sideways" directions I was able to travel in.

"I think Blaine and I have been to maybe less than fifty in the past ten years," she said, "we spent a lot of time exploring each one. It takes a while to get your bearings. Plus, we got into trouble several times and couldn't get back home easily," she said.

I couldn't help but think of how much not having Denny or myself around stunted their development in building out Draw Bridge tech for travel.

"I mean, it kind of sounds like you could have had some good adventures, at least," I said.

"Yeah," she said, "we certainly had some adventures. Some great ones. Once, we accidentally lost our portal opener in the back of an auto-auto in New York City after getting a little too drunk one night. Good thing we could track it, and that no one could use it without our biometrics, but it still took a week to get it back."

"Seriously?" I asked. I couldn't imagine losing the Draw Bridge. That thing was a part of me.

"Yeah... we thought we'd be stuck in that dimension forever and were prepared to live out our days there if it came down to it. It wasn't too bad there. Michael Jackson was alive much longer there, and got help with his mental health issues, and made like five more albums," she said matter-of-factly.

"Dang. Did he make a Thriller 2?" I asked.

"Yep," she said.

"Awesome," I said, "oh, hey. Epiphany. There's gotta be a way to build an interdimensional music service. Hal, take a note on that."

"Okay. We must talk about this thing you do where you talk to someone else, someone no one can see, but don't really prepare people for it..." she said with a grimace turning into a smirk.

"Fair enough. Hal is my personal AI. I can talk to them whenever I need to because I have a constant open channel with them," I said pointing towards my ear.

She leaned closer trying to look into my ear. I gave her a side-eye with a grin.

"What are you doing?" I finally asked.

"Trying to see the earpiece. Sheesh, how small is it?" she asked still inspecting.

She was very close to the side of my face now. I turned my body so I could face her less awkwardly.

"I've missed you," I said, "I know you're not the you I got to know specifically, but you are still you."

Tabitha rested her head against the couch and stared into my eyes and smiled.

"I've missed you too," she said, "I've missed your face, missed your eyes, your...lips."

I moved my head a little closer.

"Would it be... weird..." I said trailing off while moving my head closer. Lowering my hand to rest atop her hand that was on the cushion. She licked her lips gently.

"Would what be weird..." she said trailing off softly.

We melted into each other and kissed.

The next morning, I was awakened by the sunshine brushing my eyelids. Tabitha lay next to me, still sleeping, her naked body pressed against mine. I slipped from the covers and dressed. Down in the kitchen I made tea and sat at the kitchen table. I drank slowly while watching the sun slowly travel up through the windowpane. The view was clear, so I could see the sun fully. Our safe house was down a dirt road and you could only see the neighbors' houses in the winter. This view was clear any time of year though.

My pocket pulsed a brief vibration and I retrieved my handheld. Dr. Zine had sent me a message. He wanted me to return to the +10 West safe house immediately; he wanted me to return alone.

I finished my tea and went to the basement.

Other Max, er, Kel, and I had set up a small workshop auto factory to stand up a small reserve of drones. In case we needed them in a pinch. On one of the work benches was a small round device, with a projector lens on the top and speaker wrapping the body. This was capable of projecting a holographic image above it and playing the audio from the speakers, giving the perfect illusion of a tiny version of a person talking to you. I pocketed it and returned to the kitchen.

I retrieved my coat and hat and was dressed to leave. I placed the holo-device in the center of the kitchen table and synced a message from my handheld to the device. It explained that I needed to leave suddenly and gave instructions on how to leverage the resource we stood up in the dimension to track down the +3 South Blaine. Kel would know how to reach me if needed.

I pulled out my Draw Bridge and opened a Bridge between the kitchen and living room.

"That's it, huh?" I heard Tabitha's voice say. I looked around the kitchen but couldn't see her. I closed the Bridge, and she was standing on the other side – standing in the living room with her arms crossed, sheet wrapped around her tightly like a dress.

"I got an urgent message from Dr. Zine, my Dr. Zine, and he said I needed to return immediately," I said, "I set up this little thing on the kitchen table that would have explained everything. And hopefully make you hate me a little less for leaving."

"Why are you running away, Max?" she asked, clearly not buying my poor justification.

I was running away.

"I'm sorry... last night was special..." I started to say.

"Stop," she interrupted, "save it. That wasn't a wedding night. I'm lonely, too."

"I'm not sure who to trust anymore," I said.

"I get it," she said, "I'm not sure who to trust either. I can't spend time worrying about that though. I haven't shared anything I can't recover from."

Dang, I loved her. Any version of her. Even though I felt the strongest connection and subsequent pain when it came to my original Tabitha. This was some sort of emotional quantum conflict I suppose. I let out a sigh and looked at the floor. There was silence and I walked over to the holo-device and pressed the red button on the side. A tiny version of me popped up, looking exactly like I did right now: dressed for harsh conditions.

"Hey guys, sorry to step away without warning, but I got a message from Dr. Zine that was urgent. He needed me to return home immediately. He told me to come alone and to not try to open a channel to communicate. You three should try to track down the Blaine of this dimension and find out why she's doing what she's doing. Kel will help with the resources," little me said and then was sucked back into the lens. I smirked and I looked back at Tabitha.

"Cute," she said, "is that supposed to make your bailing on me better?"

I had hoped.

"I guess the answer is no..." I said losing my smirk and confidence in my plan.

"Yeah. No. It doesn't make me feel better," she said, "look, I know we technically just met, in some unexplainable way, but we do have history. I'm not suggesting you should have taken me with you, but you could have at least been honest with me."

"You're right," I said.

"And we did get close last night, following some innate attraction and following the path that was carved out years ago. I wasn't nothing," she said.

"I agree. I got scared. I haven't felt that way in a long time," I said.

"Me either," she said.

"Where does that leave us?" I asked.

"Can we stay on this path? At least until we trip?" she asked with a smile.

I smiled and nodded.

"Okay then. Go off and do what you do, "she said," and I most'll try to keep Kel alive." She winked.

"I didn't want to call him out, but he's new to all of this," I said.

"It's pretty obvious," she said, "it's okay. I kind of feel responsible for Blaine. In any dimension. But my Blaine needs me, so I feel protective of her. I wouldn't have let what happened between them happen last night happen, if it wasn't a version of you with her."

"That sounds super weird," I said, "never going to get used to hearing us describe things like this."

"Yep," she said, "should I move?"

"What?" I asked confused.

"Out of the way, so you can open the portal?" she asked.

"Oh. Yeah. Come over here," I said.

She walked over next to me, holding her arms crossed, but mainly to hold her sheet tight against her body.

"Ready?" I asked. She watched the threshold.

"Yes..." she said, side eying me, waiting.

I turned and wrapped her up in my arms and kissed her, catching her off guard.

"Well. That's better than a hologram," she said.

I released her. Causing her to lose the grip on her sheet slightly and needing to readjust it.

Then I redrew the Draw Bridge and opened the Bridge. It glowed to life, and she stared.

"I'll see you in a bit," I said, then walked forward and through.

I turned back from the other side and brushed my finger across the brim of my hat with a nod and we winked out of existence to each other.

Chapter 18 - Something Very Concerning

"Max, we've detected something very concerning in another universe," Dr. Zine said as soon as I stepped through the Bridge, back to +10 West.

"What is it?" I said as the Bridge winked out behind me.

"With data collected via the multidimensional communication system, BridgeAI has detected that the universe +137 has what appears to be the beginning of a major power struggle going on. Multiple groups are fighting over a device that opens multiple Bridges at the same time," Dr. Zine said.

"+137 South?" I asked.

"All directions of +137," Dr. Zine said.

"As in, North, South, East, West, Northwest, Southwest, etc.?" I asked with bits of shock running like sweat from my eyes.

"Yes," he said.

"Usually, we see differences in dimensions directionally," I said.

"This is one thing that isn't different," Dr. Zine said, "there are subtle differences, but this major event is taking place in all of them. Yet, not in any other universe going forward or backwards, relatively speaking. This event doesn't seem to be occurring in +136 or +138."

"What could this mean?" I asked.

"Let's go back to the house. Denny is there running some programs he created against this new data," Dr. Zine said.

When I walked through the front door, I immediately noticed the differences. They had redecorated my house. Large fluffy area rugs sprawled beneath the living room furniture and beneath the dining room table. There was more lighting: standing lamps in the corners and the chandelier above the dining room table was different. Two little robot vacuums zoomed around cleaning the floors. Jasper and Jenkins had some new companions, and all were busy in the kitchen.

"Made some changes, I see," I said as I hung my coat and hat on a set of new wooden built-in coat hooks to the side of the front door. Enough for many more coats and hats than just mine.

"We spruced it up a little; made it homier," Dr. Zine said, hanging his own coat and hat.

I nodded and pursed my lips in approval. It felt more like home now.

"Where's the workshop now?" I asked.

"We leveraged the construction resources you created to finish the basement. Don't worry, we preserved a space for your quiet room," Dr. Zine said with a big smile.

I followed him into the basement; command center 2.0.

"While you and other Max were playing detectives in +3 South, we've been busy tracking data across the multiverse," Denny said. I walked up alongside his chair and gazed at the screen before him. Several windows were running programs, and I watched as lines generated in a flow of strings and numbers cascading downwards, some readable, some encoded.

"Hey buddy, you guys have been busy," I said, looking to him placing my hand on his shoulder and squeezing gently.

"Yep," Denny said, glancing briefly at me, then back to the screen, "I'm starting to see a convergence of, um, well, Maxes, in the +137 dimensions. Like, a lot of them."

"Can you tell which dimensions they are from?" I asked, focusing on the screen.

"Not really," Denny said, "just seeing them on several different surveillance feeds."

"Interesting," I said, "what about Bad Max? Or Bad Tabitha?"

"We haven't specifically found Bad Max, based on scent analysis, but we have detected one 'Denny' in that dimension," Denny said doing air quotes around his name, "and..." he paused for a second and looked over to me, "he was with a 'Max' and they seemed to be working together."

"This is the concerning part I wanted to tell you, and why I wanted to do this in person," Dr. Zine said, from the other side of

Denny, "they appear to be trying to activate the device. They appear to be working together."

I grimaced and took in a deep breath and let it out slowly. Am I a bad guy there?

"Okay..." I said, "this is getting crazy. How are we going to keep track of who's bad or good?"

Both Dr. Zine and Denny looked over at me with slight shrugs. I looked to Dr. Zine.

"We are operating in the best interest of trying to bring home our loved ones. That in itself means we're the good guys," Dr. Zine offered.

Yes. We were just trying to bring home our loved ones. We were just trying to find Tabitha... to find Michael. I'm so caught up in trying to deal with the immediate concern, which is bringing back Tabitha, that I get lost in that and forget I started this journey trying to find and bring back my brother Michael.

I sighed and looked at the floor.

"How urgent is this concern in +137?" I asked after several seconds, looking back to Dr. Zine.

"If they trigger that device, it could rip the fabric of space and time," Dr. Zine said.

"That sounds bad, obviously," I said, "but how will that impact us, here?"

"I've been trying to calculate the effects, and I've fed several calculations into Denny's prediction programs. We won't know for sure, not yet, but..." Dr. Zine said and paused, "if my theory is correct, that device will start destroying universes it opens up to, by 'causing branches to shatter,' for lack of a better description. It's theoretically possible the device was created to open two branches simultaneously causing them both to collapse into each other, because one universe can't handle both outcomes at the same time."

"Holy hell," I said.

"Yeah," Denny said, "my sentiments exactly."

"So, the device is built, and people are fighting over it? Or people are fighting over building it?" I asked.

"It's not entirely clear yet," Denny said, "we've seen video for the designs for it, and what looks like a device, but it could be just a prototype."

"We've also heard some people speaking about it and describing that it will open multiple universes simultaneously. However, I think we'd have seen evidence of it being triggered, and we haven't seen any mass implosions yet, so that's some good news at least," Dr. Zine said.

"Yes, still existing is good news," I said, shaking my head.

Quiet fell like fog between us again.

"Okay, can we just keep an eye on this?" I asked, "because I think I need to go back to +3 South to help them find the Blaine that tried to kill us."

"You found a Tabitha and a Blaine there?" Dr. Zine asked.

"Yeah, but not from +3 South. They said that +3 is +2 to them, so my thought is they are from +1 South by our dimension numbering."

"That's a good guess," Dr. Zine said.

"And I think their dimension might be where Bad Max originated from," I said. Dr. Zine touched his chin and thought, and Denny's eyes grew wider.

"Really?" Denny asked.

"It's my best educated guess," I said.

It was quiet again for a bit.

"How was it being with Tabitha, a close version of her?" Denny asked to break the silence.

"It was good," I said with a smile.

"Was it weird with other Max?" Denny asked.

"No. He seemed to connect with Blaine," I said, "also, he goes by Kel now."

Denny donned a confused smile.

"Tabitha insisted we have different names to go by, and Kel leaned into using our middle name," I said, "let's just hope I don't befriend another me anytime soon." I winked. Denny smiled.

"I think you should go back," Dr. Zine said, apparently having mulled over a plan in his head, "the Blaine that tried to kill you, might be connected to the events of +137."

"Interesting. What makes you think that?" I asked.

"You are of interest to them, as apparent from that trap set at the Under Belly in +21 South, in addition to the attack in +3 South. Also, I'm speculating this, but it might be because you are the originator of Bridge travel."

"We all invented it together," I said.

"From an origination perspective, we all wouldn't have come together to invent it without you. You hold things in your mind that no one else does."

These esoteric conversations with Dr. Zine could go on for a while, so I had to move on.

"Okay. I'm going back to +3 South to find +3 South Blaine," I said, "I'll find out the connection, if there is one."

I pulled out my Draw Bridge, aimed against the wall, and opened the Bridge. I didn't have time for ceremonies right now.

"Good luck, son," Dr. Zine said as I stepped through.

"Don't get anyone pregnant," Denny said with a huge grin, just as the Bridge winked out, leaving me with gaped mouth that turned into a smile and left me laughing to myself.

"Brooklyn, where are my friends?" I asked.

We hadn't finished the basement in +3 South, so I stood in dimly lit dankness.

"Kel, Tabitha and Blaine are back at +3 Blaine's garage," Brooklyn said, "They have +3 Blaine tied up there."

Wow. They worked fast.

I got to the garage as fast as I could and stepped in through the side door to an unusual scene.

Both Blaine's were tied side-by-side in chairs.

"Max!" Tabitha said running over to me and throwing her arms around me to suck me into a hug.

"So, what the Scooby-doo is going on here?" I said reciprocating the squeeze quickly and releasing.

"Apparently, Bad Blaine had a camera in here, saw Good Blaine and dressed up exactly like her. When we came back here, after we got an alert she returned to the garage, a true comical ordeal seems to have ensued. Yeah, it was a Scooby-doo scene for sure," Kel said. I noticed he was holding a gun pointed down at the ground.

"And you guys mixed them up and can't tell who's who?" I asked. I wasn't surprised, this was bound to happen at some point.

"Yep," Tabitha said, "Blaine is my best friend, I know everything about her, known her since we were little. But I can't tell them apart right now."

"Tabitha, I'm Blaine, your Blaine," Blaine One, the one on the right side in front of me, said leaning forward in the chair towards Tabitha.

"You sound like her, but..." Tabitha said frowning.

"Well, this is kind of hilarious, I can't believe we're having an actual Scooby-doo moment, but we don't have a lot of time," I said. I had all their attention. I noticed Blaine on the left had a more worried look than Blaine on the right, but we would know for certain soon enough.

"Hal, settle this please," I requested of Brooklyn. The group looked amongst each other.

"Running scent analysis, Max," Brooklyn said in my ear.

We all awaited the results in silence for a minute.

"Blaine on the left is from this dimension. I've marked her," Brooklyn finally reported.

"That's Bad Blaine," I said pointing to Blaine on the left and I walked over and freed right-side Blaine.

"What? No, I'm not," Bad Blaine said, fighting against her restraints.

"Yes, yes you are," I said, "we have your scent-markers, and they match with what we know Blaine's markers from this dimension are."

"How?" Tabitha and Good Blaine asked in unison.

"We have a piece of Tabitha's clothing from this dimension, and it had traces of this dimension's Blaine on it, which is her," I said matter-of-factly.

I was met with amazed stares.

"We also don't have time for me to explain much more than that, so let's get to it," I said walking in front of Bad Blaine. She stared up at me looking nervous.

"Get to what?" she asked.

"Why are you here? Why did you try to kill me?" I asked.

Bad Blaine just glared at me.

"If you think scent detection is my only trick, you're sadly mistaken," I said with no movement in my face.

Bad Blaine mulled this statement over, then visibly relinquished.

"I was sent here to get your device," she finally said.

It wasn't exactly me they wanted, like Dr. Zine speculated. I knew they had Draw Bridges. Anyone traveling to other dimensions had some version of one. Yet, mine certainly was more powerful. I stepped back from Bad Blaine eyeing her, then looked at Tabitha and Good Blaine. I backed up to Kel and got close to his ear.

"Did you run any scans before coming here?" I asked him at an audible level only he could hear. Kel looked at me and shook his head letting me know we might have trouble coming.

"Hal, any threats?" I asked still keeping my voice low. Tabitha and Good Blaine looked at each other, then at Bad Blaine, then around the room.

I looked at Tabitha, partially wishing she was hooked up with our AI.

"No immediate threats, Max," Brooklyn responded.

"Open party line, Hal," I said.

"Opened," Brooklyn said.

"We're going to move the party," I said. I couldn't risk the next part being heard, so I pulled out my handheld and typed 'open bridge behind chairs to +2 east' into my BridgeAI application. Then returned my handheld to my pocket. Still holding all eyes on me.

The Bridge opened behind Bad Blaine.

"Now!" I said and rushed forward pushing Bad Blaine with the chair forward through the Bridge, guiding her down to the floor the best I could, then stepped to her side and yelled back, "let's go!"

I needed to get Bad Blaine clear and could only hope my team would follow my lead.

They did. They rushed through behind me emerging on the other side.

"Hal, close the Bridge!" I shouted.

The Bridge winked closed, and we were all in the empty semi-dark garage of +2 East. I had accepted the risk that it might not be empty, but being ambushed in +3 South, with the bad guys having the upper hand, was not an option. I looked around the room and got my bearings. Then walked over to the door and peered out. Nothing looked like an immediate threat.

"Hal, scan for threats," I requested.

The others' shock wore off and finally sensed the defensive urgency and started to scope out the area, looking through windows and checking darker areas for hidden threats.

"We're definitely going to have a postmortem on whatever the heck all that was, but later," Tabitha said as she tested that the garage door was locked.

"Yes," I said, "later."

I pulled out my handheld and called for a seven person auto-auto. We escaped the garage without incident.

I sat with Kel in the very back of the auto-auto, Tabitha and Good Blaine sat near the front. Our prisoner, Bad Blaine, was seated between us, hands and feet tied with electrified zip ties (I always kept electrified zip ties in my coat, they were so handy). Bad Blaine didn't really put up much of a fight. I think she realized she was outnumbered and outgunned by our tech.

"Who sent you?" I asked, tapping Bad Blaine who was staring down.

"Denny, who do you think?" she said looking up. I looked over at Kel, he raised an eyebrow.

It was odd she thought that was obvious.

"What did he tell you or offer you, to get you to come after me?" I asked.

"He told me if I brought your portal device back to him, he could put my timeline back to normal. Bring back Tabitha, my Tabitha," Bad Blaine said.

Curious.

"How could he bring me back? What does that mean?" Tabitha asked, causing Bad Blaine to turn towards her.

"He didn't explain it, really, he just said he had a device that could do it," Bad Blaine said, "but he insisted it would only work with Max Prime's portal device."

He was calling me 'Max Prime,' that's obnoxious.

"What's so special about Max's portal opener?" Tabitha asked. Bad Blaine furrowed her brow.

"It's the most powerful one," Bad Blaine said.

Tabitha furrowed her brow now and grimaced. She was just realizing I wasn't just another Max from another dimension. Knowing we still didn't have a lot of time to chit chat, I pressed forward.

"How were you going to get it to him?" I asked. Bad Blaine turned back to look at me. She paused, thinking about how to answer.

"Denny gave me a dimension to travel to, one thirty-six, and a place to leave it," Bad Blaine said.

"Things will never be the same, you know?" I said with a slight frown, "this dimension will never be the same as before he took you and Tabitha. Even if he does return Tabitha, your Tabitha, it will be different."

She looked back down at the floor of the vehicle.

"Why are you telling me this?" Bad Blaine asked, without looking at me.

"Because it doesn't mean your life is over. You can start over, move on," I said opening my hands towards her. She looked up with tears glistening her eyes.

"If I don't bring your device to him, he won't return Tabitha," she said. I nodded accepting the predicament.

"We're going to figure something out," I said, then leaned back and pulled out my handheld.

"Where are we going?" Tabitha asked.

"We need to find a safe house," I said. I was communicating with Brooklyn through my application on my handheld, going over our options. Once she pinpointed a location, we made the arrangements, and the auto-auto did a U-turn, took the west bound route, and headed for our safe house. I queued up some deliveries of resources we'd need, as well as an electronic lock, as a way to contain Bad Blaine in a room once we arrived.

"We have a place, about twenty-five minutes away," I said and returned my handheld to my pocket. I saw Tabitha nod and settle back in her seat. Good Blaine seemed to relax a bit too. Kel looked at me with concern. I pulled out my handheld and typed up a message for London to deliver to his ear. He nodded after he listened and settled back and watched the scenery pass by.

The auto-auto cruised along and as I closed my eyes for a second, listening to the whiz of air flowing past, then the road exploded in front of us, and we flipped over.

Chapter 19 - She Dead

Calm was suddenly chaos.

The windows of the vehicle were like all white stained glass, shattered, yet held in place because it was laminated glass all around. We couldn't see anything outside through the opaqueness. I was hanging upside down, held up by my seatbelt. Kel was too, hanging, motionless. Tabitha was hanging the same as me, as well as Good Blaine; both looked to be unconscious. Bad Blaine was bleeding from her ear, her arm at an unnatural angle, her body very still. I pulled my knife from my belt and cut my seatbelt and dropped down to the ceiling bracing the fall with my shoulder.

"Brook... Hal, what happened?" I asked.

"A missile was fired from a drone and struck the road in front of us as we drove, causing the front of the vehicle to dip down, catch in the hole and flip. The vehicle rolled several times before settling on its roof. I dispatched four of our Guard drones and took out the one that fired on us as well as two others close by that were readying to fire. There are no more threats I can detect," Brooklyn said, "I'm sorry, Max. I should have detected them sooner. I was able to slow the auto-auto down right before the missile hit us, and that's why it hit ahead of us and didn't impact directly."

I could hear sorrow in her voice.

"It's okay, I think we're okay..." I said feeling Kel's neck and finding a pulse.

"Bad Blaine is dead, Max. I detect no heartbeat," Brooklyn said solemnly.

I didn't respond.

I cut Kel loose and lowered him down to the ceiling, then crawled over Bad Blaine and carefully cut Tabitha loose. Feeling her faint breath as I cradled her in my arms.

"Tabitha," I whispered. She opened her eyes and panic set in. She tried to pull away, but I held her tight, "it's okay, you're okay."

She looked at me and recognized me. I slowly lowered her lower half, so her rear was on the ground.

"We were attacked, and the vehicle crashed," I said. Tabitha got her balance and rose to her knees and immediately noticed Good Blaine hanging and reached up for her. I put my hands out to slow her down and moved my knife to cut the seat belt. I nodded before I cut, so Tabitha knew to help catch Blaine. We lowered her down gently and Tabitha leaned her ear to her mouth, to listen for life. She detected it and touched her face gently.

"Blaine. Blaine, can you hear me?" Tabitha said just above a whisper.

Blaine opened her eyes.

Both the women got their bearings and then froze at the sight of Bad Blaine.

"She's dead," I said flatly and moved back over to help Kel.

"Hey bud, can you hear me?" I said patting his cheek. Kel gasped and sat up quickly.

"What the! Max, what happened?" Kel said looking around confused. He felt his face and body and tried to stand up but bumped his head on the floor. He dropped back down on his rear.

"There were three drones following us, and one fired a missile at us. Hal shifted our path slightly, so we didn't take a direct hit," I said working the door handle to try to open it. It wasn't budging so I started to kick at it until it finally opened. I pushed my way outside and extended my hand to help each of the others through. We all stood on the side of the road, looking around. A large auto-semi rushed towards us and blew past, seamlessly dodging us and the distressed vehicle. These large haulers were programmed to go from point A to point B without any unnecessary stopping, so it wasn't a surprise it didn't come to our rescue.

"Hal, how far out is another auto-auto?" I asked Brooklyn.

"About twenty minutes away," Brooklyn said, "I recommend moving away from the wreck."

"Got it," I said, "thanks, Hal. Take care of the clean-up. Okay, we need to move down the road as far as we can, and we'll be picked up in twenty," I said to the group.

"Max, need some assistance with the trunk, so I can get our resources free and airborne," Brooklyn said in my ear, "also, a couple nanos scavenged Bad Blaine's clothing and took anything of interest."

"Roger that," I said, "hey Kel, need your help."

Kel and I walked over and fought with the trunk until it was open. The drone resources took to the air. Then we all walked about three quarters of a mile down the road before our next transport arrived. We all climbed in and headed off, with air support guarding us this time. I looked back briefly and saw a plume of smoke behind us, signaling that the charges went off to finish covering up evidence of our presence.

It was about fifteen minutes before we approached the safe house. It was a simple, tan, one story house. Kel and I had stepped out of the vehicle and took up positions on either side, doing a visual inspection of the surrounding area. I had showed him how to use his handheld to check for heat signatures, with the help of London, and our surveillance drones. No signs of threats. Brooklyn/London confirmed. We got back in the vehicle and went to the house. Since we were being extra vigilant, we didn't enter the house until a pair of Cloaked drones and their tiny minions inspected practically every inch.

"We're all clear," I said as I went in through the back door.

"Finally," Blaine said with a sigh.

"It got real. I'm sorry," I said.

My three companions followed me into the mud room. We fanned out and inspected the whole place ourselves. I headed for the basement and Kel followed. The resources I had ordered were already busy at work building more resources.

"This approach to building out more drones is amazing," Kel said.

"Indeed. It's way better than cranking them out by hand," I said with a wink, "I didn't invent the process though, I got the idea from the Bobiverse: auto-factories."

"Ah, that's right! I love Dennis E. Taylor," Kel said with an approving nod. (Look him up, he's great.)

We inspected the progress.

"Since this is getting pretty serious, I had to pull out a lot of tricks. We have raw materials being piped in from other dimensions," I said, pointing to the edges of the basement where several pipes were literally protruding from small Bridges.

"Many of these are just for our protection. As soon as these Guard drones are 'born' they fly outside and contribute to the 'iron dome' now fortifying our location. It's why I paid extra for a safe house sitting on twenty acres this time. Especially since we didn't have time to do reconnaissance.

"Check those stations over there and make sure no error codes are showing," I said pointing, "I'm going to start up the 3D printer and then check those over there."

We reconvened in the center of the room once the inspections were complete.

"How did those drones find us?" Kel asked.

"I'm not entirely sure," I said.

"Well, that's concerning," Kel said.

"If you want a theory, I have one," I said, "those drones were in the garage and followed us through the Bridge."

Kel's mouth opened mouthing a "whaaa."

"It's a theory," I said.

"It's a good one though, but why didn't the AI detect them?" Kel asked.

"Hey!" Brooklyn and London said in Kel and my ears causing us both to jump. (They could open a group channel when there was imminent danger or they were pissed off.)

"Sorry, er, London," Kel said. I smirked. He was acclimating.

"It's possible they had cloaking tech," I said. That didn't help settle down Kel's face.

"Listen, Kel," I continued, "I know a lot has been thrown at you in a short period of time. But I need you, man. We are going to need these resources, as many as we can generate, because we have to go to the drop point and try to catch Bad Max. I need you to get ready, mentally. This will probably get dangerous."

I placed my hand on Kel's shoulder and smiled. He looked very concerned but nodded.

"Not to sound too 'Hallmark,' but we're all going to have to work as a team. All of us. Tabitha and Blaine included. And we're definitely going to have to have a moment where we all stand in a circle and stack our hands and cheerfully yell something corny. You feel me?" I noted with a big grin. This elicited a light chuckle and a smile.

"Yes. I feel you," Kel said, "...such a weird phrase."

"Now, we do have some ways to prepare," I said, walking towards the farthest corner of the basement. Kel followed. His eyes got wide when we came to the booth-like objects in the dark corners. As we approached the area became illuminated.

"What are these?" Kel asked.

I smiled big and winked.

"Our training simulators," I said waving him forward, "step inside."

I moved close to the one on the left and tapped the screen on the side, and it came to life. It could be likened to a vintage photo-booth, except twice as big and spherical inside, but with a lot of haptic controllers for most of your body parts, that auto-attached when needed. It was hard-shelled and had transparency tech, either outwardly or inwardly, when the configuration was set to make it that way, with a door that slid into the shell for access. The neat thing about the transparency tech was when set inwardly, it was like a two-way mirror in that we could see in from the outside, but the user inside could not see the outside world; when set outwardly, the user could see the outside world through the door. Everything was voice controlled.

"How come you're just telling me there's training for all this?" Kel asked, stepping inside.

The interior lit up to show a 360-degree spherical display; you could look in any direction and see the simulation unit display.

"Engaging sim config," the unit voice modules said, "choose your persona."

"I've been giving you bit sized meals, so you don't throw up," I said leaning in to point at the configuration options on the screen, "you can choose London here if you want."

Kel tapped the name London.

"Hello, Kel, fancy meeting you here," London said via the system speakers, in her British accent, "I'm going to ease you into the tutorial. As soon as Max leaves us alone."

I took my cue and backed away.

"Keep it transparent through the tutorial. I want to make sure he doesn't pass out," I said.

"Right-o, Max," London said closing the door with a whitish.

"Want to take bets on him passing out?" Tabitha said causing me to jump. I turned to see Tabitha and Blaine standing on either side of me.

"Oh, hey. Sorry, we got a little distracted down here," I said, "and thanks for reminding me I have skin that can be jumped out of."

"No problem," Tabitha said, lightly fist bumping my shoulder and smiling.

"Once I got him going, I was going to find you two, see if you wanted to train up. We have another unit on that side," I said pointing to the opposite dark corner.

"Yeah, sure. Boys and their toys," Blaine said rolling her eyes.

A color explosion emanated from the simulation unit and the three of us on the outside stepped back a bit. I forgot about the color and brightness during calibrations: 281 trillion colors from 48-bit color depth were hard to fathom still. Kel flinched and looked around, like he was trying to see every color at once.

The calibration settled down and the floor moved slightly under Kel's feet. He would be hearing London explain the movement capabilities (we couldn't hear anything since the unit was completely soundproof). In theory, you could move in all directions with the floating transparent flooring that would slide all around in any directions, keeping your feet attached via enhanced electro-static controls drawing tight the graphene-based shoes everyone wore these days.

It was like suction-cupping your feet to something without the special suction-cups attached to your shoes. (Boy, the first time I saw someone run up a building leveraging this special tech, I thought superheroes might be real. Nowadays, everyone did it.)

Kel started to run as instructed and jump out of the way of objects being thrown in front of him. He thrust his arms out defensively to push through anything in his way. The objects were actually there, we could see them too, all materialized graphically with perfect likeness to real world items. He made it through the first stage and stopped and bent over with his hands resting just above his knees, panting to catch his breath. After a two-minute break, he stood up and watched a Draw Bridge materialize in his left hand.

Tabitha and Blaine looked at each other in awe and back at Kel. Kel configured the Draw Bridge based on the instructions he was receiving from London, then hit the trigger and opened the Bridge and moved forward to step through to the simulated alternate dimension, without actually moving an inch forward in real life.

The scene on the screen changed and he inspected his new surroundings. This tutorial stage called for him to deploy assistive resource drones to help with his mission, so he grabbed two from inside his coat and released them one at a time.

He went through several more warmup guides and reached the end with a satisfactory rating. Kel hit a button we couldn't see which opened the door. It whiisshed open and he emerged.

"That was intense," Kel said blowing out a heavy breath.

"That was just the tutorial," I said furrowing my brow.

"I know... I just needed some fresh air to catch my breath," Kel said, looking at Blaine and seemingly realizing how he might look, "I'm ready for the real simulation now."

Kel didn't wait for reactions and popped back into the simulation unit.

The simulation took him into a real simulated training mission. He was sweating when he exited.

"Is it always transparent?" Tabitha asked.

"No, it's a setting," I said.

"I want to try," Blaine said. I motioned for her to enter the unit. No more secrets.

164

They would all know everything about everything. We were preparing for something big now.

"I guess I'll try this one," Tabitha said walking over to the other unit and stepping inside.

The girls gave them a try and breezed through training, showing they had a little more fitness to them than Kel. I guess without Bridge travel, I would have gotten a bit lazy. (I was so glad everyone could call it the Bridge and the Draw Bridge now.)

We were going to be as prepared as possible for the danger that stood ahead of us now.

Chapter 20 - The Drop

After a couple days of physical training and mentally preparing, we were as ready as we could be. The ask for Blaine, the Good one, was going to be great though.

"I appreciate you doing this, Blaine," I said, as the four of us sat at the kitchen table, all geared up. Kel was looking more like me, but without a hat, he just didn't like them (we can't all have style). Tabitha and Blaine looking like Lara Croft from Tomb Raider, but with more clothes on. They wore warmer gear with coats, because it was cold and the practical thing to do (why do we think it's sexy to be cold).

"Sure. I just hope he doesn't kill me at first sight," Blaine said with a frown.

"You can't think that way," Tabitha said.

"Yeah, we got your back," Kel said.

"But you guys won't be that close," Blaine said looking around at us.

"We've gone over the logistics, Blaine," I said.

"I know, but how quickly can a drone take him out if he decides he doesn't need me anymore?" Blaine asked with pleading eyes.

"We're employing drones with sniper barrels," I said, "they are accurate to within a millimeter."

"I hope so," Blaine said brushing both her hands up and across the hair on the sides of her head and stacking they back in front of her on the table.

"Like I said. We've got your back," Kel said reaching out with his right hand and resting it on top of hers. She looked at him and smiled and nodded. Tabitha and I looked at each other and gave each other "aww" looks.

"Alright. We need to go," I said, "see you all on the other side."

I crossed alone into +136 East, having stepped along dimensions all the way from +2 East, leaving the others behind. Once in +136 East, I stepped to the South. I wanted to carefully cross dimensions through each one to ensure it was safe. All we knew was the drop was supposed to happen in +136, and I assumed South, but we didn't know anything for sure.

We hadn't learned the exact location for the drop but did have Bad Blaine's handheld that held a cryptic message. Brooklyn was able to leverage images from Bad Blaine's face to unlock the device, but there was a non-biometric passcode locking an application for anonymously sharing location points, and that most likely would lead us to the drop point. Brooklyn was working on the decryption.

I was heavily guarded by mechanical companions, trying to anticipate everything, ready to fight anything. I holstered an E-Glock under my coat for the first time in a long time. No threats met me though. I was still in the basement of our safehouse, just forward many dimensional versions. Crossing through that far and that fast was interesting. The structure never changed, it was always there, but the contents of the basement changed.

The BridgeAI adjusted my entry point a few times to avoid landing on Christmas decorations, family artifacts, gym equipment and even pools of water from basement-flooding. Yet, no other people were occupying the area each time I crossed, since I carefully crossed directionally from East to West to North to South, and sub-directions in between, to get there. This lowered the probability of running into other versions of me doing this exact same exercise. We have perfected the techniques to avoid the chaos of bumping into ourselves.

"Max, I've fully cracked the device encryption, so we can access everything now. I have the drop location," Brooklyn reported.

"Okay. Let's do this," I said.

With Bad Blaine's handheld in my hand, I pulled up a map that showed the drop location. It was a barn near Blaine's garage. Brooklyn sent the location to the Span, and everyone now had the most important location, in recent history.

I called for an auto-auto and was there within thirty minutes.

Once I was at the drop point, I activated a beacon in the app. This would signal that my device was at the drop and draw Bad Max to me. I put Bad Blaine's handheld inside the cargo bay of a

Cargo drone and launched it up into the barn loft. It didn't appear that this app could differentiate elevations, so this would work to our advantage. I didn't know how long until Bad Max would arrive but wasn't waiting around just being vulnerable. I retreated to the familiar hill where Kel and I first staked out the garage, just a dimension far, far away.

Now the waiting game began.

Once Bad Max presented himself, we'd wait for the call to Bad Blaine's handheld, which was connected to all our comms, so our Blaine, Good Blaine, could answer. We were anticipating that he would be annoyed having expected her to be at the drop, with my Draw Bridge in hand, but Blaine will play it off that she was in her garage and was scared for her life and wanted to "talk first" before meeting.

Fingers crossed this would work.

We were still going to have her meet him in person, with a Draw Bridge in hand. Only it would be a replica. We just needed enough time to act.

It was curious that my device was so coveted. Obviously Bad Max had a Draw Bridge, in some variation, he was traveling across dimensions. Yet, something about mine drew him to try to kill me to take it. I knew I could travel multi directionally with it, and that would be something to covet, but did he know I could do that? How would he know that? More riddles for my mind to work on. When was the last time I meditated... sigh. Too much nonstop action.

"Hal, let's bring the others forward to the +136 South safehouse, and get the channel opened with all our comms on the open channel," I said to Brooklyn aloud, still protecting her true name when making requests to her.

"Roger that, Max," Brooklyn said.

I wasn't entirely sure how Bad Max was getting the notification. Maybe he had access to interdimensional communications tech. Maybe he had a minion waiting here that would go retrieve him, but I was anticipating that he wouldn't just show in the next ten minutes. If he did, well, we might learn something from that.

"We're at the safehouse, Max," Tabitha said in my ear.

"Nice to have you here," I said, "move to the garage location now."

"Heading there now," Kel said, "vehicle just pulled up."

I left my auto-auto and made my way down to the garage. All this time spent at this garage, I had to wonder what the heck Blaine's parents did all day. They never seemed to leave the house. We knew they were there because we detected heat signatures from the house. Always in the living room. It made me wonder if fighting broke out, would they even notice. Sheesh, typical extras.

"We're outside," Kel said when they arrived, over the open comms channel.

I went to the door to greet them, and they stepped inside. Not much was different about this version of the garage, except there was also a door on the opposite side and there was no apparent Bridge station in the center, like in +3 South.

"Welcome to the party, Kel" I said bumping his shoulder, as he walked by throwing me an eye roll.

"Not going to welcome us?" Tabitha asked pointing her thumb at her and Blaine.

"It's an inside joke," I said with a wink.

"Great. Can we focus?" Tabitha said, "We have the Spider things."

The three of them had carried with them large duffle bags full of Cloaked Spiders. We set them all free and let them out the door. They all converged on the barn and infiltrated it, taking up positions all around the inside; two hanging via silk, invisibly from the rafters. The two modified Cloaked Spiders with sniper barrel attachments were positioned in the opposite corners. We were ready for his arrival.

"What if he doesn't show up? Or doesn't anytime soon? Or he takes a week? How long do we wait? Can we order food? Is anyone else hungry?" Blaine rapid-fired questions.

"Chill, Blaine," Tabitha said looking concerned and exhausted by the barrage of queries.

"I could eat," Kel said leaning up against a workbench.

169

"We can't exactly order Tarzan Treats right now," I said, "Those drones would definitely draw attention."

"Right," Blaine said, pinching her bottom lip.

"We're going to be close by," I said.

"Yeah," Blaine said, still looking worried, "what if he just kills me? Or drags me with him through the open portal, um, Bridge?"

"We have a tracker in the fake Draw Bridge, and the tracker on you. Plus, you have your own personal drones in your coat. Use them," I said, "we'll have a Cloaked Spider go through the Bridge as soon as he steps through."

"Okay," Blaine said, finally breathing out and shaking her hands at her sides and rolling her head around a bit.

"We're not going to let anything happen to you," Kel said walking over to Blaine and taking her right hand ensuring to pass comfort from his eyes to hers. She smiled and blushed slightly. I wondered if Kel was secretly always into Blaine but stayed with Tabitha to avoid something awkward. We were all still humans, even if from different timelines; the interdimensional dynamics were a trip.

"Let's do something to distract me until it's time," Blaine said.

"That's a good idea," Tabitha said.

"Like play cards?" I asked.

"Cards is cool," Kel said.

"How about we learn more about each other?" Tabitha said.

(Dudes' brains versus ladies' brains.)

"How do you suggest we do that?" I asked.

"Well, it doesn't have to be mushy," Tabitha said, "we could trade 'war' stories or something like that."

"Okay, that sounds cool," Kel said, "but I don't have any." He frowned.

"Maybe telling you ours will be helpful, since you're an interdimensional traveler like us now," Blaine said with a wink to Kel, squeezing his hand she was still holding.

"Can we manifest some chairs?" Tabitha asked, "I don't really want to just stand here forever."

"We could use those," I said, pointing to the dimly lit corner where there were a dozen outdoor chairs stacked. We all took up seats in the center of the garage with the chairs positioned so we were facing each other.

Tabitha went first, telling of her and Blaine's craziest adventure.

Chapter 21 - Tabitha and Blaine's Crazy Adventure

Tabitha and Blaine had traveled to their +15 South dimension (my +16), continuing their search for their Max. The trail led them to Manhattan, New York, in the Upper East Side. Dr. Zine had given them some ideas of what types of things to look for, specifically following where Draw Bridge parts could be found. Tabitha told us that even though Max knew how to build one, he didn't have a Draw Bridge when he crossed, so he would need to build one.

Tabitha and Blaine found through searching online that Manhattan was the perfect place for someone to collect the necessary parts to build a Draw Bridge. Key electrical components could be found on the cheap. In the Upper East Side antiques district there were several shops that sold old toy parts; key parts that could be used to build one. Even though these were antique shops, didn't mean that the toys or parts were ancient.

To most kids, a lot of toys were "old" after a few months and were discarded once they were replaced with a new toy (the Toy Story movie series was a documentary all about this). And after the Better Efficiency Supplying Toys Act was passed a decade ago it was hard to find a toy that wasn't built more solid and long lasting than most household appliances these days. One of the main efficiencies was driven by better energy sources: nuclear batteries.

Incidentally, Tabitha and Blaine needed exactly these, and after having been to the area a few days back asking vendors if they saw Max, they knew this place could help them out of their bind.

"Let's check in here," Tabitha said to Blaine, pointing to entrance of the Upper East Antiques Complex. The building took up the entire block and was six stories tall. The ground floor had all glass windows wrapping most of the building, but the upper levels were brick with sparse window layouts.

"Do you think they have batteries?" Blaine asked.

"It's not just any battery, it's nuclear batteries we be needing," Tabitha said with a slight giggle, "these places sell toys, we should find a bunch here."

"Arrr. Seems like an oversight to only have the low battery warning alert us when it's down to five percent, when we need more than that to get all the way back home," Blaine said shaking her head.

"Yeah... building new technology is an iterative process I guess," Tabitha said mirroring the head shake, "but this one has some deep consequences."

The two women entered the antiques center and were hit with a barrage of sounds. They navigated a maze of vendor booths searching for a section with an electronic toys cache.

"Where are the toys?" Blaine asked a vendor they were passing.

He pointed. They headed that direction.

In the far back corner, they found the mother lode of all toys. It was dimly lit and dusty. They started turning toys and inspecting for battery ports.

"Hey, how are we going to pay for these?" Blaine whispered close to Tabitha.

"Well... we might have to... um...," Tabitha whispered back not wanting to say out loud the reality that bothered her. They had run out of money a few days ago and were planning to head back home to resupply on everything, until they noticed the low battery warning when they turned on the Draw Bridge.

"Are you seeing a lot of these battery bays, I guess you'd call them, are empty?" Tabitha asked no longer whisper-syncing with Blaine.

"Yeah, everyone I've checked has had the batteries removed," Blaine said looking at Tabitha with concern.

They started inspecting faster and caused quite a commotion in their panic.

"Hey! What are you doing?" a vendor yelled approaching quickly.

"Sorry!" Blaine yelled, dropping the toy she was holding from her hand and putting both her hands up in the air. The vendor furrowed his brow.

"What are you looking for?" he asked moving closer and seeing that Tabitha was inspecting the battery bay door on a little robot, "are you with him?! The guy that stole all the batteries for these!"

Tabitha and Blaine both looked at each other. Blaine lowered her hands, and they moved towards the man. Tabitha pulled out her handheld quickly and showed the vendor a picture of Max.

"Was this the guy stealing batteries?" Tabitha asked.

"Yes! Yes! He stole all the batteries!" the vendor yelled, "I'm calling the authorities!"

"Wait!" Tabitha put her handheld away and raised a hand to him, "we're not with him. We're investigating him." Tabitha looked over to Blaine and made eye contact.

"He's wanted for, er, battery thievery in ten states. We're trying to capture him," Blaine said with as straight a face as she could hold.

"Oh," the vendor said, visibly relaxing a bit, "okay, yeah, I want my batteries back."

"Don't worry, sir, we'll get them back," Tabitha said, walking close and putting her hand on the vendor's shoulder to comfort him. He relaxed more.

"Thank you," the vendor said.

"Now, when did you see him last?" Blaine asked, moving closer and following Tabitha's lead.

"A couple weeks ago," the vendor said, "I filed a report with the authorities, but they said it was unlikely they'd ever recover them. They just said to alert them if the perpetrator returned."

"Do you know how many he stole?" Tabitha asked, looking back at the spread of toys.

"He took the batteries out of all those toys in that bin that says, 'battery operated toys,'" the vendor said pointing.

"There are at least fifty toys in that bin," Blaine said, looking from the bin to the vendor.

"Yeah. None of those toys work anymore. I don't have replacement batteries, and new ones are expensive," the vendor said with a frown.

"Don't worry, sir. We'll do our best to retrieve them," Tabitha said and looked at Blaine and nodded for her to follow.

They left with their heads spinning.

"This isn't good, Tab," Blaine said flopping back from sitting on the edge of the hotel room bed to laying and staring at the ceiling.

"Yeah," Tabitha said, leaning against the wall with her hands behind her, gently knocking her head back to the wall to also look at the ceiling. As if the ceiling had the answer written on it.

"The room is only paid through the end of the week. We have three days to figure something out. To at least get some more money, to live," Blaine said, "maybe we should have gotten a cheaper hotel room, in hindsight."

"Yep," Tabitha said, "but we're not completely broke; we have enough money to live for a few more weeks here. It's just that new nuclear batteries are crazy expensive here. The cost of six of them would keep us booked for a month."

"Sheesh," Blaine said.

Tabitha pulled away from the wall and walked over to the window to look outside. She could only see the solid brick wall of the adjacent building. She stared blankly at it, wondering what was on the other side of it, wondering if it was an apartment, a shop, a... bank.

"Do you think there is a way to open a portal right at the edge of a wall and get to the other side of that wall?" Tabitha said, turning from the window and walking over to the bed to look down at Blaine.

"I don't know. You know more about that device than I do," Blaine said turning on her side to face Tabitha and using her hand to support her head, "why?"

"I just had this wild idea," Tabitha said. Blaine sat up spinning on the bed to face her.

"What are you thinking?" Blaine asked.

"We could rob a bank," Tabitha said matter-of-factly. Blaine's eyes went wide.

"Say that again," Blaine said.

"We could open the portal against the wall of a bank, walk through and steal some gold and walk right back out," Tabitha said, "even if they see this on camera, we're in masks and they wouldn't even believe what they are seeing."

Blaine pondered the idea.

"Maybe we should test the theory about the portal first," Blaine said, standing up with a bounce.

"Yeah. Good idea," Tabitha said and pulled out her Draw Bridge, "wait, what about the battery?"

"Oh. Yeah," Blaine said, "but it's only at five percent, so just don't keep it open for long."

"Yeah. Okay," Tabitha said walking over to the bathroom, "we can close the bathroom door and open the portal 'over' it and see if we can see the bathroom from the dimension before this one."

"Sure," Blaine said.

Tabitha closed the bathroom door and pointed the Draw Bridge at it. She opened the Bridge and saw the toilet and sink of +14 South, then quickly closed it.

"I guess it works," Tabitha said. She then inspected the battery indicator on the Draw Bridge, "four percent. Great. We're really only going to get one chance at this. We need to save some juice in case we need to escape through a few dimensions if this goes wrong. And I'm not sure if at one percent it'll even open for long or stay open for both of us to pass through."

"So, the plan is to steal some money so we can buy new batteries?" Blaine asked as they both returned to the bed area and took seats on it.

"Yeah. That's the plan," Tabitha said, "we just need to find a place to rob. Probably best to steal some gold coins or something small, but that's worth a lot. We wouldn't need many."

"Hmm. I know I've heard of places like banks that will store gold and silver for you in their vaults," Blaine said, "I think my parents did that. There must be a place in Manhattan. If not several."

"Let's do recon tomorrow," Tabitha said with a smile.

"What are we going to do for dinner tonight?" Blaine asked, looking at her stomach as if it was asking.

"Let's see if we can find someone to buy us dinner at the hotel bar. Just not in a 'sorry-for-us' kind of way," Tabitha said.

"Super maniacal, today are we, Tabs," Blaine said with a smirk, "you said we had money for food."

She just received a wink as a response.

Tabitha and Blaine walked along the sidewalk in midtown Manhattan. They found a manufacturer that made nuclear batteries and were visiting to see if they could get some kind of deal on them. They called ahead pretending to be with a start-up looking to build a prototype.

"You only need six?" the corporate salesperson named Clyde said, "Usually we sell bulk orders by lots of one hundred."

Tabitha and Blaine sat across from Clyde at a small conference table just off the main entrance hall. Lots of promotional material hung on the walls in this client sales room.

"Yes. We're working on a prototype for a new type of search and rescue drone," Tabitha said.

"It will be able to detect people at any depth," Blaine added thoughtfully.

"That does sound amazing, but I can't just crack open a lot and take out six," Clyde said sitting forward, "I could probably help you out and give you a discount on twenty-five, but that's the minimum."

Tabitha and Blaine looked considerately at each other.

"Where does that put us?" Tabitha asked.

"With the discount, eighteen thousand," Clyde said sitting back against his chair.

Tabitha and Blaine nodded, then looked at each other.

"We'll have to get back to you," Blaine said, both standing at the same time. Tabitha reached out to shake Clyde's hand, and Clyde scrambled to his feet with the suddenness.

The ladies nodded and showed themselves out.

Chapter 22 - Tabitha and Blaine Kind of Kill a Guy

"Okay. For that amount, we could stay at that hotel for more than six months," Blaine said.

"It was wishful thinking," Tabitha said, "I'm the..."

"You're the king of it!" Blaine interrupted her quickly and belting out the sentence.

"Nineties nerd," Tabitha said with a smirk, "you always beat me to it. It's not even applicable here, ha ha."

"Yes," Blaine said, then hummed the song she now heard in her head.

"I'll get over you... I know I will..." Tabitha started looking at Blaine.

"I'll pretend…" Blaine followed, curling forward to belt the last notes.

"And I'll tell myself, I'm over you…" they sang in chorus, finishing on the words: wishful thinking.

People glared, the ladies giggled like girls and laughed and moved away quickly.

"So, we need to find a guy that works at Sats Trading?" Blaine asked, while applying makeup in the mirror.

"It's the best location for us to do this. Its wall is against the vault of Precious Cargo Reserve Holding," Tabitha said, following suit next to her.

"I understand that part. How are we going to find someone that specifically works there and that's dumb enough to take us into the building after hours?" Blaine asked, blotting her lips.

"We don't have much choice. We must find him... or her..." Tabitha said, "and we must do it tonight."

"It smells weird in here," Blaine said close to Tabitha's ear, as they sat at the bar.

"That's ego," Tabitha said with an eye roll.

"How about that guy?" Blaine pointed with her pinky towards a table against the wall, while she sipped from her glass.

"Maybe. Let's find out," Tabitha said and rose and headed over to the table.

The bar was crowded, so some people just stood against the walls near the tables and chatted. You had to "know" someone to get a table. This guy seemed to be a person to know.

"...I sold it all, right from under their noses!" the guy said trying to talk over the volume of the bar. He was very animated with his arms flailing as he talked, spilling unapologetically on his party, "it's all about the sats, baby!"

Tabitha and Blaine heard "sats" and looked at each other quizzically. That was the name of the firm they needed to get into. Hopefully it wasn't a coincidence. The ladies moved closer to initiate their plan. Blaine started to wobble a bit and act a bit drunk. Tabitha pushed her a little and Blaine spilled some of her drink on her top.

"Oh no!" Blaine yelled and then leaned down to the table where the guy was sitting and dropped her glass down and picked up some napkins. She started mumbling about the spill and began blotting at the spot right at the edge of her breasts, causing them to bounce, practically in the guy's face. She had his attention.

"Here," the guy said grabbing more napkins and handing them to Blaine with a somewhat evil smile. He could barely keep his eyes from dropping.

"Thank you," Blaine said with a smile, continuing to cause bouncing, "I think it's got them, my shirt, clean."

"Of course, no problem," the guy said, "can I get you another drink?"

"Sure, you're sweet," Blaine said finally standing straight again.

"What do you take?" the guy asked.

"Sex in the park," Blaine said with a raised eyebrow. The guy nodded and went to retrieve it.

"Dial it back," Tabitha said leaning to Blaine. Blaine rolled her eyes.

The guy handed Blaine her drink and then retook his seat at his table. He stayed facing her though.

"I'm Kaplan, what's your name?" the guy asked, fully paying his attention to Blaine.

"Marcy," Blaine said leaning closer to him so he could hear her as it seemed someone turned up the volume, "sorry to interrupt your group."

"Not an issue," Kaplan said with a dismissive wave towards the two guys and three girls watching him, "they're just co-workers." He winked at them. He received fifty-percent eye rolls, the rest apathy.

"Where do you all work?" Blaine asked, doing well to sound only slightly inebriated.

"Sats Trading," Kaplan said, thumbing towards the wall behind him, indicating the company they hoped.

"Very cool," Blaine said and sipped her drink.

"I've always wanted to meet a real Wall Street guy and see where the magic goes down," Blaine said, "my friend and I are from Kansas. This is all so exciting."

Kaplan raised an eyebrow.

"I practically own the place. I could show you my office," Kaplan said with a smirk.

"Both of us?" Blaine asked as she tipped her head towards Tabitha, who was leaning closer with a smile.

"Sure. My buddy Drake could join us," Kaplan said.

"That's okay. We'd feel safer with just one person. Just you," Blaine said with a wink.

It seemed to be working up to this point. This was the moment of truth.

"Later haters," Kaplan said, standing up and guiding Blaine away with his arm finding her waist. Then he reached back and grabbed Tabitha's hand and pulled her with them. He gave a "cool guy" smirk to his coworkers and the three of them left the bar.

"It's so quiet in here," Blaine said as they walked between dozens of desks with quad-monitor setups in the open area of the floor.

"It's Friday," Kaplan said matter-of-factly.

Blaine and Tabitha nodded.

They reached Kaplan's office, and he sat on the corner of his desk in a way where his legs hung and spread a bit, to show off his subtext.

"What do you do?" Blaine asked as Tabitha hung back and swept the office with her eyes until she found the wall of interest to her. She didn't enter his office and kept to just out of Kaplan's eyeline.

"I'm a trading director for this office," Kaplan said, "so, you got me here alone now. You two looking to party?" He pulled a little clear bag from his pocket with white powder in it.

"You get down like that, huh?" Blaine said with a smile, "yeah, we like to party. You start."

Kaplan expressed a large grin and quickly traded his desk-corner for the couch off to the side that had a glass coffee table in front of it. He spread out lines, pulled out a metal straw from his coat jacket and didn't hesitate to consume them immediately, with a "woo!" He held out the straw to Blaine. She looked back for Tabitha, but Tabitha was around the corner inspecting the walls. They had found building plans that showed where the vault was in relation to this office. Tabitha was using her handheld to calculate the distance from the front of the building to where the vault would be on the other side of the wall.

"Do you have anything else, to, uh, party with?" Blaine asked Kaplan. He looked at her quizzically, then wagged a finger and bounced up and off to his desk, pulling things from his drawers and dropping them on the desktop. He was searching frantically. It seemed like all his stuff was out now and Blaine walked up and started visually inspecting the pile. She noticed a bottle of Valium and worked to get closer to it.

"Are you looking for something? Or doing some early spring cleaning?" Blaine said with a smile.

"Trying to find my heroin," Kaplan said, still frantic. He didn't notice Blaine pocket the bottle of Valium.

182

"Oh, cool," she said and turned around and worked one pill out of the bottle into her hand. She then walked around the desk over to Kaplan and got close.

"How about we make this a party with a little blue pill?" Blaine asked, showing the blue pill pinched between her fingers. Kaplan smiled, smirked and nodded. She extended her pinched fingers, and Kaplan snatched the pill away quickly and placed it on his tongue. He winked and swallowed. This was not an enhancement pill, it was Valium. Blaine was hoping this would calm him down and maybe cause him to pass out and fall asleep, but she was starting to second guess herself.

The implication was stronger now.

He took her hand and led her over to the couch, leading her to sit. He sat then pulled her down to straddle across his lap on top of him and he leaned up to kiss her. She then pushed back on his chest and started to unbutton his shirt, to slow down the kissing action. His eyes started to droop like he was tiring already. Her plan was working. Until it wasn't. Kaplan's head fell back against the wall and off to the side to his shoulder. She noticed half his face droop. Blaine stood up quickly and started to panic.

"Oh no!" Blaine said, "Tabitha!"

"Yeah?" Tabitha said from around the corner, "I think I found the wall."

"Come here, quick!" Blaine yelled.

Tabitha rushed over and her eyes grew.

"What happened?" Tabitha said moving close and inspecting the scene. She saw the mess on the desk and Kaplan slumped back on the couch.

"I was trying to calm him down. He did some cocaine," Blaine said.

"That happened after doing cocaine?" Tabitha asked.

"No. I gave him Valium," Blaine said.

"Valium..." Tabitha said, letting the word roll from her tongue while thinking about it, "that's like a downer."

"I thought you took it to help with sleeping?" Blaine asked holding her arms wrapped to her body nervously.

"You mixed an upper with a downer... I thought I read somewhere that that could cause a stroke," Tabitha said, then she looked around at the desk. She rushed over and knocked things aside to dig through the mess, quickly reading prescription bottles.

"Okay, I found aspirin," Tabitha said, holding up the bottle.

"Okay..." Blaine said looking confused.

"This will stop the stroke," Tabitha said, pill already in hand and she walked up to Kaplan. She forced open his mouth and stuffed the aspirin under his tongue.

Kaplan started to shake violently and slumped further onto the couch cushion, continuing to have a seizure.

Tabitha and Blaine stared, both frozen in shock.

Kaplan stopped his vibrating and became completely still.

Tabitha and Blaine looked at each other in horror.

"Oh my god," Blaine said.

"Did we, just, kill him?" Tabitha asked.

Both still hadn't moved.

"Okay. Okay!" Tabitha yelled, "we can't panic!" she said panicking.

"Oh no, oh no, oh no, oh no," Blaine said, "no, no, no, no. I can't be a killer. I can't go to jail."

"We need to calm down," Tabitha said, now moving, moving away from the couch and shaking her hands at her sides, "okay. Okay. We just need to... we need to get the gold and go."

Blaine looked at Tabitha in shock.

"What?" Blaine asked.

"We gotta finish what we came here for," Tabitha said, heading out of the office, "we can't bring him back." The cold statement echoed, hanging in the air. "Come on," Tabitha said after a beat.

Blaine followed numbly.

Tabitha approached the wall she had identified as the entry point. She pulled out her Draw Bridge and positioned it and opened the Bridge against the wall. The inside of the vault was dark. Tabitha pulled out her flashlight and lit up the vault. She scanned and could see transparent cabinets along the other side of the vault. They didn't appear to have any locks, just handles to open them. Inside there were neat stacks of gold coins.

"Go get them, quickly," Tabitha said, turning to Blaine, who was still in shock. She looked back towards the office but couldn't see Kaplan. She looked around the greater office area, then back at the bridge.

"Come on!" Tabitha yelled, "the battery could die any minute!"

This got Blaine's attention, she sprung forward and hurried to cross through the Bridge. Blaine rushed to open the cabinet and grabbed several packages of neatly wrapped coins. She looked back at Tabitha holding up the coins. Tabitha nodded.

"Should I grab more?" Blaine asked, but realized her hands were full and she didn't have an easy way to carry them. She walked back to the Bridge. Tabitha watched her get close and then disappear from in front of her eyes, as the Bridge suddenly shut.

Tabitha looked down at the Draw Bridge and saw the flashing red light on the side. The indicator saying zero percent. She felt her face flush and felt cold as her previous comments about dead Kaplan.

"No. No, no, no, no, no!" Tabitha scolded herself, "there was more battery life!"

She screamed.

She squatted down and slapped her hands at her head. The Draw Bridge was still in her right hand and beeped. She stood and looked at it and the indicator showed one percent now. Tabitha quickly opened the Bridge again. Blaine fell through at her. She was banging against the inner wall of the vault and her clenched fist landed against Tabitha's chest and they both fell backwards into the office together. Tabitha braced herself as they fell and her finger placement on the Draw Bridge caused her to accidentally close the Bridge. One wrapped roll of gold coins slipped from Blaine's hand and rolled away on the floor.

They were inches from each other's faces.

"Welcome back," Tabitha said with a smile. Blaine pushed herself up and shook her head in disgust, with an audible scoff.

"That was freaking horrifying," Blaine said, going to retrieve the coins, "can we just get out of here?"

Tabitha got up and inspected the Draw Bridge. It still had one percent on the indicator. She put it away in her purse which could only fit one thing.

"Yes. Let's go," Tabitha said.

"Great. It's all over the news," Blaine said from the edge of the bed as she watched the TV. Tabitha quickly dressed and applied makeup in the mirror by the bathroom, "we're murderers."

"It's fine. It was an accident. We're going to get the batteries and leave, and forget this ever happened," Tabitha said, "I'm ready. Let's go."

"Wait," Blaine said standing and getting in Tabitha's path to the door.

Tabitha stopped with a jolt.

"I want to know how to work the portal opener," Blaine said, "I'd be screwed if something happened to you."

"Okay..." Tabitha said giving a side-mouth grimace. She pulled out the Draw Bridge and demonstrated how to use it up to the point before opening the Bridge, "after you dial in the direction, you'd just press this button." She pointed instead of pressing.

"Okay. Thank you," Blaine said, satisfied.

They headed for their meeting with Clyde. With a short stop at the currency conversion center to swap their gold coins for digital currency using an anonymous automated teller. Clyde expedited getting their order, and within minutes they were walking back out the door.

"Let's go home," Blaine said as soon as they rounded the corner and entered the alley.

"Hold on a sec," Tabitha said, looking around. She spotted a more secluding spot further down the alley, "here. This is better." She knelt and quickly unwrapped the packaging for the batteries. Blaine knelt in front of her and watched Tabitha while also keeping an eye out. Tabitha broke loose one battery at a time and replaced them in the Draw Bridge. Once all six were replaced, the women both breathed out audible sighs of relief when they saw the battery indicator return to one hundred percent.

"Time to go," Tabitha said. They both stood and Blaine turned to face the spot where Tabitha aimed the Draw Bridge. The Bridge glowed to life and then both took a last look around and then at each other and stepped through.

Chapter 23 - Max Tells a Story

"You kissed that guy?" Kel asked frowning at Blaine, breaking the brief silence after Tabitha and Blaine finished telling their story.

My mouth gaped and eyes went wide as I looked over at him. Tabitha rolled her eyes and Blaine squinted with pursed lips, leaning her head forward while keeping her cross-armed body still.

"You mean, killed, not kissed, right?" I asked.

"Oh. Yeah. You killed that guy?" Kel asked trying to save face. Tabitha and I looked at each other and smirked.

"Hey, it happens," I said with a shrug. This broke the awkwardness, then led to horrified looks towards me from everyone.

"How often has that happened to you?" Tabitha said, leaning a bit forward in her chair.

"I mean, not a lot, but it's happened," I said trying to not sound so casual.

"I guess you're up next, buddy," Tabitha said kicking my leg.

I inhaled and let it out.

"Okay."

About a year after I set off in search of Michael and Tabitha on my own, from my home dimension, I got myself into some trouble in +55 South.

I was just aimlessly crossing through dimensions at that point, not even sure what I was looking for. I didn't have a plan for searching. I would just get into the next dimension and dig around on the internet there, trying to find clues of where Tabitha or Bad Max might be. Or trying to find any trace of Michael. He was always on my mind.

I was trying to track down the version of myself from that dimension to learn about him. Or sometimes I'd track down my parents and watch them, learn about their lives, see what they've done to move on.

I never seemed to find the Tabitha of that dimension, if there even was one – she was always missing.

Same with Michael.

I was drinking a little too much during this one time. Being a little too reckless.

An obvious limitation to crossing dimensions is not being able to control too much with the location on the other side. The BridgeAI helps to ensure some things don't happen, like opening a Bridge right at the edge of a cliff and preventing you from stepping to your death or placing you on top of something undesirable. However, you always run the risk of crossing and meeting another person on the other side that was out of the range of the BridgeAI's capabilities to detect.

That's what happened in +55 South.

Before crossing, though, I had traveled to Nashville, Tennessee, when I was in +40. I traveled a lot, all around the country; sometimes long rides in auto-autos, sometimes by A Real Air, my favorite autonomous aerial vehicle company. (It's pretty crazy to think how quickly the passenger pilot industry dried up, but I suppose piloting the numerous asteroid mining ships is way cooler anyways. I digress though.)

I was a gypsy, looking for lost things.

Nashville was a bad place to have a drinking problem. Too many opportunities to keep down a bad path. It was certainly fun, but it was dangerous. I'd get into bar fights and just cross forwards to walk away from my problems. It felt like the further I moved away from my home dimension, the less real the problems from that dimension were. The memories were not less real though.

At a high-end hotel downtown, which I can't even remember the name of, I crossed forward into +55 South, one night. After an angry man received a busted lip, and I was thrown out of a bar. I stumbled back to my room and decided it was time to ruin another dimension for myself, so I crossed from +54 South into +55 South. The naked couple in the bedroom screamed a little too loud for my liking and I screamed at them to shut it.

The hotel security met me in the lobby after I stumbled out of the room, leaving two shocked people gripping the same bed sheet around them to shimmy over to slam the door I left open.

Security attempted to grip me physically, but my Guard drones that suddenly popped up above me with questionable (to them) looking armaments, gave them pause. They quickly radioed for the police but could do little to stop me from walking past them, as the Guard drones extended ominous looking barrels towards them. The security guards shouted and held their hands on their holstered Tasers but wouldn't dare draw.

"It's okay... going to be leaving," I slurred.

Out the front door I walked, and down the street. The security guards followed until I passed the edge of the end of the hotel building's sidewalk footprint. I could hear sirens in the distance. When I reached an alley, I turned down it and walked until I found myself at a dead end. There was no better a place to open a Bridge, so I did. I slipped through like slime down a storm drain and banged my face against the dead-end's wall on the other side. It caused me to stumble backwards and fall over. The Bridge remained open, and I could hear the sirens getting closer. The jolt from knocking my head around caused me to throw up on the pavement. The sirens got closer, and I could hear panicked, "what the hell's" echoing through the Bridge. I started to regain myself and fumbled with the Draw Bridge, trying to remember how to work the button to close the Bridge.

A homeless man had been watching the whole thing and he walked over to the Bridge to look through. His eyes wide with amazement, he even wiped them and blinked. He looked back at me, and that's when I sobered up quicker and found the button. I still fumbled to press it, as the cops closed in, guns drawn. I must have been disobeying their commands for too long because they fired their guns. The homeless man was hit in the chest and started to fall forward as I finally hit the button and Bridge winked shut.

The bottom half of his body remained in front of me.

I decided to stop drinking.

Thinking I was dialed into +56 South when I crossed and expecting to be in a "fresh" dimension, I was unpleasantly surprised to see two cops at the end of the alley. They looked to be yelling into their radios and drawing their guns, having seen the torso. I must have dialed in +54 by accident, and they must have been looking for the guy from the bar fight, but this looked much worse than a busted lip.

I definitely was not going to drink anymore.

I sighed and lifted my Draw Bridge to dial in +54 North, when the bullets started flying at me. My Guard drones sprang into action, based on meeting these preset conditions, and shot out a flash grenade that quickly stopped the cops from firing and they scrambled out of the alley.

More police cars arrived on the street.

I returned my attention to my Draw Bridge and felt my stomach drop. A smoking hole was right through the center. I banged the side, but it wouldn't light up. I really messed up this time. And I was all alone. My drones weren't much for companionship. I couldn't communicate with back home... and I didn't have Brooklyn yet. I wasn't prepared to start a war with the cops, since I didn't have a way to summon more support, so I ran away. I broke into a sprint towards the cops' direction. I pulled out my handheld and sent a command for the Guard drones to fire smoke grenades ahead of me. In the confusion I was able to round the corner and run past the disoriented police. I ran as fast and far away from the scene as I could before slowing down to check my surroundings in a city park, several blocks away.

The sound of sirens was dull now.

Nashville's evening glow faded from view.

The auto-auto I ordered was a small neutral colored sedan, with tinted windows so I could cruise away without any concern for being easily spotted. Twenty miles down the road, I made a quick switch to another similar looking vehicle, so I could evade video tracking implications, leading them to pursue me. I followed this pattern a few more times until I was through Oklahoma City, and the last switch put me in a spacious van with a desk and a comfortable bed for the sixteen-hour drive to my destination.

I was heading to Las Vegas, Nevada.

There would be at least one place there for me to find parts to repair my Draw Bridge. After inspecting the damage, I found that the pendant was fractured and one of the energy lines from the nuclear batteries was severed. The latter was easy to find parts for anywhere that sold electronic parts, but the pendant, yeah, that was trickier to find.

My grandmother got those for my brother and me from a metaphysical shop somewhere inside Las Vegas Land. I'm sure the expansion was even greater since the last time my grandmother was in Vegas. It started as a strip, a street about five miles long and expanded outwards to form around sixteen square miles.

I made a reservation at DuelKings (after DraftKings and Fan Duel merged, this was the name they settled on) casino that was pretty much in the center. From my research, I found three promising shops to try to find the pendants I needed.

I slept for several hours.

As my auto-van recharged, at a roadside station just outside of Albuquerque, New Mexico, I was able to grab a meal. Then I returned to the vehicle and sat on the bench seat/comfy couch that was in front of the bed, centered to the van, while it finished the last bit of charging. I decided to check through some of the information that I had saved to my handheld before leaving Dr. Zine and Denny.

Denny said he was working on new AI that I could leverage if I'd follow the install steps. When I first left, I didn't get around to it, but after a while it felt fruitless. Then I started drinking and cloudiness settled into my mind, and I forgot about my friends. I was so far from them now and was hoping to find something that could help me feel at home again. I found a good proxy. This AI sounded like they had created it to be a companion for me on my long and lonely interdimensional journeys.

The vehicle dinged a tone and let me know we'd be on our way again. The voice was calm and friendly, soothing, and comforting.

I hadn't taken the time to notice before. I hadn't appreciated that the user-experience designers of these vehicles had put in the consideration of helping to make lone travelers feel safe and less alone. It certainly helped me understand I needed this. Maybe that's what the new AI companion would help me do.

I spent part of my ride to Las Vegas following the setup instructions that Dr. Zine had written. It only took five minutes to install and get the AI up and running but took over an hour to follow the training methods. It seemed that Dr. Zine had laid out careful instructions on how to specifically train the AI model through verbal sequences, so that it could know exactly how to interact with me. This way it would know all the necessary information to work as a counterpart to me during operations, but also providing companionship, I guess so I wouldn't go crazy. I worked through an options menu and found the personas I could choose from. As soon as I saw the name I knew. I set it and went back to the home screen to start it running.

"Hello, Max," Brooklyn said.

"Hello. Brooklyn," I said.

"I'm here to help," Brooklyn said out of the speaker on my handheld, "you can talk to me anytime. You can use the earpiece provided, to enable a constant open channel with me."

I sat with this for a few minutes.

It was a wild concept, even in this day and age where AI was everywhere. Where everyone everywhere was engaging with AI nonstop. Yet, I hadn't embraced it up to this point. I didn't feel I needed it, since I felt superior with my Draw Bridge at the ready. Except. Now, when I needed it. I didn't have it. Mulling over the comment Brooklyn made, I reached into my deep coat pockets and pulled out an ear bud case. I plucked out the right ear bud and stuffed it into my ear. The bud sat comfortably in the center of the canal, with the tiny speaker suspended looking like a tiny hub with spokes all around. I adjusted the volume.

"What can you help me with?" I asked Brooklyn.

"Whatever you need?" Brooklyn responded.

"Do you know what I need?" I asked, testing the system.

There was a pause for a few seconds. I tried to imagine a person thinking. Tried to imagine what Brooklyn might look like but couldn't quite form the vision. It was probably better to imagine just a bodiless voice, a floating energy echoing, a pulsing light projecting sound in front of me.

"I have many preprogrammed functions, but I am weighing the most important one. That is to keep you safe. Second to that is to provide companionship. Those are my top directives," she finally said.

"I see," I said, "can you play music?" I smirked to myself.

"Of course, but that's a little insulting, Max, I'm not one of those ancient Google Homes," she said, with a hint of actual irritation in her voice. This was going to be fun. I already liked her.

"What if I wanted some music now, though?" I asked.

"I'm better suited to recommend and play music based on what would be most beneficial to you right now," she said, "but will you consent to me reading your levels?"

I thought about this for a moment.

"Sure... what song would you play for me right now?" I asked, now curious.

"After analyzing the logs you've recorded to the BridgeAI Span for the past six months, as well as your vital signs, I would recommend a song that might help you with dealing with loss," she said.

I didn't say anything.

"After scanning your music playlist history, I think this song might help you," Brooklyn said and played Ghost by Justin Bieber without waiting for my response.

I got chills as the first lines of the song played, then froze at the most poignant line to me, the one that mentions crossing a bridge and not being able to follow.

I exhaled and rested my head back against the bench seat, staring at the van ceiling.

Tears welled in my eyes.

"I miss you more than life," I said softly.

The song stopped.

"I'm reading your levels, and your heart rate has decreased, blood pressure has dropped, and breathing rate has slowed. Just checking if you'd like me to continue playing this song for you?" Brooklyn said.

"Yes," I said. I continued listening to the song, asking for her to repeat it several more times before tiring and having her stop.

"Thank you," I said.

I let quiet linger for several minutes while I watched the landscape pass.

"How long until we're in Las Vegas?" I asked.

"Six hours and seventeen minutes," Brooklyn said, "I've hooked up to monitor the auto-van and estimate our best option is to recharge in Flagstaff, Arizona before our final stretch to Las Vegas."

"Cool," I said, "as you were," smirking to myself.

"What else would I be?" she asked, and I couldn't tell if this was an attempt at humor.

"Never mind," I said, "are you able to play a video on my handheld when I ask?"

"Certainly," she said, "you want me to load up the playback from when Tabitha was kidnapped by the other Max?"

Uncanny – valley.

"Yeah," I said with a sigh. It was exactly what I wanted to watch at this moment, "but, also, he's Bad Max, not other Max."

"Noted," she said, and the video popped up on my screen. I pressed play and watched my last moments with Tabitha, over and over, for ten minutes. Then I paused it at the point where I tried to pull her back. As she went through and I was left with a bracelet and piece of shirt in my hand, I was reminded that I had a piece of clothing from Bad Max.

"How far along is the scent tracking technology these days?" I asked Brooklyn.

"Dr. Zine fed that artifact of clothing into the system and uploaded the markers to the Span. Once we can acquire a device for sniffing out based on those markers, we should be able to track Bad Max within a fifty-foot radius indoors or outdoors."

195

"Interesting. Okay. Your first task is to help locate someone in this dimension where we can find a device to help us with that. Along with getting everything we need to fix the Draw Bridge."

"Understood, Max," she said, "glad to have something to focus on."

Un, canny.

"Max," Brooklyn started.

"Yes, Brooklyn," I returned.

"Could I suggest something?" she asked.

"Sure," I said.

"Based on information brought into my model, I see you used to meditate," she said, "when was the last time you took time to do this?"

I was slightly offended. Then slumped at the forgotten feeling. This information was probably loaded into the system for her to model from by Dr. Zine. He knew how it helped me and recommended I do it every night after our long days of experimentation. We even joined group sessions once a week... back then... back before...

"It's been a while," I said.

"I can grey-out the windows, if you'd like to sit quietly for a few minutes," Brooklyn said, almost softly, compassionately.

"You can control the window opacity?" I asked. Of course, the tech was more intriguing than the human-like sentiment at first.

"Yes, I am able to," she responded.

"That would be nice," I said assuming a cross-legged position on the bench seat, "twenty minutes would be good."

"I'll set a bell for twenty minutes," she said.

It fell silent and I closed my eyes.

The rest of the ride to Las Vegas was relatively quiet since I couldn't really think of much else to talk to Brooklyn about yet, and the recharge was uneventful.

Just knowing she was there made me feel less lonely already.

Chapter 24 - Sin City Psychics are Sus

"I don't want my fortune told," I said, frustrated with the blind woman, "I'm looking for a pendant like this." I showed her my broken pendant presented in the palm of my hand.

"I sense great loneliness in you. Are you looking for a lost loved one?" the blind woman asked. This tinged my heart slightly, but I knew it was part of their script.

When I entered her shop, I wasn't exactly the most pleasant patron. I refused her refreshing offer of relief, as I attempted to find what I was looking for on my own. Of course, the shop was a cluttered mess, and it would take way too long for my liking to sift through all the junk drawers for the pendants I coveted.

"I sense you are aware I am blind, but yet you still are presenting something for me to search for. You must have faith enough I will be able to help you then," the blind woman said, calling me out. I turned red and wondered if she could sense that as well.

"She doesn't seem to be lying, Max," Brooklyn said in my ear. Good to know that was a feature.

"I'm sorry. I'm just in a hurry," I said, trying to soften my tone.

"It is no trouble," she said, reaching out to my hand, and I yanked back instinctively.

"I think you can trust her, Max," Brooklyn said, being reassuring, again, "and if she tries to steal it, I'll have our Guard drones subdue her in seconds." Great to know THAT was a feature as well.

"It is okay, son, you have to trust me just a little," she said, seemingly feeling the wind from my quick withdrawal. I moved my hand forward and into a position, so the pendant was at her fingertips. She pulled her hand back as soon as she made contact with it.

"Where did you get this?" she asked with a wary frown.

"My grandmother gave it to me," I said with my own frown. This was odd behavior, but then again, I thought of where I was, "is there a problem with it? Do you have any?"

"I have two," she said.

"Okay..." I said, "can I buy them from you?"

"What was your grandmother's name?" she asked, like a talking statue.

"How does that matter?" I asked.

"Tell me her name, and then we can continue," she said.

"Ere," I said.

"Ere?" she repeated questioningly.

"Yes, Eh-reh," I said sounding it out phonetically.

"The palindrome. I gave her the other two. Well, she won them from me."

I held onto the thought of this for a few moments.

"Huh?" I asked confused by everything she said, "you know her?"

"She's been to my shop many times," she said, "we play cribbage."

I suddenly felt foolish for not knowing this. I suddenly felt foolish for leaving my grandmother, for leaving my parents. For chasing Tabitha and... for not searching for Michael. I had run away from home and this stranger had smacked me with the reality of this.

"Do you know how to play cribbage?" she asked, breaking the silence, yanking me from my thoughts.

"I do," I said, looking at her with curiosity, holding for the next incoming words.

"I will give you a chance to win each one," she said evenly.

I sighed.

It took two hours, but I was able to win one from the blind woman. She was pleased with the turn out, keeping her sole remaining pendant. Without much reluctance she had handed it to me but paused just briefly to tell me they were powerful and to use them wisely. I was pretty sure she had no idea.

"Where's the electrical place, Brooklyn?" I asked as soon as I was away from the blind woman's store front.

"Five blocks south of here," she said, "I'll give you turn-by-turn directions as you go."

"Thanks," I said.

"By the way, a good protocol that Dr. Zine wanted to implement, was not using the AI persona names in public, and to use an alternatively defined name," she informed me, "the default is Hal."

"Hal?" I repeated.

"Yes."

"That works for me, Hal" I said, laughing to myself, thinking of Denny.

"Cross left at the corner and head down the street coming up," Brooklyn/Hal said. This would take getting used to.

I noted as I walked how city planners created neighborhoods following themes in Las Vegas Land. I was walking through the Yellowstone district, based on the popular TV series from the mid-two thousand twenties. One building was just a gigantic cowboy hat, which was a hotel and casino, with the hat creases each being hotel penthouse-level towers. Past the hat casino was a full-blown arena where they held rodeos. From the street you could see traditional rodeo bleachers through tall glass soundproof windows. (You had to pay for the sound experience.) In fact, it was a giant rectangular glass enclosure wrapping the entire venue. From above (I was seeing it through the view of one of my surveillance drone cameras streaming to my handheld) it looked like a giant's toy set. I continued and passed a hotel that was an exact replica of the Dutton Ranch from the original show. There were unique districts like this all through Las Vegas Land.

"Take the next right ahead," Brooklyn said. I wasn't going to think her name as Hal in my head, which would be crazy.

The next right put me in the Swiss Alps. One side of the street was summer, the other side was winter. I stayed on the summer side. The hotels and casinos were all chalets, with a modern marvel that was a full-sized ski resort, ski slopes and all, nestled in the middle of that winter side row of buildings. This venue encased in glass on all sides except the front. It was actually snowing on the other side of the street somehow. The unprepared looked genuinely cold.

"How much longer?" I asked, out loud. Not worried about sounding crazy because everyone talked out loud. Many talking to Selfie drones that followed in the front and back of them.

"We've only gone one block, so, four more," Brooklyn said, sounding snarky.

"What do you mean, we?" I snarked back.

"You're doing the walking; I'm doing the thinking. Which do you think is harder?" Brooklyn retorted. I puzzled this sentiment, then left it alone.

Past the Alps, I came to the MCU district, which spanned three blocks. Marvel anything always had to be the biggest. This was where all the tallest skyscrapers were. Deadpool's Cocaine Bar looked pretty dope though. Hulk Tower was too green, in my opinion and Mjolnir Casino seemed architecturally impossible. The caps of the streetlamps were Captain America shields and the lights were scaled down faux arc reactors.

Once I dodged all the street characters trying to extort tourists for money for selfies, I reached Candy Cane Lane. I don't know how, but you could eat everything anywhere in this district. It was like Willy Wonka's Chocolate Factory, but outdoors, with regeneration. You bite the chocolate lamppost and two seconds later it was like you didn't. Somehow it was sanitary, too. I grabbed a handful of Andes Mints from a bush and kept on my way. However, had to stop a few feet further to sip from the cocoa water fountain, then I continued on my way.

The end of the candy zone was sudden. I was in a manufacturing district, and it felt like I walked into the industrial revolution district, which was exactly what the theme was apparently. I wouldn't lick these sidewalks.

"The shop is two hundred feet ahead on the right," Brooklyn said, "but it looks to be closed." Now she was running the show with the drone resources, I could focus on other things, like being annoyed.

Great.

"Any other places to get electrical parts?" I asked.

"I haven't scanned the damage, yet, Max," Brooklyn said, "we should go somewhere where I can do that analysis."

"Good idea. I booked a room at the DuelKings Hotel & Casino," I said.

"That would be a good place," she said, "want directions?"

"Sure."

"Head west through this Industrial district," she directed.

"Gross," I said, "this is appealing to people?"

"There should be a more charming section ahead," she said.

I reached the more charming section, and it was, slightly. It felt like a gray dusty film coated the area. All the resident workers were dressed as if they were from the nineteen-fifties. There were younger kids acting like the paperboys of the time. Just like in the movie Newsies. The pedestrian traffic was thick, and I noticed no vehicles were allowed on the cobblestone paths. Horses and buggies were allowed, however. A small kid tried to sell me a paper and bumped into me, but I politely refused.

"Max, that boy just stole the pendant from your pocket," Brooklyn said, interrupting my smiling.

"What?!" I exclaimed, "no. No, no, no, no, no. Hey, kid. Get back here," I yelled.

A foot chase ensued, but the boy was lost in the crowd within seconds. I spun around, looking in all directions, but could not see him. He was effectively a penny in a wishing well now.

"I don't think I can beat that blind lady again," I said to Brooklyn. I got side-eyes and scoffs from folks who overheard me. I ignored the strangers.

"You don't really have a choice," she said flatly. I sighed, loudly.

"Just get me to the hotel for now," I said, shoulders slinking forward as I walked.

"Sir, I'm sorry, it declined payment with that account as well," the receptionist said with a frown.

"I know there is money in that digital account," I said, flipping through my handheld to check on the balance. I had been leveraging a digital currency hack with crypto currency funds bought in one dimension long ago being available in each dimension I crossed into. This was the first time it didn't work. I was getting nervous as I navigated through each wallet and saw zeros in every one I checked. Then I found an old school Bitcoin wallet that had several thousand in it. Good thing I forgot about that one until now.

"Let's try payment again," I said hovering my handheld near the tap terminal.

"Okay. Go ahead," she said looking at me, seeming to be just as nervous as I was for it to process this time. The terminal glowed green, and I heard the success chime.

"That worked, sir. Sorry for the inconvenience," she apologized unnecessarily out of training habit.

"Glad we got it figured out," I said.

"You're all set," she said with a smile, "your key is now synced to your device."

I nodded, smiled and headed to my room.

"The bullet really did some damage," Brooklyn said after I finished scanning the broken Draw Bridge from every angle I could.

"Yep," I said and dropped backwards to fall laying on my back on the king-sized bed.

"The main concern is the pendant," Brooklyn said, "the battery connector is common enough to find at three different locations near here."

"We can't find it anywhere else?" I asked.

"Like the mysterious blind woman said, 'they were powerful,' meaning unique," Brooklyn said, "and as far as I can find from searching all around the available data sources of this dimension, she has the last one that will help you rebuild the Draw Bridge."

Awesome.

"Hello again," the blind woman said as soon as I walked through her storefront doors, "I knew you'd return."

"Hello. Would I be able to just buy your remaining pendant, please?" I pleaded.

"Remaining?" she said sardonically.

"Yeah, I would like to buy your last one," I said, getting a little annoyed with this game that seemed to be brewing.

"I have two left though still," she said with a smirk. WTF

"What do you mean?" I said, moving closer to the woman.

"These are powerful, even just a little bit of it, I tried to tell you," she said, "one has returned."

"Hal?" I asked to Brooklyn, feigning assistance and strength.

"I don't know how much I can help, but she is telling the truth. She doesn't appear to be a threat," Brooklyn said.

"My name is not Hal," the woman said, losing her smirk and frowning.

"What is your name?" I asked.

"Yukim," she said.

"I'm Max. Nice to officially meet you, Yukim. You know my grandmother, and hopefully you can see how important it is to me to get this pendant," I said, with pleading tones, "I lost the one my grandmother gave me, and need to get another. It's the only thing I have to keep me close to her."

"Smooth," Brooklyn said in my ear. I would have given her eyes to be quiet, but she can't see my eyes, at least not easily.

"Okay, Max. Let's have a game of cribbage for one," she said with a smile.

"You won't let me just buy it?" I asked.

"No," she said evenly.

I sighed and moved to the counter where she had already pulled out the board and set up the pegs.

I won, thankfully.

"I know these pendants can travel," Yukim said, "but I always have two."

"What does that mean?" I asked tilting my head and squinting.

"Good luck on your travels, Max," she said and made a motion to shoo me away like a little kid or pet that's overstayed its welcome. Since I had what I came for, I left without protest. I headed down the street, wondering, internally and externally.

"What do you think she meant by that?" I asked Brooklyn.

"Hard to say, but she's alluding to a magical quality to these pendants. I can only process data, and 'magical' is not a data point I can use for evaluation. I will try to find solid information about what she said, but for now. Let's fix the Draw Bridge and go home."

Chapter 25 - There is Something Wrong with +137

"Maybe the pickpocket kid brought the pendant back to the blind lady and sold it to her?" Blaine said.

"Maybe," I said with a shrug.

"It could be that kid worked for her, and followed you," Tabitha said.

"I don't know. I should have been paying closer attention," I said.

"I love cribbage," Kel said, "grandma was so good at it." He smiled, and I smiled back.

"It sounds like the pendants are the thing that make the portal opens, er, Draw Bridge's work..." Tabitha said. "What is it about them?"

"Dr. Zine suggested it's the heavy metal makeup condensed inside them," I said, "and..." All the proximity alarms went off suddenly.

"A Bridge was just opened in the barn," Brooklyn said in our ears.

We all sprung up.

"Alert our friends in +10, Hal," I said. "Ready, Blaine?" I asked, looking at her and breaking her empty stare in the direction of where the barn was beyond the garage wall.

"Uh, yeah. I'm ready," she replied.

"We'll be right nearby, outside the barn. We have the cover the twilight is providing us now," I said. Blaine nodded. "Plus, a lot of backup in the form of our mini-drone army."

I patted her shoulder.

We all went to the barn.

As Blaine walked 60 feet ahead of us, Tabitha, Kel and I kept in a tight, crouched cluster following close behind, but far enough away to remain hidden.

Assuming Bad Max didn't send out his own surveillance drones with cloaking tech. I was bringing up the rear of our march and was checking the screen on the handheld when Blaine reached the side door of the barn.

Bad Max was standing in the center of the barn, just ahead of a Bridge that was still open behind him. I noticed that the other side of the Bridge didn't appear to have a barn, but a field; darkness made it hard to tell though. There were glowing orange flickers of light beyond the field. I shook my attention back to Bad Max. Two drones hovered just above each shoulder, like armed sentries, pivoting barrels in robotic motions in mirrored synchronization. He had a black baseball hat low on his brow, making it hard to see his eyes. He was staring at his handheld. Blaine's handheld rang in our ears.

We had her device silenced in the barn, but the call was funneling to us via the Bluetooth connection to our collective earpieces.

"Hello," Blaine said, and answered the call. She spoke softly and turned away from the door, realizing she was so close, Bad Max could possibly hear her through it.

"Where are you?" Bad Max said, sounding like his teeth were gritted. I could see Blaine take a deep breath and exhale, as her body rose and fell gently in the shadows.

"I have his portal opener, but I need some assurances," Blaine said calmly.

"What assurances, Blaine? You knew your job," Bad Max said, sounding impatient. "It wasn't that complicated. And the deal was simple. You get me his device… you get your Tabitha back." He paused and appeared to look towards the barn side door. Then he rushed towards it.

"Blaine!" Tabitha yelled and started running to the barn.

"No! Tabitha, don't," I yelled. I grabbed the back of Kel's coat and yanked him down to the ground.

"What are you doing?!" Kel yelled back at me and tried to get up.

"Stay down," I said through my teeth.

"We need to stay out of sight. We'll blow the whole plan." He huffed and listened and watched ahead. Bad Max busted through the side door and caught Blaine spinning in shock. He grabbed her by the hair and yanked her back into the barn. I had to put all my strength into holding Kel down.

Tabitha chased after them.

"Brooklyn, send the drones through the Bridge now," I said as calmly as possible.

"It's going to be okay, Kel. We've accounted for this," I said in a low tone.

"Okay," he said.

"I'm going to go to the other side of the barn." I released his coat. He moved swiftly to the barn.

I slowly stood and headed for the side door that Tabitha now disappeared through. I watched on my handheld as Bad Max wasted no time and dragged Blaine through the Bridge with him.

Tabitha was right behind and dove through, pistol in hand, just as it winked closed. "Brooklyn, open the Bridge to +137 South. Send everything through," I commanded. Kel and I rushed into the barn at the same time and rushed through the open Bridge. As it closed behind us, we stood in a burning world. It looked like the fit had hit the shan.

Fire seemed to be all around.

"Tabitha? Blaine? Can you hear me?" I asked, speaking to our connected comms. No response. We stood next to each other, struggling to keep our mouths closed from the sheer shock of what we were seeing.

The sky was a grey haze with an orange tint. The fields were either on fire or smoldering in all directions. I could see two buildings smoldering as well, possibly houses. There was a strong smell of ash and earthiness in the air. It certainly looked apocalyptic, and I didn't see any other people around. I didn't see Tabitha or Blaine or Bad Max anywhere around us either.

"Where did they go, so fast?" Kel asked.

"Hal, talk to me," I said to Brooklyn.

"Bad Max has Blaine in a vehicle, heading east. Tabitha couldn't catch the vehicle and started chasing after it. We have drones in pursuit. They stayed with the vehicle, so we lost visual on Tabitha," Brooklyn said, an air of sorrow in her voice. "I can disable the vehicle, if you would like."

"No. Not yet. Just follow," I said.

"What do you mean?" Kel asked. "We need to stop the vehicle."

"We need to track where he's going. If we stop it, we won't know where he's going," I said evenly.

"No. Stop the vehicle. London, that's an order," Kel said firmly.

I turned and grabbed both his shoulders, startling his confidence out of him, and he looked shaken.

"Stop, Kel," I said with a stern look. "I have ultimate command of this operation, and Hal won't complete those orders. Plus, you broke protocol, using your persona's name. We will get her back, just be patient."

"How can I, Max?" Kel said with a bit of wetness in the corner of his eyes. Maybe I was asking too much of him, of everyone.

"Hal, any vehicles near us?" I asked.

"Yes. An old gasoline vehicle is about three hundred feet away, in the direction they went," she said.

"Let's move," I said.

We jogged and found a 2023 Porsche 911 Turbo inside a large Quonset hut made of corrugated steel that was starting to rust and show holes in the side. The car was partially covered by a thick canvas cover. The right headlight glass was smashed. I quickly tried the driver's side door and was able to open it. I hopped in and found a key fob tucked above the sun visor.

The fob went straight into my inside coat pocket, and I pressed the starter button. The deep hum vibrated the car and echoed in the garage.

"Pull the canvas off!" I yelled to Kel who was just staring in awe. He moved quickly to yank the canvas clear. "Jump in the other side." He tried the handle, but it was locked.

The cliché schtick ensued where I said "wait" while he tried the handle anyway. I unlocked it and this happened three more times, until I anticipated correctly and got it to unlock finally. With a few revs of the engine and a look about the interior, I got my bearings and shifted into drive.

We shot out of the door and were flying down the gravel road in seconds, Kel screaming and grabbing anything to hold himself in place, me with a huge smile and yelling "wooo" loudly.

"Slow down! Slow down!" Kel yelled.

"Really?" I said, looking at him. "How are you me?"

We reached the paved road, and I cut the wheel so we could slide from the gravel and screeched across the asphalt like I had a death wish. Also to see if Kel would pass out. He didn't. Kel regained his composure and was now smiling and laughing nervously.

"I've never been in a car like this," Kel said. I was just speeding down the road normally now, no stuntman actions.

"Me neither," I said. "I've never been in a Porsche."

"I mean, I've never been in a gas vehicle," Kel said.

"Oh," I said, frowning at him and nodding. "I guess you don't want a turn driving then?"

He gave me wide eyes and shook his head. I laughed.

"How far away is Bad Max, Brooklyn?" I asked.

"Hey, you used her name!" Kel said.

"We're alone," I said with a wink.

"Oh," he said with a slump.

"You are gaining on them, but they are still about eight miles away," Brooklyn reported.

"How about a sign of Tabitha?" I asked.

"I've reviewed some of the drone footage, and it appears she found a dirt bike not too far from where we found the Porsche," Brooklyn said.

"She might be still in pursuit, but no sign from any views behind the vehicle yet."

"Ma...x...m..ax," I heard a broken female voice coming into my ear.

"Tabitha?!" I shouted, realizing I didn't need to. "Maybe we're getting closer to Tabitha, and we'll pick her up on comms again." I looked over at Kel. He nodded.

"Max! I'm… clo…," a voice that sounded like Tabitha was starting to break through. I floored the gas pedal and pushed past a hundred miles per hour on the straight-away ahead of us.

"Tabitha, can you hear me?" I asked and waited, holding my breath.

"Max! I hear you!" Tabitha said in a shout. "I see them."

I looked again at Kel with concern. I pushed to one hundred and ten, zero worry about a auto-cop.

"Tabitha, wait for us to get there before you engage," I said, gripping the steering wheel tight.

"They're right in front of me," Tabitha said. I heard what sounded like gunshots that caused Kel and I to jump and wince, since our volume auto-adjust wasn't timed to the speed of sound.

"How much further, Brooklyn?" I asked. "Three miles and closing fast," she said.

The road was straight but rose and fell in peaks and valleys. There were less toasted wheat fields now, and even some lively growth.

We came over the ridge of the next peak and I could finally see them. Tabitha was swerving back and forth from the driver side to the passenger side of the rear of the open-air Jeep Wrangler.

I couldn't tell if there weren't any auto-autos in this dimension or what, because there were a lot of humans driving right now. I pushed the pedal even further and crossed one hundred and thirty miles per hour. I caught up fast and found us moving too quickly towards them, so I let off the gas and we were gliding. Still too fast, so I started braking, trying not to lose control in a skid.

"I'm coming in hot, Tabitha," I said. She looked back at our car.

"Holy hell," she said, looking a little longer than made me comfortable.

"Where did you get that?" Tabitha asked.

"Watch out!" I yelled as I saw a shotgun protrude out through the back center bars of the Jeep.

I finally was able to see Blaine, duct tape across her mouth, and her arms appeared to be tied behind her back. She was trying to fight Bad Max with her shoulder, to stop him from pointing the shotgun back at Tabitha. Tabitha turned back and veered to the passenger side and sped past the Jeep, causing Bad Max to jerk the gun back so he could steer.

He tried to then run her off the road but was knocked sideways by Blaine again, causing him to release the gas a little, and Tabitha went flying ahead, causing her to turn to stare back. I had to brake harder and fishtailed slightly to prevent smashing the rear of the Jeep. Puffs of burnt-rubber smoke sizzled upwards behind us.

Blaine had freed her hands during the shoulder fight and climbed to the back seat, Bad Max trying to grab her and stop her while still driving with the other hand. Tabitha had slowed enough to realign with the Jeep.

"I'm going to ditch the bike and jump in the Jeep," she said, steadying the bike alongside the Jeep. I slowed the car down and moved over to the oncoming lane.

Tabitha leapt and landed in the front passenger seat of the Jeep, startling Bad Max. Blaine and Tabitha were then able to subdue him, with Blaine wrapping her arms around his neck and Tabitha punching his gut and taking the breath out of him while she took the wheel. The Jeep started to slow and came to rest in the middle of the road.

All of us breathed out in relief. It didn't go down how I'd hoped, but at least we were all still in the same dimension. He didn't lead us to anything to help explain more about what was going on here, or what he was up to. It was okay, though. We finally had Bad Max.

"You've made a big mistake," Bad Max said. "You're in over your head, Max."

"That's what all bad guys say," Kel said. Bad Max squinted at him.

"You're the one that looks like the bad guy," Bad Max said, looking between Kel and me.

"Just stop," I said, grabbing Bad Max's arm and pulling him out of the Jeep.

"We know what you've been up to."

"Yeah? What have I been 'up to,' Max?" Bad Max said, dragging out his sentence with annoyance and arrogance with emphasis on "up to."

"You've been kidnapping people from other dimensions to build an army," Tabitha said, coming over to take Bad Max's other arm to help me move him to the right side of the road.

"Blaine, can you move the Jeep to the side of the road, before any vehicles come?" I asked.

"You have no idea what is happening here," Bad Max said in just above a mutter. I looked at Tabitha and furrowed my brow. She raised hers, but we shook off the comment.

"Kel, come hold him still, while I move the Porsche," I requested. With the vehicles safely situated on the side of the road, we circled around Bad Max who was now sitting on the ground in front of us.

I had removed all items from his pockets that could be a threat, including his Draw Bridge. He had a boxy variant, which made it look almost like an old Roku TV remote. I used my knife to cut a piece of sleeve off and pocketed it. Then I inspected his handheld.

"Hal, can you get this open?" I asked.

"Hang on, Max," Brooklyn said. The device unlocked and I quickly scanned to find an open application that had a location dialed.

"We got you now," I said.

"This isn't going to end well for you all," Bad Max said, grinning and looking at each of us.

"Hal, any threats nearby?" I asked Brooklyn, just to ensure confidence he was bluffing.

"A large vehicle is headed this way, Max," Brooklyn said in our good-guy comms.

The good guys all looked amongst each other silently.

"There are," Bad Max said with his grin growing.

"There are what?" Kel asked innocently, then realized and could only say, "Oh."

"We have to go," Tabitha said.

"Hal. Initialize protocol Z," I said. The group looked at me with confusion. This seemed like a legitimate command, but it was a nonsense request; it didn't need to be anything real.

That was the point. I had written up "nonsense" protocols years ago for just this occasion. When I used one, Brooklyn would start working through the situation on her own. I just had to say "protocol" anything to engage. Our Guard drones took up positions in the air above us, forming an aerial perimeter with a dozen of them.

"The large vehicle is a military-grade armored Sports Utility Vehicle. Two males are inside," Brooklyn said into the comms.

I pulled zip ties from my coat pocket and bound Bad Max's hands behind his back.

"Oww. This isn't going to help you," Bad Max said.

"Tabitha," I said to her once she looked. "You three need to leave. Go to this location," I tossed her Bad Max's handheld. "I'll meet up with you after. Think you can handle the Porsche?" I winked.

"After what?" Kel asked.

"After I find out why this vehicle is coming at us," I said, pointing down at Bad Max.

"Someone is on the way, and I'm going to find out who."

The three nodded and didn't argue much. Tabitha frowned, staring at me, and I could tell she was fighting the urge to resist and stay with me. She didn't.

"I'll take the Jeep. It will handle better if we need to go off road," Tabitha said. I nodded.

They all climbed into the Jeep and sped off.

"I hope your friends are ready," I said, walking over and picking up the shotgun that was left on the side of the road, and inspected it.

This dimension was full of antiques. Bad Max never got a chance to fire it, so there were still five rounds loaded in and one chambered, I noticed after inspecting.

"I hope yours are, too," Bad Max said, again in a mutter.

"Why do you keep doing that?" I asked. He just glared at me and looked away.

I watched as the Jeep cruised down the long flat stretch of road, until I was startled by the sound of dirt grinding against rocks, coming from the other direction, where there was a side road that met the main road. The large vehicle that Brooklyn had warned of appeared suddenly. This must have been an EV, but I barely heard it coming. It looked like a reinforced Jeep frame, with "blast-through-anything" bumper attachment, extra-large tires, extra layers of bulletproof glass, extra badass everywhere else. (Talk about "shut-up-and-take-my-money" vibes.)

I leveled the shotgun at them, not that it would have done anything, but it was a show of resistance. The mini drone army above was my real posture against this threat. The driver window rolled down. A long barrel slipped forward and aimed towards me. I bolted for the Porsche and took cover behind it, anticipating bullets chasing me.

One shot was fired.

Bad Max slumped to the side.

I was looking in disbelief, when a large Bridge opened directly in front of the vehicle.

It drove forward and I was finally able to get a look at the driver through the windshield. I saw myself disappear.

I looked down at my other self, who I thought I knew to be Bad Max. "Hal..." I said in a bit of a panic. "Is he dead?"

"Yes, Max," Brooklyn said.

"Tabitha, they killed Bad Max and disappeared," I said. No response. I turned and looked down the road and saw the Jeep driving away still.

They should have still been in range.

"Hal, why can't they hear me?" I asked.

"Max, they should be in range, but I'm having trouble with communication signals right now," Brooklyn said. "Er, what?" I asked. I ran for the Porsche and jumped in and took off down the road to catch up with the Jeep.

"Tabitha? Kel? Blaine?" I asked, trying to limit panic in my voice. "Can anyone hear me?"

I was gaining on them as I pushed the limits of the car and breached one hundred miles per hour in no time. Then a large Bridge opened ahead of the Jeep. I could see the tires smoke and the Jeep twist slightly while braking, but it slid right through.

Then it was gone.

I sped up even more until I reached the black tire marks left on the road. I braked, sliding to a stop, and busted out of the car, once in park. I stood in the middle of the road, ahead of the Porsche, slowing and spinning and looking around for the Jeep, for my friends. It seemed like in less than twenty minutes I was now completely alone in this foreign, desolate dimension, left with nothing but questions and confusion all around me.

"This doesn't make any sense," I said to no one. It wasn't even a statement to Brooklyn.

"Max. I've lost control of the drones," Brooklyn said.

All our drones crashed to the pavement in unison. Something was wrong with this dimension.

"Can you open a channel with Dr. Zine and Denny in +10?" I asked.

"Communications are being interrupted, Max," Brooklyn said. "I'm trying some workarounds with our local network. I have the drones back online, but some are badly damaged."

Half the drones began to hover again, and half of those flew up into the sky to survey the area.

"I left Bad Max on the side of the road. Should we do something with this body?" I asked.

"I don't think that is our priority right now," Brooklyn stated. "I've scanned him against the scent database. It is him. The one that took Tabitha." The words hit me like an unexpected hard tap against the gut. I breathed out. This person, which looked identical to me, who I was chasing for so many years, was dead. It felt anticlimactic. I didn't feel satisfaction. I shook off the feeling because I had other, bigger concerns now.

I stood in the middle of the road and closed my eyes. Sucking in the air, the earthy, stale air. I inhaled it deep and held it for six seconds. Slowly, I released it. I repeated this action five more times then opened my eyes.

Slightly refreshed and ready.

"Right," I said. "Okay. Maybe I should head somewhere else. I need to see if I can find out what's going on with this dimension."

I climbed back into the car and headed the way the Jeep was heading.

The road was empty; it was eerie. I would have expected to pass auto-autos or auto-semis along this road, at least one or two, but no other vehicles were in sight. The stretch of road was cut through field after field of wheat, and the crops were in various states of burned versus thriving.

About thirty minutes later I came to a small town and pulled into an old gas station. I took note that the gas gauge on the Porsche was at a quarter tank, so I pulled up to the pump. It had been years since gas stations had started to die out in large swaths, but in the more rural places, they still could thrive. Not all roads could accommodate the electric road-lines, and the grids could still struggle. The pumps were still upgraded over the years to the point where gas station attendants were unnecessary.

You used your handheld to pay. The gas in the large underground tanks was refilled by auto-semi fuel trucks. So, pulling into a quiet gas station was not unusual. It was the lack of any other humans anywhere else, at the diner across the street, the bank next to that, the Chicken Donuts diagonally across from those, which was eerie.

I paid and filled the tank up. Then I continued driving down the road.

"I'm not sure where I'm going, Brooklyn," I said. I really didn't.

"Max, I've reworked our networks. I've been able to bring through more resources into +136, from +2 East, and more are being produced rapidly," she said. "However, there are anomalies.

There are many more resources than we left, but it would be impossible to produce that many in just a couple hours."

"Dr. Zine was right about this dimension," I said.

"Indeed," Brooklyn said.

"Have you brought new resources through to here yet?" I asked, trying to think through the scenarios.

"There doesn't seem to be anyone else around. Will we need them?"

"It's quiet, a little too quiet," she responded. I had to pause to process this.

"Are you quoting Teenage Mutant Ninja Turtles?" I asked.

"Yes, Max," she responded matter-of-factly. I shook my head at the fact that she could still surprise me.

"We should be ready for anything."

"I think you're right. We need to figure out why it's so quiet," I said. "Can we open a link with +10 yet?"

"Yes," Brooklyn said. "Max, can you hear me?" Dr. Zine asked.

"Yes!" I said, so happy to hear the familiar voice.

"We haven't heard from you in like six months!" Denny chimed in loudly. "Why is it taking you so long to reply?"

"Wait, what?" I asked.

"There must be time dilation at play there, Max. There is a delay in your messages," Dr. Zine said. "I told you there was something concerning about +137."

"Time is moving slower here...?" I asked and paused to think for a moment.

"Yes, but because of the time dilation, there is a large gap between your messages to us," Dr. Zine said. "You might hear us instantly, but an hour or more passes between messages back to us."

My mind was melting.

"Oh. Okay. I should try to respond quicker," I said, not being efficient at all. This would take getting used to, but I didn't have the time!

"Dude. We thought you all were dead," Denny said. I could hear a bit of panic mixed with relief in his voice.

"I'm alive," I said and paused. "Tabitha, Blaine and Kel went missing though. I don't know how to time this communication. Not sure what is best to say…"

"I'm sorry, Max," Dr. Zine said. "We'll do what we can to help you from here, but you are essentially on your own, unfortunately. I do see that we received the latest data upload from Brooklyn, but new data will be flowing in in increments. Then we'll need time to process it, so by the time we respond, it might be out of date."

"Do you know what's causing all this weirdness?" I asked. Still struggling to efficiently ask for the information I needed. I had to stop asking closed questions.

"My speculation would be that there is some kind of black hole in that dimension. I don't know for sure, but you most likely are near one, in some unexplainable way."

"Okay. I'm not good at this and don't want you waiting for many hours for lame responses, so I'll check back in when I can. I am worried about the others. I'm going to find them."

"Good luck, Max," Dr. Zine responded.

I drove on for a while in silence. A small army of flying drones behind me. What a wild sight it must have been if anyone was around to see. An antique Porsche with about a hundred high-tech drones flying in formation all around me. Protecting me. The daylight was carrying on as usual, heading towards its respite without concerns. The next town over was just foundations, smoldering and charred. Still no other beings. Not even drones. No vegetation anywhere. I started to notice Bridges opening and closing randomly in the fields around me. They would glow to existence, and some would snap shut quickly, not staying opened long enough for anyone to cross, while others lingered a bit longer.

"That's odd," I said out loud.

"I'm tracking the energy output on these Bridges, Max," Brooklyn said. "And I'm noticing anomalous readings."

"Like what?" I asked, slowing down to watch a mini light show out the driver's side window, looking south, as around twenty Bridges flashed open and dissipated in various sequences, some staying open for mere fractions of a second, others for several. Then it was quiet again.

I thought about trying to take the sports car offroad but reconsidered. More so because I didn't want to get sucked into a randomly appearing Bridge and get my head lopped off.

"The levels are weak," she said, "as if they are being opened with insufficient energy."

"Interesting," I said and continued driving. I finally reached a town after a while, just after the sunset, which was in relatively normal shape.

Still empty though. It was more settled, with a main street, shopping center, multiple restaurants, and a couple gas stations. I decided I would top off the tank again, not knowing how many opportunities there might be. As my drone posse and I buzzed up to the pump, I noticed a vehicle parked at a pump across the street. I started the pump filling my tank and walked to the other side of the car to look a little closer.

"Can you check the heat signature on that truck across the street?" I asked Brooklyn.

"It's warm, recently running," she responded. I started to look around for another person.

No one was near the Ford F350. It was quiet. I couldn't tell if anyone was inside the gas station store. Then I noticed several drones heading down the street from the oncoming direction.

"Hal..." I said.

"I have some of ours ready to engage. Should I send them?" Brooklyn asked.

I walked to the main street road and looked up and down it. No other cars, no other drones.

"Hold on," I said.

The drones cruised forward to the truck, rotating to pan cameras in our direction. A person walked out of the small convenience store. They were wearing a face like mine, no hat, and no long coat though. He had longer hair and was wearing a leather bomber jacket, with what looked like a rifle slung behind his back. I went right over.

"Hey," I said, getting his attention. He looked up and smirked.

"Hey," he said back. I looked around.

"What's going on here?" I asked. He twisted the top off the soda bottle in his hand and took a sip.

"I'm not sure, but I'm going to guess you're here for the same reason I am," bother me said. He was me, but he looked younger.

When I looked at myself in the reflection of the Porsche window not too long ago, I looked weathered, looked tired, and looked old. This version of me looked like he might have been through less.

"What reason would that be?" I asked, narrowing my eyes slightly.

"Looking for the weapon," he said casually.

"Yep," I said.

Trying to sound steady.

He narrowed his eyes at me.

"Vin, is he telling the truth?" he said out loud. I assumed he was talking to his AI.

"You're lying."

"I am," I said flatly.

"Why?" he asked with a raised eyebrow.

"Because I don't know what's going on here," I said, running my hand through my hair. "We came here to catch Bad Max. Now my friends are gone and he's dead." He just stared at me, then looked slightly up, as if listening to a voice in his ear. I could see a slight nod.

"Bad Max is dead?" he sought further confirmation, I guess.

"Yes," I said.

"From what dimension?" he asked.

"To me, it's +2 south," I said, making some assumptions he knew the schematics of the interdimensional multiverse, because he was a traveler like me. This other Max was thinking over what I said, doing some calculations in his head. Then his eyes went wide.

"This dimension is +137 to you, isn't it?" he asked. I nodded. "Then you're Max Prime." I sighed with my body slumping slightly.

"I've been called that, yes," I said. The concept was so odd to me: Max Prime.

Was the implication I was the first to travel through the Bridge? Obviously Bad Max was waiting on the other side; he had to know about it before I started traveling.

"You're a legend, Max," other Max said with a completely different posture now. "I go by K, to help with the confusion of meeting all the other Maxes out there."

Other Maxes.

"Oh. Have you met a lot?" I asked. "I haven't seen anyone else in this dimension."

"Yes, of course," other Max said, now known as K to me, said. "There are many out there traveling through dimensions."

Interesting.

"Why am I a legend?" I asked.

"You don't know?" K asked and tilted his head, frowning. "We're all spawned from you. You're like our dad in some weird interdimensional sense."

That hit me hard.

I didn't respond for a full thirty seconds, and the silence hung thick and awkward. K started to look around, not exactly sure what to do.

"Well, I don't view myself as anything like that," I said finally. "I just lost my three closest friends because I was too short-sighted about the trouble we were in. And I'm still no closer to finding Michael."

"We've all lost people out there. We're all looking for Michael as well," K said solemnly. I nodded in solidarity.

We held a moment of silence.

"How do you know about me though? I mean, how would you know you're in a dimension a certain number of steps removed from my dimension, what you consider the 'prime' dimension?" I started rapid-firing questions at K. "I mean, you're a split-off version of me, right? In theory, I made some choice and you're the result of the other side of the choice. How would you even know that?"

"I didn't know that at first. But, once I started to travel through the Bridge, I began bumping into other Maxes and asking about their dimensions. We record every interaction. Eventually the AI was able to detect patterns. Denny, er my Denny, assuming he's a Denny like yours... anyway, he was able to build a sort of interdimensional intranet, a MaxNet if you will, where we share the data where only other Maxes, good Maxes, could see it," K said, and paused, looking at me quizzically. "Did you not know about this?"

"No," I said. He brought his hand to his chin and rubbed it with his fingertips.

"Have you met any other Maxes, good ones?" he asked.

"Yes," I said, "one."

"He is one of my friends that I just lost into another dimension."

"Oh, he's not dead?" he asked. "No. At least, I don't think so... honestly, I don't know," I said. "Max, the intranet, or MaxNet that K spoke of, I just found it and connected to it," Brooklyn interrupted in my ear. "I'm keeping it isolated from our own though. I'm creating middleware now to help with transferring so we can combine information to expand our data."

"Thank you, Hal," I said out loud.

"Your AI?" K asked with a chin check towards me, looking at my ear.

"Yeah," I said with a nod. I thought for a second about sharing that Brooklyn found the intranet/MaxNet but decided not to say anything.

"They found the MaxNet, huh?" K said with a big smile. I just shrugged coyly.

He nodded in silent acknowledgment.

"How many other Maxes have you met?" I asked.

"I don't know, I've lost count. Maybe dozens," K said.

"You've met them while traveling through the Bridge?" I asked.

"Yeah," he said. "I can't believe you've never bumped into yourself out there."

"Only once," I said.

"Interesting," he said. "Well. Maybe you can help me figure out what's going on here?" I asked.

"Oh. We know what's going on here," he said confidently.

"You do?" I asked.

"Yeah," he said. "A version of us is starting a portal war."

I thought I couldn't be shocked anymore, but K's statement left me with a hanging lower lip.

"What the heck, a 'portal war,' seriously?" I asked, verbally emphasizing the ridiculous term. I rediscovered my normal face and then shook my head while rolling my eyes. I was back to being me again. "Why is there always a 'bad' version?"

"Heroes and Villains, I suppose. It's a symbiotic relationship," K said. "It gives us a purpose. Yin and Yang. Yada yada."

"Yeah. I don't think that's right. The words sound good; however, I don't think that's right," I said. "There must be some greater motivator in play. I became an interdimensional traveler to find someone... two someone's, that were taken from me. I didn't seek out the ability. It almost literally struck me." I paused for a few seconds and thought, looking around, then back at K.

"Did you say Bad Max is starting a portal war?" I asked. "Because I just watched him get shot in the head by another one of us, and die."

"There are other Bad Maxes, unfortunately," K said.

"Awesome," I said. Just when you think something is solved... "So, Bad Max is starting a portal war?" I asked.

"Yes and no," K said.

"This dimension is destabilized because of the attempts to create a portal war when testing the weapon. If Bad Max succeeds... it will start to take out other dimensions."

"Other dimensions?" I repeated the last of his sentence.

"Yep," he said.

"How?" I asked.

"Well. We're kind of thinking of it like the weapon would sort of 'eat' the connecting dimensions. Acting like a virus, which would cause subsequent dimensions to be eaten too. It's essentially interdimensional portal cancer."

"Holy. Hell," I said, dropping my head and holding and squeezing my forehead with my left hand.

"Yeah... it's pretty bad," K said. "But don't worry. He doesn't have your pendant to do it."

"My pendant?" I asked.

"Yeah, he needs the purest one," he said somewhat matter-of-factly. "That's the consensus at least."

I thought on this for a bit. The blind lady did say the pendants were powerful, but wouldn't they all be equal? I got my replacement pendant in a dimension very far removed from the home dimension. But that woman was kind of cagey.

She said the pendants return... maybe that meant something... it was hard to tell at this point.

"How do you know all of this?" I asked.

"MaxNet..." he said.

"Ah. MaxNet," I returned. "Okay. How do we stop him?" I asked with a hefty sigh, resigned to just get this over with.

"We've been assembling an army," K said. "Of Maxes and drones. Good Maxes, of course. It's pretty epic." He smiled huge.

"Alright," I said. "I have a lot of questions, but those can wait. I guess we should go to where that's all happening then."

"Yep. Follow me," K turned and headed for his truck, started it up and drove off. I looked around, a little shocked at the abruptness. Then I rushed for my car, removed the pump nozzle quickly and set off to follow him.

We drove for a few hours northeast, bypassing New York City, heading more north, then cutting east. We passed through towns and small cities in various conditions of fully intact or disrepair – always abandoned. It was like every person in the world had just picked up and ran away. Occasional Bridges popped open and

224

closed following that same pattern of lasting from seconds to minutes. "Are there really no other living souls anywhere, Brooklyn?" I asked.

"There's no sign of human life in any of the areas we've passed through. I've been scanning for heat signatures as far out as a fifty-mile radius as we've been traveling. Communications on a broader spectrum seem to be down. I'm suspecting EMP devices may have been used recently. Additional scans have detected the signs with shorted out satellite receivers in many places."

"That's fun," I said.

"So no broadcasts from TV or radio? No internet?"

"No. No signals from anything," Brooklyn said.

"It could be isolated to the east coast. The EMPs could have been activated in major east coast cities, such as New York and Washington D.C., but it could be country wide, even worldwide. I'm still trying to scan across all satellite signals." We finally reached the outskirts of a city in Connecticut.

The GPS showed I was near Bridgeport, although it didn't look the same as the last time I had driven the highway through it. Even in a 'normal' dimension, you only wanted to pass through it anyway. K slowed down ahead of me and pulled over to the side of the road. He climbed down from his truck as I pulled up behind him and stepped out of my car.

"We're getting close to where the original weapon testing facility was. We need to head north of it, but this is the only way to get there, and we must go by as fast as we can and try not to get sucked into a stray Bridge," K said. "You'll be fine to go fast with this, but you'll be dodging a lot of holes in the road." He patted the hood of the Porsche.

"What are we walking into?" I asked flatly.

"Ground zero. Where the first weaponized Bridge test was conducted... unsuccessfully," K said. "About five years ago. It destabilized the entire area and then spread. Most of the middle of the state became uninhabitable instantly because Bridges started to open and close randomly, disappearing people. The army tried to stop it, and they lost a bunch of guys. Scientists came to study the phenomenon. They lost a bunch of them too."

"And we're driving through here for what reason then?" I asked.

"To get to the other side," he said with a grin. I rolled my eyes; I didn't have patience for jokes.

"Seriously. I'm no closer to finding my friends and we've lost several hours," I said.

"Right," K said with a frown. "We're going to meet the other Maxes and to talk to this dimension's Dr. Zine."

Finally. Hope.

I did the best I could dodging potholes, but if the owner of this Porsche ever got it back, they were going to be pissed. I bottomed out going ninety at one point and lost part of the rear bumper. I managed to keep the rest together by getting better at dodging and we cruised past the disaster area without much incident. There was a giant crater a few miles wide that I could see from the highway that itself was a few miles from the rim. The sporadic Bridge events felt less sporadic there and steadier, as several opened and closed in varying lengths of time-open, but in larger sets of twenty to thirty at a time. The colors varied as well and made for a spectacular light show.

The most curious phenomenon I witnessed though, which made my blood go cold, was when I saw a Bridge consume another Bridge. That felt catastrophic. Another hour north and we finally reached an encampment tucked away in the tree-covered hills, several miles from the highway to the west. It looked like a makeshift military installation. Pod Houses were everywhere. These geodesic domes were reinforced with paneling and glass and solar triangles used for power and warming capabilities. Various types of vehicles were scattered throughout, auto-style and gasoline-powered. Enormous solar-flower dishes were lining three corners of the perimeter of the camp.

Tall metal sentry towers were at each corner, with several Guard drones manning the posts. I parked next to K once we drove past the armed guards at the entrance. We emerged and suddenly I felt exposed, too much in focus; everyone was looking at me. Even though most of our faces matched, we were different in many ways, some even looked younger than me somehow. I was apparently the only one with this clothing style of gambler hat and shearling coat combination. There had to be three or four dozen Maxes all around the Max camp. Each with several drone companions.

The nuances were subtle, but some had different color eyes, not brown like mine. Some had blonde hair, not brown like mine. All were mostly the same height though. I guess just the superficial recessive genes shined interdimensional.

Some were standing alone, but talking, so I assumed to their version of Brooklyn. "I think I'll show you the tech shop first. We have some impressive things, in my opinion. I want to get your thoughts on it," K said as we walked up to a large grey rectangular building in the center of the camp complex.

Two large doors hissed open, moving in opposite directions from each other, as we approached and entered without stopping. A Max with long blonde hair and glasses, wearing a black hoodie was fidgeting with something mechanical-looking at a table against the wall. He turned as we approached, and his mouth gaped slightly.

"Hey, Mix," K said to the Max in glasses, whose name was apparently 'Mix.'

"Hey, K," he said with a smile. "So... this is him?" Mix moved a little closer and was inspecting me. I looked at K wondering if this Max was serious, and back to Mix.

"Fascinating," Mix said.

"Yes," I said. "So, you wanted to show me something?" I looked at K again. He nodded and walked to the large table ahead of us. It was covered with gadgets of all shapes and sizes.

"Mix, let's show him some of the latest stuff," K said with a smile.

Mix smiled back and grabbed a small pen-like gadget.

"This is our latest creation, just came out of the testing lab and is ready for general use," Mix said and slowly turned the device over with his fingers.

"It's known as the Express Acclimation Pen. You first press the button to create the baseline and then inject a chip here," Mix pointed to the soft area behind his right ear, "and create the baseline dimensional reference.

Then you inject the next set of chips in whomever you want to catch up to speed on the current dimensional information." My mouth hung.

"What?" K asked me.

"That's insane and amazing. How does it do that?" I asked in awe.

"You don't have anything like this where you're from?" Mix asked and looked at K then back at me. I felt flush with embarrassment and slight annoyance as he deflected my question.

"No," I said honestly. "I mean we have some cool drones and of course the Draw Bridge tech and BridgeAI, but I guess we haven't taken measures to expand into other areas yet. We spent a lot of time and energy chasing Bad Max. And now..." I paused. The other two paused with me for a few moments.

"Well, necessity is the mother of invention, and we kept running into scenarios where we needed to knock other Maxes into our dimensions to help us with various situations, and often had to scramble around just to give us enough time to explain the situation. This is a game changer," K said.

"I was talking about needing something like this just recently," I said.

"Well, here you go," Mix said with a smile, proudly. He handed me the pen and then went and grabbed a couple more and handed me those as well. I looked down at them for a few seconds, inspecting them, then put them in my coat pocket.

"Thank you," I said. "What else you got?" I grinned large. Mix blushed and went back to the gadget table. He walked around the table to the other side and picked up a sports rifle. He pointed it at the window and pulled the trigger.

I flinched and expected the loud pop of the gun and shattering glass sounds, but the only sound was a dull click. Mix looked at me and smiled, but didn't say a word. He placed the gun back on the table, then he picked up a small ring from the table and placed it on his pinky finger. He picked up the gun again.

This time he walked over to the corner where there was a gun testing setup. He sat down and set the gun in the stand and leaned forward with his eye looking down the top rail sights. I heard a soft pop when he pulled the trigger. The muzzle was suppressed in the testing unit, so it saved our ears. The gun remained when he stood and walked back over to me showing off the ring.

"Biometrically paired weapons," Mix said, and then handed me the ring to inspect. "We can pair that ring to other weapons, and that ring will be tied to only those who have also been paired to it." He grabbed a round gadget that looked like a lady's compact mirror and put the ring inside it and closed it. He shook it and the ring rattled and then he opened it again.

"Here," Mix said, moving the case towards me. "Take the ring out and put it on one of your fingers. It will adjust to fit if needed, just put pressure on it as you push it on." I did as he instructed and placed it on my middle finger.

It grew slightly and went right over the knuckle and shrank then slid into place just past it. "There you go. It's now paired to you and only you," he said with a smile. "And that rifle is now yours as well, since the ring is already paired to it." I stared at the ring and rotated my hand, then eyed the rifle.

"I haven't carried around a rifle before," I said. "I've had a few opportunities, but then thought better of it, because I thought it would become cumbersome."

"You'll need it here. Unfortunately. So, it belongs to you now," Mix said.

"Thanks," I said with a nod and took it from Mix after he retrieved it and handed it to me. He slipped me a couple of loaded magazines as well.

"You also could pair the ring to other things," Mix said. "Like vehicles. It helps slow down opponents in the thick of it.

We invented it for the battlefield advantage. There was some argument about it becoming harder for swapping weapons, but since they have become so much more efficient, you can rely on one. Plus, parts swap out so easily, the repairs are a breeze." K cleared his throat. "But I digress," Mix finished. I nodded. K smiled and eyebrow flashed playfully and looked over towards a mysterious cabinet in the corner.

"Let's show him the prototype," K said. Mix nodded and walked over to the cabinet. We followed. He tapped the lock with his pinky ring, and it made an unlocking sound of bolts retracting quickly. I guess that was also a use case.

"Oh. This is another use case," Mix said, looking back at me briefly. Then he opened the case and pulled forward a drawer that had another, slightly larger, injection pen.

"A... larger Express Acclimation Pen, with more Acclimating capabilities...?" I asked.

"No," Mix said flatly. K laughed. I smirked.

"What is it then?" I asked.

"This is an injection pen to deliver an injectable Draw Bridge chip," Mix said. I didn't say anything. I couldn't say anything.

This was wild if it was what he suggested.

"How would that even work?" I asked.

"The advancement of efficient inductive coupling powered by biofuel from the glucose in the bloodstream made it possible," Mix said. "All figured out by Dr. Zine, of course." I stood with wide eyes but nodded when I heard Dr. Zine's name.

"Mixy boy did the engineering part, though," K said and winked.

"Wow," I said. "So, you inject the chip and how do you dial in a dimension and open a Bridge?"

"You just think it up," Mix said casually.

"Um, what?" I asked.

"You bring the dimensional coordinates to mind, and think 'open' and it opens," Mix said, so casually, I knew he was not messing with me.

"Okay then," I said, leaving it alone.

"What do you call it?"

"An injectable Draw Bridge, I guess," Mix said. I grimaced.

"You haven't named it?" I asked, raising an eyebrow.

"No. It's still a prototype. I just finished building it yesterday," Mix said. I nodded.

"Well, I like naming things, and what just came to mind was 'Synaptic Draw Bridge' or 'SDB,' since we need acronyms for everything, because they are not annoying at all." I smirked.

"Sure," Mix said, then pulled the SDB off the drawer and handed it to me.

"You should take it."

"Why?" I asked with a confused look on my face. "You said it's a prototype."

"I think we're going to need all the help we can get..." K said. I looked between the two of them. Then pocketed the SDB with a shrug.

"What are you not telling me?" I asked.

"Let's go see Dr. Zine," K said. Mix nodded. I gave an 'alright' eyebrow raise and shrug.

Mix and K led me to a large freight elevator door, and we stood in front of it as K called for it. The buzz vibrated the air as the doors wooshed open. Mix stepped inside first and K and I followed.

I took note of the panel of available floor options and my eyes grew wide when I noticed there were twenty.

"This goes twenty stories down?" I asked with surprise.

"Yes, from this elevator," K said with a smile. "There's another at twenty down that will take you another five to the safe zones." Wow. I was saying that a lot. There was so much more to this dimension than I could have imagined. I thought about my lost friends at that moment. Wondering where they were. If they were alive. Was losing people through dimensions just my life...?

"Do you think Dr. Zine will know where my friends went?" I asked with soft sadness in my voice.

"Your friends...?" Mix asked.

"Yeah. They slipped into one of those random Bridges that opened while they were driving," I said. Mix just nodded solemnly.

"I'm sure he'll have some idea about it," K said after a few seconds of silence. "But those Bridges are not normal Bridges."

I nodded.

The doors wooshed open. We exited the elevator into a hallway. I followed K and Mix to the right. We walked for a bit until we came to an office door that had a small label that said 'Zine' on it. Dr. Zine was busy scribbling on a digital whiteboard. He heard us walk in and spun with a huge grin. "Max, my boy!" +137 Dr. Zine said, pulling me into a hug.

"Hey, Dr. Zine," I said, slightly apprehensively because he wasn't my Dr. Zine.

"I'm so glad you're finally here," Dr. Zine said. "I do hope to meet my other version soon." He smiled big.

"I can certainly arrange that," I said. "But I'd love to know if you can help me find my friends first." I flashed an earnest smile. Dr. Zine's face turned serious.

"Ah. Yes. Let's see about that first," Dr. Zine walked over to his desk and moved his desk chair out of the way. "Sydney, pull up our large screen," Dr. Zine said out loud, to what I assumed was his AI assistant.

"Yes sir, Dr. Zine," Sydney responded with an Australian accent via speakers mounted in the opposite upper corners of the back walls.

A transparent screen grew from the desk, like it was blossoming and expanded outwards to a large rectangle, around one hundred and twenty inches in size. Several boxes filled it, each different windows of information. One in the upper right corner looked to have some kind of program running with cascading messages flowing. A few were video feeds showing the outside of the Max camp from different angles. I could see Maxes coming and going, some carrying rifles, others moving equipment on large trucks, some converged around a fire burning in a barrel, which I was pretty sure was just for effect, because it wasn't cold out and they were roasting marshmallows.

"Where did they disappear?" Dr. Zine turned to ask me.

"On a highway, in Pennsylvania.

Through a random Bridge," I said. Dr. Zine nodded. Then turned back to his screens. "Can you get me coordinates from your AI?" Dr. Zine asked without turning around.

"Hal?" I asked Brooklyn. She stated what I needed, and I repeated out loud.

"Sydney, run a dimensional check on the latest +137 Bridges in that area," Dr. Zine said. "Max, we're all friends here, not the enemy."

"Okay. That's good to know," I said.

"You don't have to use your AI's code name. If you don't want to," Dr. Zine said, focused on watching the scans that Sydney was facilitating in one of the boxes on the screen.

"Okay," I said. "I'll consider that next time."

It certainly was hard for me to know who to trust, but at some point, I had to learn to trust someone. These other versions of me and other version of Dr. Zine had taken me in, trusted me, without any questions.

"I'm having trouble, still, with all these 'bad' versions lurking out there. Especially hearing that a Bad Max was behind the dimensional disaster he caused."

"It's okay, Max," Dr. Zine said.

"I hear you and understand. I'm only letting you know you're in a safe place." Dr. Zine started to write on the whiteboard, which was affecting the scan on the screen.

"Thanks," I said.

"We have large data models collected for the stray Bridges. You can have your AI tap into it via the MaxNet. I've just pushed out the latest," Dr. Zine said, turning to me and smiling softly.

"Brooklyn. See what you can learn please," I said out loud. All in now.

I saw Mix and K smile at each other as they watched, both leaning against the wall. It was quiet for a few minutes while we waited.

"Max, I found the dimension that Tabitha, Blaine and Kel were pulled into," Brooklyn finally said. "It's +132, but I'm unsure of the direction. At this point, I've only found data from scent tracking that suggests they entered that dimension from a Bridge on +137."

"+132?" I asked out loud. "How did they skip? Did they just keep crossing?"

"The stray Bridges are not normal, Max. They are very unpredictable," Dr. Zine said.

"Are they still alive?" I asked.

"I believe so, Max, based on how long ago the scents were traced," Brooklyn said. "But I can't open a communication channel to confirm for sure."

"Okay, thank you, Brooklyn," I said. "She's telling me they are most likely alive, but she can't communicate with them."

"Yes, that has been our biggest challenge," Dr. Zine said.

"Okay, I'm going to go there and look for them," I said, turning and pulling out my Draw Bridge.

"Max, you can't do that," Dr. Zine said.

"Why not?" I asked.

"Your Draw Bridge won't work accurately here," Dr. Zine said.

"Here, as in, down here, in this building? Or in this dimension?" I asked, turning back to Dr. Zine.

"In this universe," Dr. Zine said. "Bridge travel is very unstable through the personal Draw Bridges. That's why we created a central Draw Bridge that we can control with more accuracy."

"I see," I said. "What happens?"

"You don't end up where you think you're going," K said from behind me.

"The BridgeAI doesn't work here?" I asked.

"It works, it's just that the signals it gets from the connecting universes are wrong," Dr. Zine said.

"How's that possible?" I asked.

"When the Bridge weapon was activated, it created a severe disruption to the dimensional timelines that connect to this one," Dr. Zine said. "Since there is direct reliance on other universes in order to create those connections." K, Mix and I just stared at Dr. Zine. A bit in awe of his ability to explain complex subjects without going too far over our heads.

"This is because those universes have a parent-sibling relationship to each other," he continued. "What happened when the event occurred, is orphan universes were created because some parents were extinguished. Now, the BridgeAI can't connect to identify the metadata about the universe."

We just nodded with understanding. It did make sense, but it also didn't. I was intelligent, I knew that. I could assume that Bad Max would be as well, but so smart he could create a weapon of mass interdimensional destruction... I had a hard time believing he did this alone.

"Who was Bad Max working with?" I asked flatly. It was quiet for a few seconds. I looked between each person in the room, feeling an unsettled feeling as more seconds passed.

"There's a Bad me here, Max," Dr. Zine said. Now.

In true super hero movie fashion, I half expected Dr. Zine to say 'and that Bad me is Me.'

"I see," I said, squinting with interrogative eyes, and tensing slightly, feeling around my body for weapons with my mind.

"I'm not Bad, Max," Dr. Zine said with a straight face.

"I didn't suggest it," I said.

"Not with your words," Dr. Zine said. I nodded.

"I can't tell anymore," I said.

"I understand," Dr. Zine said.

"Where's the magical Bridge?" I asked after a brief silence.

"Yes. Let's see if we can get you to your friends," Dr. Zine said. He walked past me, tapped my shoulder, and smiled, and then headed out of the room. K, Mix and I then followed.

"It has occurred to me that no one might have mentioned to you, the potential time dilation issues with the universes, the ones that are connected from here," Dr. Zine stated as we rode the elevator down to the extra lower basement.

"I figured out something wasn't right with it, but no one has explained anything to me," I said.

"This universe is running slower, for lack of a better explanation," Dr. Zine said. "Almost like when you get closer to a black hole. Time compared to other universes has slowed down across the entire dimensional set. Max, this means that every day you are here, five years passes in all the other universes."

"Five years?" I asked, incredulous. "Dr. Zine, my Dr. Zine suggested it could be time dilation, but he didn't know why. I never realized it was that long."

"That's correct, it is time dilation," Dr. Zine said. "And yes, it's five years."

"Okay, but does that mean it has been five years since Tabitha, Kel and Blaine were knocked out of this dimension, to them?"

"It's very likely," Dr. Zine said.

I stopped walking and took a deep breath in and released, pressing my thumb and index finger across my forehead.

"Five years..." I said out loud. The others just looked at me, solemn expressions across their faces. After a few quiet moments standing in the hall, I continued, "Okay. I need to get to them. I need to know if they are okay. Also, if it's been that long, could they have tried to come back here?"

"It's possible," Dr. Zine said. "We shouldn't waste any more time, though. Let's go see what we can learn. Once we open to +136, and you cross, you should be able to attempt to establish communications with them."

"Okay. What the heck are we waiting for?" I asked with a smile.

We headed on down the hall. We reached a large room at the end of the hallway, which contained a central Bridge-zone in the center. Along the walls were control stations, where a few Maxes sat.

All looked our way when we entered.

"Karl, please open a Bridge to +136," Dr. Zine said, pointing to a version of me sitting at a large control station to the left, as we walked forward in the large room.

That must have been the central Draw Bridge at that station. Karl nodded and after a few presses of buttons on screens, the Bridge glowed to life. I rushed immediately to step through, but Dr. Zine grabbed my arm.

I jolted and looked at him with confusion.

"Max. You should expect things to have changed," Dr. Zine said. I eyed him with caution, then looked at K and Mix, who caught up to us.

"What do you mean?" I asked.

"Five years is a long time. Many things could have happened to your friends," Dr. Zine said with earnest and concern in his eyes.

"Okay," I said. "I'm not too worried... I'm ready for what I find."

"They might not trust you," Dr. Zine said flatly.

I thought about that for a second. I'd have to deal with it as it came though.

"I haven't changed," I said. "I'll just have to hope they know that." Dr. Zine nodded.

"Wait," Mix said and ran over to a large closet and yanked it open. I looked at him then at Dr. Zine and K. They shrugged. Mix grabbed a medium Cargo drone (that was effectively the size of a large duffle bag) from the bottom of the closet. Then he grabbed several items from the shelves, stuffing them in succession into the cargo hold. He ran back over to me and angled the Cargo drone so I could see what was inside.

I saw a dozen of the EAPs inside, a few dozen rifle magazines and several boxes of bullets. There were also a few other gadgets I hadn't been introduced to yet. I looked up at Mix with a questioning expression.

"A couple things for the road. These EAPs could help you in a pinch, to get people caught up to speed on this dimension and all the other fun history, if needed. They sync data constantly, but only back to this dimension while you're in it. The other gadgets are logged in MaxNet, so you can ask Brooklyn to help you figure those out later, if you are so inclined," Mix said with a warm smile. He patted my right shoulder quickly and said, "Good luck."

Then he looked down at the Near Field Communication spot on top of the drone and did a head nudge for me to sync. I tapped the face of my watch and found the sync menu, then tapped the watch on the NFC spot. Mix nodded with satisfaction. Then Mix boosted the Cargo drone into the air, and it steadied itself just behind me and above me, ready to follow, digitally tethered to me until I gave a command to disconnect it. I nodded and smiled at Mix and then at Dr. Zine and K.

"This will place you in +136 South, Max," Dr. Zine said. "You and Brooklyn will need to figure out where to go from there.

Be safe and hurry back, we really need you."

"Why do you need me?" I asked.

"We need you here, to stop the war," Dr. Zine said. "We have allies all around the country, fighting the enemy and searching for the weapon. They will check in any second now to let us know if they found it."

"But, why me?" I asked.

"From all we know, only the Prime Max can stop it," Dr. Zine said, paused briefly before continuing. "I know we've been throwing a lot at you though, and we haven't had a chance to tell you everything. We'll catch you up soon. Find your friends. Get them to safety. Then Return. We'll most likely be right here. Brooklyn will know how to reach us." I just eyed Dr. Zine, very concerned, very confused. I nodded. Thought for a second, then shook my head, as if shaking away the heavy thoughts.

"I'll cross that bridge later," I said, then, I pushed out a breath, I readied myself and turned and stepped through the Bridge, my flying cache close behind. Hearing chuckles due to my timely pun drifting behind me.

Chapter 26 - BK's in the house

I stood in the middle of the woods, after crossing dimensions all the way to +132 South. My new rifle slung behind my back crossing from my left shoulder. The goodies Mix provided hovering nearby. (I really hoped there was going to be no need for the gun here, but I was not taking any chances not carrying it at this point, and it wouldn't fit in the Cargo drone.)

I was surrounded by nothing but forest. Damp, moss-covered trees were all around, some were laying down. Thickets of prickers created annoying fencing throughout. Birds sang, bugs burped, ticks probably attached to my pants silently. It was peaceful.

"Brooklyn, let me know as soon as you can locate them," I said. "Also, where the heck am I?"

"Working on it, Max. I'm pinging out in all the directions I can, across all the channels I can find. The disruptions in +137 somehow changed the stored MAC addresses for our comm units," Brooklyn said. "And you are still in Connecticut, in the middle of the Wyantenock State Forest."

"Great," I said. "I don't suppose an auto-auto can pick me up here?"

"Nothing can get here, but if you walk a few miles southeast to the road, I'll have one waiting for you," Brooklyn said.

"That's not too bad," I said.

I pulled my handheld out and charted a route to the closest trail. I started to navigate around in a zig-zag pattern until I could reach the trail and move more swiftly. Forty minutes later I was approaching a lonely road, where my auto-auto was waiting. I climbed inside and settled back in the chair. Letting out a long breath. I watched the light passing through the trees causing them to appear to dance, like I was staring at a flip book. When we came to the highway, my trance was broken.

Not many other vehicles were around, but I did see a couple cruising normally, so that was a good sign I most likely wasn't in an apocalyptic world any longer. "Anything yet, Brooklyn?" I asked. "I haven't found anything yet, Max," Brooklyn said. "Since it's been five years and four months, the scent data is too old to be reliable."

"Okay. Then I have a crazy idea," I said. I pulled out my handheld and started to scroll through our drone inventory.

"Maybe that statement should scare me, but it does not," Brooklyn said. "What's your idea?"

"Let's scramble as many Surveillance drones and Bloodhound AI drones as we have. Across the freakin' planet if we must," I said vehemently.

"I see the last count was two hundred and twenty-five that were ready in standby in +3 South."

"There are four hundred and fifty now," Brooklyn said.

"Send them all," I said.

"Done," Brooklyn said.

"They are initiating launch protocols and will be filing into this dimension in sets of ten. They are in Pennsylvania, so it will take time for them to spread out. We should have more data in a few hours."

"Thank you," I said and rested my head back against the seatback. "Let's just head that direction. It's the last relative location we know they were in."

"Already are," Brooklyn said.

"Awesome," I said.

"I can't believe this happened again."

"You can't believe what exactly?" Brooklyn asked. I'm sure she could have attempted a guess, but she was humoring my emotions.

"I can't believe I keep losing people like this," I said, leaning my head against the window while looking outside. "It's not like people die in front of me. They just disappear." Brooklyn didn't respond. I was glad. Then I closed my eyes to try to rest for a bit.

"Max. I have detected a trace of Tabitha's scent," Brooklyn said, somewhat gently in my ear. I opened my eyes and sat forward.

"Where?" I asked, looking around outside to see if I could figure out where we were. I checked my watch and saw that two hours had passed. We were still cruising along on the highway, and

I was pleasantly surprised to see we were passing through a populated city, and plenty of other living beings were around.

"I have found a sweatshirt with her scent in a safehouse," Brooklyn reported. "But there is no sign of Tabitha, or the others."

"Okay," I said. "Keep scanning for them."

"Max, I sent in a Cloaked Spider, and it recovered broken pieces on a table.

They appear to be from a Draw Bridge. There's a microchip among the pieces," Brooklyn said. "I'm attempting to connect to it now."

"I'm pulling up the footage now from the Cloaked Spider," I said, flipping quickly through my handheld at the footage, and I could see in real time the Draw Bridge pieces it was holding. There was no sign of the pendant.

"The pendant isn't there," I said out loud. "This could mean they are stuck here."

"I'm unable to connect to this chip at the moment," Brooklyn said. "But, I have found a camera in the room. Scanning the storage on those now."

A few moments of silence passed.

"I've identified that the recordings started roughly five years ago. It would have been about a week after they entered +132."

"Let's watch the first recording," I said.

Tabitha came into view as she backed away from the camera that was angling down from the ceiling. I could make out that the camera was in the basement and was placed closer to the stairway. The wide lens allowed for almost a full view of the basement, with precise quality in all directions.

Kel and Blaine stood a little further back from Tabitha.

"Okay. So, I guess this is a message for the future," Tabitha said and then grinned and looked back at the others. They laughed. "But seriously, Max. This is the situation. We are in +132 South, following your location scheme. We're not exactly sure how we ended up here, but when we crossed through the Bridge that suddenly opened, we were here."

"Yeah, no having to cross dimensions to get here," Kel said and moved closer to the camera and stood next to Tabitha. Blaine stepped forward as well, probably to not feel left out.

"It was weird," Tabitha said. "We're not sure how the Bridge opened, but suddenly it was there, and we were through it. Almost crashing into oncoming traffic."

"We were all screaming, and it was terrifying, yet it's comical now, I suppose, when I say it out loud," Blaine said. "And thankfully Tabitha got her senses quickly and steered us back into the right lane."

"Once we got our bearings," Tabitha said, "we were able to recognize that we were only a few miles from Blaine's garage. We headed there. It was empty and quiet, but we had no plan. I thought we should just try going back to +137 from there."

"I didn't think that was a good idea," Kel said. "We didn't know enough about why we were booted from there." Good. He thought like me.

"So, we came back to this safehouse," Blaine said, "and we're going to go back to +3 South where all the equipment is. Hoping that somewhere amongst all that stuff we can find out how to contact Dr. Zine."

The three looked solemnly amongst each other.

"I guess this will be like a diary for a Big Brother, Survivor, Living in Cell, insert any other old-fashioned reality TV show here, and we'll check in regularly," Tabitha said. "I think our AI systems are also listening, so check that too."

The clip ended.

"Can you assess the footage and see if they could use the Draw Bridge to leave before it broke?" I asked Brooklyn. I checked the map and saw we were still about forty minutes away from the safehouse.

"I have brought all the footage into the span and I'm scanning through it now. There is footage from the past five years, from multiple camera feeds, some continuously running," Brooklyn said, with a little bit of contempt in her voice. "This is going to take a little time to sift through... even for me."

"Roger that," I said. I didn't interrupt again, didn't let my impatience get to me.

I stared out the window and watched a living civilization thrive and started to think about what had happened in the past forty-eight hours.

"Could we open a feed with +10, so I can chat with Dr. Zine and Denny?" I asked. Maybe pushing my luck, but of course I knew Brooklyn could run concurrent tasks without digitally sweating.

"Channel open," Brooklyn said, as if distracted.

"Hey guys," I said into the comm.

"Hey there, buddy... long time," Denny spoke first.

"Hey, man," I returned. "I know... long time for you guys."

"How are you holding up, Max," Dr. Zine asked.

"You know, searching for lost friends. Same ish different day," I said with intentional dramatic overtones. "Have you looked over the data from +137 yet?"

"Can I just say...that place sounds insane. I can't believe the time difference is like five years," Denny said.

"But I bet you look so young now." I could hear his smile.

"Well, I guess I'm a time traveler now, so I can add that to my resume," I said. "Sorry, you want to video chat, now?"

"No need, Max," Dr. Zine said.

"Indeed, Marty McFly," Denny said. "We don't need to see you live. We have plenty of video of you, so I'm sick of lookin' at ya." I laughed out loud.

"Thanks, Denny," I said. "For always being able to cheer me up."

"I got your back," Denny said. "Max, I have looked at the data. I've very thoroughly gone over the earlier data but have only had the data on that weapon for a few weeks," Dr. Zine said at the natural pause. "If that weapon is, in fact, destroying neighboring universes, then it is more powerful than anything I could have imagined. I believe that Dr. Zine of +137 is going to be our best resource to help stop it."

"It sounded terrifying when I heard about it," I said.

"How the heck are we even going to stop something like that though? +137 Dr. Zine said they needed me to help stop it."

"That I'm unsure of, Max," Dr. Zine said, and I could hear defeat in his voice. "We'll need to understand the weapon better to assess the proper strategy to stop it. It is possible you hold the key somehow, but I'm not certain in what way."

"Max, I found some footage you should see right away," Brooklyn interrupted the comm. "I've loaded it on your handheld."

"Okay," I said.

"This sounds interesting," Denny said. "I'm glad we're here in 'real time' and not waiting months to see this."

"I've marked the file 'important' in the video feed folder on the Span with synced playback," Brooklyn said. "So you and Dr. Zine can watch as well."

"Let's see it," I said.

Tabitha, Kel and Blaine stood in the barn near Blaine's garage. The feed showed the data about the dimension in text in the bottom corner. Courtesy of Brooklyn's awesome video processing skills. It read +132 South. Kel looked strange with fabric slung around one shoulder and running across the front of his body to his opposite side.

There was a small bulge at his pectoral area. The feed changed angles, and I could see the bulge was a baby. My heart sank.

"Are you sure you're okay going through first, Blaine?" Tabitha asked with concern lacing her face.

"Hey, we all agreed to honor the straws, and I drew the short one," Blaine said with a wink. Tabitha and Kel looked at each other and then nodded. "Guys, we've been over the plan several times. I'm going to +137 to find Max." The phrase echoed in my ears: to find Max.

Blaine turned and raised the Draw Bridge to dial up a dimension, ready to open the Bridge, but paused and turned back. She walked back to Kel and leaned in and kissed the baby on its forehead. Then kissed Kel on the lips. Tabitha smiled and looked away briefly.

"If anything happens, it's up to you to take care of little BK," Blaine said with a smile. Kel did not return the smile.

"I love you," Kel said and looked down at BK and cradled the back of his head from the outside of the makeshift baby sling. Blaine nodded gently at Kel and then at Tabitha, who returned the nod, and then she looked at BK one last time and turned. Blaine opened the Bridge and stepped through.

The next few seconds were challenging to watch.

From the other side of the Bridge, we could see electrical flashes and dark spots forming. It almost looked like well-defined square black pixels were forming in different areas behind Blaine. She turned to rush back through, but then her arm vanished. Her other arm, the one holding the Draw Bridge, still existed and she quickly tossed the Draw Bridge back through the Bridge to the floor of the barn. Then her right foot vanished. She wasn't screaming in pain, like it looked like she should be, but she was glancing with massive confusion at the missing extremities. Staring at where the parts of her body that disappeared from existence should have been. Her other foot was gone, then both her legs. She didn't fall or sink downwards. She was just disintegrating. Tabitha and Kel watched in horror, not processing what was happening.

When Kel finally did think to move forward, Tabitha stepped in front of him and hugged him and turned him, as gently as she could, to protect him and the baby. Blaine quickly disappeared from existence and then the Bridge followed the same fate, with it vanishing in sections until nothing was left but the heavy air of stunned silence. Tabitha released Kel, who was forcing himself out of the hug. He stepped to where the Bridge was and looked down. He leaned down carefully and scooped up the Draw Bridge. He quickly dropped it and stood and shook his hand as if it burned him.

"Why is that so cold?" Kel asked. Tabitha shook her head. He fell into a dazed stare at the Draw Bridge.

"What. Just. Happened?" Kel asked. "I don't know," Tabitha said.

"Is Blaine dead?" Kel asked and looked down at his baby who was sleeping quietly.

"I don't know, Kel," Tabitha said. "I know as much as you." Kel wanted to scream, but didn't want to startle BK.

"We need to open the Bridge again and find her," Kel said after a few moments.

"I don't think we can," Tabitha said. "It looked like something destroyed the Bridge from the other side."

"We have to try," Kel said and gently slipped the baby sling from his body and handed BK to Tabitha. She took him and cradled him. Kel leaned down and rushed a touch of the Draw Bridge and snapped his arm back. "It's not freezing anymore."

Kel lifted the Draw Bridge and stood. He looked back at Tabitha.

"Maybe step back a bit," Kel said. Tabitha did.

Kel pressed the button to open the Bridge.

Static crackled in the air and a glow snapped in and out of existence, but no Bridge appeared. He tried again a few more times with the same result. Kel lowered his hand and stared at the empty space for several seconds. Then he changed the dimensional position from +133 South to +131 South. With a quick press he opened the Bridge. With glowing glory, it stood before him. Tabitha gasped from behind him and he turned to look at her. "It still works," Tabitha said.

"This dimension works apparently. It's not crumbling away from existence," Kel said, looking back at the Bridge and then closing it. A few seconds passed as he thought, crossing his arms with the Draw Bridge pressed into his armpit. He brought the Draw Bridge back in front of him and dialed +133 West and opened the Bridge. It glowed to life. (It was a good thing I upgraded Tabitha's Bridge before going to +137.)

Kel looked back at Tabitha again and shrugged. Then he stepped through. "Don't," Tabitha whispered and sucked in a breath. Kel stood on the other side and looked around inspecting the safehouse basement from that side. He held up his hands and looked at them. He inspected his feet. He looked back at Tabitha and shrugged and stepped back through the Bridge to +132 South. She released her breath.

He closed the Bridge behind him without looking back.

"That dimension seems fine, as well," Kel said evenly, almost apathetically. "I guess Blaine just picked the wrong one."

"I think there's more to it, Kel," Tabitha said and walked closer to him. He looked numb. She reached out and slowly took the Draw Bridge away and pocketed it.

"We should just try to connect with Dr. Zine as soon as we can." Kel gave a cheap nod and walked away and went out of view at the stairway. Tabitha watched and when he was out of sight, looked down at baby BK. She squatted to the floor and started to cry silently, cupping her mouth to silence herself.

Chapter 27 - Time for Some Action

"Blaine is gone..." I said out loud and stopped the video. Silence roared. "The interdimensional cancer is spreading," Denny said after a few seconds, not trying to layer humor for levity like he usually does, just saying out loud what we all were thinking. "It's all the way down to +133 South, and apparently deleted it." It was a heavy moment and lasted. "Are you able to locate Tabitha and Kel yet, Brooklyn?" I asked after I couldn't handle the silence any longer. "I found footage where Tabitha tells Kel she's going to Las Vegas to try to get another pendant," Brooklyn said. "It's the last time I see Tabitha in any of the footage."

"Let's see it," I said.

Kel sat on the basement couch feeding BK through a baby bottle. He had a spit-up cloth draped over his shoulder. Tabitha was at the workbench hovering over the Draw Bridge. The basement was pretty barebones; the couch and workbench were the only furniture. "I feel like we should make these things more durable," Tabitha said as she separated the Draw Bridge's front casing from the back.

"What happened exactly?" Kel asked. "Remember when you dropped it because it was so cold?" Tabitha asked. "Yeah, it felt colder than grabbing an ice cube," he said. "I think that somehow weakened the pendant and when you dropped it, it shattered," Tabitha said. "Oh. Crap," Kel said, slumping slightly. "Yep," Tabitha said. "So we're going to have to go get another one. Good thing Max told us where to go."

"Tabitha," Kel said, removing the bottle from BK's mouth and lowering his arm, "I'm not going to go with you. I can't do this anymore."

"Do what?" Tabitha asked, going to the couch to sit next to Kel. "I can't do this adventure stuff anymore," Kel said and looked down at BK. "I have to take care of him now."

"Oh," Tabitha said and grimaced and nodded. "I understand. But I can go, get the pendant, fix the Draw Bridge, come back and then take you wherever you want to go."

"Maybe I can just stay here," Kel said. "That might not be a good idea, Kel," Tabitha said. "What if this dimension is next to be erased?" Kel sighed and leaned his head back against the wall. "Okay. We'll wait for you to return and then you can take me back to +3, my dimension," Kel said, looking at Tabitha. "Definitely. That sounds good," Tabitha said and leaned to Kel and gave a side hug, and gently brushed the top of BK's head. BK was peacefully sleeping.

"I'll be back as fast as I can." Kel nodded. Tabitha rose and went to collect and scoop up the pieces of the Draw Bridge. She placed them all in a shoulder bag she had lifted from the floor. "I'll see you in a bit," Tabitha said and headed upstairs. "I will keep him safe, Blaine," Kel said after a few moments, looking at the location in the basement where he saw her last.

"I'm at the safehouse, guys," I said out loud as the auto-auto pulled into the driveway. The house looked exactly the same as the +3 South version: tan siding, single level, with nothing distinct about it, but quiet because it was in the middle of twenty secluded acres. Exactly what we needed. I had flipped my rifle around to in front of me to ready myself to sweep the house. "Hal, ready support," I said. "Ready," Brooklyn said. I headed to the back door and pushed it open and let my support fly through. The Cloaked Spiders had already done a sweep, and they were still idle in the basement, but I wasn't taking any chances. The kitchen looked clear, so I rushed through to the living room, then cleared the bedrooms and bathroom and all closets. There was no sign of anyone.

"It appears to be clear," I said, walking back into the kitchen. Craving some caffeine, I retrieved a mug from the cupboard and filled it with hot water from the dispenser near the sink. Then I grabbed a tea bag and dropped it into the mug to steep. "Maybe you're on edge, Max. I already had cleared the house," Brooklyn said. "Well, it's extra clear then," I said. "You missed something,

Max," Brooklyn said. I looked around the kitchen and looked towards the living room. I put the mug on the counter and walked to the living room. "Colder," Brooklyn said. "What?" I said. "You're getting colder," Brooklyn said. "Ah," I said and turned back towards the kitchen. "Warmer," Brooklyn said. Sometimes I forget she's always watching, because my drones are usually floating near me watching. I stepped into the kitchen. "Very warm," Brooklyn said.

I looked at one of the drones in the corner, giving her the stink eye. The drone floated forward and tipped towards the kitchen table and back to level two times. I looked to where it appeared to point. Finally, it was right in front of me, I noticed the hologram projector sitting right in the center of the kitchen table. "If that was a bomb, I'd be dead," I said. "Yep," Brooklyn said. I pressed the button on the side and Tabitha appeared in front of me. "Hello, Max," Tabitha said.

"I thought you might appreciate this, and now I appreciate your attempt a lot more." Tabitha winked. "You might have found the video recordings, but in case you didn't... I'm sorry to say, we lost Blaine," Tabitha said and paused and looked down for a moment. "Kel has their baby now. They named him BK." She paused again. "The Draw Bridge broke. The pendant shattered; seems to be the most vulnerable part.

You can see what happened in the video footage," Tabitha continued. "Thankfully you told us where to find replacements, so I'm headed there." Curious she didn't say where. She was very aware of protecting our secrets. I smiled. "Come find me," Tabitha said and then dissolved. I pressed another button on the hologram and displayed some metadata about the recording. She recorded it three days ago. "I can make some assumptions, but I'd guess she's close to Las Vegas Land by now. I need to get there fast," I said. "You can go by auto-air," Brooklyn said. "It's a calculated risk."

"I'm willing to take the risk. I don't have any more time. I need to get back to +137 as soon as possible to stop the destruction of the multiverse," I said. "Wow. That was a superhero speech, man," Denny said via the comm. I was caught up and almost forgot

Denny and Dr. Zine were still connected. "Yeah, well. I guess I have to be a hero now," I said. "Or at least fake till I make it."

"That's the spirit," Denny said with a titter. "Max," Dr. Zine said breaking the banter, "this universe you are in, +132 South, is fading."

"What?" I said, perking alert. "Am I about to dissolve?" I looked around and headed to the closest window to peek outside. Nothing looked to be dissolving. "It hasn't hit this area yet. It started on the other side of the world," Dr. Zine said. "I can see Australia is gone."

"How's that possible? Doesn't it happen fast? We saw Blaine wiped out quickly!" I said. "Yes, but that was probably because she had stepped through into the end of that universe," Dr. Zine said. "So, this thing moves slow?" I asked. "I'm only working with the information I have, and I can see that it's dissolving areas of this universe at a relatively slow pace," Dr. Zine said and paused briefly.

"I'd have to do out the calculations, but I'd guess..." he paused again, "you have less than twelve hours."

"Holy hell," I said.

"Brooklyn, how quickly can that auto-air be here?" I asked.

"It's en route. ETA fifteen minutes," Brooklyn said.

"Have you located Kel?" I asked.

"He's about to walk in the back door," Brooklyn said. I turned with a jolt and Kel walked into the kitchen.

"Kel!" I yelled. Kel jumped a little at the surprise.

"Hey," Kel said. He was carrying grocery bags, and had BK slung across his chest. "Can you help me with the groceries?"

"No time!" I said excitedly. His eyes grew.

"What?" Kel asked.

"This dimension is being erased," I said. Kel looked around and out the closest window, like I did. His shoulders relaxed a bit.

"Doesn't look to be," Kel said.

"It is. Dr. Zine just confirmed," I said. "We have twelve hours." Twelve Hours.

"Great," Kel said. "Send me back to +3 South."

"Send you back?" I asked.

"Yes," Kel said flatly.

"You don't want to go and help me save Tabitha?" I asked, not even thinking fully about the situation.

"Why?" Kel asked.

"I thought we were a team?" I asked. I was hurt.

"Not anymore," Kel said, lifting and dropping the bags on the table. "You probably know. Blaine is dead."

"I know. I'm sorry," I said with a frown.

"I have only one responsibility now," Kel said and looked down to gesture with his eyes to BK in a car seat, sucking gently on a pacifier.

"Okay," I said. I didn't have time to try to convince him of anything, and couldn't argue. It would nearly impossible to guarantee the safety of BK. I pulled out my Draw Bridge and aimed at the living room.

"Let's get you home," I said. Kel gave the hint of a smile. I crossed him back to +3 South, along with his groceries, and baby equipment. It took a couple of trips. I set him up with some resources, drones and mild weaponry just in case. I figured he'd be safe for a while, since the dimension eater was at least a few hundred dimensions away from him – for now.

"Good luck," Kel said and reached out to shake my hand. "I hope for BK's sake you can save us all."

"Wish him luck, from us, Max," Dr. Zine said.

"Dr. Zine and Denny wish you luck as well," I said. Kel nodded.

I shook his hand, smiled and left him to return to +132 South.

"I have some surprises for you," Brooklyn said after I was settled into the pilot seat in the front of the auto-air. Not that I would be flying, but it was a first-class view. The craft was small. It could fit six people comfortably. The outer skin was shiny and reflected its surroundings, since it was mostly made of photovoltaic cells to power it. The batteries were efficient enough to carry passengers' from coast to coast on one charge, and with clear skies, you could make it all the way back without skipping a beat. It had two sets of wings; the larger set was positioned at the back of the craft and those held the engines.

It was very sleek looking with its aerodynamic shape and was often called a flying chameleon. On a clear day you could see several hundred flying through the sky like air trains spaced out only a few hundred feet apart. Immediately after taking to the air Brooklyn took over the craft.

This alerted the Auto-Air Authority as soon as she did. I was a flying felon instantly. Good thing this wasn't my dimension. Hopefully the Max of this dimension could Bridge travel... not my concern at the moment. I'd help him later if necessary.

"What you got?" I asked.

"Oh, this should be good, tell me what she did," Denny said in my ear. "Dang, I wish I could see."

"Chill," I said. "Hey, I think I should concentrate. I'll dial you guys back in if I need you."

"Good idea, Max. Focus. Let us know what we can do, when you need it," Dr. Zine said, and a subtle tone indicated they were disconnected.

The auto-air shook and startled me, as I heard two loud metallic-sounding clomps hit the left and right sides of the craft.

"I've brought us some help to get us there faster," Brooklyn said. The auto-air accelerated and my head hit the seatback headrest. We doubled our speed instantly. I could see from the wing-view on the dashboard that two large silver tubes had attached to the craft.

"Dang," I said. "You have tricks up your sleeve." Brooklyn was improvising now.

Sentience was wild. I wasn't scared though – at least not yet.

"I have no shirt, Max, so no sleeves," Brooklyn said.

"Yes. Figure of speech," I said, rolling my eyes.

She dreams up this supersonic auto-air plan but doesn't know about the colloquialism.

"Don't roll your eyes, Max, they might get stuck that way," Brooklyn said. I just smirked.

"Were those modified drones?" I asked.

"Yes, some new ones I cooked up by modeling off of the drones we've been using to send up our satellites," Brooklyn said.

"Neat. I should probably look over our inventory to see what other cool stuff you've 'cooked up' recently," I said.

"Yes, yes you should," Brooklyn said.

"How long until we're there?" I asked.

"Two hours and twenty-one minutes," Brooklyn said.

"What's the best outcome after hijacking an auto-air?" I asked.

"The military has scrambled Velocity drones," Brooklyn said.

"Oh man, seriously?! What timing... but I have wanted to see those things up close for a while," I said. "Maybe not this way... but if that's the last thing I see. It'll be pretty cool."

The military's Velocity drones were legendary.

They were like giant black, supersonic, flying bullets (they kind of looked like slimmer Bullet Bills from Mario), that carried payloads of smaller black missiles. When those were not enough, they would turn kamikaze and finish off their targets.

"Max, I will do my best to maneuver our way to Las Vegas Land, but we should prepare an ejection plan," she said.

"Wait, what?" I asked, sitting up straight.

"As in, I might need to eject out of this auto-air?"

"That's a possibility. Velocity drones are the fastest and most weapons-heavy drones in existence," Brooklyn said. "It's best we prepare now."

"Okay..." I said. "I have the seat-chute connected to me already." Those are standard in auto-airs, but I haven't heard of anyone actually using one or needing one yet. Outside of test dummies, and those internet guys being stupid.

"I'm readying to use the Draw Bridge if it comes down to it," Brooklyn said. "I can open a Bridge to move you to safety."

"Ok..." I said. "How would that work in the air?"

"Let's hope we don't have to do that," Brooklyn said, and I swore I heard her say that while smiling.

"Yes... let's," I said. "Hey, do we have Bloodhound AI drones out ahead of us searching for Tabitha?"

"Yes, Max," Brooklyn said. "They are searching now."

"Thanks," I said. "How much longer?"

"You're welcome," Brooklyn said. "Two hours and ten minutes."

"Ugh, only ten minutes passed," I said, then mumbled under my breath, "are we there yet." In no time an hour and a half passed with no sign of the Velocity drones. Then we cruised over Oklahoma City and two appeared.

"They have caught up to us, Max," Brooklyn said.

"Only two?" I asked. Two more appeared. "I jinxed us," I said.

Brooklyn had changed the screen on the auto-air's dashboard screen, so I could see the drones relative to our craft. They were in two-by-two patterns to the left and right of us, trailing only slightly.

A voice suddenly came through the speakers inside the cabin. "This is USAF Commander Marks, please respond in acknowledgement," the voice said. I just stared at the screen.

"I don't want to engage," I said.

"You don't have to," Brooklyn said. "I'm about to try to lose these tails."

I looked up in a quick thought to try to figure out what phrase she was trying to replicate, then was jerked violently to the left when the auto-air spun to its side and dropped down five thousand feet in seconds.

"Broooo...kkkll...lllyy...nnnn," I said, trying to say her name while hanging on for my life and trying to hold back vomit.

"Hang on, Max," Brooklyn said, and the craft spun right and dropped further down.

Tears were welling in my eyes, and I was gripping the cross-chest seatbelt straps tightly like I was on a land-based roller-coast (sky-based ones were pressurized pods to hold you in place). I could see the Velocity drones twisting and flying and turning to try to realign with our craft. Then the auto-air shot straight up into the sky, and I felt my teeth squeezing together in my mouth causing an awkward *Chandler* smile.

Two more drones appeared on the screen, but they headed towards two of the Velocity drones and the four vanished from the screen in a flash.

"Got two," Brooklyn said. I couldn't talk yet. The auto-air leveled back out and I just watched the screen. Two more drones appeared and took the remaining two Velocity drones to their fate. The screen was clear.

"That wasn't too hard," Brooklyn said. "We should be there very soon now."

"Wow. Okay," I said, trying to will my head to steady. I rested my head back and tried to relax and mentally prepare for the next part of the adventure.

We had no other trouble until we hit the outer limits of Las Vegas Land. Ten Velocity drones swarmed our craft and started firing missiles. The craft started with evasive maneuvers.

"It's looking like I'm going to have to do that ejection plan, huh," I stated.

"Yes," Brooklyn said.

"How's this going to work?" I asked, fearing any response, fearing any scenario.

"I'm flying us towards the buildings, so you can jump from the plane to the roof of one," Brooklyn said, with zero humanity in her voice. I wished for a second that she had legs and realized what she was saying.

"I'm going to fall from the sky onto a building??" I asked emphatically. "Seriously? Your plan is to let me fall from the sky?"

"Do you trust me, Max?" Brooklyn asked. This was the first time she's ever asked me this. I paused and thought about it.

"Yes. I trust you," I said after a moment.

The sound of a piano started playing music through the speakers.

"What the hell?" I said. Brooklyn didn't respond. The music continued as the auto-air flew towards downtown at super speed, twisting and turning and dodging missiles.

Then the words from a familiar song came through the speakers. "Seriously!?" I yelled.

"You put on 'Don't Let Me Fall' by B.o.B? Now! Right now! You thought it was a good time?" The music continued and Brooklyn didn't respond. I just watched the firefight going on outside the craft as missiles exploded into drones that Brooklyn had scrambled.

I watched in shock.

We closed in on the skyscrapers and a missile finally clipped one of the wings. The song's hook "don't let me fall" echoed.

"Get ready, Max," Brooklyn said. The floor of the auto-air suddenly had a hole, where a Bridge appeared, and I was falling out of the craft.

My hands involuntarily flew up as I dropped. I could hear an explosion above me, but the Bridge closed and snapped the sound out of existence. The next thing I knew I was splashing into a rooftop pool and scrambling to get my head above water. Once I reached air again, I swam to the edge and pulled myself out. The poolside spectators were screaming. A woman instinctively moved to help me out of the water, then realized how insane it was and moved away quickly like I was suddenly radioactive.

I did a shake like a wet dog and took my hat off to shake off the water. Good thing I had waterproof lining for all my pockets in my coat and pants, but I was a little mad about my hat. The Cargo drone returned to floating above my head and I looked up at it and then towards where I fell from.

"Seriously," I said. "A pool. I didn't even get to use my parachute!"

"I had to work with what I had at my disposal," Brooklyn said in my ear, zero remorse in her tone. "Head downstairs quickly."

I didn't hesitate as this shook me back to the moment. As quick as I could, I went down the stairs, all twenty floors worth. When I burst out onto the sidewalk in front of the building I got more shocked looks.

"Where am I going?" I asked, looking around. Just then the Bridge opened. "Right through there," Brooklyn said.

"Okay. Breaking all the rules today," I said and rushed through.

I received mirrored shock on the other side, but just started running down the sidewalk as the Bridge snapped closed behind me. I could hear a cacophony of sirens echoing in all directions.

I looked around and didn't see any emergency vehicles in the near vicinity.

"The auto-air debris crashed into several buildings and landed on some pedestrians on the street below. It's chaos right now in several areas," Brooklyn said matter-of-factly. "This will be good cover for you. Head east down Batman Boulevard." (Yep.) I followed the direction in a sprint. My coat flapping awkwardly due to the retained water.

"The blind lady's shop is about a mile from here," Brooklyn said. I followed her directions, and after a couple lefts and rights, I was at the front door. Tabitha was staring at me from the inside, through the glass of the front door.

Chapter 28 - Pendants

"Took you long enough," Tabitha said as she embraced me and kissed me on the lips with full action. After about a minute of kissing, I heard the blind lady clear her throat.

"I've met your friend," Tabitha said and took me by the hand to the counter.

"Hello, again," I said with a smile, then a frown. "Although, err, I haven't met you specifically." I wondered if her name was still Yukim, but didn't want to waste time asking.

The blind lady smiled but stayed quiet.

"She just told me something very interesting," Tabitha said to break the awkward silence.

"What's that?" I asked.

"We can destroy the world-eating weapon by altering the pendants," Tabitha said with a big grin. Woah. I didn't react right away, but so much was said with that little statement.

Tabitha talked to this lady about the weapon. Maybe about the pendants; maybe about the Bridge.

"How much did you tell her?" I asked.

"Just enough," Tabitha said with a wink. "Don't worry. Sometimes we need to ask for help." I grimaced slightly.

"Okay... so how?" I asked, looking between Tabitha and the blind woman.

"May I have one of your pendants," the blind lady asked, reaching out her hand to me. I looked at Tabitha with concern and she smiled and shrugged and mouthed 'it's okay' to me. I did as I was asked. I pulled out my backup pendant from my pocket and handed it to the blind lady. She held up my pendant along with a pendant of her own.

And acted like she was a magician teasing before a trick and placed them on the counter. It was amazing how precise she was with her movements. She took out a cigar cutter from a drawer behind the counter. With flair she picked up one pendant and showed it to us and then slid it into the cigar cutter. She was definitely adding entertainment value to this little show.

Then she snapped the pendant cleanly into two halves. After one side of the cut pendant dropped to the counter, she placed the other side off to the right. She picked up the other pendant and performed the same trick. This time she retained the opposite half from before. From the drawer she retrieved a small torch lighter.

"When we bring together two opposites, we create a negative energy to destroy the positive input, or the other way around," the blind lady said.

"Say what?" I asked, staring at the pendants in her hand. She proceeded to hold the two pendants pressed together by pinching each end and fired up the torch lighter and ran it under the middle of the pendants.

I heard a sizzle as she spun them and suddenly, they were one pendant again. The blind lady then heated the tip of a fat needle and poked it easily through one end of the newly formed pendant.

She then threaded a leather cord through and tied it off to form a necklace. The blind lady repeated the process with the two positive ends next.

"They fused together, the similar sides?" I asked.

"Yes," she said.

"And these 'new' pendants will destroy the weapon?" I asked.

"Yes," she said.

"How?" I asked. "And which one?"

"I already explained," she said.

"When?" I asked. The blind lady sighed gently.

"Max, she explained to me before," Tabitha said, tapping my arm lightly and smirking.

"Okay... can you re-explain, please?" I asked.

"Yes," Tabitha said. "Because this is the second time I've heard this. Let me say it back to see if I got it right this time. By breaking the pendants in half, and taking each opposite side and fusing them together, you've created one fully negative pendant, and one fully positive. Did I get that right?"

"Yes," the blind woman said. "Fully negative will implode, while fully positive will explode." Tabitha crossed her arms and leaned very cockily and smiled.

"Ah. I see..." I said. I really didn't, but would need to lean on Tabitha. "And we just replace one of these with the other pendant in the weapon and, it, what, destroys itself?"

"Yes," the blind woman said.

"Alright," I said. "We don't have a lot of time, so I hope you're right." I reached out to take the pendants from the blind lady's hand, but she pulled it back as I got close to it. "May I please have the pendants?" I asked with a verbal eyeroll.

"I'll play you for it," the blind lady said. My jaw hung.

"Are you kidding me?" I asked. "The fate of the multiverse is..."

"She's joking, Max," Tabitha said and reached out to the blind lady's hand with her hand cupped palm up. The blind lady lowered the pendants into Tabitha's hand and smiled at me. I certainly felt like I was being played, but could never prove it, and didn't have the time. Tabitha put the fully positive one around her neck and then handed me the other one. I noticed the one she handed me was slightly darker.

"Great. Thank you," I said.

"We should probably go save the multiverse now."

"This universe cannot be saved," the blind lady said. "It is already too late. You must hurry to leave. The end is near. Bye bye."

That's when the screams started outside.

"I thought we had twelve hours, Hal?" I asked Brooklyn out loud.

"It's been almost three hours since that forecast, but it appears that the interdimensional cancer has spread faster than calculated," Brooklyn said with concern in her voice. "That or..." she trailed off and paused. "No, it wasn't linear. It didn't spread from one origin. Broken Bridges are popping up all around the world and effectively sucking the life out of this dimension."

"Time to go," I said, tapping Tabitha's arm and heading for the door. "Thank you, mysterious blind lady," I said, projecting my voice backwards.

"Yes, thank you so much," Tabitha said from behind me.

"You two are powerful like the pendants. Stay close together and you'll be stronger," the blind lady said, and I looked at Tabitha, who was narrowing her eyes playfully and smiled, then we headed out the front door of the shop into the chaos.

Sirens echoed from every direction. We headed left towards the east and faced a throng of people rushing away from something we couldn't see. I grabbed Tabitha's hand and moved us closer to the building and forced our way up the block.

"Hal, what's the situation?" I asked Brooklyn.

"There's a major pileup ahead, and several vehicles crashed into the buildings up the block," Brooklyn reported. "People are fleeing the area."

"How? Were there vehicles other than auto-autos?" I asked.

"They were all auto-autos," Brooklyn said. That was odd. We didn't have many accidents anymore since the auto-autos governed driving. Very motivated people (or ones with sophisticated AI like mine) could override the auto-auto controls, but it often wasn't worth the consequences.

I imagined the only way it would be necessary is if people were panicking and trying to rush out of the city.

"Look," Tabitha pulled at my sleeve and pointed up at a large screen on the front of a building. It was normally just running ads, but a news station broadcast was airing now.

Reports from around the world are stating some unknown force is tearing apart the fabric of reality as we know it. People are being dissolved before our eyes. Property damage is incalculable. In London, we saw the London Bridge as the epicenter in that region; nothing remains of that city now. Boston Times Square was dissolved in a matter of minutes. This very well could be the end as we...

The broadcast went to static.

"Do you have your comm still in?" I asked Tabitha as I turned to her.

"Yes," Tabitha said.

"Hal, pipe in Tabitha to my comm, please," I requested.

"Done," Brooklyn said.

"Nice to see you again Tabitha."

"Missed ya, Hal," Tabitha said. "Do you know what all this craziness is about?"

"This world is being destroyed by the weapon from +137. It has started to tear apart this dimension everywhere. At first it started on the other side of the planet, but then the Broken Bridges started to pop up all over. Wherever they materialize, they start to rip apart everything in their path," Brooklyn said. "Las Vegas Land has just been hit on the far side of the city."

"We need to get out of here as soon as possible then," I said. "I'll open a Bridge right now. It doesn't matter who sees." I pulled out my Draw Bridge and dialed up +133 South then paused. "+133 South doesn't exist anymore..." I said out loud. "We don't know if other directions were affected. How are we going to get to +137?" I had always had a solid handle on Bridge travel. Even with the madness of being in +137, I still felt relatively in control. Not knowing if I could go up dimensions was making me anxious now, however.

"Is there a way to go up dimensions, Hal?" I asked Brooklyn.

"You are correct, you can't go to +133 South," Brooklyn responded. "And you two will need to exit this dimension very quickly now. Our Surveillance drones are spotting large sections near here dissolving rapidly."

"Great," I said. "How much time do we have?"

"Roughly, ten minutes," Brooklyn said.

"What do we do, Hal?" Tabitha asked with a tinge of panic in her voice. She leaned in close to me and gripped my arm.

"You won't be able to open the Bridge here, due to the pull from the Broken Bridges. You are too close," Brooklyn said. I noticed all the people were gone now and we were standing alone on the sidewalk. An auto-auto very sloppily pulled up next to us, partially on the sidewalk. "Get in," Brooklyn said.

Tabitha and I didn't hesitate. The auto-auto sped away and we looked behind us to watch the chaos in the sky through the back windshield. The tops of the skyscrapers were being sucked into blackness.

Fragments were flying everywhere like an invisible tornado was sweeping through the city. We were racing away quickly, but it didn't seem fast enough.

"Brooklyn, can you get us an auto-air? Maybe from the nearby airport?" I asked. "There is one on the way," Brooklyn said. "You'll meet it in one minute." Tabitha and I both looked from the chaos to the front windshield.

We saw the auto-air come into view twenty feet ahead of us and begin to hover briefly, before lowering itself to a few feet above the ground. I now saw several people running towards it.

"We have to get to it fast," I said. I opened the auto-auto door, grabbed Tabitha's hand and we raced to the auto-air.

The people were clustering below the auto-air and two men were trying fruitlessly to jump and grab the footrest below the entry door. I let go of Tabitha's hand and flipped my rifle in front of me.

"Back away!" I yelled out.

The group of people suddenly looked scared. None of them had weapons. The two men that appeared to be leading the group, turned towards me with angry faces.

"Now! Back away!" Some of the group started to back away, women who were protecting children grabbed the children and ushered them away. The last to move were the two men, who had apparently just noticed the large drone hovering above us, since one pointed at it. I moved closer to the auto-air and Tabitha was close behind.

"Are we going to just leave them here?" Tabitha whispered behind me.

"What can we do? We can't bring them to another dimension," I said.

"I know, but... it just feels immoral," Tabitha said.

"We'll have to figure out another way to save them," I said, but knew it wasn't likely.

"Okay..." Tabitha said.

"Hal, lower the auto-air," I requested as we approached the area just to the side of where it would lower to.

The auto-air started to lower, and I eyed the two men that hadn't quite moved far enough to make me comfortable. I pointed the rifle off to the left and up in the air and fired a shot. They jumped, Tabitha jumped, I jumped (I hadn't fired a gun in a long time), and they relinquished and turned to head to where the rest of the group had retreated to. The auto-air got to where we could climb in. The Cargo drone went in first and we followed suit quickly and were off into the sky in no time.

It was just quick enough, because the city was dissolving faster now.

"Let's go to +131 South and figure out our next steps," I said.

"I'll open a Bridge in the air," Brooklyn said.

"Sounds good," I said. We flew through dimensions and didn't even get to see +132 dissolve from existence.

"If we go to +131 West, and then go to +132 West because it's still there... maybe we can go to +133 West and all the way up to +137 then?" I asked out loud.

"We only have one way to find out unfortunately, Max, because the interdimensional communication channels are not showing any issues with that path yet," Brooklyn said. "I'm only now starting to get fail connection messages with other dimensions in that network. The cancer is spreading more rapidly now."

"This is bad, Max," Tabitha said. "All this time I've been traveling through the portals to other dimensions I've never really felt scared. I feel scared now." I reached my hand out and placed it on her shoulder and nodded.

"I'm feeling the same way," I said.

"Thanks for saying that," Tabitha said.

"Let's go fix this," I said. "Brooklyn, let's follow the path as far as we can."

The Bridge opened ahead of our auto-air (theoretically it was ours now, since the owners no longer existed), and we flew through to +131 West without issue.

"How's it looking, Brooklyn?" I asked.

"No concerns at this point," Brooklyn said.

"Let's go all the way then, baby!" I said. Tabitha smacked my shoulder and rolled her eyes.

"I mean to +137, chill." I smirked.

"Sure," Tabitha said with a matching smirk.

The Bridge opened again, and we continued our ambivalent journey.

We reached +136 West, and things started to get a little wobbly. The readings were that some Broken Bridges existed, but they were not spreading like in +132 South. This dimension wasn't being dissolved away, but Broken Bridges sat idle.

"Why isn't this dimension being destroyed?" Tabitha asked as we flew over an area where there was a large Broken Bridge open on the ground below. We could see a bend in the air, like light was having trouble with its identity around it.

"I don't know," I said. "But we should leave it, and not stick around to find out."

"Opening Bridge to +137 now," Brooklyn reported.

"You know, it could be a long time before we're back here," I said.

"What do you mean?" Tabitha asked.

"I mean, since time moves slower in +137, and the rate is one day for five years... a lot of time could pass while we're there," I said with a frown. "It might be a long time before we see anyone familiar." I paused. "I didn't get a chance to say goodbye to Dr. Zine or Denny."

"Do you want to before we go?" Tabitha asked.

"We don't have time," I said with a frown.

Tabitha just nodded.

And we crossed to +137.

Chapter 29 - Portal Wars

We crossed into the +137 air space above Las Vegas Land. Tabitha and I both looked out the windows on each side of the auto-air to try to see the city below. It looked terrible. Some of the buildings were crumbling from their pinnacles downwards. Spires were cracked. Windows were missing. We saw people in clusters near barrels with fire coming out.

"Brooklyn, can you take us lower and slow us down a little?" I asked.

"Yes, Max," Brooklyn said.

We circled the city a few times.

We could see encampments on the outskirts of the city, with tall razor wire topped fencing around the perimeter. We were near the largest one.

"Brooklyn, can you zoom in on that area down there?" I asked.

"You can see a close-up of the area on the screen now," Brooklyn reported, and Tabitha and I both turned to the center dashboard of the auto-air and could see the close-up of the area.

Maxes were at the guard posts, and it looked like they were protecting the people inside the fencing. Some children were playing soccer in an open area. Some adults and children were eating at picnic tables. It looked relatively calm. Until several SUVs kicking up dust and toting machine guns mounted to the rooftops came streaking towards the camp. We couldn't hear sounds from up here in the air, but the silent show still spoke volumes.

"Brooklyn, do we have any resources available to help?" I asked.

"No, Max," Brooklyn said.

"All our resources were left on the other side of the country." We were helpless. Maxes took up defensive positions and the armed SUVs opened fire. The civilians took cover as fast as they could, but some children and adults were hit with the gunfire and dropped to the ground. Several drones took to the air, flying out from a building inside the encampments and immediately took out half of the SUVs. Tabitha and I both cheered out loud as we watched, shifting from watching the screen to viewing the sad chaos from the windows. Brooklyn kept us steadily circling above the action and safely out of range of gunfire. With the drone support the tide quickly turned.

There was only one SUV left suddenly. One Max rushed to a sentry tower and aimed a large shoulder weapon. It was a rocket launcher. The last SUV exploded. The dust began to settle shortly after, and Tabitha and I breathed out a sigh almost in sync.

"Wow," Tabitha said. "That could have been so much worse." We both watched as people began to attend to the injured.

"Yes," I said. "But that was still bad. I think a few people died." We watched a little longer in silence.

"Is this happening all around this dimension?" I asked after a period of time passed.

"Yes, Max," Brooklyn said. "The MaxNet reports this is happening worldwide."

"Let's track down Dr. Zine. He'll still be at that camp with K and Mix," I said. "And let's head toward the east coast."

"Trying the connection now, Max," Brooklyn said. "I've been able to connect." Brooklyn was able to open a connection with Mix, based on instructions left on the MaxNet. We started to fly out towards the city limits of Las Vegas Land. Away from the sad shell of a city it had become.

"Hello, Max," Mix said. "Can you hear me okay?"

"Where are you?" Mix asked. As soon as we hit +137 our data from our Span synced out to MaxNet, but they would need more than a few seconds to parse through it though.

"We're in Las Vegas Land," I said.

"That's wild," Mix said. "It has been less than a minute since we last saw you and spoke with you. I'm expanding the channel on our side so you can speak with Dr. Zine and K as well."

"Thank you for returning, Max," Dr. Zine said.

"We're here to help," I said.

"Did you find your friends?" Dr. Zine asked.

"I found Tabitha and Kel," I said, then paused a second and looked at Tabitha with a frown. "We lost Blaine."

"I'm very sorry to hear that, Max," Dr. Zine said. "Are Tabitha and Kel with you?"

"I'm here, Dr. Zine," Tabitha spoke up from our group comm. "Just me though. Kel is back in +3 with his baby. Long story."

"I see. I'm sorry, Tabitha," Dr. Zine said.

"Thank you," Tabitha said.

"Let's stop this thing, so we don't lose anyone else we love."

"I know it hasn't been very long, but do you know where the weapon is yet?"

"We've been chasing a lead that it might be hidden inside the Hoover Dam, incidentally," Dr. Zine said. "It's quite fortuitous that you are nearby now."

"We're just a few minutes away from there," I said, looking at Tabitha with raised eyebrows.

"I see Brooklyn's report that you have a way to disable the weapon?" Mix asked.

"Yes. We have custom pendants that should do the trick," I said.

"That's great to hear," Dr. Zine said. "I'll go through the data Brooklyn uploaded to try to understand the customization. In the meantime, if you can head there now, we'll have our allies connect with you."

"My boy Rex is there now, heading up the team," K chimed in. "He'll help get you inside."

"Okay, we'll head there now," I said.

"We'll have to close this connection," Mix said, "to reduce the risk of unfriendly-ears listening in. Have Brooklyn indicate when you're there, and I'll send Rex to pick you two up." Brooklyn then closed the connection.

From the air we could see smoke billowing ahead of us for a few miles before we got close enough to see where it was coming from. Brooklyn brought the auto-air down closer to the ground to help hide our presence behind some large boulders.

"We should probably land away from the fighting and move on foot," I said.

"Maybe Rex has a vehicle to pick us up in?" Tabitha suggested.

"Hopefully," I said.

"Brooklyn, get Mix on the comm," I requested.

"Hey... (keerrrsh)... Max... (keerrrsh)," Mix said through broken communication waves.

"What's with the static, Brooklyn?" I asked.

"Jamming waves," Brooklyn said.

"Gotcha, we're very close," I said. "Is Rex nearby?"

"I let him know your location," Brooklyn said.

"Okay," I said.

"Yes... (keerrsh)... (skeeetch)," Mix said, then there was a loud screech that made Tabitha and me jump and the comm automatically cut off the connection before our eardrums burst.

"Ow," Tabitha said and cupped a hand over her right ear for a second.

"Does that mean he is on his way?" I asked.

"Rex will be here shortly," Brooklyn said.

With that she lowered the auto-air from the sky and landed us on the desert floor, a few miles from the action. As we exited the aircraft, a vehicle pulled up. It was a large, armored vehicle with six wheels.

A man, who I assumed was Rex, jumped out and headed up to us.

"Max, long time no see!" Rex said excitedly and approached to give me a fist bump. This must have been some Max humor, since we saw ourselves every day. He eyed Tabitha with a smirk.

"Which dimension are you from, Tabitha? I'm Rex." He pushed his fist forward for a bump with hers. Tabitha gave me a side glance and looked back at Rex and slowly bumped his fist.

"It's +3 South to Max over here, so not sure which one to you... Rex" Tabitha said with a raised eyebrow.

"Ah, gotcha, cool, cool, nice to meetcha," Rex said a little awkwardly. I wondered how long he had been in this dimension; he certainly was at least several years younger than I was due to the time dilation.

A large explosion could be heard in the distance. Tabitha and I flinched, but Rex was steady.

"What's the situation at the dam?" I asked, wondering how he was so calm.

"We've been tracking the weapons. They were inside the Hoover Dam. Bad Max had actually built two there. He was able to escape with one and head to the East Coast. Another team is tracking that one," Rex said. "We stopped them from moving the second one before they could escape though, and pinned them down, so they can't get out."

My eyes grew large at the thought of two of those weapons.

"Why here?" Tabitha asked.

"Because of the depth and the water surrounding it, it made it nearly impossible to trace it," Rex said. Tabitha and I nodded. "And all the powerline infrastructure came into play as well, to funnel enough energy. Of course, when the 'brain team' started to think of places to hide it, they found it."

Another loud explosion echoed.

"Should we go help?" I asked, eyeing the area the sound came from.

"Yes. Hop in," Rex said, turning and rushing to jump into the vehicle. Tabitha and I followed and climbed into the other side of the six-wheeler, with me taking the front seat like a gentleman (to protect her).

"Put on those gloves and boots. Mix cooked them up," Rex said, thumbing towards the back seat.

Tabitha and I looked at the items sitting in two piles on the seat.

"What do they do?" I asked.

"Some cool things, but mainly provide full body protection," Rex said. I was trying to wrap my head around how casually these guys referenced what I would consider advanced technology, and I helped make advanced technology.

They also did a poor job fully explaining things. Tabitha grabbed a pair of gloves and boots that quickly fit to her shape, then handed me the other pairs from the back seat. I slipped mine on and they fit perfectly. It was hard to not notice the electrical burst that ran from fingers to wrist and toes to ankles after I put them on.

I didn't feel any physical sensation, but innately knew they were scanning and adjusting somehow to my body.

"Hey," Tabitha said from the backseat, and I turned to look at her smiling and to check out her new gear. The gloves had turned a tangerine color. "I found some color settings."

"Yeah, that's the 'cool things' part I mentioned," Rex said, looking up in the rear-view mirror briefly. Tabitha had a big grin.

"Let's go!" Tabitha shouted, causing me to flinch and then smile. I shook my head. Rex raced us off to the battlefront.

As we approached the chaos of the firefight, we could see what looked like military troops lining the edge of the road that led across the bridge, which ran across the top of the dam. There were a lot of familiar faces, since they were like mine. Although, it was like seeing myself when flipping through a photo reel timeline across the years. Some were very young faces; I assumed those Maxes were led to +137 much sooner than I was. Some were just like mine now, weathered and much older, probably more recent versions. I wasn't even that old, but my travels aged me faster.

A rocket sailed past the six-wheeler, exploding somewhere behind us, and caused me to snap out of my facial evaluation.

"Woah," Tabitha said. "That was close."

"It's all good," Rex said. "The vehicle adjusted." I hadn't noticed. I needed to focus. "Okay. How do we get inside?" I asked.

"Hang on to your posteriors," Rex said and pressed a button on the dashboard touchscreen. Tabitha and I looked at each other and the six-wheeler accelerated. We gripped our seatbelts and pulled them tighter to our bodies. Tabitha started screaming as we went airborne. The vehicle crashed through a series of cement barriers the enemy placed in the road to slow us down. Troops from our side spun and recognized the vehicle and rushed to clear out of the way as we started down towards the welcome center.

The enemy troops were protecting the stronghold from the inside. The six-wheeler barely lost any speed as it blasted through bollards in front of the welcome center, as if they were made of paper, and plowed into the glass front doors. The six-wheeler abruptly got stuck and the three of us whiplashed forward against our seatbelts with audible 'ughs' from our throats. Dozens of drones exited the six-wheeler from outside compartments and immediately started to take out enemy troops.

The Max troops rushed in in formations that funneled through the opening we made and started to fan out and clear the remaining threats in the lobby. Rex forced his door open and popped out with a fluid motion of grabbing his rifle from the backseat floor and beginning to sweep his weapon to anywhere there was movement.

"Can you see any weapons in the back?" I asked after turning to Tabitha urgently. I lifted my rifle up, which I had put next to my leg when

I climbed into the six-wheeler.

"Oh my," Tabitha said, leaning back and climbing into the back.

"What?" I asked.

"Yeah, there's a butt load of guns," she said.

"Load up," I said and opened my door and stepped out carefully, holding my rifle at the ready. The cacophony of warfare sounds had dulled and turned more distant. I backed up slowly and opened Tabitha's door to use it for cover, backing into the protected space it created.

"Ready?" I asked.

"Ready for some action," Tabitha said and used her hand to nudge me forward to let me know she was stepping out. We stood side-by-side, rifles raised.

"Rex!" I shouted out.

"Max," Rex shouted back, but I couldn't tell from where, because of the way the room bounced sounds.

"Where are you?" I asked.

"Right here," Rex said as he crossed in front of the six-wheeler towards us.

"You could have asked me where he was, Max," Brooklyn chimed in in my ear.

"Yes. I know," I said out loud directed at Brooklyn.

"Know what?" Rex said, then realized, "Ah yes, talking to your AI."

"Yes, you *should* be talking to your AI, Max," Brooklyn said with snark in my ear.

"Okay. Let's all open a channel, so we don't have issues," I said.

Wondering how we didn't just do this in the first place. But things were moving fast.

"Let's get to the weapon and stop it."

"Follow me," Rex said without hesitation. We carefully swept our rifles around the area as we moved close together up to an elevator bank.

"This is where it's going to get interesting," Rex said. He pulled out his handheld and pressed a few times on the screen and one of the elevator doors opened. "Here we go." Rex stepped in first, then I heard a rush of buzzing as two dozen drones flew forward and over my head and a dozen flew into the elevator with Rex.

The other dozen held hovering above Tabitha and me, joining our one Cargo drone that was much larger. The other elevator door then opened, and they flew in.

"You two take that one," Rex said. "We don't want all the eggs in one basket." I nodded to Rex as the door closed and I could see through a slight sliver that the elevator had slipped down into the earth. I sucked in air to take a deep breath, and then released. Tabitha placed her free hand on my back.

"Are you okay?" Tabitha asked.

"I'm good. Just preparing myself to end this," I said. "Time for the ride of our lives."

I winked and entered the elevator. Tabitha followed, smirking and shaking her head at the cheesy hero line. The drones crammed above our heads. I pressed the button for the lowermost level. The doors closed and we dropped smoothly into the earth. After forty-five seconds we began to hear the faint echo of gunshots. Then they became louder. We both flinched at the pops, but readied ourselves, as we reached the bottom, and the doors opened. Immediately we saw a couple Maxes in fatigues, and they were startled to see us.

They turned their weapons at us, and I fired rapidly at two, and Tabitha followed suit and dropped the other Max. The fighting drones filed out after and flew off ahead.

"Oh no," Tabitha said. "Crap, crap, crap," she said with more panic.

"I just killed you, killed a Max, a version of you!"

"It's okay," I said. "He was about to fire at us." Tabitha wasn't satisfied with my response.

"If he was a good one, and was on our side, he would have lowered his weapon and told us," I said, trying to reassure her as much as myself.

"Okay..." Tabitha said. I didn't wait for more concerns and stepped out of the elevator carefully, sweeping my rifle left at the wall and then right towards the hallway.

"Rex, where are you?" I asked.

"Just down the hall from the elevators," Rex said in my ear. More gunfire rang out. Crashing, tinging sounds echoed, most likely from drone-on-drone combat. I took off running towards the sounds.

Tabitha was close behind. We turned a corner, and bullets whizzed by causing us to jump back to the protection of the other side of the corner. I peeked carefully to look for Rex. I could see him lying on the ground unconscious.

"Rex, are you okay?" I asked urgently. There was no response. I tapped Tabitha and pointed for her to take a quick look.

"Oh no," Tabitha said. "He isn't moving."

"Can you try to cover me from here?" I asked. I wasn't military trained but had many hours in the simulator.

I was about to see how equivalent the training was. I crouched and readied my rifle and used the wall to guide me down the corridor towards Rex. Gunfire started again, and I dropped to the ground and started to crawl as Tabitha returned shots to distract the shooters.

"Since you seemed to have forgotten again... I'm sending you some help," Brooklyn said over the comm, loaded with the dramatic pause and everything. A few drones provided some air cover. I got close to Rex and put my hand on his shoulder to shake him. The firing was sporadic, and Tabitha returned shots, the drones returned shots.

Rex's body rippled with electricity from his gloves to his boots and a shell casing slid from the side of his neck. Rex shuddered and popped up, gripping his rifle, then got into a crouch and readied himself to continue.

"Hey, Rex? You okay?" I asked. Rex flinched and turned to me.

"Max!" Rex shouted and it echoed through the corridor.

The gunfire stopped all together.

"Crap."

"What?" I asked.

"I just let them know you're here," Rex said with a slight slump. "Dang it." Rex stood up and pressed his eyes with his finger and thumb.

"Let who know?" I asked.

"The bad guys," Rex said.

"Oh, ha," I said. I looked forward and could no longer see any sign of the bad guys ahead of us.

"Why would it matter?"

"There is no one that goes by Max on our side, other than you, and they know this," Rex said. "Any Max that joined our effort changed to go by a nickname. Out of respect for you."

"Really?" I asked.

"Yes," Rex said. "And maybe slightly out of fear. On the other side, Bad Max forces any Max that joins his effort to change their names."

"What's with my name?" I asked.

"When they've heard it, they would know when you arrived in this dimension," Rex said. "Now they know."

"But, why?" I asked. These people were confusing AF. "That still doesn't help me understand my importance."

"You still don't get it," Rex said. "You're the One, like in the Matrix. The Special, like in the Lego Movie. The only, like in the Kliffsbury Saga. You are Max Prime, the only person that has the power to cut off the branches. Because of you and your pendant. The combination of both." I just looked at Rex blankly. He sighed.

"You see that the bad guys stopped shooting as soon as they heard your name, they left, because Bad Max needs you. He needs you to be in the home dimension when he activates the weapon. Those guys are running to alert him," Rex said. "If Bad Max can get the weapon back to your dimension, with you in it, then he can affect all the branches, in all directions, and effectively become the new Prime Max when new branches are formed. He can also erase all of us. Then it would be just you and him left. Until he kills you, so he can become the new Max Prime."

"Holy hell," Tabitha said as she came up to us. I looked back at her then back to Rex.

"But we can stop the weapon," I said. "We have the pendants."

"What does that mean?" Rex asked with a confused look. It felt good to not be the only confused one now.

"It just means we know how to stop the weapon," I said. "And we should probably do that now." I started to walk away.

"Max," Rex said, grabbing my arm. "Since we only have one of the weapons here. We were actually going to confirm that and then destroy the dam and bury it inside here."

"What?!" Tabitha exclaimed. "That would be devastating, to a lot of people."

"We didn't think we'd have a choice," Rex said.

"But now you do," I said and pulled away from his grip. We all started walking down the corridor.

"What's the plan though?" Tabitha asked from behind Rex, who was behind me.

"I don't know, I guess I'll just shove the pendant into the weapon's pendant slot, and activate it and then it destroys it...?" I said without turning around.

"Wait, you don't even know?" Rex asked. I stopped and turned around.

"No. There isn't exactly a manual for shutting down a multiverse-destroying weapon," I said, gesturing towards Rex with open palms. "Do you know how?"

"No. I just told you our plan was to bury it," Rex said with a grimace.

"Okay, hold on guys," Tabitha said. "Let's take a beat and come up with an actual plan."

"Didn't blind lady say we use the pendant to destroy the weapon?" I asked, looking at Tabitha.

"She didn't say that specifically..." Tabitha said. I pursed my lips and didn't know how to respond. The blind lady's words drifted through my mind: *Fully negative will implode, while fully positive will explode.* Using the weapon with one of the special pendants had to be the key. But maybe she wasn't talking about destroying the weapon.

Maybe she was talking about destroying the dimension the weapon is in... If I were to speculate, I could guess that using the negative pendant would erase all the dimensions created as branches off of the dimension the weapon was in, because it would implode them. I didn't know what "exploding" could mean though. Maybe expanding and creating new dimensions simultaneously? There were two weapons. Could the blind lady have known this? Was the intention to implode all the dimensions, and then recreate them? Too many questions.

"I think the way to destroy the weapon, is to destroy the dimension it is in," I said calmly. Tabitha and Rex looked at each other and then at me in silence.

"You're suggesting destroying this dimension?" Rex finally said after a few seconds.

"Yes," I said. "I think that's what the blind lady was trying to tell us." I looked at Tabitha.

"She said negative imploded," Tabitha said.

"Exactly," I said. "Implode this dimension with the weapon in it. Destroy it."

"What about the other weapon?" Rex asked.

"Yes, well. If we implode this dimension with that one still in it, it will destroy that one as well," I said.

"Yeah, along with us," Rex said. "K, Mix, Dr. Zine..."

"Yes," I said. "We can try to evacuate everyone first."

"I guess so..." Rex said, looking down at the ground.

"But… we can't be here when we activate the weapon. We need to do it from the dimension before this one," I said. "So, we can go to +136 and have everyone else go anywhere else."

"Let's talk to Dr. Zine first," Tabitha said.

"Okay. Yes, that's a good idea," I said. "Let's connect with him now."

"Already on it, Max," Brooklyn said before I even got the "now" out of my mouth.

"Max. Are you close to the weapon?" Mix asked.

"Yes," I said.

"Nice work, Max," K said. "Is Rex there?"

"Hey, K," Rex said. "Long time, no talk."

"That's for sure. Hope you're taking care of my friends there," K said.

"Of course, except, now they want to blow us all up. So, I'm having mixed feelings about my first impressions," Rex said with a smile. I rolled my eyes and Tabitha smiled.

"Not with you all in it," I said.

"What's your thinking, Max?" Dr. Zine said, joining in.

"We have a potential way to cause the weapon to implode the dimensions. If we go back one, and then activate it, it should take out this dimension and destroy the other weapon, before Bad Max can leave with it," I said.

"That's a sound theory, Max," Dr. Zine said.

"I wish we could have tried that."

It got noticeably quiet.

The three of us stood silently in the dimly lit corridor, as the evidence of a gun fight settled around us. Utility lights were broken and swaying, hanging by the single thread of electrical wires. Dust lingered in the air. Bits of concrete chips were scattered all around. Poor drones lay dying, fried circuits zapping their last signs of life away. I looked at Tabitha and crinkled my eyebrow.

"Why can't we try it?" I asked finally.

"Bad Max has left +137, with the second weapon," Dr. Zine said calmly. Tabitha faintly gasped.

"Oh," I said, breathing out and looking up. "Do you know where he went, where he is taking it?"

"The logical place is to take it to your home dimension, Max," Dr. Zine said. I could tell Dr. Zine was leading towards something. He tended to do that. At least my version did that. I knew he was going to say I needed to follow the second device. As I looked at Tabitha again, and then at Rex, they knew too.

"So, that's it, then?" I asked. "There's nothing we can do to stop him before he gets there?"

"I didn't say that, Max," Dr. Zine said. "Now we will need to execute the contingency plan."

"What is the contingency plan?" I asked.

"I think you already know, Max," Dr. Zine said. "Why is everyone being so cagey?" I asked, almost yelled, and huffed in frustration.

"There's always eyes in the sky, man," K said. "You stated the exact plan earlier that we had been defining as a contingency plan for weeks," Mix said. "Taking one of the weapons to the dimension below, and activating it in a way to take out +137, along with the second weapon. It has obvious consequences for everyone that remains here though." I didn't say anything right away, and no one else spoke.

"I can see why this is a sensitive subject then. And I'm guessing you thought I was the one that needed to do this?" I asked finally.

"Yes. Because you are the only one that can activate the weapon in your home dimension and take out Bad Max. His dimension would be wiped out, thus wiping him out. And from the home dimension, you would wipe out every branch off it," Dr. Zine said and paused, causing an ironic dramatic effect he didn't intend.

He wanted this to sink in with me, but it already had.

"So, pretty much everyone would die," I said. "Except me. And my Dr. Zine and my Denny." No one spoke. I looked at Tabitha who had tears welling in her eyes.

"Let's say I don't," I said after a few moments. "What could Bad Max do with that weapon in the home dimension? And... where are these branch-making decisions going by-the-way?"

"Dang, I hadn't thought of that," K said.

"That decision affects the home dimension, ultimately, so branches from that would be created from the decision to stop him or let him do it," Dr. Zine said. "And to answer your first question. He could potentially do exactly the same thing and destroy all the branches from the home dimension. It's unclear however what could happen if the opposite happens."

"Aren't we wasting time debating this?" Tabitha asked, blinking away wetness as she appeared to have turned frustrated. I looked at her with a frown that turned into an anxious expression. I looked at my watch.

"Wait!" I yelled. "We've been talking about this for a few minutes. How long has passed outside this dimension?"

"About five or six days, Max," Brooklyn said in my ear almost instantly, but only to me.

"Maybe five days," Mix said.

"We have to do something, now!" I shouted and took off down the corridor. "Is the weapon right down here?"

"Max, hold on," Dr. Zine said. "You need to go to the home dimension and stop Bad Max from using the weapon. Rex and Tabitha can retrieve the weapon and meet you there in case you can take control of the other weapon," I slid to a stop. "I thought I can't use my Draw Bridge?" I asked.

"You'll have to try," Dr. Zine said.

"You might end up jumping over dimensions," Mix said. "But you should be okay."

"Great," I said. "So glad we have our crap together." I pulled out my Draw Bridge and dialed in +136 East. Hoping it was still there. The readings seemed fine on the screen.

Tabitha ran up to me and hugged me, then pulled back and kissed me.

"We'll get there as fast as we can," Tabitha said after she pulled back from my lips.

"I will see you again." I could grip a feeling I would see Tabitha again, but would it be this version...? I gave half a smile and a slight nod.

"You should go up to ground level before crossing, Max," Dr. Zine said. "Good luck to you, my boy. It's been a pleasure."

I was silent for a second, but seconds were precious.

"Thanks, Dr. Zine," I said. "I'm sure I'll see you again." Then I looked at Rex.

"We got this," Rex said and tipped his head at me. With that I took off running down the corridor to the elevators, the Cargo drone racing behind me. Feeling each second as a lifetime back home, more time for Bad Max to ruin everything. It took me ninety seconds to get to the lobby, open the Bridge and cross.

I lost about two more days.

Chapter 30 - Appreciation

"Can you connect with Dr. Zine and Denny in +10?" I said out loud, as soon as I was in +136 East. My voice echoed. I was standing inside the empty lobby for the Hoover Dam welcome center. It was nighttime. I looked at my watch and it had adjusted to say it was 01:25. I looked around for doors, I'm sure they were locked, but I was going to use the "wall trick" to exit to the other side.

I began scanning with the Draw Bridge for my next destination in +135 East, because it was still going to take me several hours just to get to the east coast, where I would travel through the Bridge East until I got to +1, then head South.

"Connecting," Brooklyn said.

"How long has passed since I last spoke with Dr. Zine and Denny?" I asked.

"It's been over five years," Denny said as he connected at that moment.

"I won't get used to this," I said.

"Sorry, man. So, you're like ten years older than me now, or something like that. You gonna say how much wiser you are now?"

"Max," Denny said with no humor in his voice, "Dr. Zine is sick."

"Sick?" I asked. "Like he has the flu...?" Hoping.

"No. Cancer," Denny said solemnly.

"Dang," I said.

"Yeah," Denny said, and I imagined I could see his long face and hear a quiver of the lip. "It's throat cancer. He can no longer talk. We went to an oncologist and the cancer was so advanced they had to do surgery on his larynx."

"Is he there with you?" I asked.

"No, he's resting in his room," Denny said. "The hospice nurse just left."

"Hospice..." I said. The word stung my tongue.

"Listen, Denny," I said, thinking this situation was about to get so much worse for him.

"Things are really bad. Bad Max escaped +137 with the weapon and he's taking it to the home dimension. There's a high probability the dimension you're in gets destroyed very soon."

"Awesome," Denny said.

"I'm sorry, Denny," I said. "I'm sorry I haven't been able to be with you while you two were going through that. I had no idea."

"Yeah. I know," Denny said. "Do you think you two can get back to the home dimension?" I asked. It was quiet for a few seconds.

"I don't think so," Denny said.

"Maybe I can come and help you," I said, running through scenarios in my head fast, trying to imagine if I could pull this off and still stop Bad Max in time.

"No, Max," Denny said. "You know you can't do that. You can't try to save two people and risk losing millions... billions, actually." He paused, then continued, "Max, we're okay. He's made peace with dying. I've made peace him dying, and I'm at peace in general. It's been a hell of a ride."

"Are you kidding me?" I yelled. "You're still young, you have so much more to do!"

"Maybe, but I'm not leaving Dr. Zine's side," Denny said.

This couldn't be how his story ends.

I had to do something.

"I'm going to stop Bad Max. And then I'll bring you home," I said.

"Okay. That sounds good," Denny said. "I have to go wake up Dr. Zine to try to get him to eat. I'll talk to you later."

"Denny cut the connection," Brooklyn said.

"Okay. This is unbelievable," I said. Denny sounded numb. I couldn't blame him. The person without the cancer that's taking care of the person with the cancer has the noble job of staying strong. Even when an adjacent person knows this, they sometimes still need to go off and save the world, leaving the only thing they can with the one that remains: appreciation.

I had to do something. I couldn't lose another person to all this madness.

"I'm sorry, Max," Brooklyn said.

"Thank you," I said. "Can you get an auto-air for me to travel to the east coast?"

"It's already en route," Brooklyn said. "ETA five minutes."

It was refreshing to be back in the relatively normal multiverse, where my sophisticated AI could order auto-airs across dimensions. With some caution, I moved up to the large glass window at the front of the building and leveled my Draw Bridge.

I opened the Bridge right on the glass and could see the other side where the sidewalk ran in front, on the +135 East side. An interesting thought occurred to me.

"Brooklyn, what are the chances we could vertically align multiple Bridges like this, almost like stacking them against each other?" I asked, staring at the Bridge and its edges.

"Let me see what adjustments I need to make to the software on the Draw Bridge," Brooklyn said and about a minute later I felt a pulse in my hand. I lifted the Draw Bridge to look at the screen and a new dimension of the menu was present. There was an inner digital dial now nested as a ring inside the dimensional direction dial. There was also a tab I could slide down with my finger, to expand a new ring inside the other ring. I swiped it down and could see the new ring of numbers. It was forming a target with the rings and the bullseye was the final dimension.

"Wow. This is awesome," I said. "Let's give it a try." I closed the Bridge to +135, then configured the rings to take me to +130 East. In theory, I'd skip five dimensions in one shot. Necessity is the mother of invention.

I needed to travel fast.

I triggered the Bridge, and it opened.

Slightly more moonlight illuminated the area, and the light direction was slightly different. Possibly the phases of the moon were different, five dimensions removed. I never stopped to think about it, but didn't spend much more mind power on it. I crossed.

Nothing felt inherently different here, and I quickly closed the Bridge.

"I guess you can cancel the auto-air in the other dimension. I'm going to ride this bad boy all the way to +1 East now," I said.

"Copy that," Brooklyn said.

After a few moments of configuration on the Draw Bridge – I was ready. I opened the Bridge and could see sidewalk, moonlight, and no other beings, so I crossed.

"Impressive," I said.

"Thank you," Brooklyn said. "An auto-air is ten minutes out."

"Okay, thanks," I said. I turned and looked around. I was seeing something most people would never see; I was on the Hoover Dam at night. I headed to the bridge and looked over both sides, taking both in with fulfilling breaths.

I'm sure security guards would try to swarm me any minute, but the auto-air arrived and landed on the bridge, and I stepped in. I was airborne in no time, no drama to be had. I settled in to sleep for a bit while we traveled high above the unknowing world below.

It could all be quantum dust soon.

I didn't have Denny and Dr. Zine any longer to help me. I didn't have anyone. Well, no humans. I had Brooklyn. She was enough. She had evolved to do everything combined that all my companions were doing individually. And she had yottabytes of data from our Span as well as MaxNet to work with now. It was no surprise when she just started suggesting the strategy I should follow, after I woke up from my nap.

"Mix uploaded recommendations for gaining human resources quickly to help you. You can pull Maxes from immediate branches across several dimensional directions and use the EAPs to get them up to speed quickly," Brooklyn said. "I recommend that once we get closer to where we think Bad Max is, we execute this procedure."

"Thank you, Brooklyn," I said. "I'm glad I have you."

"You're welcome, Max," Brooklyn said. "We make a good team."

"We do. We certainly do,"

I said with a smile. "Do we know where Bad Max is yet?"

"I scrambled Bloodhound Drones around several areas of the east coast, so they are searching for his scent. Although, we don't know his scent exactly, we can detect the scent of a 'Max' and when we detect one, we can use process of elimination based on all the scents of all the, quote-unquote 'Good Maxes,' we have scent records of from the MaxNet," Brooklyn said.

"Alternatively, we have the potential visual of him from +137 when he arrived to shoot Bad Max, which I'm running against any surveillance systems I can tap into."

"Can you pull up pics of him for me, please?" I asked, rising from the auto-air couch I was laying on and moving to the front left seat, so I could view the dashboard screen. Brooklyn loaded the screen with four quadrants so I could see three different still pictures of his face, as well as the video in the bottom right corner.

I tapped the video to play it on a loop. Of all the Maxes I've met; he looked the most like me. He was wearing a Gambler hat just like I did, except his was all black with a small red feather sticking up from the right side. He didn't wear a shearling coat; he had a leather bomber jacket from what I could tell from the collar.

He also had a marking just above his cheekbone, a slightly faded scar. Was that all someone needed to become a bad guy in this life? Scars are beautiful unique nuances on the body, like a tattoo, they add character, so there's no need to be bitter about them. Sheesh. People need to love themselves more. You are beautiful, just the way you are. Okay. That sounds judgy or preachy or both. But also, just be a good human to other humans... and AI – (heart hands).

"How much longer until we're in that area of the east coast?" I asked.

"One hour and fifteen minutes until we reach New York City," Brooklyn said. "That will be our starting point. If Bad Max is planning something for maximum effect, he would attempt it in a large city."

"Let's start building the team now," I said.

"We are just outside of St. Louis," Brooklyn said.

"You should define a decision." Brooklyn was setting up a scenario that I hadn't worked with in what felt like a long time. I pulled out the Draw Bridge and configured it to open a Bridge to the back half of the auto-air, to +2.7 as the base, but wouldn't be able to open anything yet. I needed to create somewhere to go first. "Mother may I, stop right now and switch seats to the back of the auto-air?" I asked.

"No, you may not," Brooklyn said.

"Fine," I said and quickly dialed +2.7.1 and opened a Bridge. I stepped forward and poked my head through to find a version myself sitting in the back of the auto-air. That me looked surprised and then alarmed. I grabbed that me from the other side and pulled that me back into my dimension, pushing him down onto his back and kneeling on his stomach to keep him from moving. With one motion I jabbed the EAP into the side of his neck, behind the ear.

It stunned him at first and his eyes went wide and then his body relaxed and let out a breath. I closed the Bridge and stood in one fluid motion, then took a seat back in the front of the auto-air turned to watch him. Patiently I waited, staring at the other version of me on the ground, as his breathing started to even out.

He sat up, looking at the back of the plane. Then he turned to me and smiled.

"It worked," other me said.

"Mix, wherever you are... you're a genius," I said. "Welcome to the team."

Other me slowly steadied himself and moved onto the couch.

"What should I call you?" I asked.

"I'm Max," he said. "You know that." I guess this method Mix created didn't take into consideration the naming conundrum we faced.

"When other maxes cross paths, it's been customary for the new Max, brought into the new dimension, to choose a new name," I said, fibbing a bit. He narrowed his eyes at me, but then sighed. "Okay. Yes. I'm remembering that now. Call me... Beck," other me said, establishing his new name as Beck. I nodded. He smiled.

"Nice to meet you Beck," I said. "Maybe slide over, so I can do this a couple more times."

The auto-air felt crowded, with four of us now.

"What's the plan?" Kip asked. Kip sat in the seat next to me, up at the front of the auto-air. Beck and Dex sat opposite each other on the couches that ran on each side of the auto-air.

"We stop Bad Max," I said.

Chapter 31 - What Happened With That Shootout

It took us two and half years to find him, but here we were.

The blackness began to fade, and I started to see bits of clear views through my foggy vision. Bad Max had activated the weapon, thus opening several Bridges at once, and the effect caused the space and time around us to slow. I could hear screaming in the distance. Beck was very still with a thin line of blood running from his ear, only a few feet away from me.

I rolled to my side and pushed up slowly from the ground and got to my feet. Swaying slightly and holding the side of my head as if trying to steady my body from the top down. My ears were still ringing. My upper lip felt wet, and I tasted the salty flavor with my tongue. With my other hand I touched at its stickiness and pulled away to see it was crimson.

There was slight movement to my right and I could see it was one of the new Maxes I had yet to learn the nickname of (not that I would have remembered since we looked so identical). Cautiously, I started towards him, but realized my ankle was a bit tweaked, so I limped up to him. The Bridges hung in all different positions around the van, some higher than others, some facing in different directions.

Through one, I could see the scene of an accident beyond: a version of our vehicle and the auto-van stuck front-first together, a Max resting lifeless, partially through the windshield. I forced myself to look away. The Max by my foot moaned.

"Are you alright?" I asked, lowering down to kneel next to him. He didn't have any visible physical injuries.

"Yeah, what the hell happened? What was that?" he asked, then seemed to just now notice the Bridges floating in space all around the van. "How did that happen?!"

"Bad Max activated the weapon. I'm not sure yet what this means," I said.

"Hal, what's the situation?" I asked out loud.

"It was not an implosion," Brooklyn said. "It also was not an explosion. The readings say this was just a mass Bridge opening, for lack of better terminology, because there is currently no exchange of energy between dimensions."

"What caused the explosion then?" I asked.

"Opening all the Bridges at the same time expended a lot of energy, in a condensed space," Brooklyn said. "It was the action of pushing out all the Bridges away from the weapon to open them that caused the blast wave." I walked up closer to the auto-van. Now I could see two other "new" Maxes laying lifeless on the ground towards the rear. They were the closest when the weapon was activated. I looked in through the driver side window and was surprised to see that no one was laying on the floor.

My memory was vivid. I had a clear shot of Bad Max. The bullet hit him in the head. A faint memory was now coming back though.

"Where did Bad Max go?" I asked.

"He went through one of the Bridges," Brooklyn reported.

"Which..." I started, but something hit my right shoulder with severe force. I looked down and saw a pulse of electricity flare out across my body and realized the protection gear Rex gave me had activated. Another hit me in the stomach and though it didn't pierce me, I curled over from the impact and dropped to my knee, slapping a hand against the pavement. A shell casing dinged on the ground by me.

Siren echoes had started in the deep distance.

The Max that I had briefly tended to, was nursing similar impact pain and was turned on his side. He appeared to be vomiting. Bad Max had stepped through the Bridge with his rifle at the ready, swinging towards anything that was moving and firing.

He fired at Beck who was to my left, on the ground in front of the auto-van. Another Bad Max stepped through another Bridge, and then another. Within seconds there were half a dozen Bad Maxes. I leapt forward to the driver side door of the auto-van and pressed up against it. Quickly, I opened it and rushed inside but kept my head low and out of range of any shots that could come through the windshield.

I moved to the center, off of the seat, so I could get even lower. I looked back and saw the weapon. A bullet whizzed over my head and tinked off some metal in the back. I couldn't help but peek out the windshield. That's when I noticed that one of the Maxes, it appeared to be Dex, from his dark purple fedora, had survived and was knocking new Maxes into our dimension to help with the fight.

This was going to be fruitless because this could be endless. I lowered back down and lifted the negative pendant from under my shirt and I held it for a second. It was a dull and muted black. I thought of Tabitha, from +3 South, the Tabitha that helped me get this pendant. The one I came to know better than my original Tabitha. I thought of how what I was about to do was going to erase her from existence – if our theories were accurate.

Another bullet clanked louder against the metal sidewall and knocked me out of my daydream – the only thing that would be left of Tabitha after this. I focused on the weapon and saw there was a clear plastic cover with a latch, straight in front of me. The pendant was visible. I moved closer and lifted the cover open. The slight stickiness of my gloves helped me pull out the pendant with fast ease. I pocketed it and then yanked at the negative pendant necklace from around my neck.

The leather cord broke and allowed me to slide it loose from the pendant. With it pinched between my fingers I placed it in the pendant slot and returned the cover to protecting it. I found the button to activate the weapon and didn't hesitate.

Whoomph was the next sound I heard.

The windows on the passenger side and driver side shattered almost instantly. My ears popped like when descending a ten percent grade hill on a highway at full speed. I felt pressure inside my head and tried to use my hands to squeeze the sides of it to try to prevent it from bursting outwards.

The sounds of metal clanking on the roof echoed throughout the inside of the auto-van. My head started to level back out and I steadied myself so I could retrieve the negative pendant. It was fractured in half. I stowed the two halves in my coat pocket. Then I moved back to the front of the auto-van and climbed into the driver seat. There seemed to be a bunch of Bridges in front of me, but one by one they were fading from existence. The sound of cut off screams and muted gasps could be heard outside the van.

I opened the driver door and stepped out. Bad Maxes looked to be frozen in time, or moving very slowly, but only briefly, because they started fading from existence. I walked around to the front of the auto-van and could see a scene all around me where Bridges and Maxes were disappearing. In some cases, the Maxes would vanish with whatever they held, but in other instances they'd vanish and what they held would just drop to the ground. I heard my name faintly and turned.

"Max. I did this to bring back Michael," Bad Max said. He looked like the picture I had studied. His hand was red and pressing against his abdomen.

"What are you talking about?" I asked, moving closer to him to try and hear him better.

"Opening all the Bridges at once was supposed to bring him back," Bad Max said.

"How?" I asked, staring at his face.

"Dr. Zine, the one from my dimension, said Michael's dimension was locked, because it was before Bridge travel started. So, we created this device to unlock it," Bad Max said, falling to a knee now.

"This weapon was destroying the entire multiverse!" I shouted at him. I felt my cheeks were hot. "We were losing everyone we knew – all my friends!"

"No. Well, yes. Because we activated the device in the wrong place. We needed to do it here. Where we lost him," Bad Max said, on both knees now, breathing heavy.

"We," I said through gritted teeth.

"It's the only..." Bad Max started to speak but fell forward. Falling face first to the pavement. Then he dissolved away.

It took less than five minutes, to be standing completely alone.

I turned three hundred sixty degrees slowly to take in the scene, then stared at the disfigured vehicle.

"We probably shouldn't leave that here," I said out loud.

"You're probably right," Brooklyn said in my ear.

"What should we do?" I asked.

"I can push it into the ground through a Bridge," Brooklyn said. "Then we can figure something out later."

"Okay," I said. I was too numb to think too much more about it. Brooklyn sounded the same.

I listened as sirens blared louder and I could tell they would be here shortly.

I walked back over to the auto-auto we had left at the edge of the driveway. Behind me, I heard metal creaking as the demolished auto-van slipped through the Bridge Brooklyn had opened. I climbed into the auto-auto, gripped the steering wheel and took control, to back out of the driveway. I started to drive away, opposite from the auto-van, when a Bridge suddenly opened twenty feet in front of me. Tabitha stepped out. I jolted the vehicle to a stop and rushed out towards her.

This seemed impossible.

"How are you here?" I yelled forward, while rushing up to her.

"Max!" Tabitha yelled back. We collided into an embrace. We kissed. I pulled back to look at her. Her jacket was different. I gave her a curious look. The Bridge dissolved in the background.

"I activated the weapon with the negative pendant," I said. "I had no choice. It wiped out the branches... it should have wiped out you too..."

"Not me though," Tabitha said with a slight frown. "It wiped out the other Tabitha." I looked at her in dismay. Not fully comprehending. "She found me at the dam and rushed to fly us here, with the weapon. She opened the Bridge, and we were stepping through. One second, she was behind me. The next, she wasn't. And neither was Rex who was moving the weapon on a cart."

I lowered my head and released a breath. The cacophony of emergency sounds rang against the trees and flashing lights decorated them. More were coming from the direction I was about to head, as I saw them come into view cresting over the hill in the distance ahead.

"We have to go," I said and took Tabitha's hand. I didn't have time to figure out if I was about to take a trap with me.

"Where?" Tabitha asked as she came with my pull.

"Have the car follow us," I said out loud.

"What?" Tabitha asked, looking around for another person.

With my free hand I pulled out the Draw Bridge and flicked across the topmost digital ring to +1 and swiped a bit more to home in on the direction, which was North (+1.10.1). I waited for the BridgeAI to do its analysis, which only took seconds. The checks passed and the next action opened the Bridge. It appeared in front of us, and I stepped through and pulled Tabitha with me. I navigated us off to the side and the auto-auto came through after us.

I closed the Bridge and silenced the chaos.

Chapter 32 - In the End

Tabitha and I sat in the auto-auto, parked in an empty lot, designated for daytime hiking. I was in the driver seat; she was in the passenger seat. I was staring forward through the windshield into the darkened woods.

"Aren't you even going to say anything?" Tabitha asked.

"Sorry," I said, smiling and resting the side of my head on the headrest and looking at her. "It's been a long day."

"Yeah. I know. Same for me," she said. "But, we haven't seen each other in how many years?"

"I know," I said. "This doesn't seem real though. I was searching for you for so long," I paused for a moment. "And here you are." She mimicked me and rested her head on her headrest. Then smiled and reached for my hand.

"And here I am," she said. We looked at each other for several minutes, weaving our fingers, tethering and untethering them.

"Were you the one at the bar, when Bad Max shot at me?" I asked with a grin, gently disrupting the stillness.

"What bar?" she said, lifting her head from the headrest and frowning. "What do you mean?"

"I was in this dimension, one time, chasing down a bad version of myself, at the Underbelly Bar. He tried to kill me," I said. "Afterwards we saw playback and a version of you appeared in the Bridge and was talking about me... I figured I had to ask." Tabitha breathed out a laugh and squinted her eyes.

"Seriously?" she asked. "That sounds nutso." I held my smile and kept looking at her. "That wasn't me, Max," Tabitha said to break the awkward silence. "You have to believe me." I raised my head off the headrest and brought my hand up to my face to tap my finger on my chin to show thoughtful consideration.

"Okay," I said. "I'm glad to hear that." I would have to trust her. We leaned together and kissed.

The morning light woke us, even with the full window tinting.

"Maybe we should find somewhere to get breakfast?" Tabitha suggested as she sat across from me on the other couch, dressing.

"That sounds nice," I said as I pulled my shirt over my head.

"Hal, where is the closest place that serves breakfast?" I asked.

"Umm, who is Hal?" Tabitha asked. I gave her a raised eyebrow.

"My AI's name," I said. Tabitha nodded.

"There's a highly recommended farm-to-table breakfast place about ten minutes from here," Brooklyn said in my ear. "You can pick your own eggs for your omelet."

"Great," I said. "There is a good place ten minutes away."

"Let's go," Tabitha said and took a seat in the passenger spot. I stepped over and into the driver seat and the auto-auto took us to the breakfast place. It was a quaint farmhouse that was converted into a restaurant.

"Bad Max said he was using the weapon, or device as he kept referring to it, as a way to bring Michael home," I said after the waitress left us with our drinks. "Do you know what he could mean?"

"I'm not sure exactly. He didn't talk about much when I was around," Tabitha said.

"Did he... umm... did he keep you locked up?" I asked and looked down at the table when she made eye contact with me.

"He didn't hurt me," she said, "if that's what you are wondering. He just wouldn't let me go. He kept telling me that he needed me to draw you to him. To get you to follow him."

"So that I would eventually end up following him back to the home dimension," I said, making eye contact again. Tabitha nodded.

"I did overhear him and Dr. Zine talking one time about the 'backwards' dimension," Tabitha said while swirling her apple juice before sipping it.

"A 'backwards' dimension?" I asked.

"Yeah. Not sure what that meant," Tabitha said.

"He did mention to me before he died that the dimension that Michael was in was locked," I said.

"I don't think I heard that mentioned before," Tabitha said. I leaned back in my chair and looked at the ceiling.

The waitress came by and dropped off our food. We both had ordered omelets and picked out our eggs (that had to have a significant effect on the taste). After I was halfway through my omelet, I had a thought.

"If something did 'unlock' the dimension Michael was pulled into, maybe now we can open a Bridge to it," I said.

"You think so?" Tabitha said without looking up and proceeded to cut new pieces to eat.

"I think it's worth a shot," I said. "But I think we need to try to do it where I lost him."

Tabitha stopped chewing and looked up at me. She raised an eyebrow.

"You haven't been back there in a long time, right?" she asked.

"Yes, I know, but I have a gut feeling that that might be where I need to go to find him," I said. "Or at least I need to go there to try."

"It's been so long," I said as we exited the auto-auto in front of my childhood home.

In +1 North, my old home was abandoned. We walked to the side of the house and could see a clear path to the tree line, so we continued. Once we were through the thickets and into the clearing under the powerline towers, I stopped and surveyed the area.

"We can cross here," I said and pulled out the Draw Bridge.

We crossed without incident into the home dimension.

The dilapidated fencing was ahead of us. I looked back towards the house and noticed it was abandoned here as well.

"Where did it happen exactly?" Tabitha asked as she slipped through a large opening in the fencing, to get closer to the tower footing.

"Right there," I said after I followed her through and pointed to the spot a few feet above our heads. Tabitha started to climb the tower, but I pulled her back down.

"Please don't," I requested. She *tsked* with her tongue but could see I wasn't joking.

"Okay," she said and returned to the ground next to me and adjusted her bunched shirt.

"I just don't want... you know... you to fall or something," I said choppily.

"I understand," she said. "So, what now?"

I pulled out the Draw Bridge and stared at it. What would I dial in?

"What's wrong?" Tabitha asked.

"I'm not sure what to do," I said.

"Try to open a Bridge," she said.

"Yeah, but to where?" I asked.

"Good question," she said and stared along with me at the Draw Bridge screen. We did this for a few moments.

"You said 'backwards' dimension, right?" I asked, looking at Tabitha.

"Yes," she said.

"Hal, can you update this so I can dial -1," I requested.

"Certainly, Max," Brooklyn said. I waited a minute and felt a vibration in my hand.

"All set," Brooklyn said.

The Draw Bridge had received an update, and I inspected the screen. I was now able to dial -1, so I did. I pressed the button, and the Bridge appeared in front of us. We held our breath for a few seconds. Nothing happened. I walked closer and slowly pushed a hand through. Nothing bad happened. Then I tipped forward to look through. I could see the same tower on the other side. Then I was pushed backwards by a hand. Startled, I bumped into Tabitha, causing her to push backwards as well. We locked our steps, and both of us moved further back together, to make room for whoever was about to come through.

Michael stood before us.

He was much older than when I remember seeing him last and was much older than me now. (Because of that craziness with +137).

299

"Michael!" I exclaimed once he was fully through and I moved to hug him, but he stopped me, again pushing against me with his hand. I stepped back to return to next to Tabitha.

"Hello, Max," Michael said. Even with his age being greater than mine now, his face still looked familiar like the day I lost him.

"I can't believe you're here," I said in a bit of a whisper now.

He inspected me by looking me up and down. Then he eyed Tabitha the same way.

"Yes. Looks like you finally found me," Michael said with an air of something I couldn't quite put my finger on, but it didn't sound like love.

"I'm sorry it took so long," I said with a frown. "All I've done since I lost you was search for you."

"Is that right?" Michael said and eyed my Draw Bridge. He turned and looked at the still open Bridge then turned back to me and took the Draw Bridge from my hand.

"Don't let him Max," Brooklyn said in my ear, and I flinched as the Draw Bridge had left my hand. I watched Michael inspect it and hit the option on the screen to close the Bridge. It winked from existence.

"Yeah. Of course, Michael," I said. "I've never stopped trying to find you." Michael looked to my eyes, his narrowed and flicked them briefly at Tabitha and back.

"You found her," Michael said with emphasis on 'her.'

I looked over at Tabitha, who was visibly nervous with the sting from the word, with a slight quiver forming in her bottom lip.

"Only recently..." I said feeling slightly embarrassed. "Are you okay, Michael?"

"I'm great, Max," Michael said with a robotic smile. "I'm finally home."

"It's really good to see you, man," I said, stepping a little closer to him. Trying to break the tension that was pushing us apart.

"Stop," Michael said, raising his free hand and eyeing me, then the Draw Bridge. I stopped.

"I don't understand what's wrong," I said.

"What's wrong? What's wrong!" Michael shouted. "I'll tell you what's wrong, Max. You have no idea what I've been through, what I've lived through. All these years. I was just hoping you would find me. I fell through that hole in the sky. I was a little boy. I just hoped my big brother would save me. But he never came."

"I'm sorry," I said with a crack in my voice.

"You are sorry," Michael said. "You let this *girl* distract you." I looked at Tabitha and back to Michael and furrowed my brow.

"I still looked for you, even when I was looking for her," I said. "You don't understand, Michael. When I lost her, it was another person I was responsible for losing. I had to find her. If not for me, for her parents."

"What about our parents, Max?" Michael said. There was gravel in his voice now. I stared down at the Draw Bridge – it was suddenly a weapon.

"When you went missing, they changed. They cast me aside," I said, matching his tone now. I moved my body to be more in front of Tabitha now and hooked my right hand behind me to touch her, to assure her I was going to protect her. Something was building that was more than the tension now.

I looked to Michael's eyes and attempted to inch closer. His eyes narrowed and he smirked. Before I could grab the Draw Bridge from his hand, he had dialed in a dimension and opened a Bridge behind Tabitha. I noticed it out of the corner of my eye and turned my head to it.

I wasn't sure how he could control it so easily. There was a buzz suddenly from above and I looked up behind Michael and saw a Guard drone rushing down towards him. Michael moved his hand quickly and pushed me, causing my body to bump Tabitha through the Bridge, and she fell backwards onto her butt. Without hesitation, I went after her. I helped her up and looked back at Michael.

"Goodbye, Max," Michael said.

The Bridge closed before my eyes.

Tabitha and I stood in silence, at the base of the metal powerline tower.

"Hal, where are we?" I asked.

"I don't know, Max," Brooklyn said. "I've lost connection to... everything."

We were in an unknown dimension, without a Draw Bridge.

Thank you

I appreciate you taking the time to read my story, *Knocked*!

Please take a moment to leave a review :)

Search *Knocked: Into Another Dimension*

Or type the following URL into your favorite browser:

https://www.amazon.com/dp/B0FHF58DHC

Also, stay up-to-date with the latest from me by checking in on https://www.derekchance.com regularly.

Or scan the QR Code below:

More of the *Knocked* story is coming soon.

The rules and tools of the multiverse
according to Max

The rules of the multiverse

This should help explain how this multiverse thing works in case you didn't know already.

First things first... I poppa, freaks all the honnies... er... one, two, three, and to the four, Snoop Doggy Dog and Dr. Dre are at the door... yeah, I get sidetracked easily... Hit Em Up!... Okay, seriously, a universe is created every time a bell rings... No wait, that's not right; that's angels.

Sorry!

Here we go.

Much of this is courtesy of Dr. Zine's brain, with the help of Denny's technical acumen, and translated into pseudo layman's terms by me, Max. Forgive me for stumbling through this complex topic, as I attempt to break down its nuances.

The multiverse concept

A universe, or dimension (these terms can be used interchangeably, although I prefer 'dimension,' but Dr. Zine prefers 'universe,' such is life), is created whenever a two-sided decision is brought to light. For instance, you come to a fork in the road and must decide to go left or right. That moment splits off a new universe for you, as you move forward in the one you're currently in. I say "for you" with emphasis because it's a key point here. There are billions of people in this world, and each one creates a new universe with each decision point. Each dimension is "spun up" for that person; it's very myopic, in reality, but consider how our consciousness works. We are very selfish because we have a

304

selfish view of the world; we can only see out of our own eyes. As Jay-Z said, "what you eat don't make me sh*t."

A key distinction here, though, is that even though *you* spin up that new dimension, when you meet people in that new dimension, they are still tied to you going forward.

In a binary sense, it's all zeros and ones. Consider *left* is a zero-or-one scenario where choosing *left* equals one because it's true, and since left was chosen, that makes *right* zero. This sets up the current universe to continue down the one path, and the zero path begins anew to the side. To conceptualize the scale, imagine it is tracked on a spreadsheet: the columns are set up with date and time as the first, followed by a decision summary in the next column, and then true or false for the choice. Each zero-row in the spreadsheet is a new universe tied to you. Your spreadsheet app would break pretty fast, considering all the choices you make so often, and Microsoft Excel has a limit of 1,048,576 rows.

You can see the immense size of possibilities.

All that is to say, the main idea is that the decision points are created from that decision, and from that point forward, the trajectory of your life, in that new universe, is completely open to different outcomes. It's a pretty insane concept when you think about it, but it means limitless possibilities. And if you've lost someone in a parallel dimension, it seems like it would be impossible ever to find them.

Surprisingly, that's not necessarily true.

Imagine these universes, being parallel, connected to your origin universe, and being tethered together, like apartments in a giant apartment complex (you're the apartment complex). Your universe shares a wall with other universes. Consider that the walls, ceiling, and floor had hidden doors, and also note that there is only this access point, with no "front door" to enter the apartment, for simplicity in this analogy. Each wall (or ceiling or floor, but let's call them all "walls" for simplicity's sake) leads to another apartment, which has a unique address, and each address could be located in a cosmic mapping application if one very smart individual had created one (Denny's awesome). You can travel to what are called sibling universes, and then from those, jump to that universe's sibling universe. It's similar to taking available roads to get to your destination in another town. <u>You cannot go "as the crow flies" to other parallel universes very easily, sadly.</u>

In this apartment analogy, think of being able to move around the complex easily because you can pass through walls without much trouble, given the close proximity of everything. However, traveling to the next apartment complex over is a bit more complicated. Generally, many universes in the same complex share similarities because they were designed by the same architect and interior designers, who influenced layout and decor, often borrowing ideas from neighbors. You don't see many significant changes: TVs are usually mounted in similar spots because of limited options, and toilets in bathrooms tend to be placed similarly or mirrored due to plumbing needs, and so on. However, in the neighboring complex, a different architect and designer were involved, resulting in a distinct design. Basically, if you pass into a universe other than this one, you might find yourself going from a living room onto a toilet.

That's when things get interesting to navigate.

The scientific elements are the same: you can breathe the oxygen there, and gravity won't be any different, but robots might be ruling the world sooner than expected.

Generating a door to another universe

There appear to be special qualities in some heavy earth elements; *at least, we think it's an earth element.* The combination of magnetic characteristics, heavy metal material, and the effects of high concentrated energy all coming together in a single instance opens the interdimensional door, the Bridge (as we call it). Condensed into the form of a pendant, where several elements come together, this is the catalyst through which high energy is sent to create the opening.

Some believe Electromagnetic Frequencies cause cancer, and an industry has sprouted around creating products that help protect against the negative effects. A condensed protector comes in the form of a small pendant, which can consist of Orgone and/or Shungite, and is occasionally interlaced with copper. In rare cases, a creative product design, in an attempt to add a twist, may create matching pieces for this EMF pendant where they join magnetically at their center. Send a jolt of the right amount of highly concentrated energy, and *presto*, you generate a Bridge, a hole that acts as a door to another dimension.

Traveling through the Bridge

The sensation of traveling through the Bridge isn't as disorienting as one might wonder. It's like walking through a doorway, just not having a physical door to handle. You also don't feel any sensations, even though you might expect to feel one, because your brain is telling you you're passing through something that looks like a vertical puddle, but it's not wet. It's the same as walking through a framed doorless entryway from a kitchen to a dining room.

The experience of traveling through the Bridge and emerging into a different universe, however, is astonishing, to put it mildly. When your brain begins to digest the understanding of being in a parallel universe, that's when you experience euphoria.

It's best to try to test this experience for the first time in a quiet corner of your world, if possible.

It is essential to note a phenomenon we initially overlooked: time dilation. It wasn't until we conducted tests with clocks that we realized that opening the Bridge caused time to slow down. We suspect that this is due to intense gravity at the nexus of the Bridge. Although we don't feel intense gravity when we pass through, we have no trouble stepping across the Bridge. We classified this discovery as "needs more data" from experimentation.

Time dilation

Slight spoiler alert. Proceed if you've already read about +137. The dimension +137 experiences time dilation due to extreme dimensional strain. The time difference between +137 and the other dimension ranges from 1 day to 5 years. One day on +137 equals 5 years elsewhere. This means that for every 1 second that passes in +137, about 30 minutes pass in all other dimensions. There is also an impact on multidimensional communications due to the delay.

The tools of the multiverse

When you refine the process and operationalize your approach to traveling between dimensions, you will find that you have created some specialized tools to help you.

Tools of the trade

To ensure portability, we created a handheld device to generate the Bridge. This device resembles an old-school tool called a pocket watch. We've packed a lot of power into this small device that fits in the palm of an average person's hand. We call it a Draw Bridge. Inside, there are multiple small nuclear batteries and copper wiring to connect the electrical components to an arc current that encapsulates lightning when enough energy is supplied. At its center is the pendant, with copper wrapping around its middle, where the magnetic pole is located. When activated, the concentrated electrical current travels to the pole and opens the Bridge. There are an even number of nuclear batteries; half send positive electricity down one path, and the other half send it the opposite way. When the current meets the pendant, there's a fifty-fifty chance that the positive current's direction comes from one side or the other.

There are mirrors angled at the front, back, and right side that effectively "push" the Bridge out of the side of the device. When you press the button on the side to fire up the Draw Bridge, the Bridge will appear on the left side. (Of course, the configuration could be changed to cast the Bridge to the right side if desired, but most of the population is "righty" and would like the Bridge to present from the left.)

The face of the pocket watch is digital, unlike its earlier predecessor, which had an analog face often featuring Roman numerals around the edge and a large hand and small hand indicating the hours and minutes, respectively. There is more than just a clock included, though. The most important feature is the battery life indicator, which shows the percentage remaining on the nuclear batteries. This is critical because at ten percent battery life, if you keep the Bridge open for more than three minutes, it will run out of power and close.

In place of the traditional numbers running along the outer perimeter of the watch face, there are many more than twelve numbers. There are one hundred digital numbers in a format similar to old radio station dials, representing frequencies. These can be "tuned" using an adjustable bevel that rotates along the edge of the face, with a tiny triangle protruding slightly over the face to indicate which frequency you've settled on. The reason for this is to dial in on a frequency of the universe to open the Bridge to.

The device has voice connectivity, so you can communicate instructions and questions with it when you're "feeling lazy" or your hands are tied up. With its Bluetooth capabilities, you can pair a single earpiece or multiple earpieces. Within its one-mile range, it's sometimes helpful to have a backup person connected.

Custom software has been built to help manage the device's critical functions. It will also emit an audible alert when the battery is running low and display a countdown. The software also helps determine which set of 100 frequencies to display at any given time.

The software is powered by another useful tool called BridgeAI, but that deserves a dedicated section.

BridgeAI

BridgeAI (BAI) is the artificial intelligence built into the Draw Bridge and all related systems. This AI can predict the best Bridge to open for a given scenario, and suggest the best direction to point the Draw Bridge in. You want to avoid opening the Bridge on the edge of a cliff, for instance. It's not an issue in adjacent universes, but when you're opening a Bridge three universes over, having to cross through each one to get to the final destination, it can be challenging, and BridgeAI can be a literal lifesaver. The system can also help detect people on the other side of the Bridge, which is especially useful when looking for a version of yourself.

Via the voice capabilities, you can speak with BridgeAI, otherwise known as Brooklyn (with a softer female timbre) or as Fremont (with a deeper male timbre), depending on which persona you choose in the settings. The bone-conduction earpiece rested, centered in the ear canal, with small arms made of high-capacity, flexible rubber-like material, molded against the ear and hooked around to the back, where it stuck to the skin. You can imagine the earpiece as a tiny, misshapen wheel, like a small aluminum hub supported by rubber spokes, all connected by a thin outer ring. This allows vibrations to transmit sound through the bones and pick up sound without requiring the speaker to speak as loudly.

The companionship of your AI assistant is comforting on those lonely adventures where Fremont and Brooklyn are the only familiar voices you might hear for extended periods of time.

Drones

There are numerous drones, more than can be named, due to the numerous potential uses. Here are some of the favorites:

Cargo drones

As the name suggests, they carry stuff. There are varying sizes available, allowing us to deploy the suitable ones depending on the mission. They also carry other drones, often acting like Russian Nesting dolls with drones inside drones inside drones.

Cloaked Spiders

These Cloaked Drones are like cargo-carrying drones that have weapon systems, while also carrying up to one hundred nano-drones.

Guard drones

These are the most commonly used drones, as they follow operatives in the dimensional field in packs, like digital bodyguards.

Surveillance drones

These do what the name implies: survey whatever is needed. They are equipped with the latest high-definition camera technology and are connected to the Multidimensional Communications network for quick syncing with the Span.

Communication drones

The specific purpose of these drones is to establish multidimensional network connections. They are generally small and can generate their own Bridges to slip between dimensions with ease. They also maintain open Bridges in order to facilitate communication.

<u>Bloodhound AI drone</u>

The most prized drone in the fleet is the Bloodhound AI Drone, which utilizes the latest scent tracking and processing technology across the entire multiverse. With long-range capabilities, scents can be detected from many miles away.

MaxNet

A network created by Maxes from other dimensions, used primarily in dimension +137. Then it's been connected back to the Span for full data syncing into the closed network.

Span (A.K.A Bridge Span)

The Span is a closed network for storing and processing data from all dimensions. It is one of the data sources for the BridgeAI. It also syncs with MaxNet as well.

Glossary

Bridge: Interdimensional portal between universes, dimensions, and timelines (terms used interchangeably).

BridgeAI: Artificial Intelligence embedded in the Draw Bridge and related systems to help with Bridge enablement. Also used for general generative AI assistance for any possible requests.

Digital Currency: a form of currency that is available only in digital or electronic form. Such as Bitcoin, Ethereum, Ripple, etc.

Draw Bridge: A device for opening a Bridge to another dimension. It has precision capabilities for homing in on exact locations in the multiverse.

Knocked: describing someone unexpectedly falling from or being knocked out of their home dimension.

Nuclear Battery: an energy source (also known as atomic batteries or radioisotope generators), they are devices that generate electricity from the decay of radioactive isotopes. _**Unlike traditional batteries, they don't rely on chemical reactions and can't be recharged.**_

Span: Closed storage and processing network system. Also known as the Bridge Span. _See the Span section above for further details._